The intelligent creatures who had created the statues and raised the temples and built the city were all dead. Extinct. Gone forever from the universe. Every form of life on the planet, from the simplest virus to the tallest trees and largest beasts, were all wiped out, killed without mercy and without exception. Their dead bodies could not even decay.

It was a planet of death. It had existed this way for millions of years. It would remain preserved in death until its star collapsed and exploded.

Why show me this? Stoner asked his star brother, while every nerve in his body screamed to be released from this grisly vision.

Because your world could become this, the presence in his mind replied. The human race could destroy itself and every living creature on Earth. Your people have that power in their grasp.

And Stoner realized that the terror he had felt in his star brother was not merely fear. It was shame.

BEN BOVA

VOYAGERS III
STAR BROTHERS

Mandarin

A Mandarin Paperback

VOYAGERS III: STAR BROTHERS

First published in Great Britain 1990
by Methuen London Ltd
This edition published 1991
Reprinted 1992
by Mandarin Paperbacks
Michelin House, 81 Fulham Road, London SW3 6RB

Mandarin is an imprint of the Octopus Publishing Group,
a division of Reed International Books Limited

Copyright © Ben Bova 1990

A CIP catalogue record for this title
is available from the British Library
ISBN 0 7493 0532 0

Printed and bound in Great Britain
by Cox & Wyman Ltd, Reading, Berks

*This book is dedicated to
that wonderful moment on
that historic day, March 12, 1971.*

Come lovely and soothing death,
Undulate round the world, serenely arriving, arriving,
In the day, in the night, to all, to each,
Sooner or later, delicate death,
Prais'd be the fathomless universe,
For life and joy, and for objects and knowledge curious,
And for love, sweet love—but praise! praise! praise!
For the sure-enwinding arms of cool-enfolding death.

And death shall be no more; death, thou shalt die.

ACKNOWLEDGEMENTS

The epigraphs used in this novel are from Walt Whitman, "When Lilacs Last in the Dooryard Bloom'd"; John Donne, "Holy Sonnet X"; The Gospel According to St. Matthew, 5:21–22; *The Sacred Pipe*, by Joseph Epes Brown; the *Bhagavad Gita*; *Genghis Khan, Emperor of All Men*, by Harold Lamb; and *Caesar and Cleopatra* by George Bernard Shaw.

The lines quoted from David Gates's song "If" are copyright © 1971 Colgems-EMI Music, Inc.

The concept of nanotechnology is best described by its originator and leading proponent, K. Eric Drexler, in his book *Engines of Creation* (Anchor Press/Doubleday, 1987). The basic work is his, but he is not responsible for the liberties that I have taken with his innovative ideas.

PROLOGUE

LATE in the afternoon of the longest day of the year a solitary man drove a sleek electrically-powered sports car southward from the city of Lima. Once past the growling snarl of urban traffic the car lifted off its four wheels and began skimming across the glass-smooth road surface on a layer of invisible energy that held it suspended a few centimeters above the ceramic-coated concrete highway.

A cruel joke of nature had placed the Earth's driest desert between the surging expanse of the Pacific Ocean and the snowcapped peaks of the Andes. The car sped down the curving coast road past the high sand dunes that heaped along the restless ocean shore, a shining silver projectile alone on the empty road. A late springtime mist clung to the huge ridges of sand, cold gray tendrils sliding in among the rugged seaside cliffs like the ghosts of long-forgotten ancestors.

The man, middle-aged, balding, plump, wore a strange expression on his round, mustachioed face: as the slanting light of the afternoon sun flickered in through the fog he seemed at one moment to be utterly serene, completely at ease with himself, yet a moment later totally intense, concentrating with almost superhuman determination upon a task that he alone could understand.

Hour after hour he drove, the speeding car tearing through the clinging fog as a bullet tears through living flesh. The car's motor was as silent as death itself; the only sound the driver heard in all his long journey was the whisper of the wind rushing by. The road swung inland and the dunes dwindled behind him. The car climbed through passes carved into bare rock, higher, always moving higher as deep gorges of river valleys fell away from the twisting road's edge. The sky

1

cleared into a perfectly cloudless cobalt blue. Past fields already green he sped; past long irrigation canals dug a thousand years earlier.

Up onto the *altiplano* the car surged, into a barren flat world where fields of bare pebbles stretched endlessly out to the dimly-seen masses of the mighty Andes, their great bulk a hazy violet in the distance, their snow peaks shimmering on the horizon as if floating disconnected from the world.

The stony desert of reddish brown seemed utterly lifeless. Completely barren. Not a blade of grass, not a hint of green. Like the planet Mars, nothing but stones and pebbles and the empty sky overhead. For kilometer after kilometer. For eternity, it seemed.

Finally the man brought the car to a stop near the foot of a steep bare rocky hill. Its wheels came down crunching on the stony ground. Then silence, except for the eternal keening wind.

He got out, shivering slightly as he realized that the breeze was cold; the night was coming on. Zippering up the light windbreaker he wore over his corduroy slacks and thin cotton shirt, he slowly, patiently began to climb the hill. The loose scrabble of dark pebbles slipped and clattered beneath his suede boots. He dropped to all fours and doggedly made his way to the crest, some sixty meters above the roadway.

At the top he straightened and looked out across the waterless plain. Despite himself, his breath caught in his throat. As far as the eye could see stretched the lines and figures, hundreds of them, thousands of them, extending in every direction across the stark plain of Nazca. Animals, birds, triangles, circles, an enormous rectangle, all crisscrossed by lines as straight as any modern surveyor could draw. The work of countless centuries ago, the only sign that life had ever existed beneath this empty copper sky.

With eyes that went beyond normal human vision the man saw the drawings with perfect clarity in the last rays of the dying sun. The giant spider, the monkey, the frigate bird with its puffed-up throat, the killer whale.

He sought one particular line, as straight as the division between good and evil. In the dying golden light of sunset he found it, bright as silver against the darker rocky desert. It stretched out toward the flat emptiness of the western horizon.

The man felt his pulse racing as he waited. Slowly, with the dignity of a god, the sun came down and touched the horizon. Exactly where the line touched it.

The man breathed a long sigh of contentment. Midsummer's day. He could sense two of his brothers, each of them half a world away, sharing this moment of serenity and cosmic understanding. We have done well, my brothers, he said silently. And he felt their answering smiles in his soul.

It was hard to believe that only a year ago he had never heard of the man Stoner. Only a year ago he had been an ordinary human being, no better or worse than billions of others. But then Stoner had changed him. And the whole world.

BOOK I

Ye have heard that it was said by them of old time, Thou shalt not kill; and whoever shall kill shall be in danger of the judgment:

But I say unto you, That whoever is angry with his brother without a cause shall be in danger of the judgment: and whosoever shall say to his brother, Raca, shall be in danger of the council; but whosoever shall say, Thou fool, shall be in danger of hell fire.

CHAPTER 1

THE sudden heat was like a sodden, muffling blanket that weighed so heavily he could hardly breathe.

Jõao de Sagres gasped and felt sweat streaming from every pore of his body as they struggled through dense jungle foliage. Fronds slapped at his face. Birds cawed and shrilled overhead. The ground was spongy, squelching underfoot. His expensive silk suit was drenched in seconds, stained and ruined. He dared not even to glance at his muddy shoes. Yet the man Stoner seemed perfectly at ease in this dripping, raucous, sweltering tropical forest. Hardly a gleam of perspiration showed in his intense, dark-bearded face.

"Where are we?" de Sagres asked in a whisper.

"Almost there," said Stoner.

"How did . . ."

Stoner silenced him with an upraised hand. On a branch high above, a long-tailed monkey stared solemnly at them, then disappeared among the leaves in a blur of motion.

"Get down," Stoner hissed.

Dazedly, de Sagres did as commanded and dropped to his knees in the bushes. The grass was alive with insects. De Sagres saw ants the size of his thumbs crawling busily across the leaves a few centimeters in front of his face. He shuddered and began to itch all over.

"I don't understand . . ."

"Shh!"

He wanted to get up and run away, but to where? What was he doing in this strange dank oven of a jungle? How did this man Stoner bring him here? We should be in my office, speaking politely to each other over a civilized drink, with the air conditioning and ice cubes at hand, with my aides and servants and security guards protecting me.

Yet he was kneeling in the mud of a tropical forest, bedraggled and sticky with sweat, certain that poisonous insects were devouring his flesh, trembling with fear. And totally unable to get away. It was as if he were chained to Stoner, shackled to the man like a prisoner.

Stoner was peering intently through the dense foliage. De Sagres studied the big man carefully. A fierce, uncompromising face, like an Old Testament patriarch. Patrician nose, strong cheekbones, a full dark beard that now showed drops of sweat in it, dark hair trimmed neatly. Powerful body, tall and lean and flat-bellied as an athlete's beneath the simple khaki jacket and whipcord slacks that he wore.

It was Stoner's eyes that unsettled de Sagres. They were gray, as gray as a distant thundercloud or the tossing stormy sea. Yet his eyes did not look troubled at all. Rather, they were as serene as any saint's, and terribly, terribly deep; there were depths in them that seemed infinite. When de Sagres had first looked at Stoner he had been startled by those strangely fathomless eyes; it was like the first time he had peered into a telescope and seen the universe of stars beyond counting.

For all his broad-shouldered build and fierce appearance, it was Stoner's compelling gray eyes that held de Sagres in an unbreakable grip of steel. The eyes of a madman. Or a mystic. They had fastened onto de Sagres's soul and they would not release him. De Sagres had received no hint, when he had welcomed Stoner to his private office in the capitol, that he would end up in this rotting infested jungle. Stoner had led and he had followed, as helpless as a lamb.

The forest went suddenly silent.

Stoner turned toward him. "Look. They're coming."

Despite himself, de Sagres hunched closer to Stoner and leaned on his strong back as he stared out through the concealing foliage at a sun-dappled clearing in the thick tropical forest. Massive rough-barked trees rose all around the clearing, their boles soaring like the pillars of a cathedral, their canopies a solid green carpet as far as the eyes could see. But this clearing, about the size of a football field, was open to the hazy, searing sunlight.

A line of grotesque dark-skinned men was forming on the farther side of the clearing. Naked except for scraps of dirty cloth covering their groins, each man was elaborately painted in garish designs that covered face and body. Each man carried a long, sharp-tipped spear.

Another line of forty-some men appeared on the opposite side of the clearing. Also naked and painted and armed with spears.

"Where are we?" de Sagres pleaded.

Stoner shook his head. "Does it matter? Watch."

The two lines of warriors confronted each other, separated by the width of the clearing. They waved their spears and stamped their feet, chanting and yelling back and forth.

"Notice the ground between them," whispered Stoner.

"It is worn down to bare dirt," de Sagres saw.

Grimly Stoner nodded. "This isn't the first time warriors have faced each other at this spot."

"They're going to fight?"

"They are from two different villages. One of the men from one village has kidnapped a woman from the other village. Her kinfolk have raised this army to recapture her. And to steal as many of the other village's women as they can. The kidnapper's village has brought their own army here to defend themselves. If they kill enough of their enemy they can raid the enemy village itself and steal pigs as well as more women."

"How do you know all this?"

Stoner merely shook his head slightly and whispered, "Wait . . . I think—yes. The elders have arrived."

Half a dozen wizened old men, bent and grizzled with age, stepped into the sunlight between the two armies. Their naked bodies were unpainted; they bore no weapons. They walked slowly, with great dignity, to the middle of the clearing and stood for many minutes, speaking earnestly among themselves.

"What are they doing?"

"Trying to prevent the war," said Stoner.

One of the white-haired men raised his hands above his head and spoke in a loud quavering voice to the line of warriors at one side of the field. Then he turned and spoke to the other side. The warriors shuffled their feet, looked at the ground, glanced at one another.

Another of the old men spoke to each side. Then a third.

Finally the two groups of warriors turned and disappeared into the jungle as silently as snakes. The old men waited several minutes more, then they broke into two smaller groups and went their separate ways, each group following the path of the warriors.

The birds began to call and whistle once more.

Stoner's bearded face broke into a broad smile. "They did it! They talked the warriors out of fighting. They prevented the war."

De Sagres realized his legs were cramping painfully, he had been kneeling for such a long time. He let himself fall back on his buttocks—

—and found himself sitting in his own office chair, behind his imposing, immaculately gleaming desk.

CHAPTER 2

"HYPNOTISM!" snapped Jōao de Sagres.

Stoner made a wintry smile. "Something like that."

De Sagres glared at his visitor as he peeled off his sopping, stained silk suit jacket and pulled his once-immaculate tie loose from his shirt collar. His hands still trembled, even though he was safely back in his spacious office. Through the long windows he could see the reassuring gleaming towers of Brasilia.

I am the president of the most powerful nation of Latin America, he told himself. And this man before me is a nobody. But he avoided Stoner's eyes.

He felt better, although his mind was still in turmoil. He was a smallish man, with a high forehead and round face that would have been bland except for the luxuriant black mustache and his probing dark brown eyes. This office was his sanctuary, where he could sit on his elevated platform and look down on the supplicants and schemers who came to beg favors from him.

"You tricked me," he accused.

"Not really," Stoner replied. "I showed you something very important."

"A band of savages in the Mato Grosso," de Sagres sneered.

Stoner, sitting in the leather armchair in front of the president's imposing desk, replied, "They are men. And they are in New Guinea, not the Mato Grosso."

"New Guinea! Impossible! One moment we are here in my office, and then suddenly ten thousand kilometers away? And then back here again? It was a trick! Admit it!"

"I wanted to show you that even so-called primitive men have ways of preventing war. Those elders, they are called 'the Great Souls' by their people. They talked the warriors out of fighting."

De Sagres reached toward the intercom.

But Stoner suggested mildly, "Don't you think you could make your own drink?"

He pulled his hand back as if scalded. For a moment he simply sat in his high-backed swivel chair, looking troubled, undecided, almost frightened. Then he rose and walked shakily across the thick carpeting to the mirrored cabinet that served as a bar.

"If you have some Jamaican dry ginger ale," said Stoner, "I'll have it with brandy. On ice."

By the time de Sagres mixed the drinks and returned to his desk he had pulled himself together somewhat. His hands barely trembled; the ice in the glasses clinked hardly at all.

"You somehow talked your way into my private office, past

all my staff and security. Why? Merely to show me a conjuring trick?"

Stoner sipped at his brandy and dry. "Not entirely."

"Then what it is that you want?"

"I want you to become one of those 'Great Souls.'"

De Sagres's dark eyes flashed. Then he threw his head back and laughed. "You want me to live naked in the jungle with those savages? No thank you!"

But Stoner was deadly serious. "I want you to prevent your military from intervening in the civil war in Venezuela."

The president's mouth dropped open.

"Your general staff thinks they are clever enough to move their troops across the border without having the Peace Enforcers intervene. Perhaps they are right. I can't predict how the Peace Enforcers will react. The political situation is murky, after all."

"We have no intention . . ."

"Don't lie to me. Your army has been supplying the Venezuelan insurgents for more than a year. It was your army's agents who fomented the civil war in the first place."

"That's not true!"

Stoner said nothing. He merely stared at de Sagres.

The president felt like a little boy under the awesome presence of a sternly uncompromising priest. "We merely . . . the Venezuelan insurrection was a genuine movement, we did not create it."

"You armed those farmers. Trained them. Led them to believe they could accomplish more with guns than they could with negotiations."

"The government of Venezuela has ignored their farmers for generations!"

"And to rectify that injustice you are helping those farmers to slaughter one another."

De Sagres ran out of arguments. He felt strangely empty, hollow. He tried to turn away from Stoner's infinite gray eyes and found that he could not.

"You must exert your authority over your own military,"

Stoner said. His voice was soft, almost a whisper, yet there was implacable iron in it.

"You don't understand how difficult that would be."

Stoner smiled slightly. "Yes I do. Would I be here otherwise? Would I have taken you to that jungle if a simple request would have been sufficient?"

"The military . . ."

"The military will take over your government unless you stop them now. Their plans include not merely annexing Venezuela. They want their chief of staff to sit in your chair."

De Sagres's heart constricted with fear. He realized that he had known it all along, but had never found the courage to admit it, even to himself.

"What can I do?" he whimpered.

"Stop them now," said Stoner. "The people of Brazil will support you. The Peace Enforcers and World Court will support you."

"But the army is too powerful."

"Only if you are too weak." Stoner leaned forward in his chair, stretching a hand over the desk to grasp de Sagres's wrist. It was like being held in an inhumanly powerful vise.

"You can become a 'Great Soul,'" Stoner said urgently. "You can save your people untold grief and pain. And the people of Venezuela, too. If you don't, the military will take over your government and you will be lost and forgotten."

De Sagres wanted to run away and hide. But Stoner had him pinned down like a helpless insect. His arm began to tingle.

"You have the power to do it," Stoner insisted. "Do you have the strength?"

The president wanted to admit that he did not, but he heard himself saying, "I can try."

Stoner's smile beamed at him. "Good! That's all that anyone can do."

"If I fail . . ."

"You won't be any worse off than you are now. The army won't kill you; they'll keep you as a figurehead for their puppet government."

"A figurehead? Me? Never!"

Stoner considered the Brazilian president for a long, silent, solemn moment. De Sagres felt as if his soul was being stripped bare and examined, atom by atom.

"Will you do me a favor?" Stoner asked at last.

De Sagres arched his brows. It always comes down to a favor, he told himself.

But Stoner extracted a small straight pin from the breast pocket of his khaki jacket and pricked the tip of his thumb. A drop of blood welled up.

"This is as primitive as those 'Great Souls,'" he said, "but I'd like to make a blood bond with you, to seal the understanding between us."

Unwilling, but unable to resist, de Sagres held out his trembling hand and allowed Stoner to grasp it in his own warm, firm grip. The touch of the pin was painless, and then they were pressing their thumbs together like little boys sharing a solemn, sacred oath.

"You have the strength to stop your military adventurers," Stoner said. "You have greatness in you. One day you may even win the Nobel Prize for Peace."

The president of Brazil sank back in his chair as his unannounced visitor strode purposefully to the door and disappeared from his sight.

CHAPTER 3

THE island of Cyprus, once torn by bloody conflict between Greeks and Turks, basked in the Mediterranean sunshine and the money spent by ten thousand members of the International Peacekeeping Force who made the island their Middle

East headquarters. Clerks, computer specialists, missile technicians, sensor analysts, bureaucrats, warriors by remote control, each of the ten thousand men and women who wore the
sky-blue uniform of the Peace Enforcers was paid well and
regularly.

They had brought peace to strife-weary Cyprus, as Greeks,
Turks, and even the descendants of displaced Palestinians
found more to be gained by earning Peace Enforcers' money
than by shooting at one another. Prosperity did not end hatred
and long historical grudges; it merely put them to one side
while everyone put their best energies into the scramble for
steady money.

Banda Singh Bahadur, commandant, IPF Cyprus, was a huge
Sikh, still strong and fierce-looking despite his eighty-odd
years. His proud curly beard was as white as the immaculate
turban wound around his leonine head. His back was unbent,
his shoulders wide and square as a castle gate. In bygone eras
he would have wielded a heavy curved sword against his foes,
or fired a high-powered rifle with merciless, deadly accuracy.

Now he sat in a padded leather chair, surrounded by younger officers in a comfortable air-conditioned office as they
pored over satellite pictures of poppy fields in Turkey. The
picture table was one large horizontal display screen, and the
false-color imagery he studied was being relayed in real time
from an IPF surveillance satellite several hundred miles above
the Earth's surface. Four young men and one woman officer
were hunched around the table, bending over, scrutinizing the
imagery.

The entire span of the table top glowed with harsh colors
that showed steep jagged ravines deep in the Taurus Mountains, near Lake Van. The face of an old man, thought
Bahadur as he studied the seamed craggy display. Much like
my own.

"*Papaver somniferum,*" said Bahadur's imagery_analyst, a
blonde young woman from California. "I'd recognize that sig-
nature anywhere."

Bahadur looked up at her with eyes of cold steel. The young

officer touched a few buttons on the keypad built into her side of the display table. A spectral analysis of the region they were examining appeared in a box at one corner of the horizontal screen. Alongside it appeared a laboratory spectrum that matched it so closely Bahadur could not tell the difference.

"It's poppy fields, all right," said the intelligence chief, a stocky oriental. "And illegal as sin."

Bahadur nodded a ponderous agreement, yet still brought up the display that showed all the legal poppy fields in the region. They were small and under the relentless control of the Turkish government. The fields in the satellite views twined through tortuous valleys far from the eyes of government inspectors.

"They even tried to overgrow them so the satellite sensors would miss them," said the blonde imagery analyst.

"We'll have to move against them."

Bahadur said, "Standard procedure. Notify the Turkish authorities after we have sterilized the fields. Offer our assistance in arresting and interrogating the farmers."

One of the young officers stepped swiftly across the office to a red command phone.

To his intelligence chief the Sikh said, "Trace the method of processing."

"Probably minimal," said the Asian. "Just enough to make some potent opium. They wouldn't dare to try to operate a sophisticated processing plant."

"They could have made arrangements with a legal medical house to produce extra, unregulated amounts of heroin," said Bahadur, his voice heavy, slow, weary.

"That is possible," the intelligence chief admitted. "I will check on it."

The younger officers left after straightening up to attention and making casual but correct salutes. Bahadur leaned back tiredly in his chair, alone with his thoughts.

In his mind he saw Peace Enforcer planes swooping low over those rugged valleys, spraying a nearly invisible mist of biological agents that specifically killed the poppy species and nothing else. He saw poor Turkish farmers running from the IPF helicopters and paratroopers that dropped out of the sky to round them up and turn them over to their government police. He saw smug men in expensive business suits suddenly arrested for their part in processing illegal heroin.

After all these years they still have not learned, Bahadur thought. The money is irresistible. The lure of enormous amounts of money, if only they can avoid the notice of the Peace Enforcers. But they cannot. Year after year, decade after decade, they continue to try. We find them, we catch them, we kill their crops and destroy their factories and put them in jail for life. And still others try.

The world is at peace, and even the lowest of the low are getting richer instead of poorer. Yet people still turn to drugs. Bitterly the old Sikh realized that global economic growth provided a larger market for the forbidden pleasures. The wealthier the world becomes, the more people can afford to play with narcotics. How the gods must weep at our folly.

Is there no end to it? he asked himself. Will fools and devils always attempt to make themselves rich by crushing the lives of their brothers and sisters?

The old Sikh got up slowly from his chair and walked to the window, where the port of Larnaca gleamed in the high Mediterranean sun, white and clean and prosperous. The streets were crowded with businessmen and women striding along purposefully, while others ambled more casually through the shaded shopping arcades. Down on the docks, laborers worked half-naked and sweating. How many of you, Bahadur asked them all, would sell your futures for the chance to make illegal millions?

Too many, he knew. There were always more, every year, every generation. Selling their souls to the path of evil.

He went back to his comfortable old chair and sat slowly in it, scarcely noticing its groan beneath his weight. Still, he thought, there are other young men and women who join the

Peace Enforcers, who dedicate their lives to the path of righteousness.

Bahadur was glad that younger men and women were willing to take up the challenge, to bear the burden that he had borne almost all his long life. For a moment his memory flickered back fifteen years to Africa and the day he had met Keith Stoner. A strange man, mysterious, powerful in spirit. Bahadur smiled and leaned his head back and closed his eyes. His last thought was of Stoner.

When his aide found Bahadur dead, the smile was still on the old Sikh's face.

Paulino Alvarado knew there was trouble when he saw little Ramón racing down the village street as fast as his nine-year-old legs could carry him, straw hat clutched in one hand, face red with exertion.

"Soldiers!" Ramón bleated. "Soldiers coming to the village! I saw them from the hilltop! Coming up the valley road!"

A lightning bolt of fear hollowed Paulino's chest, took the air from his lungs. Throwing down his half-smoked cigarette, he leaped up from the chair on which he had been sitting, his mouth suddenly as dry as the Moondust he had taken only half an hour earlier.

The village looked perfectly normal. Perched on a hillside at the base of the Andes, it looked down on *la ceja de selva*, the edge of the tropical rain forest, the valley where once coca had been cultivated to the exclusion of all other crops. Its one curving street was quiet in the late morning sunlight. The houses, built of solid stone from the mountains, stood silent and enduring as they had for centuries. A few women in black shawls gossiped idly by the well in the square. Children played up by the church yard. Most of the men were in the fields with the yellow tractors and other implements the Peace Enforcers had given the village.

And soldiers were coming up the valley road.

What we are doing is not illegal, Paulino repeated to himself. There is no law against Moondust. But he remembered his father's bitter anger when he had first brought the strangers into their village.

"They will bring ruin down on our heads!" his father had warned.

"But Papa," Paulino had replied, "this is not like growing coca. All these men want is a place where they can manufacture their pills."

"The soldiers will come and kill us all!"

Paulino had gotten very angry with his father and called him terrible names. There was money to be made, much money, more money than the whole village had ever dreamed of. More money than Paulino had ever seen in his entire twenty-three years of life. Money enough to buy a beautiful new automobile and an apartment in the city. Money for women and good restaurants.

But his father saw through him. "I labored all my life so that you could go to the university and become an engineer," his father had said. "And you come back a drug addict. I am ashamed of my son."

Paulino had cursed his father and screamed that he was not going to spend his whole life tinkering with computers while others made millions. His father, worn thin and coffee-brown from a lifetime of laboring over potatoes and corn in the Andean sun, bent and old before his time, bore the proud aquiline nose and strong cheekbones of the true Inca. But in the end he swallowed his pride and allowed Paulino, his firstborn and his only son, to have his way.

Strangers came to the village, six men in tee shirts and faded jeans and dark glasses. They brought truckloads of chemicals in big jars, cartons of evil-smelling powders, and crates of odd-looking equipment made of glass and shining metal.

Paulino's father shook his gray head. "The soldiers will come, you'll see."

His son snorted contempt for the old man's fears.

"Many years ago," his father said, "in my own father's time, *Norte Americano* soldiers came out of the sky in their noisy helicopters and burned the whole valley, everything, coca, potatoes, corn, everything. As a punishment for growing the coca."

Paulino had heard the story many times.

"Growing coca was against the law, they said. We were bewildered. Since time immemorial we had grown coca. The men from the capital who bought it told us that they sold it to *Norte Americanos*. Now Yankee soldiers had destroyed the year's crop and the men from the capital said growing coca was illegal."

"That was years ago," Paulino said impatiently.

But his father went on, "Within one month other men from the capital came and told us that the Gringo soldiers had gone home and we could resume growing coca next season. In the meantime we nearly starved."

"But then . . ."

"But then we were told to plant the whole valley in coca. So we did, and for years all was well. Until the day the Peace Enforcers arrived."

Paulino felt the inner trembling that signalled the need for another hit of Moondust.

His father droned on, oblivious, "The Peace Enforcers carried no weapons. Not even *pistolas*. There were even women among them! They told us that the coca crop was going to die, and it would never grow in this valley again. In its place, they would help us to plant the valley in corn and potatoes and squash, food crops they said were needed by hungry people thousands of kilometers away.

"The Peace Enforcers kept their word. The coca withered, blackened, and died. No matter what we did, coca refused to grow in our valley anymore. The Peace Enforcers gave us tractors and tools and the generator that turns sunlight into electricity."

"I need to go," Paulino said. His hands were beginning to shake.

"One moment," said his father. "Today we live in peace . . ."

"You live dirt poor!" Paulino spat. "Those men from the city, they take your crops and give you so little you can barely stay alive!"

"We live simply, the way we have always lived, since the time when the Great Inca ruled all the world."

"That's not good enough for me," Paulino said.

His father saw how the young man shook and sweated. "Yes. I understand. Because you cannot control yourself, one day the soldiers will come and destroy us all."

Now Paulino stood rooted by the closed wooden door of the old stone barn, staring in the direction of the valley road, as if he could make the soldiers go away if he stared hard enough. In the distance the Andes rose to snow-capped magnificence. The sun burned hot in the cloudless sky, but the wind from the mountains was cool and dry.

And Paulino saw a cloud of dust rising above the valley road. He wanted to run.

Instead he pushed through the creaking barn door. Inside, six men in goggles, breathing masks, and stained plastic aprons were bending over a complex apparatus of glass and heavy metal levers.

"Put on a mask!" yelled one of the men.

"Soldiers!" shouted Paulino. "Soldiers coming to the village!"

All six men froze for an instant. Then they rushed for the door, throwing their masks and goggles to the floor of the barn.

Outside in the sunlight their leader, a wiry hard-faced Frenchman, dashed across the village street to the ramshackle shed where they kept their truck. He came back with a pair of binoculars in his hands. And a heavy black pistol jammed into the waistband of his pants.

Clambering up the rough stones of the barn like a monkey, he flattened himself on the roof and peered through his binoculars.

"*Merde!* It must be a whole battalion of them! Armored cars and everything!"

The others raced to the truck and jammed themselves into it. The motor coughed twice and then roared to life as their leader scampered down from the roof.

"But you said what you're doing is not illegal!" Paulino clawed at the Frenchman as he hurried across the road.

"You knew that was not true," the Frenchman snarled, twisting free of Paulino's grasp and climbing into the truck's crowded cab.

"But you told me . . ."

Paulino found himself staring into the muzzle of the gun.

"Get away, you stupid fool, before we run you down."

The truck lurched out of its hiding place and down the street, coughing and sputtering, throwing up a little storm of dust and grit as it raced for the road that led out of the valley. Paulino stood in a daze, wondering what he should do. By the time he heard the engines of the approaching government troops, he had made his decision. He ran.

Just as he had done when he was a child hiding from his mother's wrath, Paulino dashed up the slope of the hillside behind the village's houses, scrambled past the terraced gardens where the women grew their kitchen vegetables and the men cultivated a few wine grapes, and hid in the secret cave beneath the lip of the moss-covered hilltop.

It was no more than a low niche in the hillside, but from that hiding place he could see the entire village and all the valley. As a child he had spent long hours there, flat on his belly, watching the villagers at their work while he daydreamed whole afternoons away. Now he lay in the low narrow cave, trembling in the damp darkness as the soldiers entered the village in their trucks and armored cars. The trucks stopped in the village's only plaza and the troops jumped to the ground. These were not Peace Enforcers, they were troops from the capital. Their uniforms were ugly brown battle dress and they carried automatic rifles, deadly looking with their curved magazines and flash suppressors on their muzzles.

Paulino watched as two of the armored cars sped down the

road after the Frenchman's truck. Watched as a squad of troops raced straight to the old stone barn, kicked in the door, and tossed in half a dozen grenades. The ancient stone walls held, but the explosions blew out the roof and started a fire that sent oily black smoke bubbling into the pristine sky.

Then the soldiers went to every house and pulled out every person. Truckloads of soldiers trundled out into the fields and rounded up the men working there. Paulino watched in sickening shame as the fields went up in smoke, the yellow tractors were blown to pieces, and a dozen of the elder men of the village put against a wall and shot before the horrified eyes of the whole village. One of the old men was Paulino's father.

Then the looting began. And the raping. Paulino cried bitterly and clawed at the grass until his fingertips bled. It was all his fault. He had brought this destruction down upon the village just as his father had warned.

But he did not move from the safety of his cave until long after dark night had fallen and the soldiers had left the wailing, bloody, burning, sorrowful village.

CHAPTER 4

THREE months later the Brazilian ambassador to the United States gave a lavish dinner party at the embassy's newly-finished complex of buildings in suburban Bethesda.

Ambassador Branco, a cousin of the president and a more distant relative of a general who had overthrown the government of Brazil half a century earlier, graciously accepted compliments from the stream of guests flowing past him in the reception line. The men were in traditional black dinner clothes, the women in the most expensive gowns and jewels they possessed. The ambassador himself wore a conservatively-tailored tuxedo with the sash of his office bearing merely a few of his huge collection of medals and decorations.

Jo Camerata, tall and stunning in a low-cut strapless gown of midnight black, reached the ambassador and allowed him to take her hand in his.

"A beautiful new embassy, Miguel," she said, in a carefully modulated voice. "You must be very proud of what you have accomplished."

"Its beauty pales to insignificance now that you have graced us with your presence," said the ambassador, in English.

Jo smiled at him and moved to the next flunkey in line. She was a strikingly beautiful woman, a centimeter or two taller than the ambassador, with dark hair to her bare shoulders and even darker eyes. The lush figure of a Mediterranean empress. Her fingers and wrists and throat flashed with gemstones and precious metals; over her heart was a diamond pin in the shape of a stylized V.

The crowd mixed and milled as Jo, unescorted but never alone for very long, wandered through the opulent rooms admiring the rich draperies, the exquisite furniture, the paintings and sculptures that adorned every wall, every corner. Brazil was a rich nation, and this new embassy proudly proclaimed its nation's wealth and newfound power.

"Don't you think the ambassador looks tremendously relieved?"

Jo turned to find Sir Harold Epping standing beside her: lean, dignified, bushy white eyebrows, trim white mustache and ruddy cheeks. He held two slim crystal flutes of champagne. Jo deftly handed her empty one to a passing waiter and accepted Sir Harold's.

"Thank you, Harold."

"You're quite welcome. It's good to see you here."

"Bored already?"

Glancing at her cleavage, "Quite the contrary, dear girl. Quite the contrary."

Sir Harold was one of the few men on Earth who could call Jo "girl" without risking emasculation.

"You said you thought Miguel looked relieved?"

The English diplomat smiled and dabbed at his white mustache. "You are the only person I know who can get away with calling everyone by their first name. I've known you for years, yet I never know if I should call you Ms. Camerata, or Mrs. Nillson, or perhaps Josephine. Or is it Josette? Are you descended from Frenchmen?"

Jo laughed. "You may call me Jo," she said graciously. "I haven't been Mrs. Nillson for more than fifteen years."

"Widowed?"

"Divorced," Jo answered stiffly, "although my first husband died shortly after."

"Can't say I blame him. Probably broken-hearted."

"Hardly!"

"And you never remarried? There's hope for me?"

Laughing again, "I'm afraid not. I remarried almost fifteen years ago."

"Really? I had no idea. Who's the lucky fellow?"

"No one you'd know."

"H'mm." Sir Harold sipped at his champagne. The dinner guests drifted from room to room, chatting, laughing, telling each other stories they had all heard at similar parties, but pretending they were amused and amusing. Jo wondered why Sir Harold was showing interest in her marital status. *Surely he has access to all the information he wants. Is he trying to get to Keith?*

"The Brazilians have done themselves proud with this place," Jo said as she and Sir Harold paused before a marble fireplace with a huge portrait of President de Sagres above it. "It must have cost half their gross national product."

"Hardly. But did you observe that there's not a military uniform to be found anywhere among our hosts? And how relieved the ambassador appears to be?"

"You mentioned that before."

"Yes. De Sagres thwarted the army's coup attempt in Brasilia, you know."

"So I heard."

"The president appears to have gained the upper hand over the generals. His cousin seems happy about it."

"Shouldn't he be?"

"I had always wondered about him," said Sir Harold. "Which way he would jump when the fire got hot."

Jo gave him a sly smile. "Miguel doesn't jump at all. He merely stays here in Washington and waits for the smoke to clear in Brasilia. Whoever is in power, that's who he supports."

"You think so?"

Jo nodded.

"I suppose you have better sources of information than I do," Sir Harold admitted. "You have the farflung operations of Vanguard Industries at your beck and call. All I have is British Intelligence."

A series of musical tones chimed out over the hubbub of conversations.

"They're calling us to dinner," Jo said. "Just like on a cruise ship."

"How gauche!"

The crowd streamed in to the formal state dining room with its three magnificent chandeliers, where a dozen circular tables had been set with flawless damask, sparkling crystal, and beautiful figured chinaware from Coimbra. Liveried servants showed the guests to their tables. Jo was placed next to the ambassador and his wife, an overweight former video star in a grotesquely green gown with a plunging neckline and enough emeralds to make a maharajah jealous. Seeing that Sir Harold was being seated several tables away, Jo spoke briefly with the ambassador, and the Englishman was asked to change places with one of the Brazilian flunkies at the ambassador's table.

Senora Branco glared at Jo, who ignored her and welcomed Sir Harold to their company.

* * *

Less than twenty kilometers away, but more than thirty meters below ground, three technicians sat at their monitoring stations, exchanging exaggerated tales of their daring and bravery to pass the long hours.

"So there I was," said the youngest of the three, traces of acne still blemishing his jovial round face, "at the top of the jump with a busted fitting on my right ski and nowhere to go but down the chute."

On the other side of the steel walls that enclosed their station, a thermonuclear fusion generator quietly converted isotopes of hydrogen and helium to energy. Deep in the heavily shielded heart of the fusion generator blazed a man-made star, a core of plasma a hundred million degrees hot that duplicated the unimaginable forces existing in the heart of a star. Incredibly powerful magnetic fields held the fierce blazing plasma in a cage of energy. The forces at play inside the fusion generator, if let loose, could have destroyed the city of Washington in an eyeblink.

But the monitor screens showed that everything was under control: more energy than the entire power grid of the United States had been able to produce a mere generation earlier was routinely created and used while the three technicians swapped stories.

"There were three of 'em," the second technician was saying, unconsciously toying with his thick red mustache. "Mako sharks, and man did they look hungry!"

A fraction of the energy generated by the fusion reactor was converted into the electricity that powered most of the government buildings in Washington. The White House, the Capitol, the Library of Congress, the office buildings for the House and Senate and all the administrative departments from Agriculture to Space, all the agencies from FBI to IRS—their lights, their air conditioners, their coffee makers and paper shredders and computers and even their pencil sharpeners were all powered by electricity from the man-made star.

The largest part of the fusion-generated energy, however,

powered a strangely small device that made no noise, no vibration, and seemed to be doing nothing. Energy went in, but to the unappreciative eye, it seemed that absolutely nothing came out. The device, little more than a hemisphere of polished metal gleaming in the overhead lights, seemed to swallow the energy and give nothing in return.

Except that the city of Washington, and all its suburbs out to a twenty-kilometer radius, were shielded by an invisible, impalpable bubble of energy. Airplanes could fly through it. Cars could drive through it. People could even walk through it without feeling a thing, except perhaps a slight momentary tingling along the skin, as if the tiny hairs on the back of one's neck had been stirred.

But a nuclear bomb could not pass the energy bubble. It would explode, and the protective screen would absorb the heat and blast and radiation the way a sponge soaks up water, only more efficiently. Much more efficiently. The best physicists on Earth still did not completely understand how the energy screen worked. It was a gift from the stars, from the alien spacecraft that had entered the solar system more than thirty years earlier. As was the fusion generator.

Together, the fusion generator and the energy screen had ended the Cold War. Removing the threat of nuclear holocaust and providing cheap, abundant energy had changed the world enormously. Gifts from the stars.

"Our command post was being overrun," the third technician was saying, "so I took the automatic rifle from the sergeant who had just been hit and sprayed the bastards a good, long burst. Then somebody threw a grenade . . ."

She was older than the two males who worked with her; almost a full generation separated them. The two young men listened with envious eyes and mouths hanging agape to her tale of valor in Central America, while the gifts from the stars quietly, unobtrusively protected them all.

Dinner was pretty much of a bore, Jo thought. The ambassador spoke glowingly of a "new era" in Brazil.

"Our president has a unified congress behind him. The army has been purged of its more adventurous elements, and the people support our president totally." Jo knew it was an optimistic view of the situation. The Brazilian congress was far from unanimous and there were still young military officers who harbored dreams of glory.

But, undeniably, Brazil had avoided an army takeover and President de Sagres was starting to move in the direction of devoting the nation's immense wealth to raising the standard of living of the people who created that wealth.

Sir Harold leaned close to Jo and whispered, "What on Earth is so amusing?"

"What do you mean?"

"You're smiling like one of Rubens' pink little cherubs."

"Was I? I had no idea." Jo consciously kept her face straight through the rest of the dinner. She had no intention of telling Sir Harold or anyone else that President de Sagres's newfound strength had been a gift from her husband.

But as she said goodnight to the ambassador and his green-eyed wife and headed down the broad marble steps toward the line of limousines waiting for their owners, Jo was accosted by two other dinner guests.

Li-Po Hsen looked distinctly out of place in a tuxedo. The Hong Kong industrialist, head of Pacific Commerce Corporation, would have been more at home in a flowing silk robe or even in a lightweight tropical suit. The tuxedo was too formal, too western, for his ascetic oriental face with its hollow cheeks and menacing hooded eyes.

Wilhelm Kruppmann, on the other hand, looked more like the bouncer in a rough Hamburg rathskeller than the financial genius behind a multinational banking cartel headquartered in Geneva. His neck bulged out of his collar; his tuxedo jacket seemed to strain across his shoulders and thick chest.

"Do you mind if we ride downtown with you?" asked Hsen. Despite his oriental looks, he was completely westernized; none of the painfully indirect eastern politeness for him.

"Both of you?" asked Jo. "Your drivers on strike?"

They laughed, but it was uneasily, Jo thought as she allowed her chauffeur to help her into the plush rear seat of her limo. Hsen and Kruppmann took the two seats flanking the TV console, facing Jo.

The car pulled smoothly away from the Brazilian embassy and started toward the corporate office towers in the heart of Washington, its electric motor whisper-quiet. For several moments Hsen and Kruppmann remained silent as the limousine whisked down tree-lined Bethesda streets. Jo watched their faces carefully. This was not a social visit.

"You can speak freely," she told them. "There are no recording devices in here and the partition behind you is soundproof. Besides, my chauffeur speaks only Italian." Two of her three assertions were true.

Kruppmann and Hsen glanced at each other. Jo smiled patiently.

"This business of Brazil," the Swiss financier blurted. "It has me very worried."

"We had expected the Brazilians to proceed with their plans of expansion," said Hsen. "Now, suddenly, abruptly, de Sagres has thrown out the military leaders and threatens to invest the better part of his nation's wealth in internal improvements."

"Unbearable," muttered Kruppmann.

"It *is* something of a surprise," Jo said carefully. "But we can all do business with de Sagres. Brazil will still be a major market . . ."

"For Vanguard Industries' fusion generators, yes. For Vanguard's electronics and pharmaceutical divisions, yes. But what about the armaments that Pacific Commerce was going to sell them? What about the increase in their exports that would have been necessary to support their expansion program?"

Jo knew that Hsen's term, "expansion program," was a euphemism for the planned invasion of Venezuela.

Slowly she said, "Brazil will still be increasing its exports of coffee, metals, petrochemicals. Pacific Commerce will still carry those cargoes in its ships. The export program will shift emphasis, it will be aimed at different markets, that's all."

A splash of bright glareless light from one of the street lamps at the entrance ramp to the automated highway briefly illuminated Hsen's face. In that flash of a moment Jo saw undisguised fury in the oriental's eyes. Then the shadows concealed him once more.

"They have cancelled the negotiations for new loans," Kruppmann said, his voice heavy and dismal.

"They'll need new loans soon enough, and they'll come to you for them," Jo soothed. To herself she added, But you won't have those greedy generals to fleece; you'll have to deal with people who know something about finance.

"Ja, but when?"

"And when will they need shipping? I have six container ships sitting in Brazilian ports now, idle. Do you realize how much that costs? Every day?"

With a shrug of her bare shoulders, Jo replied, "But these are normal business problems. You didn't hop into my limo just to tell me your everyday troubles."

Another long silence, while the light of the highway lamps flickered among the shadows in the back of the limousine like a stroboscope. Jo saw flashes of the two men's faces: grim, angry, worried. But not uncertain, she decided. They knew exactly what they wanted.

"This business of Brazil," Kruppmann repeated. "All of a sudden de Sagres has become a strong man. His people look up to him. Other leaders in Latin America are seeking his advice, his help."

"Like Nkona in Nigeria," said Hsen. "And the upstart Varahamihara in Bangladesh."

"One minute they are nobodies, and the next they are being called 'Great Souls' and having millions kneel at their feet," Kruppmann grumbled.

"De Sagres was never a nobody," Jo countered.

"He was a malleable politician until a few months ago. Now he is becoming the leader of the continent."

Hsen added, "Nkona came from nowhere and somehow stabilized all of sub-Saharan Africa. Varahamihara was an obscure lama."

"Who averted nuclear war between India and Pakistan," Jo pointed out.

"And now is being compared to Gandhi."

"His political influence is as great as Gandhi's," Kruppmann said. "Greater, even. Both the Hindus *and* the Moslems revere him. Even the Sikhs follow him!"

"It was Nkona who started the movement to restructure southern hemisphere debt," said Hsen, almost accusingly. "And the Bangladesh lama is leading the struggle for family planning throughout Asia!"

Jo remained silent, but her heart was racing so hard she feared they could hear it in the darkness of the limousine. Did they know that each of these men had been visited by Keith Stoner? Her husband.

Hunching forward, burly arms on heavy thighs, Kruppmann said, "These events are not random. They follow a pattern. They represent nothing less than a deliberate move toward realignment of the world's financial structure."

"A realignment of the international power base," said Hsen.

Realignment. What a bloodless word, thought Jo. She recalled what the world had been like fifteen years earlier, when the great multinational corporations were running roughshod over the world.

Keith had made her see what was happening. And why it had to change. Forests ripped down in Brazil; farmers and even scientists who dared to protest killed by mercenary soldiers. War tearing central Africa apart; whole tribes annihilated, genocide so routine that it was hardly newsworthy. Terrorists striking blindly in a blood lust that seemed endless. Greenhouse effect turning farmlands into deserts, raising sea levels everywhere. Population growing, swelling, bursting beyond the capability of the world to sustain so many human beings. Six billion people. Eight. Ten. Most of them starving, diseased, born in miserable poverty and dying in miserable poverty; surviving only long enough to make still more babies, half a million more each day.

Keith Stoner struggled to change that world. With Jo beside him, he quietly, fiercely, unceasingly worked to save the human race from self-destruction. With the drive of an implacable force of nature, with an intensity and single-minded strength that went far beyond ordinary human abilities, Stoner worked invisibly, beyond the sight of the world's intelligence services and news media, to improve the human condition. Jo helped him, shielded him, put the enormous resources of the world's largest corporation at his disposal.

Thanks to Keith Stoner, and his wife, central Africa was now an interdependent economic zone that sold its natural resources on the world market and invested in raising the standard of living for its people. Terrorism dwindled as true wealth began trickling into the hands of the poorest of the Earth. Fusion energy desalted seawater and pumped it along thousands of kilometers of irrigation channels. Blind exploitation of the planet's resources was slowing, a little more each year, as a new economic balance was painfully attained.

Hardly anyone knew that Stoner was the man behind this monumental change. But have Hsen and Kruppmann found out? Jo wondered. Have they learned the role I've been playing in all this?

If they find out, Jo told herself, they will try to stop Keith. And the only way to stop him will be to kill him. That was why her heart pounded beneath the cool surface she presented to the two angry men riding in her limousine.

With a small nod, Jo said to them, "Your computer forecasts must be telling you the same things mine do. The old days of East-West competition are gone. Today it's the North against the South. The industrialized nations against the nations that hold most of the world's natural resources."

"The rich against the poor, as always," Kruppmann agreed.

"But the poor are making rapid strides," Hsen pointed out.

"Is that so bad?" Jo asked lightly. "The more money they have, the more they can spend on what we have to sell."

"They are moving to create a world government," Kruppmann insisted. "First the Peace Enforcers, then this *verdammt* International Investment Agency . . ."

"Which you helped to create," Hsen accused.

Jo arched an eyebrow at them. "The IIA has forestalled god knows how much terrorism by channelling investment money to the nations that need it."

"Extorting blackmail from every major corporation, you mean!" Kruppmann groused. "Blood money!"

"Do you want to go back to the way it was ten or twelve years ago? Would you like to have your factories blown up by terrorists, or be kidnapped and tortured to death?"

"We are not here to argue about the International Investment Agency," Hsen said. "Although it troubles me that you so often vote against us at board meetings, Ms. Camerata."

Masking her fear with a cold smile, Jo replied, "I don't want the IIA board split into two intransigent camps. If every vote comes down to 'us against them,' the Third World and the environmentalist zealots will defeat the corporations every time. A bipolarized board would be very bad for us."

Kruppmann shook his head, making his beefy cheeks waddle. "You are *proud* of kowtowing to the Greens? Do you know how much the ridiculous ecological constraints your IIA insists upon are costing us?"

"Vanguard complies with those environmental constraints, just like everyone else," Jo replied.

"For how long?" asked Hsen, as softly as a cobra gliding toward its prey.

Jo stared at his shadowed face, its expression hidden in the darkness as the limo sped silently along the highway. So that's what this is all about, she realized. He wants to take over Vanguard.

"For as long as I'm president of Vanguard," she said mildly.

"Which means," Hsen replied, "for as long as you control

your board of directors. Some of them are not as pleased with
your IIA as you seem to be."

Kruppmann nodded. "This is true. Many of the directors
dislike your infatuation with those environmentalists and
Third World beggars."

"Do you want to put the matter on the agenda of our next
board meeting, Wilhelm?" Jo asked, the sweetness of cyanide
in her voice.

Kruppmann glanced at Hsen, then evaded with, "But the
IIA is just the tip of the iceberg. These are merely preliminary
steps. They mean to form a world government and to tax us
into the poorhouse. I know this!"

"Who means to start a world government?" asked Jo.

"They do. The Third World. The Greens. The Arabs and
Africans and Latin Americans. I am certain of it."

"But who in the Third World?" Jo insisted. "Which nations? I haven't heard anything at all . . ."

"It is not a nation that is fomenting this idea," said Hsen.
"It is some small group of special people. Some elite organization, some hidden *force* that works through the Third World
nations and organizations such as your International Investment Agency. We can see them at work in Brazil, and India,
and elsewhere. These so-called 'Great Souls' are nothing more
than the front men for the *real* organization working against
us."

"Aren't you confusing a few random events with some international scheme?" Jo countered. "There's no movement to
create a world government. That's pure paranoia."

"There *is* such a scheme afoot!" Kruppmann slammed a
heavy fist on the padded armrest. "And it is extremely dangerous for us."

"It must be stopped."

As calmly as she could, Jo answered, "But our companies
are still profitable. None of this has harmed us very much."

"We have lost billions!" Kruppmann snapped.

"And made billions elsewhere," Jo pointed out.

"Pah! You'll think it's a necklace when they come to slip the noose around your throat."

"Perhaps you don't understand the long-range implications," Hsen protested. "A world government would be dominated by the overpopulated nations of the southern hemisphere—including, I must add, several Asian nations above the equator, such as India and the Philippines."

"And China," Jo snapped.

"Their first order of business will be to squeeze taxes out of us until we go bankrupt," Kruppmann grumbled. "And then they will take over all our factories and other facilities. They want to *control* everything, the entire world! They are dangerous!"

"And your IIA is helping them," insisted Hsen. "Perhaps you do not realize it, but the International Investment Agency is part of our problem. You have supported the IIA blindly, and this must stop."

Jo fought to keep her face from showing her thoughts. You little yellow bastard, you don't like what the IIA is doing, so you're threatening to push me out of Vanguard if I don't play the game your way. She knew that Hsen had his own little clique on her board of directors, including Kruppmann. If I don't do what they want, he's going to try to muscle me out. Very neat.

Almost, she relaxed. Handling her board of directors was not frightening to her. They had even elected her chairman, unanimously, two years earlier.

"Still," she said softly, "I think the IIA has been a net gain for us. We're in no real trouble."

"We will be if this keeps on!" Kruppmann grumbled.

"Then what do you propose to do about it?"

Hsen now leaned forward too. "First, we must find out who our enemies are and how they are organized."

Jo nodded.

"Then we must eliminate them," said Kruppmann, with implacable finality.

Making her lips smile in the shadows, Jo asked, "Have you taken any steps along those lines?"

"Yes, we have. We want you to help us, though. We need the support that Vanguard Industries can give us."

Hsen added, "And we need you to work *for* us at the IIA instead of against us."

"I won't do a thing unless you bring me proof that this—this cabal actually exists."

"The proof we will bring you."

"We must work together on this," Hsen insisted. "You are either with us or against us."

Very carefully, Jo said, "I don't want a world bureaucracy taxing us to death any more than you do."

As she listened to their plans, Jo knew that these men meant to seek out her husband and kill him. They think they can control me by threatening to take over Vanguard and throwing me out. But they mean to kill Keith, once they find out who he is and what he's been doing.

And when they find out that I've been helping him, they'll want to kill me too.

CHAPTER 5

IT was lunchtime in Sydney. Cliff Baker sat half sprawled in the imitation wicker chair at a corner table in his favorite restaurant, the oh-so-posh and totally phony Bombay Room atop the tallest skyscraper in Australia. Fake Hindus with bogus turbans waited on the tables with feigned humility and fraudulent politeness. Wog-waiters, Baker called them: phony as a virgin in a cathouse. Bowing and scraping and speaking in whispers. Not a robot in sight. But you paid for all the servility; the prices were even higher than the room's altitude.

From his corner table Baker could see the magnificent harbor with its graceful old bridge and the breathtaking opera house. But his attention was riveted, instead, on his luncheon companion.

She was a Magyar beauty, with honey-colored hair, high cheekbones, a heart-shaped face with slightly asian eyes the color of a lioness's. Flawless skin. Delightful bosom straining the buttons of her mannishly tailored blouse.

Baker was halfway drunk, not an unusual condition for him in the early afternoon. He had started their luncheon with three whiskeys, then consumed most of the wine that the servile, bowing wog-waiters had poured for them. Now the restaurant was nearly empty and the turbaned crew stood clustered near the kitchen door, whispering among themselves as they waited for the last luncheon customers to leave. The dishes had been cleared from their table by still other dark-skinned fakes in turbans, but Baker had called for a bottle of cognac and two snifters. His glass was now empty. Temporarily.

He had been a ruggedly handsome man fifteen years ago, with golden blond hair and a lean muscular body. Now his face sagged and there were pouches beneath his blue eyes. He was going to bloat, and even his hair looked a thinning, unhealthy graying blond.

"So you want to know about Stoner, do you. That's what this is all about?"

The woman nodded, holding her snifter in both hands, where it caught a glint of afternoon sunlight.

"Dr. Ilona Lucacs," muttered Baker. "Doctor of what?"

"Neurophysiology," she said, in a voice that was almost sultry. "At the University of Budapest."

"And what's your interest in Stoner?"

Dr. Lucacs was clearly uncomfortable, but she forced a smile. Luscious lips, thought Baker.

"My interest is purely scientific," she said, with the trace of an exotic accent. "My research is in the area of cryonics, freezing people at the point of death so that they can be revived later, when medical science has learned how to cure the ailment that is killing them."

"Ahhh," said Baker, reaching for the cognac bottle. "So Stoner's still the only one to make it out of the deep freeze, eh?"

"So far as I have been able to determine, no other human being has ever been revived successfully from cryonic suspension."

Baker splashed five centimeters of golden brown liquid into his snifter and downed half of it in one gulp. "Then An Linh's mother is still on ice," he muttered.

"I beg your pardon?" Dr. Lucacs leaned forward slightly, a motion that roused Baker's heart rate.

"An old friend of mine," explained Baker. "Her mother was dying of cancer so she had the old lady frozen—god, must be twenty-five years or more."

"Would this be Ms. An Linh Laguerre?"

"You've met her?"

"I interviewed her a few weeks ago, in Paris."

"How is she?"

"Very successful. She is a vice president of Global Communications."

"So I heard. Haven't seen her in more than ten years. She was a close friend of mine, back then. A *very* close friend."

Dr. Lucacs caught his meaning. "She is married now, and has two children. She appears to be quite happy with her life."

Baker grunted. "Global's a subsidiary of Vanguard Industries, isn't it?"

"I wouldn't know."

"It is. She's working for Vanguard, same as me."

"You did know Dr. Stoner fifteen years ago . . ."

But Baker was muttering, "We all work for Vanguard, dearie. You, me, An Linh, everybody. They own us all."

Ignoring his implications, Dr. Lucacs tried to get the conversation back on subject. "How well did you know Dr. Stoner?"

"Not well. But too well, if you get my meaning."

"I'm sorry?" She shook her head.

Baker gulped the rest of the cognac in his glass, then leaned his head back as if inspecting the high ceiling with its slowly-turning fans.

"I knew him well enough to damned near get killed," he said, bitter anger in his voice. "I knew him well enough to get kidnapped and tortured. Too damned well."

She said nothing, but glanced at the purse in her lap where a miniaturized tape recorder was hidden.

"You don't know about Stoner, not really." Baker hunched forward in his chair, leaning both arms heavily on the table and bringing his face close enough to hers so that she could smell the liquor on his breath.

"He's not human. He can see right through you and make you do things you don't want to do. I saw him make a bloke go blind, just while we were sitting at the dinner table. Made his eyes bleed, for chrissakes! Drove him dotty." His words were blurring together now, coming out in a half-drunken rush, frenzied, urgent. "He turned the owner of Vanguard Industries into a basket case just by saying a few words to him. He never sleeps! He spent months with An Linh in Africa and never touched her—for sex, I mean. I think he can walk through walls if he wants to. He's not human, not human at all!"

Dr. Lucacs's tawny eyes were glittering. "He spent several years aboard the alien spacecraft," she whispered, almost to herself.

"That's right. He was frozen up there in space, and when they brought him back to Earth it was another ten years or more before they figured out how to thaw him and bring him back to life."

"And no other human being has ever been thawed successfully and revived."

"Because he ain't human," Baker insisted. "While he was in that alien spaceship, I think they grew a clone of him or something. He's just not human. A human being can't do the things he can do!"

"He won't let me examine him," Dr. Lucacs said.

"'Course not. Then you'd find out what he *really* is."

"But I have all his medical records from the Vanguard Research Labs, where he was revived, fifteen years ago. They are the records of a normal human being."

"Faked."

"They match his earlier records, from the years before he went into space."

"Faked, I tell you."

She looked doubtful. "Why would . . ."

"Don't be a naive fool!" Baker snapped. "He's the property of Vanguard Industries, the most powerful corporation on this planet, for god's sake! He married the corporation president . . ."

"Ms. Camerata? I didn't know that."

"Don't you see? *He's* secretly controlling the biggest corporation on Earth. Through her. He killed off her first husband and set himself up in his place. He paid off An Linh with Global Communications and stuck me with this bloody IIA."

She looked surprised. "But I thought that you were the chairman of International Investment Agency."

"Sure I am!" Baker made a sound halfway between a laugh and a snort. "It's like being the mascot of a rugby team. You get treated well and everybody admires you. But they don't take you very seriously, do they?"

Dr. Lucacs looked uncomfortable.

His voice rising as he reached for the cognac bottle again, Baker went on, "Sure, they made me chairman of their bloody IIA. And all the big multinational corporations send their flunkies to sit 'round our table. But who runs the IIA? Actually runs it? Jo Camerata, that's who! Vanguard Industries, that's who! And who runs Vanguard? Stoner, the bloody alien freak. Her husband."

The scientist leaned back in her chair and tried to sort out all this new information.

"You'll never get to Stoner," Baker predicted. "He's better protected than the bloody Pope."

"I've interviewed almost everyone who knew him when he

was first revived," she mused, as if reviewing the options left for her next move. "Most of the medical team has died over the past fifteen years."

"You bet they have!"

Dr. Lucacs raised her brows. Baker smiled a crooked, knowing smile and poured more cognac for himself.

"Ms. Camerata won't see me," she said.

"'Course not."

"There is only one other person that I know of. A Professor Markov, of the Soviet Academy of Sciences. And he's very elderly."

"Better get to him right away, then," said Baker. "Before Stoner finds out you're after him."

Her beautiful eyes widened. "You don't think . . . ?"

Baker's smile turned cruel. "All those medical blokes kicked off, didn't they? You don't think those were all natural deaths, do you?"

Yendelela Obiri staggered to a halt along the forest trail and doubled over from the nausea. She was close to complete exhaustion, her khaki slacks and shirt soaked with sweat, her head swimming with the strange double vision of the biochips.

Gasping in the thin mountain air, she almost sank to her knees. Almost. But when she closed her eyes she saw what Koku saw, heard and smelled and felt what the young gorilla was experiencing.

Koku was being chased. Hunters were pursuing him. And the young male was too inexperienced, too tame, to realize what danger he was in.

"You are not alone," Yendelela muttered, knowing that Koku could hear her through the biochips implanted in their brains. "Lela is near, Koku. Lela is coming."

Fighting down the bile burning in her throat, she adjusted the straps of her heavy backpack and staggered up the steep wooded slope, pushing through brush and nettles that flailed at her from both sides of the narrow mountain trail. The sun was warm, but the cool mountain breeze chilled the perspiration that beaded on her dark, intent face.

Her teachers, back at the university, had been doubtful about allowing Lela to do a field mission with a male gorilla. Even Professor Yeboa, who had been her advisor, her sponsor, her secret love, had expressed doubts.

"The hills can be dangerous for a city girl," Yeboa had said. He had smiled, as he always did when he reminded Lela of her urban upbringing.

"City streets can be dangerous, too," she had retorted, also smiling. "I am not afraid."

The aim of the project was to repopulate the area that had been set aside as a safe reserve for the mountain gorilla. Over the past half century the gorillas had been driven nearly to extinction, but now at last an ecologically viable tract of uplands had been set aside for them, thanks to Nkona. Three female gorillas had already been placed in the reserve by other students and rangers, waiting for a male to complete a viable group. Lela's task was to guide Koku to the females, using the biochips to help control the young male.

Lela had even met the Great Soul of Africa, Dhouni Nkona himself. He had come to the university to see personally how they were rearing the infant gorillas from the zoo population and teaching them to survive in the wild.

As a graduate student, Lela had been concentrating on theoretical studies of ecological change and environmental protection. But once she looked into those fathomless eyes of Nkona she was swept up in an irresistible frenzy of dedication.

"The work you do here is the best that human souls can achieve," Nkona had told the eager students. He smiled at them, a sparkling bright smile in his deeply black African face. "You know that we must learn to control our behavior, to think before we act, to accept responsibility for the consequences of our actions. We cannot live by exterminating others, that much you have learned in your studies, I know. By saving the gorillas, you help humankind to save itself."

"Many oppose what we do," said one of the students.

Nkona closed his eyes briefly. Then, "All life is linked to-gether, from the humblest forms to the most grandiose. Thirty-three years ago the human race made its first contact with an alien intelligence, a race from another world, another star. I say to you that our contacts with the life of this world are just as important—no, more important—than our link to other races in space."

He turned a full circle to sear each of the students crowded around him with his compelling gaze. "We are all links of the same chain, the chain of life, which extends out to the stars and the farthest reaches of creation. Your struggle to save the gorilla is the struggle to preserve that chain, to keep faith with all the forms of life that share this universe."

Theory could never be enough for Lela after that. Aflame with Nkona's passion, she volunteered eagerly for the biochip operation that would allow her to maintain sensory contact with a selected gorilla. She battled the entire faculty and field staff for the right to work with one of the animals through its difficult transition from the human environment of its child-hood to the wild mountain forests where it would live as an adult.

For nearly two years Lela had trained hard, both physically and mentally. Out of a soft, self-indulgent adolescent cocoon there emerged a leggy, lean-muscled young woman with lus-trous brown eyes and a smile that dazzled.

She was not smiling now. Out here in the thick brush of the forest, with the early morning sunlight just beginning to filter down through the trees, with the sweat of near-exhaus-tion chilling her, Lela knew that Koku was in danger.

She should have been the only human being within a hun-dred square kilometers of the young male gorilla. But she was not. Through Koku's eyes she saw a band of hunters thrashing through the brush. White men and black, carrying rifles.

"Run Koku!" she directed. "Run!"

Startled by her abrupt warning, the big gorilla crashed off through the brush. Lela felt his sudden fear as her own. Looking back through the gorilla's eyes, she saw the hunters dwindling in the distance until they disappeared altogether in heavy green foliage.

Lela sighed out a breath of relief. Koku could easily outdistance them in the thick brush. But within minutes he would feel safe and slow down or stop altogether. Lela knew she had to reach Koku before the hunters did.

CHAPTER 6

JO dropped the two men off at their hotels, then instructed her chauffeur to drive to Washington National Airport. A Vanguard Industries executive jet was waiting for her there, and shortly after midnight she leaned back in an utterly comfortable leather lounge chair and watched the stately monuments of Washington glide past her window as the plane climbed to its cruising altitude. Once above the normal traffic patterns of commercial airliners, the plane's wings slid back for supersonic flight and the cabin lights dimmed for sleeping.

But Jo had no intention of sleeping. Not yet. Hsen and Kruppmann were threatening her. Now she knew why the board of directors had suddenly insisted on a special meeting to review Vanguard's participation in the IIA. Hsen was making a power play. The sneaky little bastard must have nearly half the board in his pocket already, in addition to Kruppmann, Jo said to herself. While I've been helping Keith he's been maneuvering to acquire leverage on my board.

She dictated a memo to the computer outlet built into her seat's armrest: "Check all board members and executive staff to see which of them also sit on the board of Pacific Commerce." Then she added, "Also, I want a complete list of all

Vanguard executives above the level of divisional vice president who have been involved in any transactions whatever with Pacific Commerce."

What about Kruppmann? Jo decided that the Swiss banker was more bluster than anything else. He never made waves at board meetings. He would loan money to Vanguard no matter who ran the corporation, as long as Vanguard showed profits. Hsen was the dangerous one. Kruppmann made most of the noise, but Hsen was the kind who knifed you in the dark.

She nodded to herself. First rule of business: find out who your enemies are, and then keep them as close as possible—until you're ready to chop their heads off.

Leaning back in the deep luxurious chair, Jo felt satisfied that she had done all she could do for the moment. She allowed herself to relax and fall asleep.

Her dreams were troubled. She was in the lobby of an exclusive hotel, carrying heavy suitcases in either hand and trying to get into an elevator. But she could not get the suitcases through the elevator doors before they slid shut and left her behind. No one in the hotel lobby offered to help her. She was frantic, because Keith was somewhere on one of those upper floors and she had to find him before he went away and left her all alone.

She awoke to a pert young stewardess smiling over her. "We land in half an hour," she said.

Jo saw that the sky was aflame with the rising sun. Then, brows knitted, she realized that she had to be looking toward the west. The sun was setting, not rising. Lifting her wrist close to her lips she said softly, "Hawaii." The watch's digits quickly shifted from 0328 to 1928. Almost 7:30 p.m., Jo realized.

The drive from Hilo Airport to her sprawling home in the hills above the city was swift. Keith Stoner was at the front door to greet her, tall and safe and smiling warmly. She had loved him since those ancient days when she had been a student and he a former astronaut. They had worked together on the project to make contact with the alien starship that had appeared near the planet Jupiter. When Stoner had flown out to the starship and remained in it, frozen in the cryogenic cold of deep space, Jo had clawed her way to the top of Vanguard Industries to gain the power to reach the distant spacecraft and return the man she loved to Earth and to life.

But he was not the same man that she had known eighteen years earlier. Frozen in the cryogenic cold of space aboard the alien starship, he had somehow been changed. It was strange. Keith seemed more human than he had been earlier, more attuned to life than the self-contained, solitary scientist she had once known. He could open his emotions to her and love her as he had never been able to do before. Yet he was somehow beyond human, endowed with abilities that no human being had ever known, burning with the urgency of a demon-driven fanatic—or a saint.

But he loved her. Loved her as she loved him. For Jo, nothing else mattered.

Now she felt his strong arms around her and relaxed for the first time since she had left their home, four days earlier.

"I thought you'd stay the night in Washington," he said, smiling down at her.

Jo said, "The party was pretty much of a bore. I decided I'd be much happier at home."

"I'm much happier, too."

They walked arm in arm into the house while the chauffeur handed Jo's overnight bag and briefcase to one of the squat, many-armed household robots.

Stoner stopped at the foot of the stairs that led up to the master bedroom suite. On their right was the spacious living room; straight ahead along the corridor was the kitchen.

"You must be still on Eastern time," he said. "Do you want some dinner or some breakfast?"

"I'm not hungry at all," Jo replied.

He pursed his lips slightly. "You know, the best way to adapt to a change in time zones is to go to bed and sleep until you've caught up with the local time."

She grinned up at him. "Sleep?"

"There's iced champagne waiting in the bedroom." He grinned back at her.

"How about a nice long shower first?" she suggested as they started up the steps.

"Sounds good to me."

Hours later Stoner lay on his back gazing up at the stars. Jo was curled next to him on the waterbed, warm and breathing in the slow regular rhythm of sleep. All of Stoner's childhood friends were in their places in the night sky: Orion and the Twins, the Bull, the glittering cluster of the Pleiades. A slim crescent Moon hung in the darkness like a scimitar, with the red jewel of Mars nearby.

There was no ceiling to their bedroom, only a bubble of energy that kept out the weather and served as a soundproof barrier. Yet it was completely transparent; like having the bedroom outdoors. Flowered hangings both inside and outside the room filled the dark night air with the fragrance of orange blossoms and magnolias, completing the illusion of being out in a sighing, whispering garden.

The energy screens that had ended humankind's nightmare fear of nuclear holocaust could also serve more romantic purposes, Stoner mused. A gift from the stars. From my star brother.

He felt no need of sleep. Instead, as he watched the stately motion of the stars arcing across the dark sky he murmured the command that turned on the record player, keeping it so low that only he could hear it. The muted, moody opening of Villa-Lobos's *Bachianas Brasileiras No. 8* filled the room faintly, violins and cellos dark and sensuous.

The best invention the human race has ever made, Stoner thought. The symphony orchestra. And so typically human: a hundred virtuosos voluntarily submerging their individuality to produce something that no one of them could produce alone.

A meteor flashed across the night sky, silent and bright for the span of an eyeblink. Stoner sank back on his pillows and clasped his hands behind his head, content to lie beside his sleeping wife and wait for the dawn while the orchestra played for him.

Jo murmured drowsily, "Go to sleep."

"I'm sorry," he whispered. "I didn't think it was loud enough to bother you."

"Big day tomorrow."

"I know. My surprise party."

She bolted up to a sitting position, suddenly wide awake. "Who told you?"

"You did." He laughed softly. In the shadowy darkness, Jo's naked body was washed by the pale moonlight, her skin glowing warm. He could not see the expression on her face, so he reached up and pushed back her shining dark hair.

"The household staff has been fussing and making phone calls for a month or more. You cut short your stay in Washington to come home in time for tomorrow. And you just told me tomorrow's going to be a big day."

Jo leaned over him. "You're the only one in this house who knows how to keep a secret."

"I have no secrets from you, Jo. You know that, don't you?"

Nodding, she began to tell him of her conversation in the limousine with Hsen and Kruppmann. Stoner listened patiently, quietly until she finished.

"About what I expected," he said at last. "They're not interested in the global picture. They only see their own needs."

"Their own selfish interests."

"They just don't understand what's going on. Maybe they don't want to understand. They want the power to control events, to keep themselves at the top of the heap. They don't understand that it's not a zero-sum game anymore. The world's economy is completely interlinked; it's not even just a global economy, not if you consider the Moon and the asteroids and the factories in Earth orbit. If the Third World gets richer, we all get richer. That's what they don't see."

"They're willing to commit murder," Jo said.

Stoner gave a bitter little laugh. "If they're willing to bankroll wars and insurrections, what's the murder of one man to them?"

"But it's *you* they want to kill!"

"They don't know who I am," Stoner said, "and it won't be easy for them to find out. Especially when I have such an excellent Mata Hari in their camp."

"I can't protect you forever, Keith. There's no such thing as absolute security."

"I'm more concerned about you," he said. "How serious is their move to take over Vanguard?"

She shrugged her naked shoulders. "I don't know yet. But they'll get their guts ripped out if they try to take over *my* corporation."

Stoner chuckled in the darkness. "That's my woman! What'd *Business World* call you: 'The tigress of the corporate jungle.'"

She laughed too, but there was anxiety behind it. "Keith, I can handle the corporate battles. And I can balance Baker and his Third World friends against the corporate interests on the IIA. It's you I'm frightened about."

"I'll be all right."

In the darkness her voice took on a sharper, harder note. "Don't you understand? Hsen's out to kill you! I'm going to strike first, before he gets the chance . . ."

"And be just like him? What good would that do?"

"It'll keep you alive, Keith!"

He shook his head. "Hsen is not the enemy. He's just acting out of fear."

"Dammit, Keith! Sometimes you carry this sainthood crap too far!"

Startled, "Sainthood?"

Jo was immediately sorry. More softly she said, "Okay, so I'm a tigress. I know you're not a tiger, Keith. Not a street fighter. But you've got to protect yourself, got to let me protect you."

Stoner countered, "Look. Even if you could kill Hsen someone else would take his place. So there'd be another assassin coming after me, with the added excuse of avenging Hsen's murder."

Jo said nothing, but he could feel her body tensing, like a true jungle cat just before it springs.

"Deliberately killing a human being is the worst thing you can do, Jo. Not because there's a rule against it written in some book, but because it always leads to more killing. Because the human race hasn't quite learned yet how to deal with its animal instincts. We're supposed to be working on the side of life, not death. Life is precious. Human life is the most precious of all."

"Oh, for Christ's sake, Keith, if there's one thing we've got too much of on this planet, it's human beings. And most of them aren't worth the effort it would take to blow them to hell."

In a near-whisper Stoner replied, "If you only knew how rare life is, truly rare among all those stars."

But Jo refused to be drawn in that direction. "What happens if Hsen kills you? What do you expect me to do?"

"Jo, we're in a race against time. You knew that when we started down this road, fifteen years ago."

"But the closer we get to the end the more dangerous it becomes."

He nodded abstractedly, as if his mind were really elsewhere. "The biochips are the next step. If the human race can absorb that technology, then we're almost finished."

"I've got our lab people working as hard as they can go," Jo said. "Biochips will be an important product for Vanguard."

"It's more than that, Jo. Much more," Stoner said. "Biochips can help us get around the limits on brain size set by the female's birth channel, the first chance to expand the capacity of the human brain in hundreds of thousands of years, Jo!"

"You're blaming women for the limits on brain size?"

He laughed. "All the great religions of the world blame women for humankind's troubles. Didn't you know that?"

"All the great religions of the world are schemes by men to keep women down!"

"But they're right, in a way."

"Really?" Jo's voice dripped acid.

"Goes back millions of years," Stoner said lightly. "Most ape females are in estrus only a couple of days a month. Our ancestors' females were sexually receptive all the time. That's how we outpopulated the other apes. It led to our dominance of the planet. But now it's a problem."

"Well, I know how to solve *that* problem." Jo pushed away from him slightly.

Stoner reached toward her and she let him put his arms around her easily enough.

"Some solutions are worse than the problems," he said softly.

"That's better," she murmured.

"But the biochips *are* important, Jo. Implanting protein chips in people's brains will allow them to link themselves directly with any library, any data bank on the planet. And they'll be able to communicate with each other directly, like . . ."

Jo interrupted, "I don't care about that! You're the only one I'm worried about."

"And the rest of the human race?"

"Let them all go to hell, what do I care? As long as you and the children are safe."

Very softly, Stoner said, "None of us will be safe, Jo, unless all of us are."

"You keep saying that. Is it really true?"

He closed his eyes and saw a different world, a planet that circled a bloated red star that hung in the sky like a huge menacing omen of doom. A world that teemed with delicate birdlike people, human in form except for feathery crests that ran along the tops of their otherwise bald skulls. A world that was dying beneath the weight of its own numbers.

Cities covered almost the entire face of the planet, their soaring towers crammed with people. Harbors were black with boats and rafts where people lived packed literally shoulder to shoulder. What little countryside remained was bare, denuded, while immense factories struggled to produce enough artificial food to feed the ever-growing masses of people. Murder and madness were as commonplace as breathing, and the only parts of the planet that were not covered with people were the waterless deserts that were slowly, inexorably growing larger, and the oceans that were all too quickly becoming polluted.

Despite famine and war and agonizing plagues the highest ethic of this race was the sanctity of life. There was no allowable way for the species to deliberately control its numbers, and as its technology and medical skills grew, billions of babies were born each year to parents who procreated in the blind faith that procreation was the ultimate goal of life.

The planet-girdling society became schizophrenic, rewarding fruitful parents with honors and blessings on the one hand, while tacitly condoning genocidal wars and mass murders on the other. Laws prohibited birth control while exacting the death penalty for minor theft. Scientists produced medical miracles for prolonging life and nerve poisons that could wipe out a city overnight.

The entire species was insane. Yet it continued to grow, continued to enlarge its numbers, spread across the surface of its world like a crawling, writhing cancer until it covered even the barren wastelands with cities bursting with overcrowded buildings where murder was as commonplace as birth.

And then the planet itself exacted its revenge. The air became poisonous, the oceans too fouled to support life. Glaciers crept down from the mountains to cover the land in glittering sterile ice. Life ended. The planet waited for eons before the first faint stirrings of protoplasm could begin again in a sea that had at last cleansed itself of the last traces of those who had come before.

Stoner shuddered in the darkness. He knew that the world

he had just seen was real, it existed somewhere out among the starry deeps. His star brother had been there.

"Jo, we're in a race against time. We've got to learn how to control our population growth. Sooner or later somebody's going to stumble onto the technology that the starship carried, discover it independently. The biochips are only the first step in that direction. Somebody's going to move on into nanotechnology, you know they will. If we haven't curbed our population growth by then . . ."

Jo leaned back on the pillows without replying.

"If we fail, the human race dies. Not tomorrow. Not even in the next decade or two. But we'll kill ourselves off eventually and that will be the end of humanity."

Jo said to herself, Maybe we'd be better off dead. Most of the human race is despicable scum. What difference does it make if we survive or disappear?

But she did not voice the thought.

Turning on his side to face her, Stoner urged, "We're close, Jo. Very close. It's all coming to a climax. The biochips are the big test. If we can absorb that technology, use it to help the human race instead of harm it, then we'll be ready for the final step."

Even though his face was shadowed in darkness, Jo could feel the intensity of purpose blazing in him. She wondered if the *we* he spoke of referred to her, or to the others.

She tried to see his eyes in the moonlit shadows, tried to peer into his soul. Keith had worked so hard since being revived, since coming back to life after being on the alien star ship. Like a man possessed, like a saint or a holy man who saw a vision beyond what ordinary human eyes could see.

"It's almost finished," he repeated, in a whisper that held regret as well as anticipation. "All the threads are coming together, the task is almost complete."

"Almost," Jo echoed.

BANGKOK

SHE was in such excruciating pain. It was necessary to sedate her so heavily that her labor stopped altogether. The delivery team performed a caesarian section, something they had done countless times before. But once they had exposed the baby the surgical nurse gagged and slumped to the floor. The two assistants stared as if unable to turn away.

The baby was already dead, and the mother died minutes later.

Now Dr. Sarit Damrong paced nervously along the roof of the hospital, the cigarette in his shaking fingers making a small coal-red glow in the predawn darkness.

The baby had been a bloody, pulpy mess, already half eaten from within. The mother also; her abdominal cavity was an oozing hollow of half-digested organs. It was the agony of having her innards eaten alive that had racked the poor woman, not the pain of labor.

The woman had been one of the millions of lower class workers who lived on barges in the *khlongs*, the canals that crisscrossed Bangkok. Dr. Damrong had immediately performed an autopsy, right there in the delivery room, and sent scraps of tissue samples to the university laboratory for analysis.

Now he stood at the parapet at the roof's edge, leaning heavily on his thin arms and staring out at the tower of the Temple of the Dawn, across the river, as it caught the first rays of the golden sunlight.

The first time he had seen a patient with her innards eaten away, a month earlier, he had been curious. It reminded him of something from one of his biology classes, years ago, about a certain species of spider that laid its eggs inside the paralyzed body of a living wasp. When the eggs hatched, the baby spiders ate their way through their host to enter the world.

How grisly, he had thought as a student. Now he had seen three such cases. And these were human beings, mothers dying in the attempt to give birth, destroyed from within.

Dr. Damrong watched the sunlight slowly extend across the teeming city. Cooking fires rose from the canals and the crowded houses and apartment blocks. He could hardly see the curving river, there were so many barges clustered on it. Another day was starting. The darkness of the night had been dispersed.

But still his hands trembled. Three women eaten away from within their own wombs. As if the fetuses within them had turned to murderous acid.

For the first time since he had been a child, Dr. Damrong felt afraid.

CHAPTER 7

"HAPPY BIRTHDAY!"

Stoner tried his best to look surprised, but everyone knew he wasn't, and he knew that they knew.

But it did not matter.

That morning Jo had begged him to stay up in his office, on the top floor of the spacious stucco house, as far away from the pool and patio as could be. Stoner spent the hours there speaking with people in Brazil and India and Thailand on the videophone. He read a few reports and tried to ignore the cars and limos that pulled up to the front door and discharged men, women, and children laden with brightly-wrapped packages.

Household robots buzzed and bumped up and down the

front steps repeatedly, discreetly scanning each new arrival for weapons as they accepted suitcases and garment bags.

No matter how hard Stoner tried to concentrate on his reading, a part of his mind reached out inquisitively to sense the people arriving. That's my son Douglas, he said to his star brother, with his wife and children. And later, Claude Appert, flown all the way from Paris. Then he recognized his daughter Eleanor and her new husband, whom he had not yet met. His grandchildren were teenagers now, and trying their best to be quiet and secretive. Stoner smiled to himself and went back to his reading.

The world's fundamental problem was the result of cultural lag. Stoner had decided that fifteen years earlier, but here in his hands was a detailed academic study by a team of researchers from half a dozen universities that came to the same inescapable conclusion—in ten thousand turgid words and computer-generated graphs.

In a world where modern medicine had reduced the age-old agony of infant mortality to negligible proportions, many cultures still drove their people to have large families. The poorer the people, the more children they begat. The higher a nation's birthrate, the poorer the nation became. There were almost ten billion people living on Earth. Too many of them were hungry, diseased, and ignorant. And with the ability to select the sex of their babies, too many lagging cultures produced an overabundance of males, far too many for the available jobs in their economies. It had been this overabundance of young men, boiling with testosterone, that had led to wars and terrorism in the past several decades.

Most of the world's experts knew the answer to this problem: Lower your birthrate, they said to the poor, and you will become richer. Balance your male/female ratio. For nearly a century this gospel had been preached to the poor. To little avail. More babies and still more babies—half a million each day—threatened to drown the world in a pool of starving humanity.

Even with the best of intentions, good-hearted but short-sighted people made the problem worse. Feed the starving poor.

Give money to help the famine-stricken people of the Third
World. The people of the rich industrialized nations opened
their hearts and their pocketbooks, and the starving poor survived long enough to produce a new generation of starving poor,
even larger than the last. The cycle seemed endless. Yet what
could an honest person do when others were dying for lack of
food?

Hard-headed analysts pointed out that giving food to the
starving without forcing them to control their birthrate was
only making the problem worse, accelerating the cycle of poverty and starvation that was threatening to drown the world.
Force birth control on them, said these experts. Make the
poor control themselves. That led to cries of genocide and
the angry blind flailings of terrorism, the one weapon that the
poor could use against the rich to satisfy their furious seething hatreds, their sense of injustice, the frustrations that
made them feel powerless.

Stoner's approach was the opposite. Instead of preaching to
the poor he worked to make them richer. Instead of demand-
ing that they lower their birthrate, he worked—through Jo,
through Vanguard Industries, through the International Investment Agency, Cliff Baker, Nkona, Varahamihara, de
Sagres, anyone else he could find—to increase the wealth of
the world's poorest. Raise their standards of living and they
will lower their birthrates: that was his gospel.

And it was working. Slowly, at first, but more and more
clearly Stoner saw that it could work, it would work. If he
were not stopped first. If he did not run out of time.

His greatest fear was that some bright young researcher
would hit upon the central idea that would extend human life-
times indefinitely. The technology that the starship had carried could allow humans to live for centuries, perhaps much
longer. If that technology were turned loose in the world before
people learned how to control their numbers, human population would start soaring out of control. Strangely, perversely,
Keith Stoner—a man of science all his life—dreaded the
thought that science would discover the real secret of the starship, the hidden knowledge of his star brother.

At last Jo appeared at his doorway, looking fresh and bright in a sleeveless miniskirted sheath of Mediterranean tangerine. Their fourteen-year-old daughter Cathy stood beside her, a flowered Hawaiian shirt several sizes too big for her slim frame thrown over her bathing suit. She was trying to appear cool and nonchalant, but Stoner could see the excitement bubbling in her.

"Are you in the mood for some lunch?" Jo asked casually.

He looked up from the report he had been reading. "Lunch? I'm not really hungry yet."

"Come on, Daddy!" Cathy yelped. "Have lunch with us!"

"Now?" he asked, grinning.

"Now," both women said in unison.

Stoner closed the report and laid it on his desk top, then went with them down the stairs and out to the patio by the swimming pool. Several large round tables had been set out beneath the gently rustling palm trees. He could see no one, but sensed the crowd huddling in the dining room, behind the drapes that were never drawn at this time of the early afternoon.

"Are we eating out here?" he asked.

"HAPPY BIRTHDAY!" roared out two dozen voices as the glass lanai doors of the dining room slid open.

They poured out and surrounded Stoner, shook his hand and pounded his back. Stoner laughed and greeted each one of the guests while his ten-year-old son, Richard, took up the official chore of accepting the gifts they had brought and stacking them up neatly on the long table beneath the big azalea bush in the corner of the patio.

The guests were mainly family, Stoner's son and daughter from his earlier life, Jo's only brother and three sisters, and their various children. A few trusted members of Vanguard Industries' headquarters staff, from the nearby city of Hilo.

Stoner was happy to see the offspring of his first marriage. Deep within him he wanted the opportunity to try to settle their relationships, square their accounts. Almost as if he were afraid he would never see them again.

He felt a puzzled tendril of thought tickling at the back of his mind. Why should I be afraid? he wondered. His star brother wondered, too.

His son Douglas came up to shake his hand, warily, almost like a stranger. Doug was well into his forties now, but the wound that had opened between them when Stoner had left his first wife, a lifetime ago, had never completely healed.

"I'm glad you could make it, Doug," he said to his son.

"I wouldn't have missed it for anything," said Douglas. "A free vacation in Hawaii for me and my whole family? Who could turn that down?"

Douglas had grown to middle age. His blond hair was thinning, his eyes had lost much of their youthful fire. He had two sons of his own nearing twenty, but the bitterness was still there. Stoner saw it in his eyes, heard it in the tone of his voice. Douglas no longer fought with his father, no longer refused to see him. But the anger seethed just below the surface. And Douglas pointedly avoided Stoner's younger children, the offspring of his marriage to Jo.

Eleanor was friendlier, more relaxed. She had remarried a genetic surgeon in Christchurch after the death of her first husband, but they had divorced after two years. Now, a dozen years later she had a new husband and seemed at peace with the world. And with her father. Stoner felt immensely grateful for that.

Stoner embraced Elly and her teenaged daughter, shook hands with her son and her new husband, a cargo specialist for Pacific Commerce's space transport division. He was startled to sense that Elly's daughter was pregnant. I'll be a great-grandfather in seven or eight months, he told himself. It seemed strange; he did not feel old enough to be a great-grandfather. I wonder if Elly knows? I'll have to talk with the girl later on.

Aside from Elly and Doug, the only one among the guests milling around the swimming pool whom Keith had known back in his earlier life, before he had spent eighteen years in frozen suspension, was Claude Appert.

The Frenchman was as dapper as ever despite his seventy-two years. Pure white hair and trim little mustache, jaunty double-breasted blazer of navy blue, pearl gray slacks, Appert was the very picture of the perfectly-dressed Parisian.

"Claude, you're looking very well."

"Not so well as you, *mon ami*. You seem ageless."

"I'm a year younger than you."

Appert laughed. "But you cheated! You spent eighteen years sleeping and not aging one minute!"

Stoner shrugged like a Parisian.

"Still," Appert said, looking closely at Stoner's face, "you do not seem any older than you did when you first recovered from the freezing. Shave off that black beard of yours and you would look no more than thirty-five or forty."

"How are you getting along?" Stoner changed the subject.

"The same as always. It is lonely without Nicole, but there are any number of handsome widows who invite me to dinner."

"Paris is still Paris, then."

"Ah yes. The one thing that remains constant in this world of change."

"Things are changing rapidly, aren't they, Claude? And for the better, I think."

"But yes! Even the government of France has agreed to stop exporting armaments. And there was hardly a peep of protest from the industrialists. *That* is how good the economy is, these days."

Surveying the assembled guests, Stoner realized that one man was missing: Kirill Markov. He hasn't been in good health, Stoner knew, but Kir would have come no matter what. Unless something really has hit him. Better ask Jo about him.

He went through the motions of the party, and soon found that he was actually enjoying himself. There were tensions, of course, especially with Doug and Elly's daughter Susan. But it was good to see his two families in the same place, good to see an old and dear friend like Claude, even if Nicole had died. Life goes on, he told his star brother. Life belongs to the living, his star brother replied.

The presence in his mind seemed to enjoy the party, as

well. The rituals of the birthday cake were especially fascinating. As he bent to blow out the candles, for a flash of an instant Stoner's inner vision saw a parallel ritual on the world of his star brother's birth, where all fifty members of his creche celebrated the day of their awakening every ten years, coming together to unite physically no matter where their individual lives had taken them.

But the vision passed in the flicker of an eye and he was back on the patio by the swimming pool, beneath gently swaying palm trees under a blue Hawaiian sky, surrounded by friends and colleagues and—Stoner looked up sharply from the smoke of the blown-out candles. There was an enemy here. A traitor. A spy.

All his senses tingled with alarm.

Certainly not Doug, no matter how deeply his bitterness ran. No one in the family. Elly's new husband? Stoner looked at the man with fresh interest, but he turned away immediately to speak to one of the other guests.

One of Jo's people? That would be more logical. And much more dangerous. Perhaps it was corporate secrets he was after. It was definitely a man, that much Stoner sensed. But which man?

The sense of danger slowly faded. Although Stoner stayed taut-nerved and wary for the rest of the party, he could learn no more. Maybe I'm getting paranoid in my old age, he thought. How much could a corporate spy find out at a birthday party? But that's not the real problem, he knew. There's a spy in Jo's inner staff. I'll have to warn her about it.

He pulled his granddaughter Susan to one corner of the patio and, still keeping an eye on the crowd of guests eating birthday cake and drinking champagne, he let her tell him about her boyfriend and how much in love they were and how afraid she was to tell her mother.

"He's Japanese," Susan confessed, struggling to hold back tears. "He wants to marry me and take me to Osaka, where he lives." Susan looked very much like her mother: chestnut hair, round face so young, so vulnerable. With a pang, Stoner recalled that he had never spent a day with his own daughter when she had been a troubled teenager.

"How did you meet him?" Stoner asked.

"At the university in Sydney."

"He's a freshman too?"

"Yes."

"And do you expect your parents to keep on supporting you once you've married him?"

With a shake of her head, "We'll take turns working. One of us will work for a year while the other goes to classes. It'll take longer for us to get our degrees that way, but we'll manage."

"And the baby?"

The tears threatened to overflow. But Susan kept her voice level as she answered, "We've talked about it and we've decided to abort it. Neither one of us is ready for parenthood yet."

Stoner felt a sigh go through him. Deep inside his mind the alien presence there felt an immeasurable sadness at the thought of deliberately ending a life. Life is so rare, so precious! But Stoner replied silently, Not on this planet. Despite our best teachings, human life is still held cheap. Jo was right: it's the most abundant thing we have.

Yet all he said to his granddaughter was, "Why did you allow yourself to get pregnant, in the first place?"

"We didn't *plan* to! It just happened. You were young once, weren't you?"

Despite himself, he laughed. "A thousand years ago, it seems."

Still wary of the danger that he had sensed, Stoner went with Susan and pulled her mother away from the crowd. With him standing between the two women, Susan told her mother about the man she wanted to marry.

"Live in Japan!" was Eleanor's first shocked reaction.

Stoner soothed, "Half an hour away, Elly. Osaka is only half an hour from Christchurch." With a grin he bantered, "And your new husband can probably get free seats for you on Pacific Commerce spaceplanes."

Elly was totally surprised and deeply hurt. Stoner felt the anguish that raced through her and reached out to his daughter to soothe her, ease her pain, help her to assess the situation calmly. Humans react with their glands first, he knew.

Only afterwards do they examine the problem rationally. It was a survival trait back when we were half-brained apes hunted by leopards. Now it's a detriment. He felt his star brother's almost amused agreement.

Once he saw that both women had gotten past the point of hormone-drenched emotion, Stoner left mother and daughter deeply engaged in talk and rejoined the other guests. Jo was off in the dining room, he saw through the open lanai doors, equally deep in earnest conversation with several of her Vanguard executives. There's no such thing as a social occasion for her, he knew.

The sense of danger tingled along his nerves again, but so faintly that he could do no more than wonder if it was real or imaginary.

Both of Doug's boys were splashing down the length of the pool, with ten-year-old Rickie matching them stroke for stroke. Stoner smiled. Born and raised on Hawaii, young Richard could swim like a dolphin. At least the youngsters are getting along all right. Swinging his gaze around the patio, he saw Doug sitting at one of the tables the servants had set up, a full champagne bottle in front of him, his wife beside him looking unhappy.

I could change Doug, Stoner told himself. I could open my mind to him and let him see all the pain and sorrow and guilt that I feel. He wouldn't be able to hate me after that.

But his star brother asked, And what would your son have left in his life, after you do that? He does not hate you, but his anger toward you is the main emotional prop of his existence. Take that away and he might collapse altogether.

For the first time in years Stoner wondered if the alien inside him was truly his brother, or was he being controlled, manipulated by forces he could not understand? He felt a shudder of astonishment within himself. After all these years, still some doubts, some ancient fears?

Stoner nodded grimly to himself. You see how difficult it's going to be to reveal the truth to the rest of the human race.

His star brother fell silent.

BOOK II

It should be for you a sacred day when one of your people dies. You must then keep his soul as I shall teach you . . . for if this soul is kept, it will increase in you your concern and love for your neighbor.

CHAPTER 8

"YOU'VE got a spy on your staff."

The party had ended hours earlier. The family guests had gone to bed in the far wing of the house, happy with champagne and a birthday dinner of grilled mahi-mahi and New Zealand lamb. The presents had all been opened to the "ooohs" and "aaahs" of the assembled partygoers; their torn wrappings had been dutifully collected by the household robots.

Now it was nearly midnight and Jo and Stoner were undressing for bed.

Jo nodded from the doorway of her closet. "More than one."

"You know who they are?" Stoner asked.

"Yes, certainly. One of them was here today."

"I sensed it—a feeling of danger."

She turned toward him with a weary smile. "Corporate espionage is one of the facts of life in the business world, Keith."

"This was more than corporate espionage," he said. "I sensed real danger. Physical danger."

"I'm well protected," she said, walking naked across the plush carpet toward the bed. "Really, I'm more concerned that Kirill didn't show up. He said he would."

"Maybe I should call Moscow."

"I spoke to him yesterday. He seemed fine."

"He would have come, or sent word if something had prevented him . . ."

"You think he's ill?"

"He hasn't been well for a long time. He's an old man, Jo," said Stoner, stripping off his undershorts. He sat on the edge of their huge bed and reached for the phone terminal.

"He's not even eighty yet. That's not so terribly old. Not nowadays." But her face betrayed the same anxiety Stoner felt.

Stoner spoke Kirill Markov's name into the phone and its computer began searching for him. Jo wrapped a glossy silk robe around herself and sat on the bench in front of her mirrored dresser.

Within seconds the phone connected. They saw a heavy-set woman with a white nurse's cap sitting before a window lit by afternoon sunlight.

Oh god, thought Jo. Something's happened to Kir.

Stoner spoke swiftly with the nurse in Russian, then disconnected. "He's had a stroke. I've got to go see him."

"I'll go with you."

"What about your staff meeting tomorrow?"

Jo made an impatient gesture. "I can postpone it, or run it from the plane. I'll decide on that tomorrow morning. If Kirill's that sick . . . I want to be there, too."

She pecked at the phone on her dresser and called the Vanguard airport to make arrangements for a hypersonic jet in the morning.

"Not a happy ending for your party," Jo said.

Stoner sank back on the pillows. "It was a good party, Jo. Thanks. With all the business pressures on you . . . getting everybody here and making all the arrangements . . . well, I appreciate it."

"My pleasure," she said, applying a brush vigorously to her thick dark hair. The brush was backed with silver mined from an asteroid by Vanguard's space metals division.

Still looking at him through the mirror she asked, "Do you think Kir . . . is he . . ."

"Will he die?" Stoner closed his eyes for a moment. "The nurse said it was very serious. He's in intensive care."

Jo sighed. "Poor Kir."

"He's never been in very good physical shape."

"Still . . . eighty years old."

"I know. It doesn't seem so old, does it? Hell, I'm seventy-one, if you go by the calendar."

"Thank god the calendar doesn't matter for you!"

God? Stoner asked himself. His star brother said nothing.

Jo silently brushed her hair, her eyes watching Stoner's naked body on the bed. "You know, Claude said to me that you don't look any older now than you did fifteen years ago, when we first revived you."

"Yeah, he told me the same thing."

"Your beard doesn't have a single gray hair in it," Jo said.

"Well, neither do you."

She turned on the bench to face him. "Keith, I've been dyeing my hair for years! If I stopped, it would grow out as silver as Claude's."

"It might look good that way," he said.

"Oh no! I'm not ready to be an old lady yet. And I'm sure as hell not going to allow anybody at the office the slightest excuse to think I'm getting decrepit."

Putting the brush down, Jo stood up, slipped off her robe, and came to the bed.

Stoner grinned at her. "You sure as hell don't look decrepit to me."

For fifteen years he had seen her almost every day. But now he looked more intently. Now he realized with a pang of sudden fear that she was well into her middle years. Jo was in the prime of health, her body taut and still totally desirable; not an ounce of fat to be seen, not a sag or a slump. But as he slid his hands across her hips and pulled her to him he saw that there were lines in her face he had not bothered to notice before.

"We're both getting older," he said softly.

But she replied, "No, Keith. I'm getting older, but you're not. You don't seem to be aging at all."

"I could give you the same thing I've got," he said, in a whisper. "Then you wouldn't age either."

Jo shook her head. "And make me understand everybody so thoroughly that I couldn't hate them? Make me a saint, the way you are? A hell of a businesswoman I'd be, then!"

"Jo . . ."

"I decided a long time ago, Keith," she said stubbornly. "I'll stay just the way I am, aging and all. I *like* my emotions. I *need* to be able to get angry enough to swat some sonofabitch who needs swatting!''

Stoner knew it was hopeless to argue with her. They had been through all this many times before. But deep within him, he felt sad that Jo refused his star gift. She's not ready for it yet, he told himself. Someday, but not yet. His star brother asked, If this woman who knows you so intimately refuses the gift, how can you expect the rest of the human race to accept it, when the time comes?

Stoner had no answer.

Markov was dying.

The Russian was in a private room in the best hospital in Moscow, surrounded by the most advanced medical technology and human care that it was possible to give. Still he was dying.

It was a small room, dark and cool with the blinds drawn over the only window. Utterly quiet except for the faint humming of the electronic monitors. Their screens showed the ragged glowing lines of an old man's struggling heartbeat, respiration rate, brain wave activity. There were no wires attached to Markov's body, but he was held in the grip of the medical sensors as firmly as a fly enmeshed in a spider's web.

"He looks so feeble!" Jo whispered.

She sat on the only chair in the narrow room, neither noticing nor caring that her long suede coat dragged on the scuffed floor tiles. Stoner stood beside her, an obvious American in his denim jacket and jeans.

Markov's ragged white beard was nothing but a wisp now. His cheeks were sunken; the skin of his face looked brittle, spiderwebbed with wrinkles and the fine red network of capillaries. His large dark eyes, which could flash from somber to hopelessly romantic in an instant, were closed. Even his eyebrows are snow-white, Stoner realized. And his hair is almost entirely gone.

Stoner remembered awakening from a sleep of eighteen years in a room such as this. But his body had been young and strong. Markov's body, beneath the thin sheet covering him, was frail and pitifully thin.

Stoner stood by the bedside, feeling totally helpless, watching his old friend slowly slip away, sensing the growing weariness of his heart, the fragility of blood vessels stiff and clogged with age, the desperate panic of electricity flickering through his damaged brain.

If only . . .

Stoner choked off that line of thought. There's no point to it. I'm standing here in the middle of all the marvels that modern human beings can create, watching my friend die, as helpless as a Neanderthal in an Ice Age cave.

Jo sat by the bed, holding Markov's hand. For years the Russian had harmlessly pursued her with beautifully romantic speeches that hid the bashfulness of an overgrown boy. They had become friends, rather than lovers, and now Jo wept as she felt the old man's fingers growing cold.

Markov's eyes opened slowly. He tried to smile, but the stroke that had paralyzed half his body turned the effort into a grisly rictus. He tried to speak, but all that came out was a tortured groan.

Jo pressed his dying hand to her cheek and sobbed openly.

Stoner did not touch the Russian physically. Instead he reached into Markov's mind.

—I'm here, old friend.

—Keith? It is you?

—Yes.

—I knew you would come . . . to see me off . . .

—I'd rather be a million miles away, and have you healthy.

—But we are here.

Stoner nodded uneasily. He felt the pain that racked his old friend's body, the terror of imminent death that flooded his mind.

—Keith, is there an afterlife?

The question surprised Stoner. —I don't know. I don't think so.

—Maria is waiting for me, angry that I've taken so long to join her.

—You haven't lost your sense of humor.

—Only my life.

—Is there anything I can do for you? Anything at all?

—A new body, perhaps?

—We could have you frozen. Jo's corporation has the facilities and . . .

—No. No freezing for me. It is time for me to leave, dear friend. Time to let go.

—But . . .

—No hope of resurrection. This old wreck of a body would not survive the freezing process. I looked into that more than a year ago.

—Oh. I see.

—My will. You . . . I named you executor. You don't mind?

—No. Of course not. I'll take care of everything.

—No one has ever come out of freezing. Only you. Of all the bodies frozen, only you have been revived.

—That is true.

—Why? What happened on that alien ship? What did they do to you?

Stoner closed his eyes and bowed his head. Markov's pulse was weakening, his heart was failing rapidly. In another few seconds the monitors would start to wail and a frantic team of nurses and doctors would burst into the room and try to keep him alive for a few agonized hours longer.

With one part of his mind Stoner kept the monitors from showing Markov's worsening condition. They hummed to themselves and repeated the measurements that they had made a few seconds earlier, despite the Russian's rapidly deteriorating condition.

As he did so, Stoner gave Markov a mental image of what had happened on the alien starship. No other person on Earth knew about it, except Jo. And Markov would take the story to the grave with him.

The starship was a sarcophagus. It bore the dead body of an

alien who had chosen to be set adrift on the sea of space in the chance that his craft might one day reach a world that harbored intelligent life. His message was simply: You are not alone. There are other intelligences among the vast desert of stars. Take my body, study it, learn from it. Study my ship and learn from it, also.

And there was more. Far more.

The alien was roughly human in shape: two arms with four-fingered hands, although its four short legs ended in soft hoofs. Head and face only slightly different from ours. But the alien was not alone.

Within its body dwelled tens of billions of incredibly tiny objects. Machines. Each of them less than a millionth of a millimeter in size. Specialized machines that coursed through the alien's bloodstream and permeated every part of his body. Machines to repair organic damage. Machines to protect against invading viruses and cancerous growths. Machines that could make more of themselves. Machines that could think, when linked with an intelligent brain.

Each of them as small as a virus, they served as an intelligent symbiote to the alien, protecting it against disease and injury, enhancing its mind.

When the alien chose to die, the machines acquiesced. They would not control the will of their host. But they did suggest the sarcophagus to be sent out among the stars. And they helped direct its design so that it would not merely drift aimlessly, but would purposefully seek out worlds that might harbor life and intelligence.

—I have a star brother inside me. During the years that I remained frozen on the alien's spacecraft, before the craft was recaptured and brought into Earth orbit, the ship's automated systems transferred those billions of nanometer devices to my body.

—That is why . . . that is why . . .

—That is why I survived freezing. They repaired the ruptures in my cells while I was being thawed. That is why I can do the things I can do. That is why I haven't aged in the past fifteen years.

—I understand now. I understand.

A feeling almost of guilt coursed through Stoner. His star brother understood and did not interfere.

—Kir . . . if I had known, if I had any inkling that this would happen . . .

—How could you? It hit me like an automobile crash.

—But I could've transferred some of the devices to you. All it would have taken would have been a simple blood exchange. They reproduce in microseconds. They might have repaired your body, made you young and strong again.

—No. My time has come.

—It still might not be too late. Let me try.

—No! Let me die now.

—You're only saying that because of the pain and the fear. Your body is tired of fighting; your brain is soaked with the chemicals of exhaustion. We might be able to reverse all that, if you'll let us try.

Stoner sensed shock, outright terror surging through his friend's mind.

—Kir, we can save you. Let us try . . .

—To be invaded by alien—*things*? To become something not human? No, never! I can't. I can't!

—But, Kir . . .

—You can stand it, Keith, being not human. But I . . . never. I could never stand it.

Stoner sensed his friend shuddering. You don't understand, he pleaded with the Russian. It's not being inhuman. It's being more than human, Kir. More than human. The next step in our evolution.

But it was too late. Stoner felt the Russian's life ebb away, like a candle blown out by a dark wind. For a long moment he simply stood by the bed, staring at the unseeing eyes of his old friend. He killed himself, Stoner realized. He let himself die rather than accept the help I was offering.

Then a surge of blackest grief and guilt overwhelmed him.

No. I killed him. I tried to force him to accept something he wasn't prepared to deal with. He allowed himself to die rather than facing it. I killed him. I killed my best friend.

He slumped down on the bed, startling Jo, who was still holding Markov's hand.

"He's dead," Stoner said woodenly. The monitors suddenly began wailing an electronic dirge.

By the time the emergency team burst in and pushed them out into the hallway, Stoner's star brother had calmed the flow of hormones raging through his bloodstream. We are still howling apes, aren't we? he asked himself bitterly. First the glands, then the brain. His sense of guilt abated, the pain in his guts eased. But still he knew that Kirill Markov, professor of linguistics, first secretary of the Soviet National Academy of Sciences, a man who had worked with Stoner all those years ago when the alien spacecraft had first been detected, his dearest friend—Kirill could not accept the idea of sharing his body with alien symbiotes.

As they walked sadly down the hospital corridor, Stoner said to his wife, "Jo, I was too optimistic a couple of nights ago. I don't think the human race will *ever* be ready to accept partnership with an alien presence."

ISTANBUL

"COME to prayer. Come to prayer." The muezzin's call was an amplified recording that reverberated through the scorching hot morning like a brass gong.

Noura Anadolu sipped coffee on the balcony of the apartment she shared with three other stewardesses and watched the ferries trudging slowly, patiently across the Golden Horn. Sunlight glittered off the oily water beneath a molten sky. Noura felt almost glad that she had to go to the airport in another hour and work the Vienna-Frankfurt-Stockholm flight. Stockholm could be fun, the Swedes appreciated a woman with dark hair and exotic eyes. Besides, it would be much more comfortable than this wretched heat and humidity.

Two days ago she had been in Bangkok. Yesterday it was Calcutta. Nothing but blazing heat and unrelenting, sodden humidity that made the very air feel like a stifling towel wrapped around your face.

Even in nothing but her sheerest robe Noura felt as if the heat was cooking her, boiling the juices inside her. It would be better inside, where it was air conditioned. Her mother still believed that air conditioning was bad for your health, that it made you weak and gave you the chills. But then her mother still walked barefoot to the market each day and refused to allow a modern freezer and microwave into her house. The only electrical convenience she put up with was the TV set that was on twenty-four hours a day. Her mother even slept in front of it.

Noura was alone in the apartment this morning, the other stewardesses were all working, so she could take her time in the bathroom with a long cooling shower.

But as she began to put on her deep maroon uniform, her stomach cramped painfully. Surprised, she sat on the bed. Another sharp burning pain made her gasp. For several minutes she sat there waiting for the pain to go away. It did not. It grew worse. Overpowering. Noura reached for the telephone, half fainting from the pain.

By the time the paramedic team got to her apartment she was already dead, her once-beautiful face twisted into a grotesque mask of agony. The police arrived at about the same moment; she had been screaming so loudly that the neighbors had called them.

CHAPTER 9

THERE were two uniformed policemen at the nurses' station at the end of the corridor, and a chunky bald man in a gray three-piece suit. Still struggling against his sense of guilt, Stoner did not notice them until the bald man called to him.

"Dr. Stoner. Kindly allow me to introduce myself. I am Feodor Rozmenko, of the Soviet Academy of Sciences. I was Professor Markov's personal aide." He held an ID card up in front of Stoner's eyes.

Jo immediately snapped, "We're on our way to the airport . . ."

"Please! One moment only!" Rozmenko begged, smiling. He was slightly shorter than Jo, but thick in the torso and arms. Younger than his baldness suggested. The two in uniform behind him were quite tall, very blond; Stoner thought of elite military police.

"Look," said Stoner softly, "Professor Markov was a very dear friend of ours. He's just died and we'd appreciate it if you could just leave us alone for a while."

"I understand. I worked with Professor Markov for several years. I would like to think that he was my friend, also," Rozmenko said with a forlorn little smile. But he pressed ahead, "Will you be staying in Moscow overnight, or do you plan to leave immediately?"

"I told you; we're leaving right away," Jo said.

"Could I induce you to stay for just one hour more?" Rozmenko was being extremely polite, smiling hopefully at them. The two uniformed men had expressions as blank as robots.

Jo was already shaking her head, but Stoner asked, "Why do you want us to stay?"

"A certain Dr. Lucacs from the University of Budapest is here. She had come to see Professor Markov."

"So?"

Almost pathetically eager, Rozmenko went on, "When she learned that you were visiting the good professor, Dr. Stoner, she asked if she could meet you."

Jo snapped, "What does this doctor want with my husband?"

"That I do not know," replied Rozmenko. "But perhaps Professor Markov would have wanted the two of you to meet—in the interests of scientific research, perhaps?"

Stoner sensed no danger in Rozmenko. No hidden motives. He was a bureaucrat sent on a mission of diplomacy. With two big military policemen to back him up.

Turning to Jo, he said, "I'll talk to her for a few minutes, see what she wants. Okay?"

Jo looked from Rozmenko to the policemen to her husband, tense, wary. "I'll go with you."

Rozmenko, delighted, led them down a corridor and into a small conference room. It was windowless, and held only a shabby, worn table and ten rickety plastic chairs. The walls were bare and gray with age, except for a big display screen that filled one wall. The ceiling panels glowed with fluorescent lights that gave skin tones a ghastly bluish cast.

"Please to wait here one moment," said Rozmenko. "I will bring Dr. Lucacs."

The two policemen stood out in the hall, flanking the room's only door.

Jo would not sit down. "I know the Cold War's over and done with," she muttered, "but I can't help thinking that *that* is watching us." She jabbed a manicured thumb toward the blank display screen. "They could hide a whole TV studio on its other side."

Smiling, Stoner eased his lanky frame onto one of the little plastic chairs. It creaked.

"Don't get nervous," he said. "The Russians won't bite you."

Still Jo paced the length of the conference table and peered anxiously at the blank screen.

"The most conservative society on Earth," Stoner said to his wife.

"Conservative? The Soviets?"

"The Russians. They like to tell themselves that they're the savior of civilization, that Moscow is the third Rome, the last bastion of Christianity."

"I'm sure Pope Gregory would be surprised to hear that," Jo countered.

"He's an American, what do you expect?"

Jo was smiling now, but barely. "I just don't see the men in the Kremlin as conservatives, I'm sorry."

"Come on, Jo! *Look* at these people. Even their architecture is a century behind the rest of the world. Deliberately. They look to the past just as naturally as Americans look to the future."

Jo turned and glanced at the screen again. Then, "We should have left for the airport. There's no sense staying around here."

"We'll just see what this doctor wants and then we'll be on our way."

"We should have gone, Keith. I *do* have business to conduct."

"Well, let's be polite to them for a few minutes, at least. You don't want to make the Russians think that capitalists are insensitive, do you?"

Then he remembered that one of the few real friends he had in this world had just died, and his smile vanished.

"Maybe I should stay for the funeral," Stoner suggested. "Kir made me his executor."

Jo started to reply, but heard footsteps clicking down the corridor outside. She turned toward the door as Rozmenko ushered Ilona Lucacs into the tiny conference room.

Stoner got to his feet.

"Dr. Lucacs," said Rozmenko with a gesture, "Dr. Stoner and Mrs. Stoner."

Stoner could feel the heat of Jo's sudden anger. Automatic

response, he said to his star brother. Competitive female. Men respond to competition by displays of aggression supported on spurts of testosterone. Women use their brains. And their tongues.

Ilona Lucacs was almost a full head shorter than Jo. She wore a simple tweed skirt and jacket, the uniform of the academic. Jo's knee-length suede coat of burnt umber was more expensive than a half-dozen such outfits. But the tweeds could not hide the curves of Lucacs's figure, any more than Jo's striking coat, slacks, and silk blouse could mask her strength.

Stoner looked from his wife to Dr. Lucacs and realized that the Hungarian must be no more than twenty-five years old. If that.

She smiled warmly at Jo, then held her hand out for Stoner to shake. He almost felt as if he should bow and kiss her dainty fingers, as a European would. Grinning inwardly, he decided he had better not. Not with Jo already fuming.

"I am very sorry about Professor Markov," said Dr. Lucacs, in a throaty voice. "My deepest condolences."

"Thank you," Stoner replied. And he found that he could say no more. He wanted to tell her what a wonderful friend Kirill had been, how he had been a true champion of freedom and the restructuring of Soviet society. But the words choked in his throat. He felt a strange inner surge of sympathy from his star brother. I know what death is, said the alien within him. No matter how inevitable, it is always a loss, always a sorrow.

Jo was saying, "You arrived here too late to help, I'm afraid. What kind of a specialist are you?"

Dr. Lucacs blushed slightly. "Oh, I am not a medical doctor. Not a physician. My field is neurophysiology—the study of the human nervous system."

Instantly Stoner felt a danger signal flash through him.

"My area of research deals with repairing damaged neural tissue," Dr. Lucacs went on.

"Like fetal grafts for repairing brain damage?" Jo asked, all business.

"Yes. And for treating Parkinson's and other diseases of the central nervous system."

"Then why did you want to see us?"

Ilona Lucacs tried to smile and failed. "I have been assigned by my superiors at the university to examine the problems in cryonic suspension of nerve function."

Stoner looked at his wife. Jo never blinked an eye. The four people stood in the shabby little conference room, facing each other: Lucacs and Rozmenko on one side, Jo and Stoner on the other.

Stoner broke the stretching silence. "Then it's me you wanted to see, not Kirill."

Lucacs looked almost ashamed. "I came to Moscow to ask Professor Markov if he would arrange some way for me to meet you. I am very sorry it had to happen this way."

Jo said firmly, "We've stopped all research on cryonics at Vanguard Industries. It just doesn't work. As far as I know, every major corporation and university has given up on cryonics."

"Not the University of Budapest," said Lucacs, almost meekly. "You see, the president of Hungary is seventy-eight years old. He is still in excellent health, but—well, our biology department has been asked to investigate the matter once again."

"So you want to examine my husband."

"He is the only case on record of surviving cryonic freezing."

Stoner almost smiled. *They're discussing me like some prize bull that's up for auction.* Yet he sensed a deeper motive in the Hungarian scientist, something unspoken, something hidden.

"There's nothing you can do that hasn't already been done," Jo was saying. "Every test that it's possible to conduct has been done. The subject is closed."

"But in the interests of science . . ."

"It's a blind alley," Jo insisted.

Dr. Lucacs took a deep breath, as if she were standing on the edge of a precipice and had to work up the courage to jump.

"Dr. Stoner . . . Mrs. Stoner . . ." She hesitated, then plunged on, "I plead with you, as one human being to another. My position at the university depends on satisfying my department chief in this matter. My career—my entire life—is in your hands."

She was telling the truth, Stoner realized, but not all of it. There was something personal, something desperate, driving her.

Jo immediately shot back, "If you're saying that your university bosses will throw you out unless you bring my husband back to your labs, then I promise you that Vanguard Industries will offer you a job at a comparable salary or better."

The young woman looked miserable. "But this means more than a job, to me. Don't you understand . . ."

"I understand," Stoner spoke up. "I remember how departmental politics can pressure a post-doc. That's the situation you're in, isn't it?"

"It will be years before I am granted tenure," said Lucacs. "Until then, my career hangs by a thread."

Jo looked utterly unconvinced.

Turning to his wife, Stoner said, "I'd like to stay in Moscow for Kir's funeral. He doesn't have any surviving relatives that I know of. I ought to be involved in making the arrangements."

Rozmenko started to say something, thought better of it, and lapsed back into silence. He had watched the interchange with wide staring eyes. Apparently he understood what was at stake.

Jo switched into Italian, "If I didn't know you better, I'd be jealous of this little gypsy girl."

He smiled at his wife and replied in the same Neapolitan dialect, "But you do know me better, and you know there's nothing for you to be jealous of."

"Maybe her age."

"Not even that," said Stoner. In Italian it sounded romantic.

"You're going to let her examine you?"

"No. But there's something involved here that she's not telling us. It could be important. I'll convince her that there's nothing to be gained by examining me. If necessary I'll go to

Budapest to convince her superiors. And find out what's going on."

"The same way you convinced de Sagres to stand up to his generals?"

"The same way."

"Then you want me to fly back to Hilo without you."

"If you don't mind."

"I mind like hell!" Jo snapped.

"But will you do it?"

"If I refuse, will you 'convince' me too?"

With a slight shake of his head, "I could never do that to you, Jo. We're partners, you and I. We have to agree out of our own free will."

She shot a glance at the apprehensive Dr. Lucacs and the eager Rozmenko. "I'll go back to Hawaii alone," she said. "But I sure as hell don't like it."

"Come back for the funeral, and then we'll fly home together."

"Is that a promise?"

"Yes. Of course."

"Okay," Jo said reluctantly. "I'll phone you when I get home."

He tapped a finger against the communicator on his wrist. "I'll be right here."

CHAPTER 10

LI-PO Hsen believed that he was a self-made man.

Born in bustling, crowded Shanghai, his father had been a street peddler, offering stolen radios and wristwatches from his ancient bicycle on the streets and alleys of the vast city, while his mother slaved twelve hours a day in a sweatshop that manufactured electronic circuit boards more cheaply that the modern roboticized factories could, thanks to the starvation wages it paid the women who worked there.

His father had died when Hsen was barely nine years old, an opium pipe clutched so tightly in his cold fingers that it took the neighborhood mortician and two assistants to pry it loose. When he was twelve Hsen ran away from the rat-infested crumbling ruin of an apartment block that had served as home for hundreds of families. He left his graying mother to fend for herself. He could work, just as his father did. He could support himself.

He had only one goal in life: to become rich. His father's example had given him a priceless nugget of wisdom: stay off narcotics—*all* the narcotics that can cripple a man and kill him slowly from within. Hsen neither smoked nor drank. He never allowed a woman to gain a hold on him. He sold drugs, when the opportunity presented itself, and women too. But he took none for himself.

He saw his mother only once again after leaving her miserable home. Through the human chain of street talk that spread information across the length and breadth of Shanghai, he learned that she had died. For one day, a few hours merely, he returned to the filthy overcrowded slums where he had been born and gazed upon his mother's dead features. He cut a strange figure, in his hand-tailored westernized suit, among all the ragged tenement dwellers. Then he went through her meager possessions, which included the key to a safe deposit box in one of the city's largest and most dignified banks.

To his utter surprise and delight, the safe deposit box contained handfuls of paper money. The old woman had amassed a meager fortune over her years of toil. He pictured her shuffling from the factory to this bank every week, shabby and exhausted, to secrete another yuan or two in this steel box.

Hsen stuffed the bills into his pockets and strode out of the bank purposefully. He had a plan.

For although Li-Po Hsen had sworn to abstain from all narcotics, he was hopelessly gripped by the most common drug of all: the desire for wealth.

With his mother's pitiful savings he bought a hand-sized computer (his mother had probably made its circuit boards) and a train ticket to Hong Kong, the city of golden opportunity for a man of strong will, strong stomach, and quick wits.

Within five years he was a successful merchant, respected by the business community and suspected by the police of smuggling, drug running, and dealing in stolen goods. But the police could prove nothing and as Hsen's fortune grew, his esteem among his fellow businessmen rose.

By the time he was thirty he, with three older associates, created Pacific Commerce Corporation out of a failed shipping line, a scattering of warehouses in Hong Kong, Shanghai, and elsewhere, and a fleet of aged jet cargo planes whose owner faced bankruptcy and disgrace. Hsen made a key decision the following year: he convinced his three associates that Pacific Commerce must enter the booming business of space transportation. They reluctantly allowed him to start a space division, and watched with no little trepidation as Hsen poured virtually all of the company's assets into it.

By the time Hsen was forty he had bought out his three associates and completely controlled Pacific Commerce and all its sea, air, and space transportation divisions.

Now he sat in his Hong Kong office, at home in a short-sleeved, open-neck white shirt and comfortably baggy dark slacks, his reclining chair tilted back almost to the horizontal. He had a slight, wiry frame, and the powered chair in which he reclined seemed almost to be engulfing him like some cocoa-brown monster ingesting its victim.

Hsen steepled his fingers over his chest as he gazed silently at the four people—two men and two women—who sat in more conventional chairs looking back at him. One of the men was Wilhelm Kruppmann, a member of Pacific Commerce's board of directors, among other things. The other was also a white man in a business suit, looking rather nervous. The two women were Chinese, although they both wore western dresses.

The office was immense, the entire top floor of one of Hong Kong's tallest towers. Heavy silken drapes covered every window. The modernistic furniture was all teak and chrome and glass; the walls were panelled in teak. Priceless vases and porcelain sculptures adorned the vast room, dimly visible in the shadows.

The only light came from tiny pivoting lamps in the ceiling that focused on each of the figures in the room and followed them wherever they moved. Although Hsen did not mention it, each lamp was paired with a small but powerful laser that could kill with an intense burst of energy, if activated. A secret little security precaution that Hsen enjoyed.

This was his stronghold, his castle, defended by faithful electronic devices and slavish robots. At his fingertips Hsen could manipulate more energy and more information than all the emperors of China's long tortured history.

"I asked you here," Hsen said at last, "to hear the result of our search for the originator of our troubles, the master conspirator who has been working against us in so many places."

Kruppmann leaned forward eagerly. "You have found who he is?"

Hsen nodded a bare fraction of a centimeter. In the beam of light from the ceiling lamp, his eyes were lost in shadow. He pointed a slim finger at one of the women.

"My director of intelligence," Hsen said, smiling slightly. "Your report, please."

She was neither particularly good looking nor all that young, thought Kruppmann. She must be good at her work.

The intelligence director swiftly outlined the procedures whereby computer banks from half the world had been searched and scanned until three matching photographs of the same man who had visited the Brazilian president de Sagres and several other key world figures such as Dhouni Nkona had been identified with ninety-percent accuracy.

"It was a difficult search," she said, in peculiarly flat unmodulated English. "Hardly anyone recalls seeing this person. It is only in facilities where hidden security cameras automatically record each visitor that we were able to find holograms of this man. And most such holos were somehow blurred or otherwise distorted."

Hsen made a small noise of impatience.

"However," the woman went on, more hurriedly, "we did obtain three barely usable holograms, and with computer enhancement we were able to identify the man in them."

She touched a button on the keypad built into the arm of her chair and a three-dimensional hologram sprang up in the middle of the darkened room.

"I know who that is!" blurted the young man sitting beside Kruppmann.

Hsen replied mildly, "I should think that you do. It is Dr. Keith Stoner, former astronaut, former astrophysicist. The man who first made contact with the alien starship some thirty years ago."

"He was frozen for eighteen years and then revived in the Hawaii laboratories of Vanguard Industries," said the intelligence director. "That was fifteen years ago."

Hsen studied Stoner's powerful bearded face. The hologram was slightly larger than life, and the face seemed to float in mid-air like the stern image of some mighty god.

"You are certain that he's the one?" Kruppmann sounded unconvinced. "A former scientist is our master conniver?"

"He is the one," answered Hsen.

"Ninety-percent certainty," the intelligence director repeated.

Kruppmann shook his ponderous head. "I find it hard to believe that a scientist would . . ."

"He is no longer a scientist," Hsen pointed out. "One might say that he is retired. And he is married, very interestingly, to the president of Vanguard Industries, and has been so almost since the very day he was revived from freezing."

Kruppmann's mouth flapped open and closed several times. Finally he gasped, "Married to Jo Camerata?"

"Do you find that as interesting as I do?"

"The bitch!"

"Indeed."

The Swiss banker's face was turning red with fury. "We should eliminate them both!"

But Hsen held up one finger. "A moment of consideration, if you please. Consider: Stoner is undoubtedly the thorn in our flesh. Also: Jo Camerata, his wife, has undoubtedly been helping him all these years."

"Her and her International Investment Agency," Kruppmann muttered. "No wonder she . . ."

"Finally," Hsen interrupted, "Stoner is the only man to survive cryonic freezing."

The room went absolutely silent.

Hsen took a breath and said, "I suggest that Dr. Stoner is worth much more to us alive than dead. The secret of immortality seems to be hidden within his body."

"*Mein Gott!*"

"Also," Hsen went on, almost lazily, "I wonder what his motives are for fomenting the changes he has produced. Is he working for some alien creatures? Is he a Judas in our midst?"

"*Gott in Himmel!*"

Turning to his intelligence director, and the younger woman sitting beside her, Hsen asked, "Would it be possible to bring Dr. Stoner to one of our special facilities?"

The intelligence director nodded. "I will need a detailed layout of his home in Hawaii."

Hsen pointed to the man beside Kruppmann. "You were there only a few days ago."

He licked his lips nervously, then replied, "I can give you the complete layout, yeah. Security systems, everything."

"Then we should be able to abduct Dr. Stoner."

Kruppmann asked, "What about his wife? What about the traitorous bitch?"

Hsen made a small shrug. "When the time comes, we will deal with her." To himself he promised, I will deal with her personally. It will be most enjoyable.

* * *

Lela Obiri sat down with a tired, undignified thump on the hard ground, her back to the huge bole of a lofty tree. The bushes were so thick that they swallowed her slight frame almost up to her shoulders. Good camouflage, she thought absently. Wearily she shrugged out of the shoulder straps of her backpack, then leaned back against the tree's rough bark and closed her eyes.

Koku was safe. That was the important thing. Through the eyes of the young gorilla she saw that he was alone now in the forest, peacefully sitting in the middle of a clump of wild celery, calmly stripping the branches clean and eating the stalks, leaves and all. She could taste the raw celery: so crisp and delicious that it made her mouth water.

The team of hunters that had been tracking him was nowhere to be seen. But they were out there in the brush, and much smarter than Lela had at first thought they could be. They had maneuvered themselves to a position between Koku and the electronically-fenced area where the three female gorillas were waiting. They had set up a trap and now they were waiting for Koku to fall into it.

I must find some way to get past them, Lela told herself. If only the radio was working . . .

With an effort of will she made Koku look up and sniff the air. No trace of human sweat or the pungent oil they used for their guns. Strange; Lela had never noticed the odor of gun oil before. But with Koku's senses transmitted by the protein chips to the neurons of her own brain, the smell was obvious and repugnant. Koku heard no sound of anything except the normal chattering and raucous calls of the forest's birds.

Earlier in the day Lela had heard a helicopter fluttering high above the forest canopy. Perhaps her radio calls back to the headquarters of the rangers who protected this reserve had finally paid off. Maybe they had caught the poachers. But she could not make contact; no one answered her repeated calls for help. Obviously she could no longer depend on the radio.

The biochips were working fine, thank god. Lela almost felt as if she *were* Koku. She felt her teeth stripping the outer layer of the celery stalks and tasted the sweet pulp of their softer centers. She felt the solidity of the ground on which the gorilla sat. She looked up and peered around the forest greenery. She sniffed the air again and grunted with satisfaction; no humans in the area.

Can Koku sense me? Lela wondered. Can I make him get up and move even when he doesn't want to? Sooner or later I must. I've got to introduce him to the females the university released in his territory. And then leave him.

The thought saddened her. It would be like leaving a part of herself behind, forever in the forest. But that was her mission, the task she had knowingly accepted: to help this young gorilla become the founder of a family. As a mother must rear its child for the inevitable day when it will leave and establish its own home.

In the midst of her ruminations she heard the faint rattle of metal upon metal, like a hunter's rifle barrel tapping against the buckle of a strap.

Lela froze, every sense alert. There should be no other humans in this area. It could only be the poachers. Instead of waiting to trap Koku, they were looking for *her*.

CHAPTER 11

NEITHER Jo nor Ilona Lucacs seemed to notice that every traffic light between the hospital and the airport turned green as the Vanguard limousine approached it. They sped along the crowded Moscow avenues without stopping once. Rozmenko and the two police officers followed them in an unmarked sedan.

The effort made Stoner perspire slightly, in the air-conditioned rear seat of the limousine. He smiled inwardly to his star brother. Did you know that sharks also can detect electromagnetic fields? Yes, the alien presence replied. I know whatever you know.

You know a great deal more than I know, Stoner replied silently. But I'm learning.

His star brother said nothing, although Stoner could sense a quiet satisfaction.

Jo and Dr. Lucacs hardly exchanged five words through the ride to the airport. Stoner had decided to manipulate the traffic signals to get the trip over with before Jo's steaming temper got the upper hand over her good sense.

Jo was staring at the TV screen, not really seeing it but fixing her eyes on it so that she did not have to look at the younger woman. Stoner saw that a Moscow ballet rehearsal was being shown: dancers in sweat-stained leotards lifting, pirouetting, leaping across a bare stage to the faint accompaniment of a solitary piano.

From her seat next to the TV console, Ilona Lucacs had to bend uncomfortably to watch the screen. But she kept her eyes fastened on it, just as Jo did. It averted the necessity to speak.

Stoner would have laughed, but he knew it would merely add to Jo's steaming anger. His star brother noted how much the contortions of classic ballet were based on simian gestures. Especially the steps that show the crotch to the audience. If an ape did that the audience would either laugh or feel offended.

The limousine swung up the airport entrance ramp at last, then drove out to the hangar apron where the Vanguard Industries jet was waiting, a nasty dead-black beast with stovepipe scramjet engines and stubby wings that were built for speed, not looks.

Stoner walked his wife to the plane, saying, "I'll make the funeral arrangements with Rozmenko or whoever's in charge and phone you when it's all set."

"You phone me tonight," Jo said, with some heat. "Or, better yet, I'll call you as soon as I get home."

"Fine." He smiled at her.

Despite herself, she smiled back. "You're enjoying this, aren't you? Making an old woman like me jealous."

He put his arms around her and kissed her soundly. "Next meeting of the IIA, you can flirt with Cliff Baker all you want."

Jo made a half-strangled growling sound, then pecked another kiss on his lips and turned to the metal ladder of her plane's hatch. Instantly a dark Mediterranean steward appeared at the hatch and extended his hand to assist her up the three steps. She turned and gave Stoner a final wave, then ducked through the hatch.

Stoner walked slowly back to the limousine, and stood beside it as the scramjet howled to shrieking life and taxied off to the runway. He waited until he saw it take off into the leaden gray Moscow sky, then got back into the limo and asked the driver to take them to Dr. Lucacs's hotel.

"You speak very good Russian," she said. She stayed on the jumpseat where she had been when Jo had shared the rear bench with Stoner.

"So do you."

"It is taught in our schools. It is mandatory to know the language of our Big Brother."

Stoner smiled at her, noting that she made no effort at all to move beside him. They rode back to the city, stopping at red lights now and then, facing each other and carrying on an utterly meaningless mundane conversation. But through the banalities, Stoner still sensed a hidden tension in Ilona Lucacs, a motivating force, an intensity that was driving her mercilessly.

When the limousine pulled up in front of the hotel, Dr. Lucacs asked, "Where are you staying?"

Stoner could have gone to the Vanguard office, near Red Square; the staff there would have put him up in one of the company's luxury apartments. But an inner voice warned him not to be so obvious. He glanced at the hotel's facade. Stolid featureless concrete and glass, as coldly impersonal as a stack of trays at a cafeteria, the kind of a building that only a bureaucrat could love.

"This looks as good as any," he said cheerfully. "I'll stay here."

Lucacs's tawny eyes regarded him with a mixture of amusement and youthful pity. "I doubt it, Dr. Stoner. The room clerk told me the hotel was fully booked when I checked in, and I had to show him my reservation form three times before he would allow me to register."

The chauffeur had opened the limo's door and was waiting on the curbside. Stoner ducked his lanky frame through and then helped Lucacs out of the car.

"I'll give it a try anyway," he said lightly.

The hotel lobby was neat, clean, and designed for efficiency. No chairs or couches for loafers to while away the hours. No newsstand or drug store. Nothing but a polished tile floor and unadorned concrete walls that echoed footsteps off the high ceiling. And the registration desk, a wooden counter that was built so low that even Lucacs had to stoop slightly when the sour-faced female room clerk placed her key upon it.

Stoner smiled at the clerk and asked for a room.

"We are entirely booked," said the clerk smugly. She was a plump woman of forty or so, with reddish hair that looked slightly bedraggled after a long day of denying requests.

"Oh, you must have something open," Stoner said.

She started to shake her head, but instead asked, "Do you have a reservation?"

"I'm afraid not."

"Then there's nothing . . ."

"Nothing?" Stoner interrupted, his voice velvet soft. "Are you certain?"

The woman hesitated. "Well . . . let me see." She turned uncertainly toward the computer at her dimpled elbow and stared for a moment at its flickering display.

"A cancellation," she announced after a few moments of frowning study. "You are a lucky fellow."

Stoner smiled broadly at her. Dr. Lucacs stared with wondering eyes. With no luggage whatever, Stoner entered the elevator with Ilona Lucacs and suggested they have dinner together. She swiftly agreed.

His room was small. Its single bed was covered with gray-looking sheets and a small pile of neatly folded blankets, no two of them the same color. The furniture was heavy production line stuff, meant for utility and hard wear rather than looks. Computer terminal built into the TV. Bathroom functional, stark white. The only window looked out on an identical building, rows of windows with curtains drawn tight.

It was all clean, smelling of disinfectant and strong detergents. Stoner nodded to himself, satisfied, and sat on the only chair as he took the communicator off his wrist.

Holding it close to his mouth, he instructed the computer built into the bracelet to contact Jo. She would be somewhere near the Arctic Circle by now, on the polar route back to Hawaii.

"Keith? What's wrong?" Even through the miniaturized speaker the anxiety in her voice came through clearly.

Smiling, "Nothing's wrong. I just wanted to let you know that I'm not staying at a Vanguard apartment."

It took almost a full second for her reply to reach him, relayed off a Vanguard satellite. "Why not?"

"A hunch. I don't want to be so easily traced."

"Then what about this call?"

He shrugged, even though she could not see it. "The Vanguard comm system is pretty secure, isn't it?"

A longer delay than the relay time warranted. "I think so. But if you're worried you ought to contact the Moscow office's chief of security."

"I'm not *that* worried," he replied. "In fact, I'm not really worried at all. I'm just . . . following a hunch."

"Can you tell me where you're staying?"

Glancing at the multilingual safety instructions glowing on the TV screen, "Hotel Armand Hammer," he answered with some surprise.

Jo laughed. It was good to hear. "Must be where they put visiting capitalists."

"No, this is where Dr. Lucacs is staying."

"You're at the same hotel with *her*?"

"There's something going on in her head that she's not telling us about. Maybe she doesn't know it herself, but there's more involved here than she's told us."

"I'll bet there is!"

Realizing her temper was rising, Stoner soothed, "Jo, she's young enough to be my granddaughter."

"And old enough to be a mother."

"You've got nothing to worry about on that score," he said.

"Then why am I worried?"

Paulino Alvarado puffed nervously on his last cigarette. His clothes were a mess, he knew. With the army and police both looking for him, he had no other choice but to go to the men in the city who had first talked him into setting up the Moondust factory in his village. They had hidden him in seamy hotels and filthy shacks, moving him almost daily, giving him cigarettes and food in exchange for odd jobs.

And Moondust. Paulino had to have Moondust; the tiny gray pills were the difference between being alive and dying by inches. They let him have just enough to keep him going.

Each time he slept Paulino dreamed of the soldiers. He saw them again and again and he wept with the shame of his stupidity and cowardice.

Beyond his shame, beyond the hatred for the soldiers who had slaughtered his father and god knew who else, there was the fear. At the very bottom of Paulino Alvarado's soul was the fundamental fear of dying, the burning terror that drove a man to do anything, *anything* in order to survive, in order to get the next one of those gray pills.

Now he sat in a shabby windowless room, filthy, unshaved, itching from the vermin that infested his clothes, knowing that he looked like a miserable worn-out peon rather than a young man with an education and a future. There was nothing in the room except the chair he sat on, some packing cartons stacked against the wall, and two doors. One from the alley, where he had come from, and the other leading to—where? Paulino wondered.

The cigarette singed his fingers and he dropped it to the bare wooden floor, scarred by countless other butts.

Waiting. The bare fluorescent lamp up on the ceiling flickered annoyingly. Paulino shut his eyes and immediately his head drooped forward. But he saw the soldiers burning, raping, killing. He snapped awake.

The other door opened and a man stood framed in the light from the room beyond. He filled the doorway: massive body, thick arms, heavy shoulders that seemed to come straight out from his ears.

"Come in here, chico," he said in a voice as heavy and rough as his looks.

Paulino stood shakily and brushed at the filth on his shirt and slacks as he stepped uncertainly to the doorway. The roughneck stood aside so that he could enter the office.

The man behind the desk wore an elegant patterned jacket over a neatly starched pale green shirt. His mustache was thin and carefully trimmed. There was a small diamond in his left earlobe and several flashing rings on his lean, manicured fingers. On his desk, next to the telephone, was a small plastic box filled with tiny gray pills, like dirty aspirin tablets.

"It looks like you've had a rough time of it," he said, in a deep baritone. "Sit down. Jorge, give him a drink."

Paulino sputtered with the tequila, but it felt warm and strengthening inside him. The man behind the desk watched with unreadable eyes. Paulino could not help staring at the box of Moondust.

"I found out how your village was betrayed," the man said.

Paulino stiffened with sudden anger. "Someone informed on us," he growled.

The man behind the desk shook his head slightly. "No. It was a Peace Enforcers' satellite. It detected the unusual heat coming from your little factory. I know how they work. They analyzed the smoke coming from your furnace and then informed the army in Lima."

Paulino held the emptied glass in his grimy hand. It felt heavy, solid, somehow reassuring.

"The Frenchman told me that the factory was not illegal."

"He strained the truth," said the man behind the desk, smiling so slightly that he actually looked pained.

The Frenchman had also said that Moondust was not addictive, Paulino remembered.

"We can't keep you here forever, hiding from the police. We have to find someplace for you to go, something for you to do."

Paulino shifted uneasily in his chair. He felt the presence of the roughneck standing behind him like the heat from an open oven. And the pills, almost in reach.

"We must find a place for you that is safe," the elegant man continued. "Someplace where you can make a living. I understand you have a degree in computer maintenance."

"Yes, but . . ."

"We will send you to the Moon, then. As a maintenance engineer. You can help us to establish our operations there. It could be very profitable for you."

"The . . . Moon?"

"Yes. The Vanguard Industries base there needs maintenance engineers. And there are several thousand potential customers there for our wares." He smiled again. "After all, shouldn't those who live on the Moon be able to have some Moondust?"

"The Moon," Paulino repeated, his voice empty.

The man behind the desk nodded, and the roughneck touched Paulino's shoulder. He got up and started for the door. But halfway there Paulino turned and begged, "Please. Just one?"

The man behind the desk pretended surprise. "Oh? The Moondust? I forgot—these are for you." He held out the box to Paulino's eager reaching trembling fingers. "To keep you company on your journey."

Paulino grasped the little box in both hands, clutched it to his chest, and shuffled almost blindly back to the windowless room from which he had come. The roughneck shut the door behind him.

"He can be very useful to us up there," said the man behind the desk, as if justifying his decision.

The roughneck gave a snort. "If he lives."

"Even if he does not, we still get the headhunters' fee for recruiting him."

"He'll never make it on the Moon," the roughneck predicted. "Too soft. He's hooked on the pills."

The elegant man shrugged. "Then we will recruit someone else. And make a headhunter's bounty off him, too."

LONDON

ENZO Massalino stared at the display screen for a long, long time. Then he rubbed at his eyes and stared at it again. His guts were churning with a frantic turmoil of conflicting emotions: the thrill of discovery, the burning tendrils of horror, the guilty pleasure of knowing that his name will be on the first paper published about this, the growing terror that this virus would kill millions before they could find a way to stop it.

If they could find a way to stop it, he corrected himself. And his fear began to overwhelm every other thought.

He was a slight, spare man who had spent most of his life in research laboratories, always doing a competent job, never distinguishing himself, one of the faceless nameless army of researchers who stood guard over the public health.

Now the chance for immortality stared him in the face. And the chance of sudden, excruciatingly painful death. The evidence was conclusive. Fourteen cases reported from around the world: Bangkok, Cairo, Istanbul, and the latest one from Naples.

The virus attacked the victim's digestive tract, devoured

the linings of the stomach and intestines so that the victim's own digestive juices began to eat away its internal organs. Death was quick and incredibly painful. The virus's incubation time was apparently only a matter of hours.

Apparently it was water-borne. Thank god for that much, he said to himself. It's not an aerial virus. You can't catch it from sneezing or coughing.

Or can you? Plenty of water droplets in a sneeze.

He ran a hand through his thinning hair. My god, my god. We don't know enough about this virus to even get started against it. The damned bug could wipe out the whole human race before we figure out what to do about it!

He thought about his native city of Rome, with its millions upon millions living cheek by jowl over hundreds of square miles. And the jet airliners that landed and took off from Rome's three airports every thirty seconds, carrying microbes and viruses to and from every corner of the world. And the rocketplanes that spread their wings even farther and faster.

We're doomed, he said to himself. The human race is doomed.

CHAPTER 12

"WHEN I was an astrophysicist, long, long ago," Stoner was saying to Ilona Lucacs, "Hungarians told strange stories about themselves."

"Really?"

They were sitting at a candlelit table for two in the corner of a quiet restaurant not far from their hotel. It had been recommended on the list that the hotel's computer provided. When they had entered, the maitre d' had looked doubtfully at Stoner's jeans and denim jacket. Stoner had smiled and apologized softly for not being in proper dinner attire. With a perplexed frown, as if he were doing something against his inner convictions, the maitre d' muttered, "*Netu problema*," and seated them in the corner farthest from the door.

"It was as if the Hungarians prided themselves on being sneakier than other people," Stoner said.

"Sneakier?" Ilona's heart-shaped face frowned slightly. "I am not sure I understand . . ."

She still wore the same tweed skirt and jacket as earlier in the day, although she had changed to a frillier, more feminine blouse. They were speaking in English. Stoner thought it best not to show that he could pick up Hungarian, or any other language, almost instantly.

"Sneakier," he repeated. "For example, a Hungarian student I went to class with told me, 'A Hungarian can go into a revolving door behind you and come out ahead of you.'"

Comprehension lit her eyes. "Ah, yes! And the Hungarian recipe for an omelet: 'First, steal some eggs.'"

Stoner laughed.

"The best one," Ilona said, laughing with him, "is this: 'If you meet a Hungarian in the street, kick him. He will know why.'"

Their waiter was a Japanese robot that was programmed to keep their wine glasses topped off. It rolled smoothly to their table, gripped the bottle of *Egri Bikaver* from their table, and neatly poured the Hungarian red wine into their balloon glasses.

"Very good wine," Stoner commented.

"The blood of the bull," said Ilona Lucacs. "That is what this wine is called."

Stoner smiled at her and asked casually, "If I met you on the street and kicked you, would you know why?"

Her lioness's eyes instantly became guarded. She replied, "Yes. Of course. I could say the same for you, could I not?"

"I'm not Hungarian."

"But you carry your secrets within you, just as we all do."

Leaning back in his chair, Stoner heard his star brother whisper, The secret within us is much different from the secrets of other human beings.

For a long moment neither of them said anything. The restaurant was quiet, half empty. No music, neither live nor piped in through loudspeakers. The only sounds were the clinks of dinnerware and an occasional whisper of conversation. The robot waiters stood mutely at their stations, and when they moved it was practically without any noise at all.

"Have you formed a theory in your mind about why I survived freezing when no one else has?" Stoner asked.

"A hypothesis," she said. "You should use the proper term."

He accepted the correction with a small nod. "I told you, it's been a long time since I did any scientific work."

"No, I have no hypothesis. No idea whatever why you were revived successfully when all the others failed."

Stoner knew it was a lie. She was hiding something, and he had to find out what it was.

"As I told you," Ilona went on, "the task of investigating you has been forced upon me. A post-doctoral student does not deny a request that comes from the president of the nation."

That much was the truth, he sensed. But what was the rest of it?

"If you weren't forced to study this cryonics problem," he asked, "what work would you rather be doing?"

Her face took on a thoughtful look. "I was beginning to study ways of interfacing neurons with protein-based semiconductors."

"Biochips?"

Nodding, "That is what some people call them, yes."

"And the idea is to interface the biochips with the nervous system."

"Yes," she replied carefully. "With protein-based chips practically any electronics system can be implanted into the human body and wired directly to the brain."

Stoner took a sip of wine. "You can carry your computer around inside your head. And your communicator with it. You can access other computers and get the information directly in your mind."

"And the information comes as sensory data," Ilona said,

more eagerly. "You do not merely see letters and numbers, you *experience* the data, taste it, hear it, smell it."

Stoner laughed softly. "I wonder what a quadratic equation tastes like."

"Communications between individuals can become like mental telepathy," Ilona said. "You can experience direct mind-to-mind linkage."

A wisp of memory gusted through Stoner's mind. Cavendish. The haunted, hollow-eyed British physicist who had drowned himself when they had been on Kwajalein. The old KGB had implanted electrodes in his brain's pain center. Markov had told him the truth of it, years ago.

"It is an enormous breakthrough," Ilona was saying, her excitement growing. "The size of the human brain has not grown since the Ice Ages. A baby's head can be only so big, of course, otherwise it could not survive birth."

"Neither would the mother," Stoner said.

"Yes, certainly. With biochips, however, we can increase the *power* of the brain by connecting it electronically to computers and other information systems."

"An evolutionary step forward," Stoner murmured, knowing it was merely the first step toward the level where all humans shared their existence with star brothers.

"Exactly!"

"You could also use such technology to pry into people's minds," he cautioned. "Even control their thoughts."

Lucacs stared at him for a long moment, her expression going from excitement to deflation to—something else. "Yes, that is true. It is also possible to stimulate the brain's pleasure centers directly. A new form of narcotic."

"Have you tried it?"

"Direct stimulation has been going on for years," she said. "It is one of the little vices that only an elite few researchers can indulge in."

"Sounds like more than a little vice to me."

"It is harmless," she said, but her face betrayed the lightness of her tone.

There's more to it, Stoner knew. He studied her face as she sipped at the wine, then lowered her eyes and returned her attention to the meal on the plate before her.

"A colleague?" he asked gently.

She looked up at him, her eyes alert again, alarmed.

"I have a hypothesis about you," he said, trying to make it sound amusing, nonthreatening, "even if you don't have one about me."

She said nothing, but there was more than wariness in her eyes now. Deep within her, Ilona Lucacs was afraid, with the terrible feral fear of a trapped animal.

"Before your superiors sent you looking for me, you were working with a colleague—about your own age, I think—on the biochip interface problem."

"That is true," she said, her back stiffening.

"He has become addicted to brain stimulation, hasn't he?"

The fork slipped out of her hand and clattered to the floor. A few of the other diners turned their heads. Their table robot rolled swiftly to the spot, deftly picked it up between two rubber-padded stainless steel fingers, and replaced it with a clean fork drawn from the silverware drawer built into its midsection.

"Hasn't he?" Stoner probed.

Ilona Lucacs made a smile that held no trace of joy. Stoner saw a hint of anger in her gold-flecked eyes.

"You are almost correct, Dr. Stoner," she said coldly. "Almost. But it is not my colleague who is addicted to the stimulant. It is me."

Stoner finally recognized the expression in her tawny eyes: defiance.

In Hawaii it was almost nine a.m.

Jo had slept poorly on her scramjet flight back to Hilo, and the fact that Keith had not phoned her yet did not improve her crankiness. It's still dinnertime in Moscow, she told herself. Then she pictured her husband at dinner with that Hungarian witch and she felt her blood seething within her.

Still, when she swept into her office at the Vanguard complex on the edge of the city, she looked as sharp and fresh as on any other day in a cream-colored sleeveless camisole and ginger-brown knee-length skirt. And makeup that covered the dark rings of sleeplessness under her eyes.

She saw her reflection in the blank display screen on her office wall and thought idly that her hair was getting longer than she wanted it to be. The longer it is the more time and trouble it takes. But Keith likes it long and why the hell hasn't he called me, it must be getting on toward midnight in Moscow.

She took in a deep breath, held it, then exhaled slowly. It should have calmed her. It did not. Looking again at her faint reflection she wondered if the time had come for cosmetic surgery. Several of her friends had undergone face-lifts and . . .

Nonsense! Jo dismissed the idea with a disdainful grimace. With all the toners and tighteners the Vanguard cosmetics division produces, if I ever need a face-lift I'll fire the whole division's staff.

Her sense of humor somewhat restored, Jo sat down in her contoured powered chair and tapped the button in its armrest that activated the comm system.

"Vic Tomasso," she said. Then she tilted her chair back slightly and began her day's work.

By the time she had scanned the latest figures on the pharmaceutical division's quarterly sales, Vic Tomasso rapped lightly on her open office door and stepped in.

Jo's office looked more like an informal sitting room than the nerve center of a powerful multinational corporation's president. Instead of a desk, conference table, and the other imposing symbols of authority, the office was furnished with comfortable chairs and two small sofas. The wall decor could be changed at the touch of a button in the armrest of Jo's powered chair. At the moment it was cool forest greens and earth colors.

Like the changeable decor of the office, Vic Tomasso was a chameleon. Neither especially tall nor broad-shouldered, he had worked hard since a teenager at maximizing his physical potential. Office gossip claimed he spent more time in the gym than on the job, and most of his evening hours in the beds of married women. In other times he would have been a beach boy, making his living by hanging around tourist hotels and offering a smiling youthful escort to lonely women.

Today he was a corporate executive, the staff assistant for security to the president of Vanguard Industries. Most of the world thought he was one of Jo Camerata's handsome young men, and there was no doubt that she enjoyed having handsome young men working for her. But each of them had to have some talent for business, or no matter how handsome or eager they were, they did not last long at Vanguard.

Vic Tomasso's real talent, beneath his perfect smile and thick wavy hair and darkly handsome face, was his ability to emulate a chameleon. For Vic Tomasso was a corporate spy.

He gave Jo his best and brightest smile as he sat on the sofa beneath the picture window that looked out on the distant Pacific. Tomasso wore a standard business outfit: collarless tunic of navy blue and light gray slacks. His shirt, though, was glittery electric blue and unbuttoned far enough to show off his muscular hairy chest.

"No jewelry today?" Jo quipped.

He grinned at her. They had a standing joke about which of them owned the more jewelry. Jo wore two gold and diamond bracelets and three rings.

"Just this today." Tomasso pushed up the left sleeve of his tunic to reveal a heavy silver bracelet studded with turquoise.

"Navaho," Jo said, making it sound disappointed.

"I'm in a cowboys-and-Indians mood," he explained.

Jo did not follow his hint. Instead, she asked, "What happened in Hong Kong? What's Hsen up to?"

Tomasso's smile vanished. "Kruppmann was there. And Hsen's chief of intelligence has come up with holograms of your husband."

Jo felt a cold fist clutch at her heart. "They've identified him?"

"Yep. They know he visited de Sagres in Brasilia, and they

figure that he's been involved in several other affairs they don't like."

"Christ! I've got to get Keith back here where I can protect him."

"They're not too happy about you, either," Tomasso said.

"I didn't think they would be. What else? What are they planning to do now that they know?"

Running a hand through his hair, "They want to get your husband out of their way. And you, too."

"How? What are they planning?"

Tomasso made an elaborate shrug. "Beats me. They pumped me for the site of the next board of directors meeting, then Hsen told me to come back here and wait for further instructions."

"Do you think he suspects you're really working for me?"

"He might, yeah, maybe."

Jo realized she was biting her lip. She straightened up the chair. "Not a word of this to anyone," she commanded. "No written reports. This is strictly between you and me."

"Like always. Right."

"We don't know who could be leaking information to Hsen."

"You think he's gonna try something at the board meeting?"

"He might," Jo said. "Maybe we'll make it a video conference; then we won't all have to be in the same place."

Tomasso got to his feet, waited a moment for Jo to say more. When she did not, he walked out of her office, leaving Jo frowning in deep, desperate thought.

I've got to start polling the board members and find out how many Hsen's got in his pocket. Time to start twisting arms, she told herself.

Tomasso had not told her that Hsen had asked about the layout and security systems of Jo's house. And Jo did not think to ask herself if her corporate spy might not be a double agent.

Stoner lay naked on the hotel's overly soft bed and stared at the ceiling for a moment. Remembering Jo's suspicions, he wondered if there were cameras or recording devices hidden behind the smooth plaster up there. He could sense none, but that did not always mean none were there.

Absence of proof, he reminded himself, is not proof of absence. The first probes of the planet Mars did not find any traces of life there, but that didn't mean there was no life on Mars.

He could almost feel the hosts of nanometer symbiotes in his blood and tissues assimilating the wine and food of his dinner with Ilona Lucacs. My alien brother protects me so well that I can't get drunk, he said to himself. He felt a wry laughter deep in his mind and remembered that he was never by himself. And never would be.

Lifting his left arm so that his wrist communicator was above his mouth, he phoned Jo in Hilo. Her computer replied that she was in a meeting, but his call would be added to her list of messages.

"I love you Jo," he said to the machine. "And my virtue is still intact."

He did not feel the need for sleep. Ilona Lucacs was addicted to electrical stimulation of her brain's pleasure center. That was the real hold her superiors had on her. He pictured her in her room now, sprawled on the narrow hotel bed, the small case that looked like a portable computer lying open on the floor, wires as thin as spider's silk leading from it to electrodes pasted on her forehead, all the world forgotten as a current of pure pleasure flowed through her brain.

No need for sex. No need for food or drink or anything. As long as the current flowed she was in ecstasy.

The machine must be programmed to turn itself off, he thought. Otherwise she runs the risk of killing herself.

I could get her off the addiction, he told himself. But what kind of harm would I be doing if I just overpowered her addiction with my own commands? Would that destroy her? It might, he decided.

He asked his star brother how he would handle the problem if he became addicted to direct stimulation. It's not like drugs or other chemicals, he pointed out. It's direct electrical stimulation of the pleasure centers.

His star brother's answer was immediate. Stop the neural
impulses of the pleasure center. No discharge of those nerves,
no sense of pleasure. And therefore no addiction.

It's simple when you have a few trillion symbiotes inside
you, Stoner said. And his star brother agreed.

Then he sat bolt upright on the bed, a powerfully-built man
in his middle years with a strong black beard and a look of
sudden revelation on his face. The question that had eluded
him ever since he had met Ilona Lucacs finally reached the
surface of his mind.

What else is she after? If they're into biochips, they're only a
step or two away from nanotechnology. From building the kind
of self-replicating machines that course through my body.

She knows! Or at least she suspects the truth about us. She
does have a hypothesis about me and it's damned accurate.

The thought filled him with unease. Why? he asked his star
brother. What is there to be afraid of? He knew the abstract
worry that nanotechnology would cause a new and irresistible
population explosion. Reduce the death rate to nearly zero
overnight, yes, but it takes generations to reduce the birthrate. With symbiotes protecting their health and extending
their lifespans, the human race could populate itself into extinction, bury the planet Earth in human flesh, even swamp
the entire solar system.

That much Stoner knew. He had worked for fifteen years to
prepare the way for nanotechnology, to get the human race to
control its numbers *before* this gift from the stars raised them
to the next level of their evolution.

But the growing terror he felt at the realization that others
were developing nanotechnology on their own was beyond all
rational, reasonable fear. What is it? he asked his star brother.

His star brother did not reply.

CHAPTER 13

"WE must be ready to strike when Stoner returns to Hilo."

Li-Po Hsen listened carefully to his chief of security. The woman's flat round face was as impassive as the westerner's stereotype of the inscrutable oriental while she briefed Hsen in precise detail on her plan for abducting Stoner from his own home.

"The man Tomasso will tell us when he returns?" asked Hsen.

"Yes," the woman acknowledged. "It should be within the next day or two. That gives us very little time to prepare."

The tabletop display screen glowed in Hsen's darkened office with an engineering drawing of the house outside Hilo. The security system wiring was shown in red.

"There is no way to override the security system," she said. "It has its own power source inside the house."

"Corrupt one of the servants, perhaps?" Hsen suggested.

"There are only six human servants, all of them drawn from Ms. Camerata's family in southern Italy. It would be difficult to sway them, especially with so little time available."

"What then?"

"Overwhelming force. We will require a mercenary attack force of at least twelve men. Twenty would be much better."

Hsen nodded. "But how will you get that large a number into the main house without raising an alarm that will bring Vanguard security forces from the outlying buildings?"

"They must get in and out before the Vanguard security teams can react."

"Yes, but how?"

For the first time since Hsen had known her, the security chief smiled. Only slightly, but the corners of her mouth definitely curved upward.

"They will arrive from the sky, like angels," she said. "And depart the same way."

Stoner met Ilona Lucacs for breakfast in their hotel's coldly efficient automated cafeteria. One entire wall consisted of gleaming metal and glass display cases, shut tight until a guest touched the button that popped that window open. No warmth of cooking, no odor of food. As hermetically sealed as a space capsule, Stoner thought. And just about as appetizing.

Other hotel guests already half-filled the austere cafeteria, chattering and clattering, the noise of their talk and eating echoing almost painfully off the bare walls. Stoner and Dr. Lucacs went through the line wordlessly, making their selections, little sighs of air gushing out when a window snapped open.

Stoner studied her face closely. *She seems to have slept well. No bags under her eyes, no nervous fidgets.* He realized that she combed her honey-colored hair down over her forehead in bangs that almost reached her brows. *Must paste the electrodes to her forehead,* he thought. *Or maybe she uses some sort of helmet that fits over the top of the head.*

Just the slightest touch of a delicate probe into her mind. She flinched instantly, but Stoner saw the flicker of a vision. Ilona Lucacs had shaved off all her hair so that the electrodes could be planted firmly against her scalp. She wore a wig to hide her baldness.

They sat at a small table along the far wall. Ilona wore a fresh blouse of nondescript beige beneath her same tweed suit. Stoner had no other clothes except the denim jacket, jeans, and light blue cotton twill shirt he had arrived in. They had been cleaned overnight by the hotel's robots, and he had instructed the hotel computer to buy two complete changes of clothes for him.

He watched her picking at the eggs and sausages she had selected, then asked, "Do you want to get off the stimulation?"

"Off the juice?" Ilona's expression showed mild amusement. She had expected this. "Why should I want to get off it?"

"It's an addiction, isn't it?"

"It has no harmful side effects."

"None?"

She spread her hands. "None at all."

Stoner leaned back in his chair and realized that she had spent the entire night in electrical ecstasy. The glow of it was still in her face. But she had no appetite for food.

"Do you program the input yourself?"

"Yes, of course."

"How long do you stay plugged in?"

She looked away without answering.

"How long was it when you first started?" he asked. "How long was it a week ago?"

Ilona refused to meet his gaze.

"It gets a little longer every night, doesn't it? You turn those dials just a bit higher every time. Just a little longer each time. Just a little more current."

"This is really none of your business, Dr. Stoner," she said, her tawny eyes snapping. "I can take care of myself."

He jabbed his fork into the thin, cream-covered pancake on his plate. "Sure, you can take care of yourself. Until one morning you don't get out of bed. Until they break down the door of your apartment and find that you haven't eaten in three or four days. Find you in the midst of your own shit, dehydrated and starving. Maybe they won't find you until you're dead."

Her nostrils flared angrily. But she controlled herself immediately and said, "I can handle the juice. I always check the cut-off time before I put on the electrodes."

Stoner made up his mind. "You want me to go to Budapest with you?"

Startled by the abrupt change of subject, "Yes, of course. That is why I came here."

"I'll do it only if you allow me to help you get off the stimulation."

She tried to laugh. "Really, Dr. Stoner, that is rather ridiculous."

"That's my deal. Take it or leave it."

Those lioness's eyes took on a sly, almost smirking look. "Very well. If that is what it takes to bring you to Budapest, I accept your terms."

"We can leave this afternoon, as soon as I finish making the arrangements for the funeral and the reading of Professor Markov's will."

"Fine."

She had no intention of letting him or anyone else take away her pleasure machine. She regarded him with the amused contempt that the young have always shown when their elders throw morality at them. Stoner knew this.

He also knew that somewhere in Budapest, Ilona Lucacs had a friend who had deliberately started her on her addiction, a friend who was moving toward the kind of nanotechnology that his star brother represented. And for some reason, his alien symbiote desperately feared that development. It was a strange sensation. Stoner had never felt fear in his star brother before.

Despite his little cache of Moondust, Paulino Alvarado was miserably sick all the long hours he was in space. He had travelled from Peru to the Brazilian spaceport at Belém aboard a Panavia jet, forged papers and money for bribing customs officials in his wallet. With a fresh hit of Moondust bolstering him, he had walked through the spaceport's boring routine of a perfunctory physical examination and the endless signing of liability waivers. The medics did not detect the Moondust in his blood; it was designed to be untraceable. Only its absence created metabolic imbalances.

Then he had joined two dozen other men and women in the spare, stripped-down passenger compartment of a Pacific Commerce spaceplane. This was no tourist flight; most of the sleek rocketplane's interior space was devoted to cargo for the Vanguard Industries base on the Moon. The passengers were mostly new hires; no comforts were wasted on them beyond the minimum required for safety. Their compartment was strictly utilitarian, windowless, scuffed and stained by years of ferrying men and women into space.

The instant the plane's engines cut off, Paulino felt his guts drop away and he became thoroughly, wretchedly sick. He felt as if he were falling, and even though he gripped the armrests of his narrow seat with white-knuckled desperation, a primitive voice inside his brain told him he was plummeting madly toward infinity. He swallowed another pill dry, but instead of helping, it enhanced every physical sensation to the point where Paulino felt like screaming. He barely controlled himself.

For only a few moments, when the ship's payload pod was detached from the spaceplane and boosted on a high-energy trajectory toward the Moon by an orbital tug, did the panic of falling disappear. To be replaced by a bellowing surge of thrust that crushed Paulino into his seat with the weight of demons on his chest.

Then it was weightlessness again, and Paulino retched into the bags they had given him until he thought he would puke up all his guts. How many thousands of Yankee dollars was he vomiting up? The contents of the paper bags were worth a small fortune.

Others were puking too. The cabin stank of vomit, and it only took one miserable person's sickening noise to start everyone upchucking all over again.

Finally the pod touched down on the dusty surface of the Moon. Not that Paulino could see anything in the windowless compartment. But he felt a jarring thump and then the sense of weight returned. Not like home, but suddenly his stomach returned to where it should be (sore from the hours of retching) and the screaming panic in his mind went away. Even the stench seemed less acrid, less sickening.

It was easy to tell the new hires from the veterans as the passengers got up from their seats and made their shaky way toward the hatch. Paulino and his fellow newcomers were ashen faced, their legs were wobbly, their hands trembling. Even though they lunged desperately at the hand grips set into each seat back along the plane's narrow aisle the low lunar gravity made them stumble and stagger. They looked awful, and the veterans grinned at them and joked to one another.

"Lookin' kinda green there, rookie."

"Don't worry, kid. A couple minutes out in the sun will give you a nice tan. Right down to your bones."

It was difficult to walk. He felt so light that he lurched or hopped every time he tried to take a step. The veterans laughed at the newcomers' clumsiness.

"You'll get used to it, kids."

"If ya don't break yer asses first!"

Again Paulino stood in line and signed the papers put before him. This time, however, there were no human beings on the other side of the desks; only computers with interactive programs on their screens. And no chairs. The desks were chesthigh; the newcomers signed and walked along as if they were on an assembly line. Paulino moved cautiously, as though teetering on the edge of a precipice, hardly looking at his surroundings. In truth there was little to see.

Vanguard Industries had established a mining center dug into the outer wall of the eighty-kilometer-wide crater Archimedes, on the shore of the broad Mare Imbrium. The base was almost entirely underground, and for his first few hours on the Moon, Paulino was guided through a maze of tunnels and winding, curving corridors, stumbling and bouncing foolishly with every step he attempted to take.

When at last he was left alone in his quarters, a spare, spartan cell deep underground, he gave no thought to where he was, or what he had seen or failed to see, or to his miserable past or his dubious future as a drug pusher. He swallowed a bit of Moondust, collapsed onto the narrow bunk and fell immediately asleep. He was so exhausted that, for once, he was not tormented by the nightmare visions of his village being destroyed. He did not dream at all.

CHAPTER 14

STONER began to worry when he realized that the government car Ilona Lucacs had obtained was not driving in the direction of the airport.

"We're not going to Sheremetyevo?" he asked.

Sitting beside him on the rear seat of the black unmarked sedan, Ilona replied easily, "No. To a military airfield out beyond the ring road."

He gave her an inquisitive glance.

"When one works for the president of the nation," she explained with a slight smile, "one does not have to travel by commercial airliner."

Stoner accepted the explanation, realizing that the Hungarian woman was holding back part of the truth. As usual, he said to himself.

It was late afternoon. Stoner had spent the day making funeral arrangements for Kirill Markov through Rozmenko, the bureaucrat from the Academy of Sciences. There had been some legal holdup about reading the will, and Stoner had decided to go to Budapest with Lucacs rather than stew around Moscow, waiting for the lawyers to sort out the difficulty. Then he had returned to his hotel, stretched out on the sagging bed, and phoned Jo to tell her he was on his way to Budapest.

He could feel the cold of ice in Jo's voice. "Is it absolutely necessary to traipse out to Budapest? Don't you think you're asking for trouble?"

Holding his wrist comm in his hand and keeping it close to his lips, he replied, "There's something going on at their university that I've got to look into, Jo. It's important."

She caught the urgency in his tone. "Biochips?" she guessed.

"Clever woman," said Stoner. "That—and maybe more."

Jo made a huffing, sighing sound the way she always did when she accepted a situation without liking it. "Stay in constant touch with me," she said.

"Yes, boss," he joked.

He put the comm unit back on his wrist, picked up the little bundle of clothing that the hotel had obtained for him, and used the computer terminal built into the room's TV set to settle his bill and check out.

Now, as he sat beside the young Hungarian scientist, their car passed through several checkpoints where soldiers with rifles slung over their shoulders minutely examined their passports and the papers that the driver had tucked in the visor over his seat. Finally the car pulled up on the concrete apron outside a huge hangar. A solitary military transport was parked there, twin jet engine nacelles hanging from swept-back wings. The plane was painted olive drab, and bore the markings of the Hungarian air force.

Almost wordlessly, Stoner followed Ilona Lucacs into the plane, ducking his head in its low, narrow interior. There were twenty seats inside, arranged in five rows, two by two with an aisle up the middle.

The two of them were the only passengers. A woman in military uniform poked her head through the hatch up front and asked in Hungarian:

"Are you ready to leave?"

"Yes," said Ilona.

"Fasten your safety belts, then. No smoking."

She closed the hatch and the engines whined to life. Stoner grinned at the brevity of the safety lecture. On a commercial flight they would have gotten a five-minute video that amounted to the same information.

They took off into the setting sun, the engines roaring so loudly that the whole plane rattled. Conversation was virtually impossible over the bellowing howl. The plane vibrated so much that Stoner kept his seat belt tightly fastened as they arrowed high into the air and sped westward.

"The flight should take only about an hour," Ilona shouted over the din.

Stoner nodded and closed his eyes, pretending to sleep. Instead, he asked his star brother once again why the possibility that Lucacs and her coworkers were developing the beginnings of nanotechnology was so fearful.

We have known, you and I, that our symbiosis is the model for the next step in human evolution. We have worked for fifteen years to set the stage for that step forward, to create the global political and economic conditions for accepting this new concept. Why be afraid of it now?

Silence. Beneath the rattling droning roar of the plane's engines Stoner heard nothing. No answer from his star brother.

He probed harder. I know the biochips carry with them the possibilities for abuse. This woman I'm with is a perfect example of that. But they are necessary. They are the first step toward the nanotechnology that will bring the human race its own symbiosis. What is there to fear?

Still no response. For the flash of an instant Stoner felt as if his star brother had gone away, abandoned him, left him as alone and separated as all the rest of the human kind. But the panic passed in less than a heartbeat. He knew his star brother remained within him, they were inseparably linked forever.

But his star brother was afraid, and this made Stoner feel fear—and an overwhelming urge to help his brother, to dig out the roots of this fear and conquer it.

Together we can do it, he said silently. Together we can face it and overcome it.

The drone of the jet engines faded away. The vibrations of the plane's flight disappeared. Stoner was back on the world of his star brother, walking across a broad field of orange motile grass. The individual leaves flowed away from his boots as he walked, baring the slightly pinkish soil to his tread, then closed again behind him. The white sun shone hot and bright overhead. And once again he saw the tower that reached to the sky.

He stopped in the middle of the field, still so far from the tower that it seemed like a fragile silver thread gleaming in the sunlight, rising from the horizon and climbing up, up, upward until he had to bend slightly backward and crane his neck to see it piercing to the zenith overhead.

The world where my star brother was born, Stoner knew. But the presence in his mind whispered, That is only partially true.

The open field slowly dissolved, like watercolors washing away, melting, flowing. The great silver sky tower wavered and then dissolved from his sight.

Now Stoner stood in the midst of a vast city. Magnificent temples of polished stone rose massively all around him. He was in some sort of municipal plaza, huge smooth flagstones beneath his booted feet, temples of immense dignity on all four sides of the square.

The sky was red. Not like a sunset. Red as blood. Red with darkness rather than light. From somewhere beyond the massive bulk of the temples bright flares flickered, almost like explosions off in the distance. Yet Stoner heard no sound.

Utterly alone, he strode across the great stone plaza in the blood-red light, heading straight for the largest of all the temples, directly in front of him. His footsteps clicking against the flagstones were the only sounds he heard. Not even the sigh of a breeze disturbed the immense empty plaza.

A splendid broad stairway rose before him, topped by rows of gigantic columns. The frieze above depicted creatures who were far from human. With a mounting sense of dread, Stoner climbed those steep stairs while the sky flashed and darkened above.

Slowly he passed through the rows of columns, almost reluctant to enter the temple itself. Something was in there that he did not want to see. Danger. Horror.

The interior was dark, deeply shadowed. Stoner hesitated at the wide entryway, waiting for his vision to adjust, wishing that the darkening red sky were brighter. He shuddered and stepped forward.

A flash of light, like an explosion or a stroke of vengeful lightning, strobe-lit the temple's interior for the briefest instant. Bodies. Twisted, agonized, horrifying bodies. Faceted eyes staring sightlessly. Alien limbs contorted in death throes. Bodies heaped atop one another as though piled up by a callous bulldozer.

Stoner blinked against the vision and darkness returned. He stood frozen at the temple's entrance, unwilling to move forward, unable to move back.

Another strobe of brilliant light. There were thousands of dead bodies, mounds of them taller than his own head. All straining in their final moments toward a colossal statue of something not human.

Darkness again. Stoner was gasping for air. He felt sweat trickling down his brow, stinging his eyes. He wanted to leave this place of death. His nostrils flared, waiting for the stench of decay to reach him.

He felt, rather than heard, a distant rumble. A volcano erupting? The ground splitting apart? The red sky glowered and throbbed. The sullen dull light grew enough for Stoner to make out the piles of dead straining toward that enormous statue with their last strength. Their god, their hero, their final desperate chance for salvation. In the blood-red shadows he could not make out much of it, but it was totally nonhuman, bizarre, with strange shape and utterly alien geometry.

Yet it was not grotesque. Somehow Stoner felt the statue had a dignity to it, a grandeur, even. It had been created by a sculptor with loving devotion.

A sculptor who was dead. The city was dead. The entire world was dead.

The intelligent creatures who had created the statues and raised the temples and built the city were all dead. Extinct. Gone forever from the universe. Every form of life on the planet, from the simplest virus to the tallest trees and largest beasts, were all wiped out, killed without mercy and without exception. Their dead bodies could not even decay.

It was a planet of death. It had existed this way for millions of years. It would remain preserved in death until its star collapsed and exploded.

Why show me this? Stoner asked his star brother, while every nerve in his body screamed to be released from this grisly vision.

Because your world could become this, the presence in his mind replied. The human race could destroy itself and every living creature on Earth. Your people have that power in their grasp.

And Stoner realized that the terror he had felt in his star brother was not merely fear. It was shame.

Stoner opened his eyes, groaning, choking, the breath gagging in his throat. He felt perspiration beading his brow, his lip.

"A bad dream?" Ilona Lucacs asked, from the seat beside him.

He was in the jet transport plane. Its noise and vibration seemed comforting now, reassuring.

Gasping, "Yes, a bad dream. A real nightmare."

"Are you all right?"

He nodded, struggling to pull himself together.

She pointed toward the tiny window at her elbow. "We are coming down for a landing. The flight is almost over."

Stoner leaned across to look out the window. Nothing but green hills and country streams. Turning, he looked out the other side, across the empty aisle. No sign of a city.

"I thought we were going to Budapest," he said.

Ilona Lucacs smiled apologetically. "Not exactly," she said. "Not exactly Budapest."

Jo swam the length of the pool slowly, methodically, using an overhand crawl stroke that provided the most propulsion through the water for the least amount of exertion.

Her mind was racing, though. Keith should have called by now. Even with the time difference he ought to be in Budapest. She had tried to reach him on the phone but the damned computer said it could not establish contact with him. Something's wrong, she knew. That wrist comm unit ought to be good anywhere, that's the reason we manufacture them. Millions of them sold all around the world. Why isn't Keith's working?

She reached the end, kick-turned, and started languidly back for the shallow end again. Maybe he doesn't *want* to be contacted? That young Hungarian bitch was damned good-looking. I know I can trust Keith. Sure. But can I trust her?

Standing hip-deep in the crystal-clear water, Jo climbed out of the pool and called to her children, sitting under the big palm tree at the end of the patio, watching the Saturday morning science shows on TV.

"Cathy, Rickie—come up to my office. Time for a fire drill."

"Aw, Mom, do we have to?"

"Again?"

Catherine was fourteen, that lean-legged coltish age when she was turning into a woman but still wanted to be a little girl. Richard, at ten, already showed his father's stubborn jaw and penetrating gray eyes.

Jo did not bother to say another word. Both children knew that when their mother gave an order she expected them to follow it. There was no wheedling with Mom.

The three of them trooped upstairs to Jo's office, just off the master bedroom, Jo wrapped in a sunset orange bath towel, Cathy in a flowered bikini, Rickie in his customary ragged cut-offs.

For more than an hour Jo drilled her children on the security measures that protected the house. Escape routes, emergency numbers to call, safe nooks for them to hide in until rescued. She called it a fire drill, but she also impressed on them that burglars might try to break into the house.

"Or kidnappers," Rickie said solemnly. "Like on TV."

"Yes," Jo nodded, equally serious, "there's always that possibility."

"Kidnappers?" Cathy looked frightened.

"Don't be upset," said her mother. "There are always at least five live servants here at the house at all times, and they know how to deal with intruders."

"You mean like Claudia and Uncle Nunzio?" Cathy looked unconvinced. "They're so *old*!"

"Not too old to protect you," Jo said. "And there are plenty of Vanguard security guards down the road, just a couple of minutes away."

"They've got guns," Rickie said, somewhat enviously.

"And we have all the electronic alarms and detectors," Jo said, still concerned that Cathy might be frightened. She wanted her children to know what to do in an emergency, but she did not want to scare them unnecessarily.

"If anything happens when your father or I are not here, you can always call Vic Tomasso," she told them. "If you see or hear anything that you think is suspicious, phone Vic right away."

WASHINGTON

THE Secretary of Defense, whose normal expression was a sullen scowl, actually smiled as he began to speak. The President sank back in her chair, realizing they were in for a scolding.

"So it's finally come," said Defense, hunching forward and locking his hands prayerfully on the gleaming broad table top. "After years of starving the Defense Department, you need the Army. After ignoring the needs of the nation and trusting to a bunch of foreigners in the Peace Enforcers to do the job Americans should be doing for themselves, you need us. You *need* the military discipline and dedication that you've scorned for so many years."

The Secretary of the Interior, who was once on the U.S. Olympic boxing team, snapped from across the table, "Cut the crap, Jerry. We got no time for speeches. This is an emergency."

Defense glared at his black colleague, but closed his mouth. The President sighed audibly.

"We've got to seal our borders," said the Secretary of Agriculture, "and prevent this virus from getting into the country."

"It's *already* here," said the Surgeon General, with some exasperation in his voice. "We've had eight cases in New Orleans, eleven in Florida, and sixty-three in the New York area."

"It's coming in from Latin America," Agriculture fumed. "We ought to go down there and wipe it out. Those damned greasers down there don't know the first thing about sanitation or public health."

Eying the three Hispanics around the table, the President replied, "This isn't the old days, Harry. We can't muscle our neighbors. Nobody can."

The old Pentagon had been transformed into the new Executive Office Building. Not only had the armed services shrunk severely over the past decade, but the other agencies of the government had slowly decreased as well, as computers and artificial intelligence systems gradually, grudgingly replaced the human bureaucracy through the attrition of death and retirement. Now most of the government's administrative offices were housed in the vast Pentagon and the old buildings in Washington itself had been turned into museums for the tourists to wander through.

The President tried to regain control of the meeting. "The facts are these," she said crisply. "This virus is carried in drinking water. It has already reached the Uni.ed States. The World Health Organization is attempting to identify it and find a way to stop it. They have asked our National Institutes of Health to work with them."

The Surgeon General nodded gravely.

"We ought to inspect every person coming into the country," Agriculture insisted. "If they object, don't let 'em in!"

The rest of the Cabinet ignored him.

"For the time being," the President continued, "the only thing we can do is have people boil their drinking water. I will declare a National Emergency tomorrow, and the Army will begin setting up emergency treatment centers across the country, starting with the most crowded areas of our cities."

She carefully avoided using the word "ghetto." In her victorious election campaign of the previous year she had triumphantly declared that there were no more ghettos in American cities.

"Panic," muttered the Vice President. "This is gonna cause the god-damnedest panic you ever saw. There's gonna be riots in the streets once the word of this gets out."

"That's why we need the Army. To keep things under control," the President replied.

The Secretary of Defense smiled again, as if they had acknowledged that he had been right all along.

The Secretary for Space, usually silent in Cabinet meetings, raised a timid hand. "Might I suggest," he said in a thin voice, "that we follow the advice of the Secretary of Agriculture as far as our facilities off-Earth are concerned. Each person bound for a space facility should be examined and, if found to be carrying the virus, should be refused entry."

"You mean for private carriers as well as government?" asked the Secretary of State. "Our commercial space lines carry citizens from all over the world."

"I mean for everybody," said Space, with unusual firmness. "If that virus gets established in the closed environment of a space habitat it will kill everybody in a few days."

He did not say aloud what he was really thinking: If the virus is as deadly as they had been told, the entire human race might be wiped off the face of the Earth in a matter of weeks. Then all that would be left was the hundred thousand or so who lived in space habitats. He was already making plans to move his entire family to the largest habitat in the L5 region.

BOOK III

Krishna: "The wise grieve not for those who live; and they grieve not for those who die—for life and death shall pass away."

CHAPTER 15

THE Hungarian transport was coming down at a military airstrip deep in the wooded hills. Stoner saw a long, narrow lake as they started their descent but it disappeared behind the tree-covered ridges.

He tapped at his wrist comm unit for a location fix. It did not respond.

"This aircraft is shielded," Ilona said over the howl of the engines. "It is a necessary precaution."

"Necessary?" Stoner asked sharply. "For whom?"

She looked uncomfortable. "It is not my doing. I am merely following orders."

"That's what the Nazis said," Stoner muttered.

Ilona pretended not to hear, but her cheeks colored and she turned toward the window.

When handed a lemon, Stoner said to himself, start making lemonade. Loud enough to be heard over the engines' roar, he asked, "Is this the country where they make that red wine we had last night, the Bull's Blood?"

"Oh no," Ilona replied, raising her voice as the engines' scream rose even higher. "The wine comes from Eger, to the east."

The plane lurched and she grabbed compulsively at the armrests. Stoner felt his stomach drop away, then climb up into his throat, and then the landing gear hit the ground with a walloping thump. The plane bounced back into the air, wobbled along the runway for an awfully long time, and finally hit the ground again with another hard bang and screeching of tires.

"Must be very gusty out there," Stoner muttered as they rolled along the paved runway, thrust reversers screaming, brakes groaning like a live bull being dragged across the concrete. Trees whizzed by and finally he saw a few hangars and other buildings.

At last the plane lurched to a stop and the engines whined down into silence. Stoner wiped his brow as the main hatch was opened from the outside. Three men climbed in, two in tan soldier's uniforms and the third a stocky dark-eyed young man wearing brown corduroy slacks and a faded blue windbreaker. The soldiers had pistols on their hips in gleamingly oiled leather holsters.

Ilona pushed past Stoner to get into the aisle.

"Dr. Stoner," she said, her eyes flashing, "may I introduce to you Doctor Professor Zoltan Janos, of the University of Budapest."

Janos was short and round, hardly taller than Ilona, with a barrel-chested torso that seemed too big for his slim arms and legs. High domed forehead, thinning hair. The dark fringe of a beard accentuated the roundness of his face. His eyes, though, were deep set and as intense as laser beams.

"An honor, Dr. Stoner." His voice was clear and as sweet as the finest Irish tenor's.

Stoner pulled himself out of the seat but had to bend over in the low confines of the plane's aisle. He took Janos's extended hand and asked, "Any relation to the legendary Hungarian patriot, Hary Janos?"

The younger man's eyes widened momentarily. He almost smiled. But he controlled himself and said a bit stiffly, "No. I deal with realities, not legends."

Stoner would have shrugged if he had not been stooped over.

"I must ask you for the communications unit on your wrist, please," said Janos. "It will be returned to you when you leave."

Stoner hesitated a moment, then unstrapped the bracelet and handed it to the Hungarian. "I would like to tell my wife that I am alive and well," he said. "She expected me to be in Budapest tonight. So did I."

Janos nodded curtly as he turned and started for the hatch. "Of course. You may telephone her from the lodge. But you will not be permitted to reveal your whereabouts to her."

"Not be permitted?"

"It is a security precaution," Ilona said hastily.

"Why all the cloak and dagger?" Stoner wondered, following them down the aisle. "I thought you people were scientists."

"We are," Ilona assured him.

Stepping down the shaky aluminum ladder to the ground, Stoner stretched his frame and felt tendons in his arms and shoulders pop deliciously. A warm wind tousled his hair; in the distance he saw the trees bending and swaying.

"Why all the secrecy?" he asked again.

Janos replied, "You will understand when we show you our laboratory."

More curious than apprehensive, Stoner let them lead him to an old forest-green sedan that had obviously gone months, perhaps years, since its last washing.

"The laboratory is up in the hills, at the lodge," said Ilona as she and Janos climbed into the back with him. The two soldiers squeezed in up front with the driver, who was also in military uniform.

"Vic, he hasn't called and he doesn't answer my calls," Jo's image in the phone screen was saying. "I want you to find him!"

Tomasso shifted uneasily in his desk chair. "That won't be easy . . ."

"If it were easy I'd have already done it!" she snapped. "Find him! Now!"

The screen went blank. Tomasso licked his lips. He had never seen the president of Vanguard so distressed. But her husband had never disappeared before, either.

Is this a test? Tomasso asked himself. A setup, to see if I'm really worth what she's paying me. Or maybe she suspects the connection with Hsen.

I've got to be careful here. Verrry careful. It's like walking through a minefield.

Victor Francis Tomasso had learned from earliest childhood that a smile and a bit of fancy footwork can move you along on the road of life. The youngest of eight children evenly divided between boys and girls, he had been babied by his mother, bullied by his older brothers, and beaten by his father whenever the old man needed somebody to bolster his machismo. A rough day on the construction job? *Wham* for little Vickie. Lost the paycheck on the ponies? Whack the kid for making too much noise.

Victor discovered early on that he could start screaming as soon as his father raised his hand, and his mother or his sisters would run to his rescue. By the time he was four he had learned to start family arguments by deliberately getting his father's goat, then screeching before the first blow landed. His father never caught on. Neither did his sisters nor, most important of all, his mother.

It seemed that no matter how much money his father earned on his construction jobs, there was never enough to go around. Buffalo was not a fast-lane kind of city, but all the Tomassos knew that they were close to the bottom of the ladder even in their own run-down blue collar neighborhood. Vic's mother worked longer hours than his father running the inventory programs for a grocery warehouse. All the kids got jobs as soon as they were able. Still they were poor, and the ads they watched on TV rubbed it in every hour of every day.

Vic's oldest brother got himself killed in a gang fight before he was sixteen. Two of his sisters got married early and moved away. Vic saw the handwriting on the wall: if he didn't make his own move soon, he would be left alone with his aging mother and father, and then he would never get away.

So he took off the day he was supposed to start high school. And he never returned. He learned very quickly that a bright young man could live nicely if he knew how to get himself a driver's license and a Social Security card. Smiling and flirting with the dumpy, dough-faced women who ran most town hall offices was a big help. But once he learned how to finagle computers, Vic had it made.

His father had given him one piece of wisdom, years earlier. The family had been eating supper, gathered around the nightly network news on TV. The screen showed six smiling, extremely well-dressed men walking away from a courthouse in New York City. Or maybe it was Washington. The sound track told how these six Wall Street brokers had been accused of stealing millions of dollars from their clients, but the judge had let them go free.

"Steal enough money and you can walk home," said Tommy, the oldest, the one who would die with a knife in his spleen four blocks from his house.

"There's more fuckin' money stolen with a briefcase," said their father, "than with a gun."

Vic remembered that. And once he had talked his way into a job tapping data into a computer for the billing department of a Minneapolis department store, Vic recalled his father's words time and again.

He never stole enough to get caught, just enough to live a little better than his salary. With his charm and the money he could spend, he climbed a ladder of women that eventually led to Vanguard Industries' headquarters in Hawaii. He was in the big leagues now, and he did not have to steal anymore. He simply became a double agent. Selling his services to more than one company was much better than stealing. More money and less risk.

Until now.

Tomasso leaned back in his chair and put his expensively booted feet on his desk. He closed his eyes and began to analyze his situation. Jo Camerata wants me to find her husband. Hsen and his people need to know where Stoner is, and when he's going to be at his house.

Okay, no conflict there. Find Stoner and they'll both be happy. The problem is, how do I find Stoner?

As they drove up into the wooded hills Stoner sensed enormous tension in Zoltan Janos. The man was wound tighter than the spring on a crossbow. One touch and he'll shoot off.

Ilona was growing tenser with each second, too. At first Stoner thought that she was merely anticipating the chance to plug herself in to her pleasure machine once more. But as the car wound up the steep twisting road he began to realize that Ilona was picking up on Janos's tension.

He studied the professor. Young for that honor. No more than thirty, thirty-two. Very committed to his work, that was obvious. He must be the one who got Ilona started on the brain stimulation. Does he do it himself? Is he addicted too? Stoner decided that Janos was not. He's too wrapped up in his work for that. He doesn't need the pleasure stimulator; he's got enough stimulation already.

Does he know how deeply Ilona is addicted? Yes, Stoner decided. And he doesn't care. Not enough to try to get her off it. She's easier to manipulate because of it. He's her pusher, her connection.

Ilona touched Stoner's sleeve. Pointing with her other hand, she said, "The lodge—where you will spend the night."

Stoner ducked slightly to look out the window on the opposite side of the car. He saw up on the crest of the wooded ridge a long, low stone building with a timber roof. An old hunting lodge, still kept in first-rate condition. At least I won't have to rough it tonight, he said to himself.

The lodge was sumptuous. Polished stone floors covered with luxurious carpets, impressive formal dining room with a gleaming long table and high-backed chairs upholstered in leather. There were no animal heads mounted on the wall, as Stoner had half expected. Instead there were heraldic crests with symbols of eagles and lions and boars against fields of blazing red and royal blue.

"In centuries past," said Janos, conducting Stoner on an impromptu tour of the lodge, "this was a hunting lodge for the Habsburg emperors and their aristocratic friends. When the empire was broken up, it became a tourist hotel, and then after the Second World War a youth hostel."

Stoner pictured hordes of red-shirted Young Communists demolishing the place just as youngsters anywhere would with all their teenaged noise and energy.

"It was refurbished as part of the great restructuring of Hungarian society," Janos continued his lecture as the three of them walked through a snug library filled with books from beamed ceiling to bearskin-covered floor. An unused fireplace and stone chimney filled one corner of the room. Stoner saw no logs in its dark and cold emptiness, but a pipe for gas instead.

As they went from room to room, Janos did all the talking. Ilona was as silent as a freshman attending her first lecture.

"The government has generously allowed us to use this lodge as our quarters," Janos concluded, heading toward the broad staircase that led up to the bedrooms.

"Quarters for your laboratory staff," Stoner asked.

Giving a curt nod, Janos said, "Each of us has equal accommodations, from the lowliest maintenance personnel to the laboratory director, we share and share alike."

"Very democratic," said Stoner as they started up the stairs. "I presume you are the laboratory director."

"Yes, that is true. That is my room there, in the corner."

Stoner guessed that it was somewhat larger than any of the other rooms. Janos came across as the kind of man who considered himself rather more equal than anyone else.

"And the laboratory is nearby?"

"Quite close."

"Under our feet, actually," said Ilona.

Stoner looked at her quizzically.

Frowning slightly, Janos explained, "The laboratory is underground, below this building, buried quite deeply."

"Why underground?"

"For security," said Ilona.

Janos darted an angry glare at her. "It was built originally in the days of the Cold War as a bomb shelter for key members of the government. In case of nuclear attack."

"I see," said Stoner.

They showed him to a bedroom where his scanty package of clothes had already been placed neatly on the rack at the foot of the bed. After telling him that dinner would be served in precisely two hours, they left him alone.

Stoner surveyed the bedroom. Comfortable enough. No

telephone, though. Jo must be climbing the walls by now, he thought. I've got to call her.

The door was unlocked. At least that's something, he said to himself. How many times had he been quietly tucked away in some remote location, behind locked doors or surrounded by security police? They always said it was for his own good, which always meant it was for their own purposes.

Stoner's star brother pointed out that they did not know what Janos's true purposes were as yet. Ilona's explanation about studying him in order to learn more about cryonics might be true, but even if it was it covered a deeper purpose. Biochips, replied Stoner, and the first steps toward nanotechnology.

The horrifying vision of the dead world flooded Stoner's mind for an instant. Nanotechnology can lead to that? he asked his star brother. The answer was immediate and implacable: Yes.

He went down the stairs to the spacious parlor and front hall. No one there. Not a soul. Closing his eyes for a moment, Stoner recalled his tour a few minutes earlier through these rooms. Not a telephone or communications system of any kind down here, he realized. Ilona's up in her room, juicing herself into paradise; there's no help to be had from her.

Only one place where a phone would be. Stoner bounded back up the stairs and rapped sharply on Janos's door.

Without waiting for an answer he opened the door and stepped in. As he suspected, this was a much larger room than the others. Windows on two sides gave splendid views of the hills and woods. A king-sized bed, neatly made up with a chenille spread. A fireplace. Even a TV set.

Janos sat behind a small desk, his mouth open and dark eyes blazing with surprise and anger. Stoner saw a computer terminal on the desk. And his own comm bracelet lying beside it.

"You said I could phone my wife if I didn't reveal my location," he said to the startled Janos.

"I will have someone call her—" Janos began to say.

Stoner walked slowly to his desk and leaned both his fists on its top, looming over the professor. "I would prefer to speak to my wife myself."

Janos began to shake his head, but stopped before he really started.

Stoner said softly, "You wouldn't deny such a simple request, would you?"

For a moment Janos seemed to be struggling within himself. Then, "No, it would be unkind to deny your request, I agree."

"May I use my own comm unit?" asked Stoner.

"Yes. Why not?" Reluctantly.

Stoner picked up the silver bracelet and spoke Jo's name into it. In less than two seconds her voice crackled through the tiny microphone:

"Keith! Are you all right? Where are you?"

"I'm fine," he said, pacing slightly away from Janos's desk. "Sorry I couldn't call you earlier."

"What happened? Where are you?"

Knowing that she could get a positional fix on his transmission from the satellite relaying his call, Stoner replied, "I'm not in Budapest. My Hungarian friends have taken me to one of their labs. Nothing for you to worry about. I ought to be on my way home tomorrow. If there's any change in plans I'll call you."

"You're sure you're okay?"

"I'm fine, Jo." He smiled at her voice. "I love you, darling."

"I love you, too. You had me so worried . . ."

"There's nothing to worry about. Kiss the kids for me."

"You'll be home tomorrow?"

"I'll probably stop off in Moscow for Kir's funeral. Can you meet me there?"

"Yes. I'll have to move my schedule around a little, but yes, I'll be there."

"See you in Moscow, then."

"All right."

"Good night, darling."

"It's seven in the morning here."

"Did I wake you?"

"I wasn't sleeping."

"Have a good day, Jo."

"You sound like a damned airline steward!"

He laughed. Her sense of humor was back and the fear was out of her voice.

" 'Bye for now."

"Take care, Keith."

Stoner held onto his bracelet for a moment, then handed it back to Janos. As if waking from a dream, he stirred, blinked his eyes, then snatched the bracelet as if it had been stolen from him.

"Thank you," said Stoner.

Janos watched with wondering eyes as the American calmly walked out of his room. He manipulated me as if I were a child, Janos said to himself. He has the power to twist a grown man around his little finger! If the president ever finds out about that he will want me to find the source of that power and give it to him. If the people in Hong Kong ever learn about it . . .

Sinking back in his creaking plastic desk chair, Janos realized, But if I can find the source of such power, why would I give it to anyone except myself?

CHAPTER 16

STILL tangled in the bedsheets, Jo eagerly tapped on the phone console's keyboard the instant Keith's call ended. The small screen showed the coordinates of the call's point of origin.

With a little whoop of triumph she ordered the computer to store the information. Then she phoned Tomasso. He was not at his apartment, but within seconds the computer tracked him down and made the connection.

"Keith phoned me a few minutes ago," she said breathlessly. "He's all right, but I want you to get a team of people ready to reach him."

Tomasso's face looked slightly puffy, sleepy. On the small phone screen it was impossible for Jo to see much of the background. In the back of her mind she wondered whose bed Vic was in and how much sleep he had gotten.

"Where is he?" Tomasso asked.

"Coordinates are on file. Get to the office and get to work!"

"Yes, boss." Despite the dark rings beneath his eyes, Tomasso grinned at her with his flawless teeth.

Instead of returning to his room, Stoner went down the corridor to the door of Ilona's bedroom. He stood there for a long moment, listening, hearing nothing.

Gently he tried the doorknob. It turned easily and the door opened.

She was stretched out on the bed fully clothed, glassy eyes staring sightlessly at the ceiling, fingers twitching spasmodically. Her honey-colored wig of thick curls lay discarded on the floor, thrown aside in her rush. A helmet made of plastic straps studded with metal contacts was cinched tightly on her shaved head. Hair-thin wires connected to a console the size of a laptop computer resting on the carpeted floor beside the bed.

Stoner's nostrils flared as if he smelled the stench of rotting garbage. His first instinct was to stride to the pleasure machine and smash it beneath his heel.

No! warned his star brother. Not abruptly.

Stoner knew he was right. He had to find the reason why Ilona could become addicted before he could truly end her dependency.

He sat on the bed beside her. She did not move, did not

blink, did not acknowledge his presence in any way. My god, I could strip her naked and screw her all night long and she wouldn't even know it. What an opportunity for necrophiliacs.

Isaac Newton had discovered that for every action there is an opposite reaction. Popular wisdom declared that every dark cloud has a silver lining. While Ilona's conscious mind was completely shut down in the tidal surges of pure pleasure coming from the machine, her unconscious mind was as wide open as it could ever be. Leaning over her, gazing into her unseeing eyes, Stoner tried to learn the who and why of Ilona Lucacs.

It was a matter of guilt. Born in an age when parents could pick the sex of their offspring, Ilona was the daughter of a proud and forceful woman who had overridden her husband's desire for a son. Yet although the passive father had acquiesced to his wife's wishes, Ilona was made aware from her earliest days that she was a disappointment to her father.

He was the nurturing parent, the one who was always there with his child. Her mother, a concert pianist, travelled all across the world. Ilona and her father remained in Budapest, where he could watch her and feed her and play with her. And make her know, hour by hour, day by day, year after year, how much he would have preferred a son.

She loved her father and broke her heart to please him. In school she skimped her studies to practice athletics. In a nation of fencers she became a champion with the foil. When she handed her gold medals to her father, he smiled and reminisced about his youth when he had been a saber fencer. Women were not allowed to fence saber in international competition. Too bad. Foil was good, of course, even though overly dainty. Now saber—ah, that was *real* fencing!

Ilona grew into a beautiful young woman. Not as tall and regal as her mother, but so obviously feminine that she felt almost ashamed of herself. She dressed as mannishly as she could when she entered the university. To please her father she took the science curriculum.

And found that she had a first-rate mind. She not only understood science, she loved it. For the first time in her young life she found that she was enjoying what she was doing not because it pleased her father but because it pleased her. At her graduation, when she placed first in her class, her father collapsed with a heart attack. She could not go on to graduate studies, she would be needed at home to take care of him.

Nonsense! her mother replied. She retired from her world tours and concentrated on video performances that she could do from Budapest. Ilona went on to get her doctorate. And her father recovered his health with stunning swiftness.

To be killed in a traffic accident. A few weeks after Ilona had moved from their apartment to begin work as an assistant to the youngest professor in the university: Zoltan Janos. He died in a head-on collision while driving to visit her in her new apartment.

She immediately fell in love with Janos and would have moved in with him if he had responded to her. But he was too wrapped up in his work to make a commitment to anyone. The old sense of guilt reasserted itself: Ilona believed she was responsible for her father's death. The man she loved would not respond to her. Her work suffered. She grew morose, depressed.

Janos introduced her to the pleasures of direct brain stimulation, more as a way of "pepping up" than anything else. He had tried it himself, found it enjoyable, but had never delivered himself to it. Ilona, needing to be told that she was loved for herself, took the electrical pleasure of direct stimulation instead.

And became hooked on it.

Now Stoner knew the why and wherefore. He sat on the bed for long moments more, considering what to do. It was bitterly ironic. You're willing to take the fate of the entire human race in your hands, he told himself, but accepting responsibility for the life of this one young woman gives you pause.

He leaned down and turned the dial that governed the

amount of current being fed into her brain. Just a bit. Then he turned back the timer dial, so the machine would shut itself off and she would awaken.

He stood up and watched as the seconds ran out and the current stopped. Ilona shuddered, her eyelids fluttered, the pupils focused and she realized he was standing over her, a tall man with wide shoulders and a grim, darkly bearded face looking down at her.

"Oh!"

"It's all right, Ilona," Stoner said softly. "It's all right. I just want you to know that you're not alone. And you never will be. Not anymore."

"I . . . what . . ." Her hands flew to her shaved head.

"It's all right," he repeated.

"Get out!" she screamed. "Get away from me!"

She ripped the electrode grid from her head and threw it at Stoner's face.

"Meddling bastard! Get out! Get *out!*"

He turned and swiftly left the room, leaving her sitting up on the bed, clothes wrinkled, dishevelled, hands trying to cover her shaved scalp, feeling utterly miserable and confused.

Stoner wore his new clothes when he came down to the library: a fresh set of jeans, shirt, and jacket, all manufactured in Bangladesh. Ilona glanced at him warily, her tawny eyes angry, suspicious. She wore a simple white tunic over plain black slacks; no jewelry except a necklace of carnelian and matching earrings. Her wig had been carefully combed. Janos was in an old-fashioned double-breasted suit of light gray with pinstripes and a formal shirt with a carefully knotted tie that bore the crest of the university.

"I have just been informed," he said, his eyes glowing, "that we will have an important guest join us for dinner. A very important guest. The president of the republic!"

Stoner saw that Janos was impressed with himself. Ilona did not seem surprised. Janos stood by the library's one window, obviously struggling with the urge to part the curtains and look outside. The gas-fed fireplace was alight with thin bluish flames; their warmth felt good in the gathering chill of evening. A robot glided in with a tray of cocktails. Stoner sipped at his and identified it as a vodka martini. Probably the president's favorite; not his own.

A helicopter thundered down on the parking lot outside. Janos gestured with both hands to keep Stoner and Ilona in the library.

"The butler will bring him in here," he said. "No need to run outside and gawk like peasants." But his free hand twitched toward the curtained window.

A few minutes later the door to the library was opened by a beefy-faced security man in the traditional dark suit. Then the president of Hungary stepped in, all smiles and nods.

He was a tiny man, slightly stooped, walking rather slowly. Arthritis, Stoner guessed. He looked sprightly, though, for seventy-eight. An elegant dark blue business suit. Still some color to his graying hair, and his skin looked a healthy pink without the waxiness of cosmetic surgery. His face was wreathed in a broad, toothy grin that squeezed his eyes to mere slits. He held an enormous cigar in his left hand, keeping his right free for clasping Janos's.

"My brilliant young friend," said the president. "How are you this fine evening?"

Before Janos could respond the president had already turned to Ilona. "And the lovely Dr. Lucacs. I see that you have been successful in bringing Dr. Stoner to us. I spoke with your mother this morning. She sends her love."

Ilona smiled and blushed as the president brought her hand to his lips. For a moment Stoner thought she was going to curtsey.

"And you," said the president, releasing Ilona, "are the illustrious Dr. Keith Stoner."

He took Stoner's hand in a surprisingly powerful grip. Janos said stiffly, "President Novotny."

The man was so short that it was difficult for Stoner to see into his eyes. They were narrow and masked by thick dark brows. And they darted about the room constantly, never meeting Stoner's gaze squarely, always shifting away as if searching for danger. Or opportunity.

Janos led them to the long dining table, where four places had been set at one end. President Novotny sat at its head, Janos and Ilona on his left, Stoner on his right. He wondered where the rest of the laboratory staff was having its dinner this evening. Equal but separate, Stoner said to his star brother. Which means not equal at all, the alien responded.

The food was good, the wine better, and dinner conversation pleasant and inconsequential. Once the dishes had been cleared away and several musty bottles of brandies put before the president, he lit a fresh cigar and began telling long, rambling stories about his childhood and early political experiences.

"Those were terrible days," he said, puffing thick clouds of blue smoke toward the beamed ceiling. "My grandfather died in the uprising, my father was arrested and held for nearly six years. They wouldn't let me join the Party until I was almost forty! That's what the rebellion of '56 left us. A heritage of suspicion and anger."

"In the West," said Stoner, "the Hungarian uprising was regarded with great sympathy. Students fighting Russian tanks with little more than their bare hands."

For once Novotny's eyes bored straight at Stoner. "The West applauded, but did nothing to help Hungary. The West praised our Freedom Fighters, but stood aside and allowed the Soviets to crush them."

Stoner admitted, "True enough."

"But—" The president's eyes began to rove again and he smiled jovially, "—all that happened more than sixty years ago. Ancient history. Hungary is proud and free today."

"And we will grow stronger," Janos added.

"Indeed we will," President Novotny agreed.

"By developing biochips?" Stoner asked.

Novotny's smile faltered for just a moment. Then, "Why, yes, biochips are what they are called. You know of them?"

"They are being developed in the West, as well."

"So I had heard."

Janos nearly sneered. "We know about the work being done in the West. Primitive, compared to our research."

"One British group is working with a team of primatologists in Africa," said Ilona. "They are trying to establish linkages between humans and apes through implanting biochips."

"Primitive," Janos repeated.

Stoner replied, "I think the research that Vanguard Industries is doing is further advanced than that. I'm sure other corporations are also working on the concept."

"The corporations do their work in secret," Novotny said, his bushy brows knitting. "They do not publish their results in the scientific journals."

"Nor do we," Ilona pointed out. "Our work is kept secret. We are not allowed to publish."

President Novotny spread his hands in the classic *what can I do* gesture. "You see that we have competition. It is important—vital—that our competitors do not learn of the advances we have made."

Stoner wondered how they intended to have him help them without revealing the advances they had made. No matter, he told his star brother, we can always talk our way out of here when we're ready to.

As if reading Stoner's mind, the president turned to him and said, "Of course, this has almost nothing to do with you, sir. Our interest in you stems from your unique experience in surviving cryonic freezing."

Stoner smiled back at Novotny. "Do you mean that you don't believe there's a connection between the two?"

Novotny looked startled and glanced at Janos.

The scientist glared at Stoner. "Until this moment, the connection was nothing more than a hypothesis of mine."

With a grin, Stoner said, "I see that Dr. Lucacs has impressed the correct word on you."

The president's head swivelled from Stoner to Janos and then back again.

"What is your hypothesis?" Stoner asked as softly as a leopard padding through the jungle.

Janos looked distinctly uncomfortable. Obviously he had not intended to speak of this in front of President Novotny, but now he was in a corner.

"It will sound . . . outlandish," he said.

"It is my idea!" Ilona snapped. "And it is pure speculation, nothing but a series of surmises."

She's trying to shield him, thought Stoner.

"I would still like to hear it, regardless of whose idea it is," said the president. His smile was deadly now. He put his cigar in the oversized metal ashtray that had been placed at his elbow and reached for the nearest brandy bottle.

"The biochips," Ilona said as the president poured for himself, "are miniature electronic elements based on protein instead of silicon or other semiconductor materials."

"This I know," Novotny said. He did not offer anyone else a drink.

"The purpose of using proteinoid materials is to allow the chips to be implanted in the body and connected to the nervous system."

"But that is only the first step," Janos took over, his clear tenor voice trembling slightly. "It is conceivable—conceptually possible—to make other devices for implantation in the body. Smaller devices. Machines that can do many different tasks, much as the cells of the body themselves. But better."

"And smaller than cells, much smaller," said Ilona.

"Nanotechnology, it has been called," Janos said. "Creating devices that are a millionth of a millimeter in size. Devices that can exist inside the human body, repairing cell damage, enhancing the body's health, counteracting the effects of aging—"

"And freezing," Ilona said, staring directly at Stoner.

"Even producing extraordinary mental powers," Janos added.

All three of them focused their total attention on Stoner.

He said nothing, merely leaned back in his chair while his star brother waited, shuddering, within him.

"I have heard of this thing called nanotechnology," President Novotny said. "My director of scientific research briefed me on its possibilities. But he said that such a development would not be possible for many decades to come."

"The alien race that built the starship must have developed nanotechnology," Janos said.

"And Dr. Stoner spent many years in cryonic suspension aboard that ship," Ilona added. "His body could have been invaded by alien . . ."

"Devices," Stoner said for her. "Not creatures. The devices are machines. By themselves they are as inert as an automobile parked in a garage."

Janos gasped. "It is true!"

Stoner said nothing. But, gazing at President Novotny, he could see the whirling thoughts behind his darting eyes. *What weapons could we make of such devices! Invisibly small machines that could invade the human body and tear it apart from the inside. What a truly incredible weapon that could be! The man who controls such technology could become the most powerful man on Earth!*

CHAPTER 17

HIS star brother fairly snarled with revulsion. *The first thing he thinks of is weaponry, killing his fellow humans. The second thing is power.*

The only thing he thinks of is himself, Stoner pointed out. *In his deepest heart he does not regard anyone else as truly* human; no one except himself. He is the center of his world. Everything and everyone else revolves around him.

And with people such as this you want to share the powers that we have?

We must share the power with them, Stoner said, or they will soon die.

Give them our power and they will kill themselves in an orgy of murder. You saw the world of death. You know what can happen when such powers are misused. That is what this man will do! He will destroy your world, utterly and forever!

Perhaps, admitted Stoner. But the time has come to face that choice.

No, said his star brother. Implacably.

We must, Stoner insisted. They'll develop it on their own and misuse it. We no longer have the option of delaying. It's got to be done now. By us. While we can observe and control.

We can't control this egomaniac! He's mad for power.

We can. We've got to.

Stoner pushed his chair back and got to his feet. "I would like to see your laboratory now," he said to Janos.

No! raged his star brother. Don't do this! The risk is too great! Everything we've tried to achieve will be smashed away.

Do you see an alternative? Stoner asked. Other than killing the three of them?

His star brother fell silent.

Janos slowly stood up, as if in a hypnotic trance. "You wish to see the laboratory now?"

Stoner nodded gravely.

"Come on then."

Ilona and the president followed them as Janos led Stoner to the rear of the lodge and down a flight of metal stairs to a concrete-walled basement. Overhead fluorescents flickered on automatically, triggered by the heat of their bodies. They walked past dusty shelves of packing crates and long rows of wine bins and finally came to a heavy steel door. Janos tapped out a combination on the keyboard panel set into the wall.

The door clicked open slightly and a gust of air sighed out from it.

It was the narrow cage of an elevator. The four of them squeezed into it and rode down in breathless silence about thirty meters, Stoner estimated. When the elevator stopped the metal bars of its door opened automatically.

As laboratories went, theirs was small. But Stoner realized that they did not need elaborate facilities nor huge expanses of equipment and offices. A few dedicated researchers, backed by a government that provided them virtually anything they asked for. That was enough. More than enough.

Janos walked them through two labs and into a third room that looked to be a combination of a surgical center with an electronics shop. An operating table, bare and cold beneath a quartet of powerful lamps. Rows of metal cabinets that held surgical instruments. Banks of computers and monitors lining the adjacent wall, their screens round and blank as the eyes of the dead. The faint odor of animal fur and excrement hung in the air despite the hum of air fans set into the concrete ceiling that sucked up Novotny's cigar smoke with relentless efficiency.

Stoner pointed toward double doors on the other side of the chamber. "Animal pens through there."

Janos bobbed his head twice. "Dogs, mostly. We have done a few procedures with chimpanzees and even gorillas, but dogs are much easier to work with."

"And you want to take samples of my blood to see if it's crawling with nanometer-sized alien machines." It was not a question.

"Blood and tissue samples, yes," said Janos.

"That won't be necessary," said Stoner. "But if you can make a small incision in your president's thumb, or one of his fingertips . . ."

Madness! screamed his star brother silently.

For the first time since he had awakened fifteen years earlier, Stoner ignored the alien presence within him. He watched, grim-faced, as Janos woodenly found a small needle and pricked both Novotny's thumb and his own.

He locked his eyes with Novotny's. The politician tried to look away, but could not. Stoner saw in the Hungarian president's eyes what he had heard at the dinner table: a man totally dedicated to himself, a man who did not truly regard other men and women as human beings, a man who felt nothing for anyone except himself.

He glanced down at the bead of blood welling from his flesh and then back into the half-fearful, half-exultant eyes of the politician. Stoner said, "You want the power that is implied by the alien's capabilities. Here it is."

You know why I'm doing this, Stoner said silently to his star brother. The alien presence replied, I understand but I do not agree.

I have more faith in the human race than you do. Perhaps that's because I know them better.

I know everything that you know, his star brother reminded him. And I am not so affected by daydreams and false hopes as you are.

You could control those hopes if you chose to.

No, the time for that is past. You have decided to act against my best judgment. We must both see which of us is right, even though the stakes are the survival of your kind and all the other forms of life on this world.

Stoner took Novotny's thumb and pressed it against his own. For a wild, insane moment a distant echo from long ago sprang up in his mind: high school, a teenager rife with acne rubbing thumbs with a girl and then announcing that he was a Martian and his sex organ was in his thumb.

Stoner almost laughed aloud. He looked up at the Hungarian president, though, and immediately sobered.

"Very well, now you have the power," he said in a deadly earnest voice. "You will find that you also have the responsibility."

Novotny blinked at him. "I don't understand . . ."

"You will," Stoner said, as much to his star brother as to the president. "You will."

*   *   *

"You signed the waiver, you work where they tell ya."

Paulino Alvarado felt his knees shaking and hoped that his new boss did not notice it.

"But I did not sign a waiver . . ."

"The hell you didn't. Everybody does. It's in the pile of forms they shove at ya when you first get here. You signed it, all right. The legal division don't make any mistakes about that."

The boss was a nervous-looking rat-faced little man, even smaller and scrawnier than Paulino himself. His coveralls were stained with grease and frayed from long hard use. Once they had been bright orange, as Paulino's new coveralls were, but now they had faded to a dull tone that was almost gray.

They were walking through a vast, echoing garage, dimly lit by panels set into the ceiling high overhead. Rows of grimy tractors with large skinny wheels stood silently in the shadows, except for one down at the end where a handful of mechanics were clustered beneath a glaring set of lights. The sparks of a welding torch sputtered fitfully, blue and cold.

"But I have never operated a tractor," Paulino protested. "I have never been in a space suit."

"Pressure suit," the boss corrected. "Don't call 'em space suits, makes ya sound like a fuckin' tourist. Pressure suit, or p-suit."

Paulino felt panic rising inside him. "I didn't come here to work outside! I'm supposed to . . ."

The boss turned on him, snarling. "You're here to do whatever the fuck I tell you to do! Got that? You signed the waiver and all the other papers like the stupid asshole you are, so you're *mine*, greaseball! If I tell you to pull your pants down and make love to an oxy tank that's what you'll do. Unnerstand?"

Paulino gulped and nodded.

More gently, the boss went on, "There's nothin' much to operatin' a tractor. I'll take you out for an orientation run. You'll get it down in ten minutes unless you're brain-damaged."

Paulino continued to nod as the boss helped him climb into a pressure suit. He was still nodding when he pulled the cumbersome helmet over his head and, following the boss's instructions, closed the seal at its neck.

And his knees were still shaking furiously.

Vic Tomasso spent the whole day going through the motions of setting up a recovery operation to find Stoner and return him safely home.

But even for a multinational corporation of the size and power of Vanguard, invading a sovereign nation was an operation that took time to prepare. Vanguard had a sales office in Budapest, and even ran the water treatment system for the length of the Danube River under contract to the various national governments through whose territories the river flowed. There was manpower available in Hungary, men and women who already were on the scene and did not have to be smuggled into the country.

But damned little muscle. Most of the Vanguard people inside the country were either engineers or administrators. Only a handful were security, and none of them were trained for special operations. Glorified night watchmen, Tomasso called them.

So he went through the motions of checking with the head of the Budapest office and then discussing the situation with the chief of corporate security, a man who had access to more troops and firepower than the nation of Hungary. But, as Tomasso had known from the start, even though the security chief had contingency plans for such operations, it would take a few days to assemble the necessary people and train them for this specific mission.

Tomasso asked the security chief to put such an operation in motion. He could not order it, since he was merely an administrative aide and the chief of a department outranked him. But being the aide to the president of the company gave Tomasso more clout than his salary level indicated. By day's end, the wheels were rolling.

Tomasso stuck his head in Jo's office before leaving for the day.

"Spoke with Guderian," he said when Jo looked up from her display screen at him. "He's pulling together the troops. We can give you a briefing tomorrow morning, say, ten o'clock?"

"Why not tonight?" Jo snapped.

Tomasso tried a boyish grin. "Give the man a chance to study the satellite photos of the area and adapt one of the standby contingency plans," he pleaded.

Jo's lips pressed together tightly for a moment. Then she said, "Make it eight o'clock. Right here in my office."

"Oh-eight-hundred hours. Yes, ma'am." And Tomasso snapped off a crisp military salute without losing his grin.

He hustled back to his office and got Guderian on the screen.

"Eight o'clock in her office," the security chief said, as tight-lipped as Jo had been. "Right."

"Have a pleasant evening," Tomasso quipped. Then he went out to the parking lot, hopped into his open sports car and headed for the beach.

The electric engine hummed softly and the wind plucked at his dark hair as Tomasso sped along the beach highway. Traffic was as heavy as any evening rush hour, but most of the cars were on the automated lanes, where the drivers could relax and watch their dashboard TVs or chat sociably with their passengers.

Trucks, of course, had their own special lanes and electronic controls. There was even talk of completely automating the trucks and having them directed remotely, the way spacecraft were. The drivers were all in favor of the idea, since they owned the trucks and could stay home while their machines worked. But the highway safety bureaucrats worried that totally automated trucks would be a problem when emergencies arose.

Tomasso drove in the fast lane, manually steering the little sportster. He turned off the main highway several miles north

of Hilo, in the bedroom town of Papaikou, and threaded the
evening traffic until he came to the Papaikou Pizza Parlor, a
shining chrome and aluminum anachronism with a garish
neon sign blinking pink and bilious green in the gathering
dusk. Tomasso parked in the farthest corner of the parking
lot, where there was a pretty view of Hilo Bay.

The inevitable strains of steel guitars and soft voices wafted
out from the Pizza Parlor's loudspeakers. Tomasso made a
wry frown: in all the time he had been in Hawaii he had
heard no more than six "native" songs, endlessly repeated by
every radio station and music service. It was enough to make
you sick.

The Moon was rising above the dark ocean horizon, and
lights from several lunar settlements were visible on its battered ancient face. But Tomasso paid no attention to the scenery. He got out of his car and walked slowly to a gap in the
steel wire fence that enclosed the parking lot.

Looking around carefully to see if anyone was watching
him, he ducked through the gap and sat on the edge of the
rocky cliff that dropped steeply down to the surf far below. He
could barely hear the music from here, and he was certainly
out of sight from the restaurant's windows. Tucked into a
man-carved ledge just below the lip of the cliff was a small
metal box. Tomasso's hand knew exactly where to find it,
even while he stared off into the gathering darkness of the
oncoming night.

Deftly his fingers inserted a tiny wafer into a slot in the
box. Tomasso counted slowly to ten, then extracted the disk
and tucked it back into his shirt pocket.

The comm unit had squirted a coded, compressed message
to a Pacific Commerce satellite orbiting overhead. In less
than a second, the information from the wafer gave Stoner's
exact whereabouts and the steps that Vanguard Industries was
taking to recover him.

Then the machine automatically erased the wafer, so that if
someone should take it from Tomasso it would be innocently
blank.

Tomasso sat there on the edge of the cliff for a few minutes more, pretending that he was merely unwinding after a tense day at the office, watching the stars come out, trying to ignore the canned music, knowing that Hsen could now take Stoner if he acted swiftly enough. He had done his job for the Hong Kong industrialist. Tomorrow he would do his job for Jo Camerata as if this night's work had never happened.

CHAPTER 18

THE strange ceremony of sharing blood with Stoner made President Novotny shake his head with wonder as he prepared for bed in the mountain lodge. He had not expected mysticism from the American. Janos had insisted that Stoner was the key to cryonic suspension; this business of biochips and nanotechnology was something of a bolt from the blue, as far as Novotny was concerned.

He slept that night without dreams, the deepest and most restful sleep he had undergone in many, many years. The first rays of the new sun awoke him, and he fairly leaped out of bed, brimming with energy and a newfound inner happiness.

The bedroom was small but quite comfortable. Novotny padded barefoot to the casement window and pushed it open. The mountain morning was chilly, the fresh air sharp and invigorating. He drew in a deep breath of it. Outside in the trees and shrubbery he could sense the presence of his personal bodyguards, even though he could not see a trace of them. But they were there, faithful men who had spent the night in the cold outdoors because it was their honor to protect their president.

Perhaps I'm a foolish old man, overly prideful, he thought. What is there to protect me against? The world is at peace.

Terrorism has been virtually unknown in Europe for years. Why do I force these loyal young men to spend a whole night so uncomfortably? It's nothing but pride, arrogant pride.

Somewhere deep in his mind that thought surprised him. But he let it pass as he gazed out on the green wooded hills of his native land. How much blood had been spilled here! Once the Magyars were fierce Asian invaders who battled the Frankish hosts of Charlemagne to win this country for themselves. Over the centuries they became the eastern outpost of Europe, constantly pressed by the Ottoman Turks whose Janissaries captured Budapest and overran the Hungarian plain, but could not quench the flame of the Magyars. These hills were our last bastion, Novotny reminded himself. We held here, and eventually drove the Turks out of Hungary.

The Austrians, the Germans, and finally the Russians had all wielded power over Hungary. The heavy treads of lumbering tanks had ripped up the ground where cavalry had once swept past. And still the Magyars survived, the fire of their independent spirit often sputtering low, but never extinguished.

He recalled the bloody days of 1956 and how his father had saved him. A fervent teenager, Novotny had fought in the streets with his friends, throwing crude gasoline bombs at the tanks that rumbled down the broad avenues of Budapest, pulling as hard on the ropes as any other student when they toppled the huge statue of Stalin on Dozsa Gyorgy Street.

All in vain. All in vain. More tanks came and turned the city into a pockmarked, rubble-choked battlefield. The Russians prevailed, while the rest of the world ignored Hungary's pleas for help. His father was arrested and jailed, while sixteen-year-old Imre Novotny swore to the police on his mother's soul that he had not participated in any of the fighting or demonstrations.

Novotny found himself in tears as he gazed out the casement window. For the first time since those long-past days he felt the fear that had made him deny his own heritage. And the shame. He had known that the authorities were watching him. They allowed him to enter the university, but he was a marked man.

He had to be better than the others, ideologically more pure, politically more loyal, because they were waiting for him to make the slightest slip. He lived in terror that one of his former friends, now in jail, would denounce him and his life would end in a dark cell with a bullet in the back of his head.

He remembered how his father looked when they had finally released him from jail: broken, gray, sick. I'm in better condition now than he was, and he was only fifty-three then. He slumped on the window seat and wept unashamedly. Papa died for me. He let them arrest him so that I would be spared. He gave his life for me.

It took nearly half an hour before Novotny could pull himself together. That all happened more than sixty years ago, he told himself. It's over and done with. Why do you linger on such matters? You are the president of Hungary, and on the verge of acquiring power that can make you the most important man in Europe—perhaps in the world!

Forcing the haunted memories away from his consciousness, Novotny went down to the lodge's dining room for breakfast.

Janos and the lovely Ilona Lucacs were there, filling their plates with sausages and eggs from the serving dishes on the sideboard. Stoner sat at the dining table in his blue jeans and open-necked shirt with nothing but a cup of coffee before him.

The American eyed Novotny as if studying a laboratory specimen, his dark bearded face solemn, his gray eyes probing.

"Did you sleep well?" Stoner asked.

"Yes, quite well," said Novotny, taking a plate from the stack on the sideboard. "Quite well indeed."

He turned away from Stoner and smiled a greeting to Ilona Lucacs. How her mother had wanted her to be a musician, like herself, Novotny thought. But she wanted to please her father so much that she went into science, instead. Now her mother lives alone without a daughter to comfort her, and Ilona works here in this guarded laboratory—because she has fallen in love with Janos! Novotny suddenly saw it in Ilona's eyes, in the way her body inclined toward the man, the way she followed him and sat beside him.

And the lout doesn't even pay her the slightest attention,
Novotny realized. A new tendril of thought touched his mind.
Somehow Stoner has interjected himself into the equation.
Novotny did not quite understand the details of it, but he saw
clearly that Stoner was involved with Ilona and her troubles.

Novotny felt as if he had been swimming underwater and
had just burst up to the surface. He shook his head as if to
clear it. Taking his place at the head of the table, he realized
that there was no conversation. Each of them was locked inside a universe of self.

Just as I have been all these years, Novotny thought. He
looked at Janos as if seeing him for the first time. A brilliant
young scientist, and I have bent his career to my own purposes. Taken him out of the stream of research so that he
could serve me personally, forced him to use his talents to
prolong my life, bribed him with all the luxuries that a head
of state can provide to become mine exclusively. No wonder
he has turned inward. No wonder he has learned to ignore
those around him, to trample over their feelings, to use others
as if they were disposable tools.

He's turning into another version of *me*! Novotny realized.
I'm crushing his soul, like a vampire sucking the lifeblood out
of him. In exchange for privilege and power he is renouncing
his own humanity.

Novotny stared at the young man, his breakfast untouched
and going cold. How many others have I done this to, over the
years? The decades? How many people have I used as tools, as
rungs of the ladder? How many have I condemned to
obscurity or poverty or even death, once I was finished using
them? Starting with my own father, how many have I killed?

The president did not notice that Stoner was staring at him
now, watching him as his hands began to shake and his eyes
filled once again with tears.

"All those souls," Novotny muttered. "All those souls . . ."

He buried his face in his hands, sobbing uncontrollably.
Janos pushed his chair back and ran toward the kitchen. Must
be a telephone in there, Stoner thought, or at least someone
who can fetch help.

Ilona stared wildly at the president, then turned to look at Stoner.

"He wanted the power," Stoner said softly to her. "But he'll never be able to handle the responsibility."

To his star brother he said, The man was not one of the Great Souls. He was a little man, a grasping politician, totally self-centered. Once he acquired his own star brother, once he began to realize that all the men and women around him are his true kin, his guilt and shame overwhelmed him.

Just as you thought would happen, answered the alien in Stoner's mind. You were right and I was wrong.

Stoner smiled grimly. There is no *you* and *I*, brother. We did not know for certain how the man would react. We were doubtful.

Both of us.

The one of us. And Stoner thought of the Christian doctrine of three persons in one God. Two is plenty, he said to himself.

Janos came back into the dining room. The president was still weeping inconsolably.

"His personal physician is on the way by helicopter," said Janos. "He will arrive here in a few minutes."

"President Novotny is suffering a nervous breakdown," said Stoner calmly. "I doubt that he will be fit to work for some time to come."

Ilona stammered, "How . . . what happened . . . ?"

Getting to his feet, Stoner said, "That doesn't matter. The important thing is that we've got to be away from here before the medic lands. There'll be all sorts of police and security troops right behind him, and we can't afford to be here when they arrive."

"Leave?" Janos gasped. "Now?"

"We'll never get past the security guards outside," Ilona said.

"Of course we will," said Stoner. He saw that Janos did not doubt his confidence for a moment. In fact, the man looked as if he were curious to see just how far Stoner could get.

Novotny is finished, Janos realized. The power is with this man Stoner. The people at Pacific Commerce will pay a fortune to learn what is in his mind, how he can control such

incredible powers. I must stay with him wherever he goes—
until I can make contact with Hong Kong.

Ilona looked doubtful, bewildered, but Janos took her by the
hand and followed Stoner out of the dining room, leaving the
president sitting alone at the head of the table, weeping inconsolably.

The head of the security team, a slim deadly-looking bald
man in a dark zippered athletic suit, burst through the front
door of the lodge as the three of them approached it.

"The president?" he nearly shouted, wide-eyed with anxiety.

"In the dining room," said Stoner, realizing that Novotny's
doctor had obviously radioed the security team.

Stoner led Ilona and Janos past the men running up to the
house and out to the parking lot where half a dozen black
sedans were lined up in neat military precision. Two more
men were standing guard there. In the cloudy sky they could
hear the distant thrumming of an approaching helicopter.

"We'll need a car," Stoner said to the nearer guard.

He was reluctant for a few moments, but as Janos and Ilona
watched in astonishment, the guard finally fished into his
pocket and handed Stoner the keys for the nearest automobile. Within a minute the three of them were driving down
the winding mountain road. A helicopter flashed overhead
and four more autos passed them, racing all-out for the lodge.

Stoner, behind the wheel, smiled slightly.

"Where are we going?" asked Ilona, sitting beside him.

"To Moscow."

"Moscow?" Janos, on the back seat, seemed startled.

"I have to attend the funeral of an old friend," Stoner explained, as if nothing much had happened that morning.
"Then we can go to Hawaii together, if you like."

They drove in silence down the winding mountain road and
finally came out on the main highway.

"Do you think you can get all the way to Moscow in this
auto?" Janos asked.

"No need to," Stoner replied, glancing up into the rearview

mirror at him. The Hungarian still seemed more curious than anything else, as if he were observing an experiment in progress. "We can take a commercial airliner easily enough."

"We don't have our passports with us," Ilona said worriedly. "Or any other identification papers."

"We won't need them," Janos said, almost laughing. "Ilona, your hypothesis about this man was more correct than you know. The alien devices within him allow him to play tricks with your mind. He'll be able to walk us through the airport, past the customs and immigration inspectors, and on to Moscow—without even paying for a ticket!"

"But . . ." She became flustered, upset. "I don't have any clothes, my travel things . . . they're all back at the lodge. I don't have my . . . my . . ."

"Your pleasure machine?" Stoner asked. "You won't need that, either."

He sped along the highway straight toward the airport without having to ask for directions.

Two travel vans bearing Swiss license plates swerved up the mountain road to the lodge, slowing as they approached an army roadblock. The soldiers waved them on, pointing toward the continuation of the road that led back down off the mountain, away from the spur that ran up to the hilltop lodge, which was blocked off by bright yellow-painted wooden bars resting on sawhorses.

The driver of the lead van stopped and lowered her window. The second van pulled in behind her.

"We wanted to take some photographs from the mountain-top," she said to the soldier. She was a beautiful oriental, high cheekbones, almond eyes, long dark hair.

"The road is closed," the soldier said firmly. "No one allowed up there today." He was young enough to grin at her from beneath his metal helmet. His automatic rifle was slung over his shoulder. Behind the sawhorse barrier stood three more soldiers, one of them with a sergeant's chevrons on his sleeves.

"But we'll only be here for today, then we go on to the capital."

The soldier glanced back at the sergeant, who scowled fiercely. "I'm sorry," he apologized to the driver. "It's impossible."

"What's the trouble?" the driver asked. Behind her, half a dozen men and women crouched, clutching burp guns and grenades. "What's going on up there?"

The soldier shrugged. "Something about the president, I think. There must be half a battalion up there by now, and more coming."

The driver gave him a flashing smile. "Thanks anyway." She put the van in gear and drove away, down the mountain, with the second van following close behind.

Picking up what looked like a CB radio microphone, the driver spoke carefully and reported that the mission to abduct Stoner from the mountain lodge had been aborted. From a transparent panel on the van's roof, a tiny laser squirted the message coded into a burst of light to a satellite orbiting high above, which in turn relayed the information to the headquarters of Pacific Commerce Corporation in Hong Kong.

The vans drove aimlessly along the mountain road for nearly an hour, waiting for a reply. When it came, it contained only two words:

"Find Stoner."

CHAPTER 19

KOKU felt lonely.

Deep in the mountain forest the young gorilla slowly pulled leafy branches off the thick bushes and laid them out in the low crotch of a tree to form a sleeping platform. Birds cawed from the high limbs and a monkey chattered at him, then scampered away through the trees. The last rays of the setting sun slanted through the trees, turning the world all gold and green.

With the massive dignity that his three hundred pounds imposed, Koku climbed up onto his makeshift pallet to sleep. But he could not. He felt lonely.

And afraid.

Gorillas have no natural enemies in the forest, none but man. But Koku did not understand that. The only humans that the young gorilla had known had been back at the good place.

Koku remembered little more than the good place. Men and women had reared him, fed him, spoken to him. He felt safe there, happy. The forest was strange and frightening.

He closed his eyes and felt fear. *Lela.* The woman he had been closest to. Koku understood nothing of the biochips implanted in his skull that linked the woman scientist with his own brain. But because the link worked in both directions, he dimly felt Lela's fear and exhaustion as she ran pell-mell along a narrow trail in the mountainous woods, terrified of something that was chasing her.

Koku whimpered with Lela's fear. And his own.

The scramjet flew so high that its cabin bore hair-thin filaments of superconducting wire on its outer skin to create a magnetic field around the plane that deflected incoming cosmic radiation particles. Streaking along at Mach 10, the plane arced across the North Pacific, entered Soviet airspace slightly above the Kamchatka Peninsula, and skirted the shore of the Arctic, heading for the Ural Mountains and the broad plains of Russia.

Jo Camerata paid no attention to the geography spinning by below her. Most of it was covered by clouds, anyway. She sat in a wide padded leather chair swivelled to face the display screen of the console built into the side of the cabin.

"I agree fully," Sir Harold Epping was saying from the screen. "Hsen is making his play for the board of directors.

His agents have even tried to recruit me to his side." One of Sir Harold's gray eyebrows rose nearly a millimeter; for him, such a ruffling of his normally unflappable exterior was an admission of surprise and disdain.

"You're the first board member to tell me about it," Jo said.

"I'm sure others will call you," said the Englishman. "Hsen's being very careful. He knows that if he tips his hand too soon you'll counterattack."

"He's got at least six board members on his side."

"Perhaps you should mount a campaign to take over Pacific Commerce."

Jo frowned at the image in the screen. "An unfriendly take-over? That would leave a lot of blood on the floor. And there isn't enough time before the next board meeting to get it going properly."

"Yes," Sir Harold admitted. "Perhaps."

The message light to one side of the display screen began blinking amber.

"Harold, I'll get back to you in a day or so," Jo said. "In the meantime, would you play along with Hsen's people and pump them for all the information you can get?"

"Of course, dear girl. I'd be delighted to match wits with the wily orientals."

"Thank you so much, Harold. You're a true friend."

"My pleasure," he said, smiling genuinely.

The screen went blank for an instant, then a message scrolled across it, telling Jo who was calling and from where. With a slight sigh of irritation she touched the keyboard pad that accepted the call.

Cliff Baker's pouchy, puffy-eyed features filled the screen.

"We've got to convene an emergency meeting," said the chairman of the IIA. "I'm polling the members to pick the best time and place."

"I don't have time for an emergency meeting, Cliff," Jo protested. "My schedule looks like a disaster area as it is!"

He made a grin that would have been charming ten years earlier. "Jo, luv, there's not much either one of us can do about it. Everybody's scared shitless about this epidemic. The Asian bloc want a meeting this week, without fail."

"Can't you put them off?"

"Varahamihara himself has asked for it."

Jo felt the steam go out of her. The Great Soul of India. No one could deny him a request.

But she heard herself asking, "This is a health problem, Cliff. Why bring it to the IIA?"

"Because the medical blokes are going to need money, and lots of it. The World Health people are asking the UN for a special appropriation, but all the national health organizations need more funding too. That's why India, Bangladesh, Pakistan, Vietnam—all of 'em are screaming for a special meeting soon's possible."

Recognizing defeat when it stared at her, Jo acquiesced with a heavy sigh. "Okay. What looks like the best time and place?"

"This Sunday, in Sydney, at local noon."

Tapping the data into her computer file, Jo realized that the entire weekend would be shot if she attended the meeting in person.

"I'll probably use the videophone, Cliff."

Baker's face took on a slightly pouting expression, but he said, "I imagine most of the members will come in electronically. Wouldn't want to spoil their weekends just because there's a plague threatening to wipe out half the world, would we?"

"Don't be an ass, Cliff."

He grinned again. "Good girl. Wouldn't be a proper talk between us if you didn't call me an ass or something worse."

"You ask for it, you get it," Jo snapped. She was tired of Baker's deliberate goading, his perpetual game of good little poor people beset by evil big rich people.

"Sunday noon then, Sydney time," he said.

"Right."

Instead of signing off, Baker asked curiously, "Where the hell are you now?"

"On my way to Moscow for a funeral."

"A funeral? H'mp."

"Good-bye, Cliff."

"Ta. See you Sunday noon."

The screen went dark. Jo leaned back in her chair and listened for a moment to the muted howl of the scramjet engines. Suddenly she snapped up straight. That bastard Cliff! Sunday noon in Sydney. He can stay on his own clock and even sleep late! The lazy scheming sonofabitch!

Baker was always playing one-upmanship games. Gazing through the tiny window at the gray featureless clouds below, Jo's tense expression relaxed into a smile. In another hour or so she would be with Keith again. And she would take him home, where he'd be safe.

His message had been terse. Just his flight's arrival time in Moscow. And the fact that he was travelling with two Hungarian scientists. That woman we met in Moscow must be one of them, Jo said to herself. Must be.

And it was, she saw, when Stoner strode out from the access ramp into the gate area at Sheremetyevo Airport. The same Ilona Lucacs, wearing practically the same outfit: tweed skirt and jacket, mannish off-white blouse, hardly any makeup or jewelry at all. Still she was beautiful. Stunning. Jo felt old and ostentatiously overdressed in her Russian-style red blazer, loose black slacks, and glossy high black boots.

Keith was wearing his usual denims. The man walking beside him, stretching his legs almost painfully to keep up with Keith, wore an old-style business suit that had seen better days. His barrel-shaped body seemed out of proportion to his pipestem arms and legs, but his moon-round face was all intensity and grim purpose, lips pressed into a thin line, deep-set eyes looking up at Keith like a caged wolf waiting to be released by its keeper. Dark hair down to his collar, little fringe of a beard that was meant to look intellectual. An academic, Jo decided swiftly. She did not trust academics; but then, she did not trust anyone until they had proved their loyalty.

All that happened in the flash of a second. Before she could draw another breath, Keith dropped the tiny bundle he was carrying, ran to her, and picked her up in his arms. Jo kissed him as hard as he kissed her, winding her arms around his neck and not letting go until he deposited her back on the carpeted floor.

Other passengers from the airliner passed by, grinning or turning away according to their personal feelings about two clearly middle-aged people exhibiting passion in the midst of a crowded airport terminal.

Stoner whispered into Jo's ear, "No questions until we're alone." Then he released her and turned to introduce Zoltan Janos.

Jo shook the scientist's limp hand, confirming her original opinion of him, and said hello to Ilona Lucacs. She looks tense, wired, Jo thought now that she saw the young woman close up.

A uniformed gate attendant picked up Stoner's bundle of clothes and handed it to him with a smile that beamed approval of romance, even among older men and women. Stoner thanked her, then slid his arm around Jo's waist and started down the long busy corridor.

"Hard to believe it's only been a couple of days," he said to her. "Seems like weeks since I've seen you."

A bald man in a gray suit pushed his way toward them against the flow of the exiting crowd. Jo recognized Markov's former aide from the Academy of Sciences, Rozmenko. At least he's alone this time, Jo thought. No policemen with him.

"Dr. Stoner, Mrs. Stoner," Rozmenko said, out of breath as if he had run all the way through the airport. "I only learned of your arrival half an hour ago."

Stopping in the middle of the crowded corridor, Keith shook hands with the chunky bureaucrat and introduced Janos to him. He already knew Ilona, however briefly. Jo nodded to Rozmenko with ill-concealed impatience as streams of other travellers flowed around them like rushing water lapping past a rock.

Looking almost ashamed of himself, Rozmenko said to the Stoners, "I am afraid a problem has arisen about Professor Markov's funeral."

"A problem?" Keith asked.

"It concerns his will. If you could be at my office tomorrow I will explain it to you."

"How long will the funeral be delayed?" Jo asked.

Rozmenko shrugged his shoulders. "Perhaps indefinitely. Professor Markov's body is being frozen."

Keith frowned at the Russian. "But Kir specifically said he didn't want to be frozen."

With a puzzled frown of his own, Rozmenko asked, "When did he say that?"

"When we visited him at the hospital, day before last."

Rozmenko shook his head. "In his last will and testament he—well, if you will come to my office tomorrow I will have the proper people there to explain everything to you."

"What time?" Jo wanted to put an end to this pointless conversation.

"At your convenience, of course."

"Ten o'clock."

"Very good, Madam. I will expect you at ten."

Jo led them away from Rozmenko, who stood uncertainly in the middle of the busy corridor, and to the Vanguard limousine waiting at curbside. They were whisked off to the corporate offices and living quarters in the heart of Moscow. On the way, Stoner asked his wife to make arrangements for clothing for his two Hungarian friends. With only a slight reluctance, Jo picked up the phone handset and called the manager of the Moscow office.

"What do you think the problem is with Kir's will?" Jo asked once she put the phone down.

"I haven't the foggiest idea. But I don't like the idea that they're freezing him. That's not what Kir wanted."

Realizing that Ilona and Janos had no knowledge at all of what they were talking about, Jo and her husband dropped the subject temporarily.

They had dinner brought in to the Vanguard conference room, on the top floor of the office building. Jo pulled the drapes back so they could see Moscow's dazzling skyline, with the river snaking through the heart of the city and the towers and turrets of the old Kremlin brilliantly lit.

Stubby little robots carried trays of laden dishes to the end of the long, polished conference table where the four humans sat. Silently the robots waited for further instructions, and silently they glided across the thick carpeting when given orders. They poured wine, removed plates, replaced silverware while the four people largely ignored their presence, except when they wanted something that was not at hand. Stoner found himself thinking that the robots were better than all but the very best of human waiters. The best human waiters anticipated the diner's needs. The fork was there before you realized you were going to need it. The robots had not been programmed to anticipate. But at least they're right there when you want them, he thought. Then, grinning to himself, he added, And they don't bother you with the fake-friendliness routine.

Ilona Lucacs grew noticeably edgier as the dinner progressed. By the time dessert was served by the silent little robots she pushed her chair back from the table and said, "I . . . I don't feel very well. Please excuse me."

Stoner stood up. "Ilona. I had intended to help wean you gradually, but it looks as if you're going to have to make a clean break."

Janos stared off at the lights of the city, looking as if he wished he were someplace else. Jo watched the interplay between her husband and the Hungarian woman.

"Sit down, Ilona, and try to relax."

As if in a daze, she did as he told her.

"There's no physical dependence to direct brain stimulation," Stoner said softly, soothingly. "It's an emotional dependence. You don't need a machine to make you feel loved, Ilona. We love you. I love you."

Jo felt her teeth grating, but she said nothing. Direct brain stimulation! The girl's addicted. What do they call it? A juicer, I think. Immediately Jo catalogued the fact in her mind as something that might be useful in handling this beautiful young woman.

Ilona was shaking her head. "Words are only words, Dr. Stoner. Nothing but air that drifts away and disappears."

He pulled his chair close to Ilona's and grasped her wrist. "Remember Hamlet's advice to his mother," he said softly.

Ilona blinked at him, puzzled.

With a smile, Stoner quoted, "'Refrain tonight; and that shall lend a kind of easiness to the next abstinence; the next more easy; for use almost can change the stamp of nature, and either curb the devil, or throw him out with wondrous potency.'"

The tawny-eyed young woman smiled back at him and said sadly, "Hamlet's Ophelia went mad and committed suicide. For lack of love."

And her gaze drifted toward Janos, who sat red-faced and utterly uncomfortable, trying to pretend none of this was happening, trying to ignore it all or to make himself disappear altogether.

She loves the jerk and he doesn't even give her a goddamned smile, Jo said to herself. For the first time she felt a surge of sympathy for Ilona Lucacs.

They took the elevator down to the living quarters, five floors below the conference room. Jo stayed beside her husband as they walked Ilona and Janos to their rooms. They were adjacent, but had no connecting door. Just as well, thought Jo.

"Get a good night's sleep," Stoner told Ilona. Jo knew it was a suggestion that was practically hypnotic.

They bid a more formal goodnight to Zoltan Janos and then made their way to the suite at the end of the corridor. In every Vanguard office complex, no matter what city in the world, Jo maintained an apartment suite that was exactly the same. Duplicates of everything, from hairbrushes to computer terminals, so that she could simply reach out her hand and find what she wanted no matter where she happened to be.

Now, as they prepared for bed, Stoner told her the whole story of Ilona Lucacs's addiction, of Janos's work on biochips, and President Novotny's lust for the power that nano-technology could give him.

"And you gave it to him?" Jo asked, sitting on the edge of the bed as she tugged off her glossy high boots.

From the bathroom, where he was brushing his teeth, Stoner replied, "It seemed like the logical thing to do. He wanted the power, but he had no idea of what was involved."

"It drove him crazy?"

Stoner rinsed his mouth and came back into the bedroom. "To outsiders it looks as if he's had a nervous breakdown. Incapable of functioning. Paralyzed emotionally. What's really happened is that for the first time since childhood he sees that there are other human beings on Earth. He realizes that he's not alone, that he's part of the whole. He'll never be able to rule again. He'll never be able to see others as tools for his personal use and aggrandizement."

"You've brought him back into the human race," said Jo.

"Maybe. We'll see. But he certainly doesn't have the personality, the mental capacity, the *soul* to be a great leader. He was only a little shit trying to make himself bigger. Now he understands who and what he's been, and it'll be years before he learns to live with that knowledge."

Jo leaned back on the bed, still fully dressed except for the boots. "See why I don't want you to give *me* some of the aliens?"

He went to the bed, leaned over and kissed her lightly. "You know I don't agree. The symbiotes wouldn't change you that much—except maybe to make you see things from other people's point of view, now and then. Might make you a little less ruthless." He grinned. "Could be an improvement, you know."

She returned him a malicious smile. "I enjoy being ruthless now and then."

Laughing, "Better get your kicks while you can, though. The game will be over soon."

"You're sure?"

"I'm positive," he answered seriously. "I don't know how it's going to end, but it's coming to a head. Soon."

"And then?"

He was silent for a long while. Finally he said, "And then we see what kind of spacecraft we've got waiting for us at Delphi."

In the basement of the Vanguard building a hatchet-faced man in a security guard uniform put in a call through one of the public telephones on the wall outside the men's room.

"Stoner is here," he said when a recorded voice answered. "Came in this evening. I don't know how long he'll be here. His wife is with him."

GENEVA

"ALL RIGHT, let's go through it one more time."

The man was in his shirtsleeves and they were rolled up above his elbows. He had kicked off his moccasins hours earlier and now his bare feet were planted on his desk top, gnarled toes hovering over the crumbs and litter of the makeshift supper they had hastily gobbled hours earlier.

Three others sat around his desk in the small office: two women and a man. One wall of the office was a series of twelve display screens, like a double row of windows. Each screen was crammed with data, photomicrographs, charts, brightly-colored maps, chemical equations.

On the wall behind the desk hung the blue and white symbol of the World Health Organization.

"God, I've got to get some sleep," said one of the women,

gray haired, matronly. "I'll never be able to keep my eyes open tomorrow morning."

"*This* morning, honey," the man behind the desk corrected. "We've got just over seven hours to get all our facts straight for the council meeting."

The others grumbled and muttered.

"Come on now, what do we know for certain?" the man behind the desk coaxed.

His assistant, the other male, started off: "It's transmitted through water. It does not appear to be an airborne virus, but that's not certain."

"Definitely transmitted by water, though. That much is certain," said one of the women.

"Sneezes?" asked the man behind the desk. "Plenty of water droplets in a sneeze."

"Apparently, yes," said the other woman.

"Christ, it must be contagious as all hell then."

"Worse."

"It attacks women preferentially," said the first woman. Grimly.

"Is that for sure?"

"Ninety percent of the cases are female. Sixty-three percent of them were pregnant. The damned bug must react to estrogen or one of the other female hormones."

"Christ on a crutch!"

The man behind the desk pecked at his tape recorder. "Action item: check estrogen levels in all male victims." To the three people in the room he added, "If they have levels of female hormones above the male norm, we'll have learned something."

"Something," said the first woman. "But what good will it do us?"

The man behind the desk shrugged. "You're sure about how it works?"

"Destroys the lining of the stomach—"

"The whole digestive tract, right down to the asshole."

"Do you have to be crude?"

"Sorry."

"It's the stomach lining that's important. The virus dissolves it, and the digestive acids get into the abdominal cavity and eat away the internal organs."

"Excruciating pain."

"Victim usually dies within hours."

"Which doesn't leave us with much to study."

"Incubation time?" asked the man behind the desk. "How long between the time the victim takes in the virus and it starts dissolving the stomach lining?"

"Unknown."

"Can't be long, not at the rate the plague is spreading."

The colored maps showed a garish red where the epidemic existed. Southeast Asia and most of India were in red. Tendrils of red extended northward into China and west through Iran. Islands of red splotched major cities across half the world: Istanbul, Manila, Naples, Frankfurt, Rio, New Orleans, Miami, New York.

"The virus likes a warm climate," said the man behind the desk.

"Yeah, but it's spreading into the temperate zones," the other male replied.

"Damn."

"Vectors?"

"Commercial air traffic," said the younger woman.

"Are you sure?"

She tapped at the remote control unit in her hand and one of the display screens showed a world map with a speeded-up presentation of where the disease had first been reported and how it had spread. The tendrils of red followed world air routes.

"Wonderful," groaned the man behind the desk. "If we want to stop the spread of the plague we've got to shut down all the goddamned commercial air carriers."

"Fat chance!"

"The virus rides the airlines. Damn! That makes it tough."

"Are we certain it's a virus?" The others turned toward the

gray-haired woman. "I mean, we haven't isolated it, whatever it is. We're just assuming it's a virus."

"You think it might be a microbe? A bacterium? That would be good news."

"Too good to be true. Whatever it is filters right through everything we've used to find it."

"Chemical analyses?"

"Inconclusive. I think whatever the bug is, it dissolves itself when the stomach acids come pouring out."

"That doesn't make sense. If it kamikazes inside its victim, then how the hell does it spread to other victims?"

"It's transmitted before it attacks the mucous layer, maybe?"

They all fell silent until the man behind the desk said grimly, "Seems to me what we *don't* know about this bug outweighs what we do know by about a hundred to one."

"But is it really a bug?"

"Huh?"

"I mean, maybe it's a chemical agent of some kind."

"A pollutant?"

"Or a biological warfare agent that's gotten out of hand."

"Jesus H. You-Know-Who!"

CHAPTER 20

FEODOR Rozmenko looked clearly unhappy. He had ushered Stoner and Jo into the office that had been Markov's, telling them that it was larger and more comfortable than his own cubbyhole.

Jo had insisted that Keith put on a real suit for this meeting. He had acquiesced, but wore a golden turtleneck shirt beneath the sky-blue jacket she had picked from the stocked wardrobe in the Vanguard apartment. Jo was in a tan military-style hip-length jacket, with epaulets and leather buttons, cinched by a wide leather belt. The skirt came almost to her knee, a length that was demure enough for a businesswoman while still showing her long legs to good effect.

Two men were already in Markov's old office, waiting. They shot to their feet as Rozmenko brought the Stoners in and introduced them. The leaner of the pair was a lawyer; the other an official from the Soviet space agency.

Curiouser and curiouser, thought Stoner as he held a chair for his wife and then sat in the one next to hers. Rozmenko took the chair that had been placed beside Markov's desk. The desk itself remained unoccupied, its worn old leather chair empty.

Jo remembered this office and how that chair would creak when Kirill rocked in it. Kir always made the same joke: "I hope that creaking is the chair, and not me."

Rozmenko coughed politely, his way of bringing the meeting to order. "Professor Markov left part of his last will and testament on videotape. Our legal counsel," he nodded toward the gaunt, dark-suited lawyer, "has examined the tape and assures us that it is a valid and legal will."

The lawyer nodded gravely.

"With your permission, Dr. and Mrs. Stoner, I will now play the tape."

Stoner could feel Jo's tension. And his own. *I'm just coming to terms with the idea that Kir is dead, and now I'm going to see him alive, hear him speaking.* His star brother smiled within him: *Life and death are not so simple, after all, are they?*

The TV was built into the panelled wall above the narrow table that held Kirill's samovar. Rozmenko touched two buttons on the desktop keyboard with his stubby finger, and the screen flickered with colors.

Markov's face appeared, his cheeks hollow and dark, his straggly little beard snow white, his soulful eyes looking somewhere off camera.

"It is working?" he asked in Russian. "Good. Good."

Markov looked straight into the camera, clasped his hands on his desk and hunched forward slightly. With a smile he said in English:

"My darling Jo, beautiful lady who fills my dreams. And you too, Keith, my old and dear friend. It must seem strange to be watching this tape, since I will have to be dead before you can see it. It seems strange to me! Like speaking from the grave."

Stoner glanced at Jo. She was rigidly controlling herself, her face showing no emotion whatever. But he could sense the feelings that were simmering beneath her outer show of composure.

"I have written out my last will and testament, so the lawyers can handle it in their usual way. But there is one request—request, not bequest, kindly notice—that concerns both of you." Markov smiled like a little boy who knew he was asking for more than he deserved.

"I have decided to have my body sent out to the stars, just the way our alien visitor did."

Stoner felt utterly surprised. Kir refused to be frozen when it could have helped him. But he had already made up his mind to send his dead body out to the stars.

His star brother said, The man was ready for death; he had given up his will to live.

"I know it's not much of a body," Markov was saying. "I haven't taken particularly good care of it, all these years. But I want to give it as a gift to some other race of intelligent creatures. I want to tell them that they are not alone, and that the universe is not a hostile arena of aggressive species.

"Jo, Keith, obviously I need your help to do this. The Soviet space agency can build a vehicle and put it on a rocket that will fling me clear of the solar system. But it seems to me that the alien starship had some form of guidance system that led it to worlds where life might exist. Can you duplicate that guidance system for my sarcophagus? I do not want to be set blindly adrift—I would like to know that I am sailing in a direction that might do some good, even if it is thousands of years from now.

"Will you do this for me? It is the last request I will ever make of you. I love you both. Be happy together. Good-bye from your devoted friend."

The screen went blank.

Before Stoner could take a breath, the space agency official leaned forward in his chair and asked, "Does such a guidance system actually exist?"

Stoner studied the man's face. There was awestruck curiosity there. And a remorseless drive to learn the secrets of the stars. It reminded Stoner of the old days, back when they had first detected the approaching alien starship, how the Russians and Americans—and all the others—had played their power games back and forth. It reminded him of how he himself had been back then, inhumanly relentless, driven to make contact with the alien visitor no matter what the cost.

"The guidance system was destroyed fifteen years ago," Stoner answered, "by a man who was terrified at the thought of meeting alien intelligences."

"My first husband," Jo confirmed. "He went insane."

The Russians looked back and forth among themselves.

"Dr. Stoner," asked the space agency official, "are you certain . . . ?"

Keith smiled, mainly because the man assumed that he should be asking his questions of another man. *He doesn't realize that Jo's the one with the clout. Or, even if he does know it consciously, he automatically downgrades her and speaks to me.*

Aloud, Stoner said, "Please don't worry about it. Vanguard Industries will duplicate the guidance system for you. It's the least we can do for our dear friend Professor Markov."

Jo put on a sweet smile also, adding, "And we will sell it to you at cost."

Operating a maintenance tractor is simple, Paulino Alvarado kept repeating to himself. His boss had given him a quick orientation ride and then expected him to be able to handle the huge machine by himself.

To a considerable degree the boss had been right. Sitting high up in the tractor's cab, surrounded by display screens and light-keyed controls, Paulino felt as if he were driving a hypersonic rocketplane rather than a massive tractor lumbering along the Mare Imbrium.

The so-called Sea of Clouds was a rolling plain of dust-covered rock, without a drop of water or a molecule of air, nothing but barren bleak rock stretching to a horizon that seemed dangerously, dizzyingly close. The undulating plain was pockmarked by millions of craters, some of them so big that they could swallow up the tractor and a dozen more, most as small as the poke of a fingertip. Beyond the knife-sharp line of the horizon hung the stars and the blackness of eternity.

It scared Paulino to be out here. Especially alone. The cabin was shielded and he was bundled into a cumbersome pressure suit, but still he felt the hard radiation streaming in from space, felt utterly naked and exposed to the meteoroids that could hit with the power of a hypervelocity bullet.

Unconsciously he pressed a gloved hand against the thigh pocket that held his diminishing supply of Moondust pills. What would my boss do if he knew what I'm carrying? Paulino was afraid of the little man's wrath. Better to try the pills on some of the other workers and keep the rat-faced boss out of it.

Out on the endless plain other tractors were placidly inching along, unmanned, automated. They scooped in the top layer of dust from the rocky ground at their front ends and deposited little squares of solar cells from their rear ends, turning the native lunar dust into glittering patches of energy farms that transformed sunlight into the electricity that powered the base at Archimedes. To Paulino they looked like enormous mechanical cows quietly grazing across the dusty plain.

His job was to repair malfunctions on the automated tractors. He received a list of malfunctioning machines each morning, rode out to each one guided by its individual radio beacon, and did not start back for home until he had completed repairs on the entire list.

Vanguard Industries' official work regulations stated that no one was required to remain on the surface, out in the open, for more than four hours at a time. Radiation badges were to be turned in to the health and safety department at the end of each four-hour stint. Paulino's boss, however, made it abundantly clear that "you stay out 'til you've finished the whole fuckin' list." And the radiation badges were turned in to him, not the safety people, at the end of the long day.

It had been a very long day. Repair jobs looked easy in the garage: just check the tractor's diagnostic display, take out the malfunctioning module and put in a fresh one. But doing such work from inside a pressure suit, with thick gloves and the limited vision that even the cleanest bubble helmet yields—that was another matter. And then there was the dust. It clung to everything with electrostatic tenacity. Paulino spent as much time wiping dust from his visor and gloves as he did actually making repairs.

Now he was heading out for the farthest tractor, which had decided to stop dead for a few hours earlier. The job was not on his morning's list; the boss had radioed the extra task to him.

"You're practically there already, just a half hour away. No sense comin' in and then drivin' all that distance tomorrow."

Paulino was too new to the job to realize that he could have argued back enough to get the boss to throw in a small bonus for the extra assignment. He sighed and, rather than risking the wrath of the little rat-faced man, pecked out the dead tractor's location coordinates on his navigational keyboard and turned his own machine in its direction.

He never found it. His tractor lumbered along, up and down the gently rolling plain, turning slowly to avoid troublesome craters, heading farther and farther away from home base. Even the highest radio mast atop the ringwall mountains of Archimedes receded below his horizon, and his only link with the base was by satellite relay.

Paulino tuned in to a powerful radio station broadcasting Andean jazz from somewhere in Latin America, leaned back in his seat and waited for the dead tractor to come into view. He could feel his own machine jouncing and wobbling as it trundled along, but even if the radio had been off he could not have heard any squeaks or mechanical groans in the soundless vacuum of the Moon.

Very carefully he took out the box of pills and shook one into his gloved hand. There was a capsule dispenser built into his helmet, originally designed so that workers could take energy tablets or even medicines while still inside their pressure suits. Paulino giggled to himself as he tongued up the Moondust pill and then, with a turn of his head, sucked on the water nipple.

All the comforts of home, he told himself as the Moondust spread its warming confidence through his body.

The first sign of trouble came when the navigational display showed that he was not heading in the correct direction to reach the malfunctioning tractor. Paulino took no alarm, he merely corrected his machine's heading. But within five minutes the nav display started blinking and beeping again. More annoyed than frightened, Paulino again reset the coordinates. Then the status board suddenly showed a glaring red warning light. Paulino's heart clutched within his chest. He touched the screen and its pictograph showed that something was wrong with the left rear wheel.

Paulino stopped the tractor and hopped down to the surface, falling with dreamlike slowness in the light lunar gravity. Clouds of dust stirred when his boots hit the ground. He nearly toppled over, but steadied himself with a hand on the tractor's massive flank.

The wheel was coated heavily with dust. The electrostatic cleaner was apparently not working and the dust was starting to jam the axle bearing so that the wheel could not turn at the same speed as the others. Paulino realized that this was why he was drifting off course; the tractor was pulling to the left instead of going straight ahead.

It was not something he could repair. He climbed back into the cab, radioed Archimedes, and told them his situation.

"Come back in," his boss's voice replied, filled with disgust. "That tractor you're in's worth a million and a quarter. Get it back here in one piece."

Paulino turned around and headed for home, wondering if the wheel would hold up long enough to get there, with all the constant course corrections he would have to make to compensate for its drift.

"You were pretty damned generous with Vanguard Industries' proprietary information," Jo huffed.

Sitting beside her in the narrow cabin of the scramjet, Stoner smiled placatingly. "Vanguard would have to share the information sooner or later; it's part of the agreement the corporation made with the Russians twenty years ago, when you worked together to rescue the starship. And me."

The plane was speeding back to Hawaii, bearing Ilona Lucacs and Zoltan Janos as well as Jo and Stoner. The two scientists had docilely allowed themselves to be bundled aboard. Stoner knew they could not return to Hungary without being swallowed alive by the government's security police, who would want to know exactly what had happened to President Novotny. Their only refuge was with Stoner, who assured them that he would straighten everything out—and even cooperate with them in their research, eventually.

Ilona seemed dazed without her pleasure machine, as if she were stumbling through the hours with no purpose, no goal, no plan to her existence. Janos stayed next to her, but kept his eyes on Stoner. Under the pretext of phoning his parents in Budapest he had managed to get off a hurried message to Hong Kong. The reply he had received was even briefer: "Stay with Stoner."

For long moments a silence stretched between Stoner and his wife. The howl of the plane's powerful engines was muffled by heavy acoustical insulation but Stoner could sense the fury blazing within them, feel the heat and thrust as they shrieked through the cold darkness of the high stratosphere.

"Can you really duplicate the starship's guidance system?" Jo asked.

Stoner tapped his temple. "Whatever was in that ship is up here."

"But will you be able to get it out of him?"

Smiling, "We're brothers, Jo. More than brothers, really, but that's the closest word in our language to express it. When we set the design parameters for the ship we're building at Delphi base, the guidance system was part of the design. It's being incubated now, most likely."

Jo stared into his eyes. "Sometimes . . . when you first woke from the freezing you were so different—almost inhuman. But then . . ."

"It's the real me, Jo. Keith Stoner, the same man I always was. Except that I have a star brother within me. But that doesn't change the original me."

"Oh no?" Jo glanced up at Ilona and Janos, sitting forward of them in the plane's cabin like a pair of bewildered school-children.

"I can do things that no one could do before," Stoner admitted. "But that doesn't change my personality. I'm still me and nobody else."

"Plus your friend."

"My brother."

"You could rule the world, Keith. If you wanted to."

For a moment he did not answer. Then, "No one should rule the world. No one person, no one group, no one nation. The human race has got to be able to rule itself. Otherwise all you get is a tyrant who'd be in constant fear of rebellion. Constant bloodshed. Constant pain."

"And you think people like Nkona and de Sagres can bring the world to that condition?"

"They're doing it, Jo. Slowly, but they're moving us in the proper direction. If they're not stopped, men and women like that will help the human race to take the next step forward."

Jo stared into his eyes, as if trying to see who was truly there.

"The step up to nanotechnology—it's a test, Jo. A test.

Other races on other worlds have tried it and failed. Wiped themselves out. Overpopulated to the point of total ecological collapse. Destroyed themselves in wars. We've got to make sure that the human race discovers nanotechnology in the right way and develops it wisely, usefully. Not for power. Not for weapons. Humanely. Then we'll be ready to meet the other races that have succeeded, that have passed this test and become truly intelligent, truly adult."

She leaned her head on the padded chair back. "Keith— don't you ever get tired of it? The struggle? It's been fifteen years, for god's sake! When do we rest, when do we get to enjoy life?"

Reaching out, Stoner touched her chin lightly and turned her face toward his. He kissed her.

"With the power comes the responsibility, Jo. I can't stop, not until it's finished."

Jo sighed. *"The Red Shoes,"* she said.

Grinning, Stoner said, "Well, at least that's better than *Macbeth.*"

Li-Po Hsen could see that Vic Tomasso was almost breathless. "Yes, yes, they'll be here in another hour and a half!"

Hsen was sitting up tensely in the comfortable lounge chair on his rooftop patio. The magnificent harbor of Hong Kong was spread out for his view, busy with boats and barges that practically covered the crescent of water from one shore to the other. Beyond lay the crowded white skyscrapers of Kowloon and the softly blue mountains of China itself. The woman who had been pouring tea for him had backed away, startled, when Hsen had bolted upright in the chair.

"You told me they would be in Moscow for at least another day!" he said to the image on the phone screen, his voice murderously cold.

"They changed their plans." Tomasso looked thoroughly frightened. "They'll be landing at Hilo and coming up to the house. I just got the word. I'm taking all kinds of chances calling you like this!"

Hsen forced himself to regain his inner calm. He closed his eyes for a moment, then said softly, "You have done well. Now go about your regular business as usual. Do not contact me unless they change their plans once again."

Tomasso nodded eagerly and cut the connection.

Before the screen went totally dark Hsen was tapping out the number of his security chief. When her sallow face appeared on the screen he swiftly told her that Stoner and his wife would be at their home within two hours.

"Is your team prepared to strike?" Hsen asked.

"Within six hours," she replied.

"Then strike! Now!"

"It will be done."

BOOK IV

"Nay," responded the Khan, "to crush your enemies, to see them fall at your feet—to take their horses and goods and hear the lamentation of their women. That is best."

CHAPTER 21

IT was just after midnight. Jo and Stoner slept together in their own bed for the first time in days, warm and moist from making love. Above them moonlit clouds scudded past the bright twinkling stars.

Outside the house, microscopically small diode lasers swept their invisible beams across the grounds. Heat and motion detectors watched patiently from every corner of the sprawling buildings. Two armed watchmen slowly padded back and forth along special walkways cunningly built into the roof to look as if they had been part of the architect's original line.

Half a mile down the only road leading to the house, dozens more Vanguard employees slept in a gate house that was part fortress, part armory, and part command center. Three security personnel—two of them women—sat by the fifteen display screens that monitored every square inch of the grounds and the house's exterior. They stayed alert because they never knew when one of their superiors would suddenly pop in to the monitoring center to check up on them. Once in a while Ms. Camerata herself showed up. God help the person who looked drowsy.

There was no other access to the house except that one road past the gate house. Like a medieval castle, the house was built on a bluff by the sea, protected on three sides by steep cliffs that plunged down to heavy pounding surf. Still, there were sensors planted in the cliff walls. And antipersonnel mines.

Stoner awoke. Ever since he had acquired his star brother he had needed but little sleep. He inhaled the fragrance of the flowers in their room, and the musky lingering odor of their lovemaking. Jo slept on her side, curled slightly facing him. The only time her face looks relaxed is when we're sleeping together here at home, Stoner said to himself. She feels safe here.

Looking up through the transparent ceiling he thought he saw a shadow flicker past. A plane, this time of night? The house was well away from the normal flight paths out of Hilo Airport, he knew. What would a plane be doing out this way?

But it was gone before he could really worry about it. Stoner listened to the quiet of the house. True silence simply does not exist. Even in an absolutely still room there is some sound, the faint sixty-cycle hum of electrical current, the Brownian motion of air molecules inside the ear, the creak of walls expanding in the sunlight or contracting in shadow, the skittering of a leaf blown across the roof.

Cathy and Rickie were in their own rooms, sleeping soundly. Stoner smiled. He and Jo had expected the kids to want to have dinner with their parents after several days' absence. But with the true indifference of youth Cathy and Rickie had preferred to eat by the pool and spend the evening swimming and watching the TV on the patio. The fact that their parents were home was reassuring enough to them; they did not want to sit through a stuffy adult dinner.

Ilona Lucacs was sleeping fitfully, Stoner sensed. Although she claimed that direct brain stimulation produced no physical effects, she had been as irritable and shaky as any junkie facing withdrawal. Stoner had tried to reassure her emotionally and had even asked Jo point-blank to help make the Hungarian woman feel at ease. But still Ilona tossed on her bed in the guest wing; perhaps she was not in pain, but she desperately missed the electrical ecstasy that she had become accustomed to.

Zoltan Janos was sleeping poorly too. Stoner could feel the nervous fear emanating from him. He was just beginning to realize that his career, his entire life, had suddenly veered off in an entirely unexpected direction. One minute he's running a high-powered research operation for the president of his country, the next he's a fugitive fleeing halfway across the world. And he's trying to keep all that fear and frustration and anger inside himself, afraid to show his feelings to anyone, distrustful of everyone.

Or is it fear and frustration? Stoner asked himself. He had come along to Hawaii easily enough. Perhaps too easily. Ilona seemed confused, frightened, but Janos . . .

Suddenly Stoner's point of view shifted. In his mind's eye he saw the house from the outside, from above, as if he were flying. The dark bulk of the roof line against the even darker edge of the cliff and the frothing luminescent surf far below. As if gliding through the soft night air in a parasail . . .

Another shadow flickered across the transparent ceiling. Stoner sat up in the bed, suddenly tense. Too big to be a bird and too low to be a plane.

The softest padding sound of feet racing across the roof. The white-hot agony of a man stabbed to death!

"Jo, get up, we . . ."

Every alarm in the house shrilled and all the outside lights came on. Stoner dived for the jeans he had tossed onto the chair near the bed.

"Stay here," he told Jo.

She had already hit the special alarm button built into the ornately carved head of their bed, sending a priority alarm to the gate house down the road. And then dashed for her robe.

"The children!" Jo yelped.

"I'll take care of them," Stoner shouted from the door. But she was running behind him, down the hall toward the rooms where Cathy and Rickie's rooms were.

Glancing out the sliding glass door halfway down the hall, Stoner saw six or seven men in dead black skintight jumpsuits disentangling themselves from the shrouds of para-sails. That was the plane I thought I saw, his mind raced. It dropped an assault team on the house.

The children's bedrooms were at the far end of the hall. Before he could reach them, the door to Rickie's room burst open and a pair of black-suited men stepped through, levelling snub-nosed submachine guns at Stoner's gut.

"Stay behind me," he snapped to Jo.

"Put your hands up," said one of the men, his voice muffled by a gas mask with big square goggles that made him look somehow like a prehistoric beast. Behind him Stoner saw two more intruders yanking a still half-asleep Rickie out into the hall. The boy wore only a pair of ragged flowered shorts.

"Rickie!" Jo screamed, lunging for her son.

But Stoner held her back as the first intruder cocked his submachine gun at her. Stoner sensed that the men were keyed to the snapping point.

"You don't want to hurt anyone," Stoner said, as calmly as he could. "And you certainly don't want the boy."

Further down the hall he saw another quartet of gun-bearing intruders hustling Cathy out into the hallway. She was wide-eyed with terror, clutching the flimsy tee shirt she used as a nightgown with white-knuckled hands.

"It's all right, Cathy," Stoner called to her. "Don't be afraid."

"You come with us!" snapped the man pointing the gun at Stoner from inside his gas mask. His voice sounded hollow, high-pitched, very dangerous.

They half-pushed, half-carried the youngsters out through the sliding doors onto the patio by the swimming pool, Stoner and Jo following as the gunmen directed them. The alarms were still hooting and screeching; Stoner knew that in another minute dozens of Vanguard security guards would come barrelling up to the house and a fire fight would erupt.

Out in the glaring lights on the patio he saw the body of one of the security guards who had been patrolling the roof. And more of the black-suited intruders clustered around a large bag of equipment that had been para-dropped with them.

For an instant he wondered where the two Hungarians were, then he saw them being led at gunpoint out onto the far end of the patio. Nunzio and the other house servants were nowhere in sight.

Stoner said to the nearest gunman, "It's me you want, not the others, isn't it?"

The gunman nodded slowly.

"So let them go and I'll go with you."

"Your family comes along," the gunman said in his muffled voice.

"That's not really necessary," Stoner said, taking a step toward the man. "You don't even need the guns. I'm willing to come along with you. There's no need to threaten anyone."

The submachine gun wavered in his grip.

"You're afraid that the security guards will be here before you're ready to leave and you'll have a fight on your hands," Stoner said softly, calmly, soothingly. "That won't happen. I'll go with you voluntarily."

He was close enough to reach the man's gun. Inside him, Stoner's mind was racing. *If I can get to the others who're holding Rickie and Cathy I can talk our way out of this before the security team starts shooting up everything.*

"Why don't you tell your men to hand the children over to their mother. Everybody will be a lot safer that way."

The man slowly nodded. It was impossible to see his expression inside the gas mask, but he turned almost like an automaton and gestured to the intruders holding Rickie and Cathy with one hand, his other hand holding the submachine gun pointed down to the ground.

Jo, meanwhile, was in a frenzy of shock, rage, and terror. In the pocket of her robe was a slim metallic rod that controlled the household robots. She watched in horror as Keith spoke gently to the bastards who had grabbed her children. Cathy looked so terrified, her face white as death. Rickie looked scared too but Cathy must feel naked and totally helpless in the clutches of strange horrible men, Jo knew.

There were eight household robots programmed to do cleaning chores and serve at table. With extensible arms operated by tiny but powerful servomotors they could even be used as lifeguards, capable of reaching into any spot in the pool and hauling out even a two-hundred-pound swimmer.

They also had built into their domed heads small but powerful lasers that could spit out pulses of light with the energy of a high-velocity bullet.

While Keith talked, Jo acted. They're not going to steal my babies! I'll kill them! All of them!

With her forefinger and thumb Jo manipulated the slipring control of the robot command rod. The eight squat machines trundled out onto the patio from both ends, their metal skins glinting in the powerful security lights.

"You are surrounded," said a preprogrammed voice tape. "A security team will arrive momentarily. Give yourselves up *now*!"

The man that Stoner had been talking to jerked around, his gun snapping toward the nearest robot. One of the other intruders laughed shakily.

Jo pressed the tip of the control rod. Each robot selected a target and fired. Eight of the intruders spasmed and smashed to the ground as pulses of laser light hit their heads and shattered bone and brain.

Before Stoner could move, all the other intruders blasted away at the robots. Who fired back at the intruders.

Jo felt herself flung to the ground. Keith had knocked her down and now he was dashing toward the men holding their children.

The one that Keith had been talking to dropped to one knee and pointed his submachine gun at Cathy. One of the men who had been holding her was already sprawled on the ground, the other had turned to fire at the robots approaching him.

"I'll kill her!" the intruder screamed.

Jo hesitated half a heartbeat, then turned off the robots. Too late. Three separate laser beams smashed the man's head to pulp. His spine arched and his throat poured out a bloody shriek. His hands twitched and the submachine gun fired a burst that flung Cathy completely off her feet and sent her reeling, tottering over the edge of the swimming pool and into the water.

Jo screamed and raced to the pool.

Stoner raised his hands high. "Come on, you stupid bastards!" he shouted. "You want me, come on and take me before we all get killed!"

The remaining intruders rushed to Stoner and pushed him

toward the lumpy bag of equipment that still lay in the far corner of the patio. The robots stood inert, half of them torn apart by bullets, their innards flickering and hissing faintly with electrical sparks.

Jo stared down into the lighted pool where her daughter floated face down, her hair spreading on the bloody water, her body torn nearly in half.

"Cathy!" she screamed. "Cathy!"

She felt Rickie's arms slide around her waist and the two of them collapsed sobbing at the edge of the pool.

Stoner watched, his insides frozen by his star brother, his mind numb with shock, as the intruders strapped a personal rocket unit on his back. In the distance, despite the horror that was trying to overwhelm him, Stoner heard the sounds of approaching cars. The security team was racing up the road.

Too late. The intruders roared off on their backpack rockets, controlling Stoner's backpack remotely. As in a nightmare, Stoner saw the brilliantly-lit blood-soaked patio receding, racing away from him, bodies sprawled helter skelter like toys thrown away by a careless child, his daughter's body floating in the reddening pool, his wife and son clinging to each other in helpless grief.

CHAPTER 22

THE control board of Paulino's tractor glared with red lights, but when the oxygen supply hit the critical level a soft female voice purred in his helmet earphones, "Only one hour's worth of oxygen remaining."

He did not think he could be more frightened than he already was, but Paulino tensed at the words so hard that he felt his teeth grinding together painfully. There was an emergency tank of oxygen on the tractor, of course, but at best that held another two hours of breathable oxy and he had been tooling around out here on Mare Imbrium for at least eight hours.

No way to get back safely, and for some reason the radio was no longer working. He felt strong and alert, thanks to the Moondust, but he could not raise the base back at Archimedes, could not even hear a homing beacon. The radio had gone completely dead.

In misery he trundled along in the massive tractor's cab, totally lost, the fear of death crawling up his spine like a loathsome poisonous insect's larva, the kind that wormed its way inside your skull and slowly, agonizingly ate your brains away.

The dusty desert of stone stretched away to the frighteningly close horizon no matter which way he looked. Not a sign of human habitation, not a landmark nor a signpost. Nothing but craters and rocks. He could not even see the Earth in the black sky. Completely alone. Paulino would have welcomed the vicious snarling of his boss; he prayed to hear the nasty little man's voice excoriating him as a fool and idiot.

But his radio yielded nothing but a crackling hissing sound with an oddly whining note running up and down the scale like a tin whistle on a roller coaster. The noise made him shudder like fingernails on a blackboard, but he dared not turn off the radio. He glanced down at the control panel and saw that the emergency transmitter was still on, beaming out its plea for help.

Rescue me! Paulino prayed to the stars that looked down at him. Save me! Don't let me die!

His vision blurred with tears as he thought about the church in his village, so far away. How he had prayed to the Virgin and the saints when he had been a child. They never answered him. Not once. Never did they grant his simple requests. What makes you think anyone is going to save your miserable life now? he asked himself.

"You in the tractor, identify yourself."

The voice cut through the whining static in his earphones like the clarion call of an angel. The breath caught in Paulino's throat. He was so excited he could not speak.

"Identify yourself or you will trigger automatic defenses that could destroy your vehicle."

Gulping down tears and fright, Paulino stuttered, "I'm lost . . . from Archimedes . . . Paulino Alvarado is my name . . . please . . . I need help."

"Stop your tractor immediately," commanded the radio voice. "Two vehicles will come out to inspect you. You have entered a security zone without authorization. You are in big trouble, buddy."

Paulino laughed. He threw his head back inside his fogged, dust-caked helmet and laughed uproariously.

Hanging in the harness of the backpack rocket, Stoner saw the lights of home dwindle in the distance. Looking up he could see the remaining intruders as shadowy silhouettes against the moonlit sky. Deep inside his brain he wanted to lash out at these murderers, kill and maim them the way they had slaughtered his daughter. Blood for blood, the ancient voice spoke to him. Kill them all, as painfully as possible.

But his star brother's voice interrupted the primeval urge to vengeance. Who are these men? Who sent them? Where do they intend to take us, and why? A cool, calculating voice. Tranquilizing. And steel-hard in its control over Stoner's body. He felt a glacial calm creep along his seething veins, cold ice replacing blazing rage. His heartbeat slowed, his breathing deepened and became more regular. The glands within him slowed their secretions of danger-generated hormones.

Leave me alone! he screamed silently at the alien presence.

So you can kill them? What will that gain?

I want to destroy them!

They're mercenaries. You know that. Professional killers. What they did they did for money. And no one would have been harmed if the robots hadn't attacked them.

They killed Cathy!

Who sent them? That's the important question. Who sent them and why?

Stoner saw the sense of it, and as his star brother soothed the animal fury within him, he realized that it was important—vital—to let these mercenary thugs take him to whoever had hired them. Yes, he finally told his star brother, I understand. I even agree, damn it.

The backpack rockets had only a few miles' range. As they flew out over the dark ocean, the rocket thrusters bellowing painfully in Stoner's ears, he spotted a tiny square of light bobbing in the distance. Sure enough, his captors headed toward it, remotely maneuvering the steering gimbals of Stoner's backpack to follow them.

It was a sizable raft tethered between a pair of trimarans, sleek triple-hulled boats shaped like jet airplanes. Two of the mercenaries landed expertly on the raft, then Stoner felt himself dropping down toward it.

He flexed his knees as the rocket gave a final roar of thrust and cut off about ten feet above the deck. Stoner hit the yielding spongy plastic with his bare feet, then rolled forward. The two men already there caught him in their arms.

They stripped the pack from his shoulders, then began to pull off their own gas masks and backpacks as the others dropped down, one by one, until eight of them stood clustered on the pitching, heaving raft.

"Is that all?" came a voice from one of the trimarans.

"That's all," said the last mercenary to land. Shrugging out of his shoulder harness he strode over to Stoner.

"Twelve men killed," he snarled. "For you." And he swung a punch at Stoner's face with all his weight behind it.

He was a big man, slightly taller than Stoner and thick in the chest and shoulders. His face was lost in the moonlit shadows, but his eyes blazed with the fury of a man who had missed death by inches and had to work off the fear and hatred boiling inside him.

Stoner's old black-belt training returned to him unbidden.

He blocked the punch with his left forearm and rammed his right fist into the man's solar plexus, stepping into the thrust with every ounce of his own raging blood lust. The man was lifted off his feet and before he even started to fall Stoner's left hit the carotid artery in his neck like a knife edge. He crumpled to the plastic surface of the raft and did not move.

"And you bastards killed my daughter," Stoner said as half a dozen guns pointed at him.

"Dr. Stoner!" the voice from the trimaran called urgently. "We did not want to shed any blood. I do not want to use any further force on you, but we will if you make it necessary."

Again Stoner felt the icy fingers of calm prickle along his nervous system.

"It won't be necessary," he said. "Unless I have to defend myself."

"Bring him in here," the voice commanded, "then drag your incapacitated friend to your own boat and get the hell out of here."

A pair of mercenaries escorted Stoner across the bobbing raft and onto the trimaran's nearer hull. Another man, shorter, wearing a sailor's pullover shirt and shorts, took him by the arm and led him across the curving wing to the central hull. Inside, only red night lights were on. Silently the man led Stoner to a small cabin and locked him in it.

Stoner peered out the cabin's tiny porthole; much too small for a man to crawl through, he saw. So he watched as the mercenaries quickly folded up the raft, four of them plunging into the water to do the job, then stowed it aboard their trimaran. They scrambled up into the boat and it pulled away, heading swiftly toward the distant Makapuu Head, as nearly as Stoner could determine.

Then the engine of his trimaran rumbled to life and he felt the boat bite into the waves. It swung around and headed straight out to sea.

Just as Stoner was turning away from the porthole, the other trimaran exploded into a red ball of flame, searing his eyes as a clap of thunder blasted across the open water.

Squeezing the burning after-image away, Stoner looked out the porthole again and saw nothing but bits of burning wreckage tracing fiery arcs across the dark sky.

The mercenaries' reward, he realized. Whoever hired them doesn't want any witnesses. Then he thought, more grimly, And how much cheaper to buy a few pounds of explosives, rather than paying the men you hired.

He watched as the trimaran put distance between itself and the pitiful few scraps of burning wreckage floating on the dark swells.

"Enjoy your reward," he muttered into the darkness. "You bastards earned it."

In the dawn's first light Jo looked out across the patio with sleepless red-rimmed eyes. A team of robots and humans were busily cleaning up the blood stains and repairing the bullet-smashed windows. She still wore the same robe she had hastily pulled on when the attack had started. It was smeared with Cathy's blood.

It had taken hours and a strong sedative to get Rickie to sleep. Half a dozen doctors were in the house now. She had refused to talk to any of them, especially the psychiatrist who offered to set up a counseling session for her. It had taken all her self-control to refrain from throwing the heaviest vase she could lift at the man. He was trying to be helpful, she knew, but she did not need counseling.

She needed vengeance. The fury that soared within her was like a volcano's lava. The longer she kept it bottled up inside the hotter it became. It would erupt, but only when she was ready to allow it to. And when it did, that lava-hot hatred would burn and roast the bastards who had killed her baby. Not one of them would be left alive. Not a single one.

She had spent hours with the Hilo police and several agents from the FBI. Reluctantly she allowed them to take away four of the dead intruders' bodies; the others had already been spirited away by her own corporate security people.

Rickie was sleeping at last and Cathy's body had been sent to the Vanguard labs nearby.

"I want tissue samples taken and cloning procedures to be started immediately," she had told the aides and assistants who clustered around her in the house's living room.

"And the other bodies?"

"Find out everything you can from them. I want to know where they came from and who they are. I want to find where they've taken my husband and how we can get him back from them. And above all I want to find out who hired them."

But she knew who had hired them, knew it without being told, knew it as surely as if the man himself had confessed it to her.

Once the living room had been cleared of everyone else and Jo was alone with Vic Tomasso, she said, "It was Hsen, wasn't it?"

Tomasso nodded numbly. "Honest to god, Jo, I had no idea he would spring this . . ."

Until that moment it had never occurred to Jo that Tomasso could have been playing a double game. She looked at him with fresh eyes. There was perspiration beading his upper lip despite the coolness of the morning. His eyes met hers only momentarily, then slid away evasively.

"Go to Hsen," she said, her voice hoarse from crying, "and tell him what happened here."

"He'll know by now."

"I want you to tell him. From me. Tell him that his people murdered my daughter."

Tomasso blinked several times. "What else?"

"That's all. Just tell him that."

"Nothing else? You don't want to ask him about getting your husband back?"

"It won't be necessary to say anything else. He'll know what the rest of the message is."

Tomasso got uncertainly to his feet, then rushed out of the living room as if glad to get away from her.

Jo sat alone on the sumptuous sweeping couch that curved around the circular green marble coffee table. Alone. Husband kidnapped. Daughter murdered. Son in a drugged sleep. Assistants fluttering around the house and the office.

Keith can take care of himself, she thought. The attackers obviously came to kidnap him, not kill him. Hsen knows Keith's the only one ever to survive cryonic suspension; the bastard wants to learn how to live forever and he thinks he can get the knowledge out of Keith.

Nothing can hurt Keith. He's not a human being, not the way I am. He'll twist Hsen's brain into a pretzel if they give him the chance. He'll walk away without a scratch while Cathy . . . Cathy . . .

She could hardly breathe. Jo wet her lips and lifted her hands to her head and held on. She felt as if she would explode. Keith would try to reason with Hsen; talk to the filthy murdering sonofabitch snake. Instead of killing him Keith would try to *understand* him and make him understand what he had done wrong.

Hsen's got to die! The thought pounded through her blood, roared in her ears. The murdering bastard's got to die. I want to hear him scream, I want to see knives slicing his guts, I want to fill the goddamned swimming pool with *his* blood!

Shaking with fury, she touched the comm button concealed in the couch's upholstery.

"Nunzio."

"*Si, Signora?*"

"Please come to the living room, I have a task for you," she said in Italian.

"Right away, *Signora.*"

Nunzio had been devastated because the intruders had gassed him and the other servants in their sleep and he had been totally unable to do a thing to prevent the tragedy that took place. He felt like a useless old man, Jo knew, instead of a ruthlessly loyal bodyguard.

Now Jo would tell him how he could redeem himself. By killing Li-Po Hsen. No matter how long it took, no matter how much it cost. No matter if Nunzio had to go back to the village of his birth in Calabria and hire every male relative of his line. The only purpose of Nunzio's existence, from this morning onward, would be to kill Hsen.

And Tomasso? She would deal with Vic herself, she decided. When he returned from Hong Kong. She would get the truth out of him and then make him pay for his part in murdering her daughter. Make him pay with interest.

Jo wanted to smile but found that she could not. In the silence of the living room she could hear, through the broken windows, the sound of the swimming pool's pumps still working to filter Cathy's blood out of the water.

The intelligence chief had never seen her master look surprised before. Or frightened.

"Killed her daughter!" Hsen shot to his feet, eyes blazing, fists clenched.

She bowed her head and said nothing.

Hsen paced to the broad windows of his spacious office and stared out for many minutes at the busy harbor. As usual, he wore a loose short-sleeved shirt and comfortable dark slacks. He clasped his hands behind his back, his wiry frame wound tight with tension.

Finally he turned back to the woman who directed his intelligence operations. "What kind of bunglers did you hire? What kind of fools would make such a shambles of everything?"

In a very quiet voice, she replied, "It was accidental. More than half the force was killed by the so-called household robots. They were equipped with laser weapons that we did not expect."

"The robots were not included in Tomasso's report on the house's defenses?"

"No, sir. Obviously he did not know about them."

"Obviously." Hsen paced nervously to his desk, flipped open a gold oblong box and put a cigarette to his lips with trembling fingers. He picked up the gold lighter and touched it to the cigarette's tip, then suddenly whirled and threw it across the big room. It banged into a bronze statue of a warrior on horseback with a loud clang.

"Sir," said the intelligence chief, "I should remind you that the mission achieved its major objective. We have the man Stoner."

"Yes, and you have Jo Camerata swearing vengeance against me with all her Italian blood!"

"She has no evidence that you . . ."

"She knows!" Hsen shouted.

The woman backed a few steps toward the door. Hsen puffed furiously on his cigarette. Even from the distance between them the intelligence chief could smell the acrid fumes of old-fashioned tobacco. There was a cloying odor too: the tobacco was laced with something, perhaps an opium derivative.

Hsen pointed a bony finger at her. "Prepare to evacuate my personal staff to the lunar retreat. But it must be done in absolute secrecy! I don't want that woman to know where I am!"

"Sir, you are scheduled to attend the meeting of the International Investment Authority on Sunday, in Sydney."

"I will attend by hologram."

"Sir, there is a two-second time lag in communications from the Moon. She will immediately know where you are."

Hsen snorted smoke through his nostrils. "Yes, yes, I hadn't thought of that." He sat at the swivel chair and drummed his fingers on the desk top. "Very well, I will move to our center in Xinjiang. From there I will proceed to the lunar retreat as soon as the IIA meeting concludes."

The woman hesitated, then asked, "Do you think that she will attend the meeting?"

Hsen nodded nervously. "She will attend it, all right. Probably by holo, but she will be there. I have no doubt of it."

CHAPTER 23

SITTING at the head of the gleaming long, broad conference table, Cliff Baker called the meeting to order. All thirty members of the International Investment Agency were in attendance, although more than half of them were holographic images that sparkled and wavered slightly, looking almost like ghosts rather than live solid human beings.

The sweeping windows that lined one side of the conference room showed the towers of Sydney's business and financial district. The beautiful harbor was hidden behind their glass and steel facades. On the far side of the room stood an elaborate sideboard of finger foods on silver trays and beverages ranging from iced tea and cola to Scotch whisky and chilled vodka.

Maybe we should have set up some photographs of food and booze, Baker thought with an inner grin. To take care of the hologrammers.

But he kept his face serious as he tapped the immaculate table top with his writing stylus. The men and women present in person quickly stopped their muttered conversations and looked toward him. The holograms also sat up straighter and looked ready for business.

"There's only one item on the agenda," Baker started, without preamble. "You all know what it is: this plague that's spreading throughout lower Asia and the western Pacific."

"It has also hit cities in Europe and North America," said the woman who represented Scandia Banking.

"And Africa, I am sad to announce." The man from the Central African Confederation said in a heavy deep voice. He was Nkona's personal emissary, a terrorist as a youth until that Great Soul captured him with his vision of a peaceful, prosperous, united Africa.

"Africa too?"

The black man nodded and folded his hands prayerfully on the table top. He was of powerful build, and in his white tribal robe the darkness of his skin radiated strength and endurance.

"Within the past few days the plague had leaped across the Sahara and is spreading through Chad, Zaire, Uganda, and even as far as Namibia."

"Good lord!"

"It hasn't hit Latin America?"

"Not yet," said the Argentinean physician who represented that continent's environmental movement.

"They call it the Horror," the slim, delicately beautiful woman from Hanoi said. She reminded Baker of An Linh Laguerre, the woman he had lost because of Stoner and his bitch of a wife.

"It is a horror," the Argentinean agreed. "I have seen the clinical reports. It must be like the tortures of hell."

What do you know about the pains of hell? Baker snarled inwardly. What do any of you know about pain? Maybe when this bug hits you, then you'll know what I had to go through. Maybe then—but then it'll be too late for you, won't it?

"The question is," he said aloud, "what can be done to stop it? And what should we be doing to help?"

The Filipino representative, also a physician, said, "Every medical service in every affected nation urgently requires our help. They need more hospital beds, more clinical facilities, supplies, personnel . . . everything."

"In other words," said the hologrammic image of Li-Po Hsen, "they need more money."

"Exactly."

"But we have already invested billions in medical research and services," said Wilhelm Kruppmann. The burly Swiss banker was also a hologram image.

"That was before this plague started," Baker pointed out.

"How many times can you draw water from the well before it runs dry?" Kruppmann rumbled.

"How important is it to stay alive?" Baker shot back, his lips curling slightly in a smile that might have been a sneer.

Jo Camerata sat in the small office she maintained at her home and watched the byplay on a flat video screen. She had been up most of the night with Rickie, who still screamed with nightmares whenever he tried to sleep. Her attempts to find Keith had so far been fruitless, but it had only been a few days since Hsen had kidnapped him. Only a few days since Cathy had been murdered.

She pecked at the keyboard on her desk and the screen zoomed in to a closeup of Hsen. A hologram, of course. Jo had half of Vanguard Industries' electronics experts at work tracking the signals that produced Hsen's three-dimensional image for the meeting. She wanted to know where the head of Pacific Commerce actually was.

Wherever you are, she said silently to Hsen's image, I'll find you. There's no place on Earth you can hide from me.

After three days of being a virtual prisoner, Paulino had learned only two things about the people who had rescued him from his errant tractor: they were employees of Vanguard Industries, and this place where they were holding him was some sort of secret base called Delphi.

It was almost entirely underground, of course. A satellite scanning the Mare Imbrium's surface would see only a pair of well-disguised entry ports, domes no larger than telephone booths and covered with rubble from the lunar soil. Even a man on foot could pass within a few dozen meters of the entrances and not realize that they were anything more than medium-sized hillocks.

"You've posed us quite a problem, son," said the grizzled, square-jawed older man who seemed to head the facility. Like everyone else in the base, he wore coveralls of faded blue with a stylized V emblazoned on the chest above his name tag, which read MATTHEWS.

"We've sent your tractor out on a course that will take it into a main traffic region. Somebody'll pick it up. They'll probably think you're dead, although they might send a ballistic rocket this way to survey the area and try to find your body."

"Why cannot you return me back to Archimedes?" Paulino asked in his hesitant English.

Matthews made a sour face. "Goddam' security regulations. Nobody's supposed to know we're here. If it'd been up to me we would of just let you trundle on by; you'd never have known we're here." He shook his head. "But I've got a gung-ho smartass of a security chief here who believes everything they wrote down in the regs. So you were stopped and detained, as per regulation XYZ or whatever."

Bewildered, barely comprehending what the man was telling him, Paulino asked, "What do you plan to . . . to do with me?"

"Damned if I know," Matthews replied. "Just your bad luck, kid. You stumbled into our area while we were testing an electromagnetic system that must've screwed up your navigational beam. Now I'm stuck with you until some genius further up the chain of command figures out what to do."

So for several days Paulino was free to wander around the underground base. It was small; there were no more than fifty men and women at work in it. Most of them were older than Paulino, in their thirties and forties. They all wore blue coveralls; Paulino's pumpkin orange seemed glaringly out of place. They seemed to be scientists of one sort or another, and almost all of them were from North America or Western Europe. Not an oriental or Latin American in the place, nor any Africans—although several of the Yankees were black.

He thought about offering some of his Moondust for sale, but hesitated. His supply of pills was dwindling, and these people looked like the type who would flush them down a toilet and turn him into the police. So he kept the pills to himself and tried to ration himself to one per day. Unsuccessfully.

They let him wander freely through the narrow tunnels and windowless chambers of the base, knowing that even with a pressure suit he was not going to walk hundreds of kilometers back to Archimedes. And there seemed to be no ground vehicles in Delphi. If there were any, they were locked away where Paulino could not find them.

The people were friendly, but guarded. They gave him a room to himself, a narrow little cell that held a comfortable bed, a TV, and little else. They provided him with coveralls and toiletries. He ate with the others in the base's only galley. Men and women talked with him freely enough, although they never discussed their work. The TV picked up programs from all over Earth; Paulino did not lack for entertainment.

He began to think that being officially dead was perhaps not so bad a thing. If these Vanguard people could provide him with a new identity and a solid job, perhaps he could truly begin life anew. Perhaps even get away from the Moon-dust. He sought out Matthews and broached the idea to him—without mentioning his addiction.

The older man grinned through his two-day stubble. "Like the old videos where the FBI protects a witness against the Mafia, huh?"

Paulino did not understand.

"Might be a good idea," Matthews said. "I'll buck it up-stairs and see what they think about it."

That confused Paulino even further. Upstairs was nothing but the barren surface of Mare Imbrium.

There were parts of the base that were locked, where Paulino was not allowed. He guessed that they might be hiding their tractors in there. As one day slid into another, Paulino began to think that if he could get away and find his way back to Archimedes, the information about this secret base might be worth something to his employers. Not as good as starting a whole new life under a new identity, but it would be a backup in case Matthews decided to make Paulino truly dead and solve his problem that way.

It was a simple matter to walk past the locked doors often

enough to watch people tap out the security code on the electronic lock. They were careless, not suspicious. Paulino memorized the combination soon enough. The base worked on Greenwich time, with only one shift. Everyone slept during the "night" hours. Paulino never saw any guards; who needed them, this far out in the lunar wilderness?

So one night when everyone was asleep he slipped out of his room and walked softly to the nearest of the locked doors. Pecking out the memorized combination he held his breath for an instant.

The door slid open. The lights inside turned on as Paulino stepped through. And lurched against the wall in sudden terror.

He found himself high on the open grillwork of a catwalk that circled an immense circular chamber. The floor was fifty meters below and for an instant Paulino felt so giddy he had to grasp the steel handrail with both hands.

The huge chamber contained a giant circular vat filled with a bubbling, frothing liquid. It gurgled and simmered like a titanic brew being slowly boiled. It must have been as high as the spires of a cathedral, at least. Waves of sultry heat flowed from it. A plume of steam rose from its top and was sucked away by vents set into the ceiling high above. Paulino did not know if the sweat that poured from him was from sudden fear or the heat that made this vast chamber feel like the inside of an oven.

The vat was transparent, or almost so. Squinting against the mist that shrouded its curving flank, Paulino tried to make out what was inside the seething circular tank. There were vague shapes in there, a glint of something, a graceful curve perhaps. But it was obscured by the steam and the bubbling ferment within the tank itself.

Paulino unconsciously leaned forward against the rail, peering intently into the giant vat. It was like trying to see a glass sculpture inside a fish tank, only worse, more difficult.

A hand grabbed his shoulder. Paulino felt his bladder give way.

Burning with fear and shame he turned to see Matthews appraising him grimly.

"You could've fallen over the damned railing, you were leaning over so hard. Don't you know curiosity killed the cat?"

"I . . . I . . ."

Matthews seemed more disappointed than angry. "Just because we don't have armed guards patrolling the tunnels doesn't mean there aren't electronic alarm systems in place. You woke me out of a sound sleep, son!"

Still Paulino could find no words.

"You've just made everything a helluva lot more difficult," Matthews said, leading him back into the tunnel. As he carefully shut the steel door and re-set the electronic lock, he muttered, "We sure as hell can't let you loose now."

"Wh . . . what is that . . . thing in there?"

With a shrug of his square shoulders Matthews answered, "Beats the hell out of me, kid. Nobody here knows what it's supposed to be."

For a week Stoner let them test him.

The trimaran made rendezvous slightly before dawn with a jet seaplane. His captors bundled Stoner into a windowless cabin and the plane flew for many hours. Stoner had the feeling they were flying roughly southwest, but other than that he had no idea of where they were going. There were fresh jeans in the cabin, socks, shorts, a pullover shirt, and a pair of deck shoes. All in the right sizes.

They've planned everything down to the last detail, he thought grimly. The image of Cathy's bloody body floating in the swimming pool flashed into his mind again, and again his star brother instantly clamped down on the visceral emotions that would have made Stoner scream with rage and guilt.

They came for me, he said to himself. Cathy's dead because they wanted me.

It is not your fault, his star brother soothed. There was nothing you could do.

I could tear this plane apart. I could kill everyone aboard.

To what purpose? What good is an animal's vengeance, especially when it's directed at hirelings rather than those responsible for the crime?

Stoner knew his star brother was right. But that did not erase the cold fury that even his alien symbiotes could not reach.

When the plane touched down in the water once more a new group of men and women entered his cabin, fitted a heavy black hood over his head, and guided him from the bobbing plane to a creaking pier and then onto solid ground. They bundled him into a van of some kind and then drove for hours. The brief moment he had in the sun felt hot and humid; the inside of the van was air-conditioned heavily enough to chill him.

When they took the hood off he was in a small windowless room that contained a narrow bunk, a wall covered with electronic monitoring equipment, and the tables, counters, glassware, and shining bright metalwork of a small but complete medical laboratory.

He almost laughed. It was nearly the same as the room he had awakened in fifteen years earlier. I'm a guinea pig again, he thought. And a prisoner.

There were four men and two women, Stoner saw, all wearing starched white uniforms. Physicians, nurses, orderlies. They avoided looking directly at him. They did not speak a word to him. Stoner thought about talking to them, influencing them to let him go or at least tell him where they were. His star brother asked silently why he did not do so. You could walk out of here and get them to fly you back home.

No, Stoner decided. I want to know who these people work for, and why they want me so badly. You were right: why deal with the hirelings? It's their masters I want to get my hands on.

The picture of Cathy came unbidden to his mind once again. Even before his star brother could clamp down on the tidal wave of grief and guilt that gushed from his glands, Stoner saw his daughter ripped apart by their bullets, flung into the pool, her young life torn from her by the intruding murderers.

The lava-hot surge dwindled, ebbed, nearly disappeared altogether. Stoner still saw Cathy die, still felt hatred for the men who had done it and the person who had sent them. But the emotion was gone. The alien presence within him damped down the inner fires almost completely. Left in its place was a cold implacable determination to find who was responsible for Cathy's murder.

The white-uniformed silent men and women left him alone in the room. There was only the one door, a conventional wooden door with an electronic lock. Not a star-given energy portal that could be solid wall one instant and an open doorway the next. I could pick the electronic lock in a couple of seconds, Stoner knew. Maybe that's what they want to see me do. It looks like they want to test me.

Instead, he kicked off his shoes and stretched out on the cot, hands behind his head, and pretended to sleep. The light panels in the ceiling dimmed. Yes indeed, I'm being watched and tested. Angrily he asked himself, So what else is new?

He thought about Jo. She had seen her daughter, her firstborn, slaughtered. And she had to bear that grief without him. Jo was tough, he knew, but could she stand up to this? He wished he could reach her, communicate with her, at least tell her that he was alive and unharmed and trying to track down the people who had killed Cathy. She's strong, Stoner kept repeating to himself. Jo is the strongest woman I've ever met. The strongest person, man or woman. She'll handle it all right. She'll come through it.

He told himself that her Italian thirst for vengeance would help to sustain her. The blood is strong. The age-old instincts boil to the surface and wash away all the veneer of polite civilized behavior. Jo doesn't have an alien brother inside her to clamp down on the emotions and control the heat that burns through the blood. She won't leave it to law and order. Her daughter's been killed; she's going to move heaven and earth to find the killers. God help them when she does.

Rickie. He's the one who needs help. It's a shattering blow to a ten-year-old. Strangers breaking into his home. His sister killed before his eyes, his father abducted. The poor kid's had almost every emotional prop knocked out from under him. All he's got left is his mother. Will Jo pay enough attention to him, or will she be too busy seeking out her revenge?

When I get back home, Stoner promised himself, I'll keep him close to me. I've got to rebuild his feelings of security and trust. All the psychologists and neural programming in the world can't do that for him. It's up to me, I've got to make him feel safe and certain of himself again. That's more important than anything else.

When I get back home.

CHAPTER 24

CLIFF Baker walked along the magnificent beach and watched the surf pounding up onto the sand. Hundreds of bathers were in the sparkling blue water, diving into the waves. Half a kilometer up the beach the surfers were riding their boards on the big breakers. Further out windsurfers leaned out from their sails and cut along the swells like over-sized waterbugs.

Once these beaches had been preyed upon by "the men in the gray suits," vicious, swift, voracious sharks that could take a man's leg with a single snap of their powerful jaws. Now a flimsy net of electrical wires protected the beaches and kept the sharks away. Hasn't been a shark attack at a protected beach since I was a teenager, Baker thought idly.

The sun was high and Baker's ragged cut-off shorts and flapping unbuttoned shirt were wet with perspiration. Soak some of the booze out of me, he thought. On the other hand, a cold Foster's would feel very good right about now.

He turned around and headed back toward the beach house. One of the advantages of being chairman of the International Investment Agency: a marvelous twelve-room house on the most expensive beach in the Sydney area. Rank hath its privileges.

Sunday's meeting had gone exactly the way he had thought it would. The regions hardest hit by the plague needed money immediately for medical services. The ecologists and the representatives of areas not so badly threatened by the Horror wanted to spend more money on research. The bastards from the corporations, who had the goddamned money, didn't want to spend their precious loot at all.

They hadn't accomplished a bloody thing. They had argued and called each other names and agreed to nothing more than appointing a bloody committee to study the problem. Study it! While thousands were dying in agony every day and the plague spread across Africa and into Europe and North America.

Baker grinned, a lopsided smirk that was far from pleasant on his bloated reddened face. Let them argue, he told himself. Let them delay. Soon enough the Horror will start to pick them off, one by one. The women first, and then the men. They all deserve it.

As he trudged barefoot through the sand he wondered about Jo Camerata. She had been strangely silent at the meeting. Usually she took charge and made things come out the way she wanted them. But she had barely said two words. It was hard to tell when you were looking at holograms instead of live people, but it seemed to Baker as if Jo spent the whole damned meeting staring at Hsen instead of paying attention to the business at hand.

Baker shrugged off his puzzlement. He had reached his house and padded up the smooth wooden steps, heading for the kitchen fridge and a cold Foster's.

In another week, he thought, the first members of the IIA

will start to get their guts torn out by the Horror. And I'll be up on the Moon, safe as houses, watching the world tear itself apart.

The medical tests they had done on Stoner were ruthlessly thorough. He thought of the stories he had heard as a youngster of the "experiments" performed by Nazi doctors in concentration camps.

His captors were extremely wary of him. No human being entered his room after the first few days. Everything was done by robots under remote control. Each morning began with a short cylindrically-shaped robot carrying in a breakfast tray of juice, cereal, and coffee. The machine was spotless and gleaming, obviously new, obviously being used for the first time.

"Good morning Dr. Stoner," the robot would say. "I trust you slept well."

It was the robot's own voice, part of its interactive programming. Immediately after breakfast another voice, human, would issue from the speakers set into the ceiling.

"I slept about the same as usual," Stoner would reply. "Where are we? What is our geographical location?"

"I do not have that information," the sturdy little robot would answer, with complete transistorized honesty.

The first two days were standard medical tests. Blood samples. Cardiac stress testing on a treadmill carried in by another robot, a taller, many-armed machine of matte-dull carbon fiber composite skin. Its long arms were of stainless steel, jointed and extensible, capable of carrying very heavy loads.

It was the blood samples that worried Stoner. He felt he could hide his star-gift abilities from his captors well enough; he had been careful not to show them anything except a normal, healthy human being. But analysis of his blood would show that it was infected with myriad particles the size of viruses. His star symbiotes.

They may think that they're nothing but viruses, Stoner told himself. But he doubted it. That many strange particles in a blood sample would set their curiosity atwitter. Chemical analyses wouldn't prove much; the symbiotes were made mostly of organic elements. But if they start photomicrographing the particles they'll realize right away that they're something no one on Earth has seen before.

At the end of the second day of medical tests it seemed to Stoner that the robot left the door unlocked when it rolled noiselessly out of the room. Stoner sat on the edge of his cot for nearly half an hour, considering what he should do. Obviously they were observing him. If the door were left unlocked, it was because they wanted to see what he would do.

There were no clocks in the room; he had no way of telling what time it was, or even if it was day or night outside. Like a Las Vegas gambling casino, Stoner thought grimly. With a shrug, he got up from the cot, wearing nothing but a pair of briefs, and padded to the door.

He turned the old-fashioned knob. Sure enough, the door was unlocked. Hesitating only for a heartbeat, he pushed the door wide open.

A very large robot stood immobile just beyond the arc of the door's swing. Its base was a pair of heavy, tanklike treads. From there it rose in a single massive column of gleaming chromed metal. Four long arms were clamped to its sides, each of them ending in metal pincers. The dome at the robot's top was studded with sensors that made it look more like a spider's many-eyed head than a human's.

"You must stay inside your room," said the robot in a voice that sounded like a top sergeant growling from inside a concrete mixer.

Stoner smiled at the machine. Obviously meant to frighten people into obedience. Probably built for military security or police patrol work.

He took a step forward. The robot rolled slightly toward him and raised one arm to block his path.

"You must stay inside your room."

For several long moments man and machine confronted each other, motionless. Stoner tried to probe the robot's computer brain to see if he could alter its programming enough to get by, but he sensed that the computer was too simple to be influenced by outside forces. There was no way to talk it into bending to Stoner's desires, as he could do with most human beings.

"You must stay inside your room," the robot repeated in exactly the same tone of voice as before.

Stoner understood that the test had been psychological more than physical. His captors wanted to see how he would react to having his hopes raised and then dashed. Also, they were testing to see if he could somehow get past the simple-minded security robot.

Acknowledging defeat, Stoner retreated back inside his room. The robot shut the door. Stoner heard the lock click as distinctly as the slamming of a jail cell's barred gate.

The third morning the voice from the ceiling asked, "You slept well?"

"Yes," Stoner lied. He had not slept at all. He did not have to. He had spent the night trying to sense the location and number of the people around him. He still had no idea of where he was. If his captors were not going to deal with him face to face, Stoner realized, he would have to go out and contact them, one way or another. And get past the security robot outside his door.

"No stomach cramps or other discomfort?"

"Should there have been?"

The voice did not answer. Stoner realized that they had poisoned his dinner. Not to kill him, just enough to give him obvious symptoms. His star brother had automatically neutralized the poison, broken down its complex molecular structure into simpler, harmless chemical components.

He wished the voice would say more to him, because it sounded oddly familiar. Even through the low-fidelity ceiling speakers Stoner knew it was a man's tenor voice, not a woman's. A voice that he thought he had heard before.

Two of the tall many-armed robots entered the room that morning.

"We have established a baseline of your physical profile," said the voice from the ceiling. "Now we must see how far from that baseline you can be driven and still recuperate. The next few days will be rigorous, but we will try to make them as painless as possible for you."

In short, they tortured him.

They began with electric shocks. One of the robots clamped Stoner into a chair with its many arms while the other applied electrodes to various parts of his naked body. At first Stoner tried to stand the pain without help from the alien symbiotes. But they kept increasing the voltage until he was screaming and his star brother intervened to shut down the white-hot messages of agony that blazed along his nerves.

He sat in the chair, the stainless steel arms gripping his bare flesh, and watched the electrodes burn away his skin. Saw tendrils of smoke rising from his chest, his stomach, his thighs. Smelled the odor of his own meat roasting.

"Remarkable," uttered the voice from the ceiling microphones. "He is able to handle intense physical pain." It was muffled, indistinct, as if the man had placed a hand over the microphone so that his victim could not hear what he said. Stoner made out the words, though, and even the slightly ragged breathing of the speaker. Was he enjoying what he watched, or did it upset him? Stoner could not tell.

"Is this necessary?" another voice asked. It was blurred even more, as if the speaker were several meters away from the microphone. "Can't you . . ."

"It *is* necessary," snapped the first voice. "We will proceed to the next step."

"Without giving him time to recuperate?"

Do they *want* me to hear what they're saying? Stoner wondered.

"No recuperation time. Not yet. The next test is a combination of physical and psychological pain," said the man's voice. "We will see how he reacts to having his manhood threatened."

"But that's inhuman!"

"We are hardly dealing with a human being here." The man's voice was cool, detached. "Don't be so sentimental. This is an experimental subject, nothing more. You must stop being so squeamish."

The other said nothing, but Stoner sensed a turmoil of emotions. And something more: the other person was a woman.

The robot held Stoner's legs apart and applied the electrodes to his penis and testicles. Stoner closed his eyes but otherwise gave no reaction. His star brother cut off all sensation, all emotion. It was like being encased in a block of ice, like being frozen again, no longer alive, inert, apart from the world of the living.

And his star brother told him, You know that whatever physical damage they do will be quickly repaired.

Sure, Stoner replied silently, his teeth clenched so hard they seemed to be fused together. Wonderful news.

After what seemed like hours the robots released him and rolled silently out of the room with their equipment. The voices from the ceiling fell silent. Exhausted, Stoner crawled to his cot and pretended to fall asleep.

They did not feed him. No robot entered with a dinner tray and the following morning there was no breakfast.

I've got to get out of here, he told himself in the dead of night.

But his star brother soothed his growing anxiety. Not yet. Wait until we can learn who they are—and who they work for.

So Stoner lay on the cot and waited for the next session. They know that whatever powers we have, we still need energy input. Without food we won't be able to heal our wounds.

We can go for several days, his star brother assured him. There is enough stored fat in the body to keep going that long without input.

The lock clicked and Stoner sat up on the cot. The tall many-armed robots came through the door. One of them pushed a gurney, the other a table full of electrical equipment.

"Today," said the voice from the ceiling, "we test the electrical patterns of your brain."

The robots strapped Stoner down on the gurney and attached electrodes to his head. In the weirdly distorted reflection from their stainless steel arms he saw his naked body, ugly red burn marks scattered about his chest, abdomen, groin.

For hours they mapped the currents flickering in his brain. His star brother remained silent as they sent tickling probes into various lobes of the brain. Stoner tried to stay completely relaxed as the electrical currents stimulated specific groups of neurons. He saw colors bursting before his eyes, heard the rushing roar of the sea, tasted bacon and then the cold metallic tang of the oxygen fed into his pressure-suit helmet. He could feel the suit encompassing him and for a fleeting moment, as in a dream that shifted like the melting scenery on a rain-streaked window pane, he was back in space helping to construct the mammoth telescope that had first detected the approaching alien starship.

The telescope glittered in the hard unfiltered sunlight, a gleaming spiderwork of bright metal against the cold black background of infinity. Stoner reached out to touch it.

And it was gone, replaced by an absurd childhood memory of trying to maintain his balance on a two-wheel bike.

Blinding white pain! Stoner could not breathe; he felt his heart stop, then start up again with thumping spasms that rocked his whole body.

"Again," he heard, as if from a trillion miles away.

The blast that shockwaved through his skull was beyond pain. Even his star brother was stunned momentarily, but then swiftly shut down the pain centers in his brain.

"There, did you see it? That blip in the EEG?"

Another powerful bolt of agony exploded inside Stoner's head, but this time he and the alien within him were ready. He knew exactly what they were doing to him: electrical shock treatments. Christ! Next they'll start lobotomies!

His star brother slowed Stoner's heartbeat and breathing rate. His whole body, rigid with the electrical shocks, spine arched, fingers and toes clenched so hard that tendons were popping, it all relaxed as if Stoner had slipped off into a deep and restful sleep. Or death.

But he heard the voices from the ceiling speaker.

"You've gone too far!"

"Not at all. Look at that EEG; have you ever seen anything like it before?"

No response.

"A normal brain would show a scrambled set of jagged peaks and troughs. His curves are as gentle as a sleeping baby's. It's fantastic!"

"Hasn't he had enough for today?"

"I want to try a couple more shocks, just to see if we can break him out of the shell he's gone into."

"You'll kill him!"

"I doubt that we could kill him if we tried."

"May I remind you that the purpose of these experiments is to determine why he survived cryonic immersion and thawing, not to chop him up into bloody little scraps!"

"Interesting choice of words, Doctor."

"What? Why do you say that?"

"Because tomorrow I'm going to see if he can regenerate significant parts of his body. We'll start by amputating a finger."

"God! You can't be serious!"

"Never more serious. And don't try to interfere. I'm in charge here, and I'm going to find out what makes that man tick if I have to take him apart like an old windup clock."

The words would have struck fear into Stoner's battered consciousness if his star brother had allowed a man's normal hormonal reactions. Instead he lay there on the gurney perfectly still, utterly relaxed, seemingly unconscious or in a deep coma.

But his mind was racing. *I know those voices! I know who they are!*

Vic Tomasso paced nervously back and forth across the length of the balcony. His apartment was two floors below the penthouse of one of the tallest residential towers in Hilo.

On a normal weekend afternoon he would have been sitting out in the sunshine, improving his tan while alternately watching the professional football games on TV and the women frolicking on the golden sandy beach in their minuscule swim suits.

This was not a normal weekend.

He could feel the searing heat of Jo's suspicions of him. Hell, even if he had been totally innocent it would be natural for her to cast a distrustful eye at the man she thought she had planted in Hsen's camp. But Jo glowered at him like the burning end of a red-hot branding iron. Even though she tried to control herself and not reveal her inner thoughts, the fury and suspicion that seethed within her glowed hot as hellfire.

He had volunteered to an interrogation under truth drugs. "I might remember something Hsen or his people said that my conscious mind doesn't recall," he had said to Jo. She had nodded and approved the interrogation. Tomasso dutifully reported to the security office and was interrogated by a team that included the physician whom he had been sleeping with for the past four months. She believed that Vic truly loved her. The drug she injected into his bloodstream was nothing more than a mild tranquilizer. Vic passed the test easily.

Still, the pressure was mounting. Jo would not be satisfied until she found the traitors in her midst. He knew that she had people backtracking every phone call he had made over the past several weeks, trying to trace every move he had made. Tomasso worried about that last call he had made to Hsen, telling him that Stoner was returning early from Moscow. The number he had actually called was another apartment in Hilo; a "girlfriend" who in reality was an employee of Pacific Commerce's intelligence operations. The call had been relayed to Hsen in Hong Kong from her phone.

That should be safe enough, Tomasso told himself, pacing endlessly across the balcony. Safe enough.

But Jo was like an avenging angel, fiery sword in hand, searching for dragons to slay. Tomasso felt like a very small dragon; more like a defenseless lizard.

If I run, that'll prove to her that I was in on the operation.
Prove to her that I've been working for Hsen.

Pace the length of the balcony, reach the end and turn back
again.

But if I stay she'll grab me sooner or later. Even if she
doesn't get any real evidence against me. She suspects and
that'll be enough for her. She'll have her own Italian bodyguards grab me and squirt *real* truth serum into my veins. Or
worse.

The far end of the balcony. Turn around and pace the other
way. Ignore the beach, the sunlight and surfers and palm
trees. Tomasso was looking inward, trying to discern his own
future.

She'll make me talk and once I do I'm a dead man. But if I
run to Hsen he'll figure I've outlived my usefulness to him.
I'm dead either way!

There was only one way out, one bargaining chip remaining
with which to buy his life. He had been holding it back, carefully keeping it to himself until the right moment. His ace in
the hole.

Well, Tomasso said to himself, if you don't use it now you
might not live to use it later.

Nodding to himself, convinced he had no other path to
safety, he drove to a shopping mall in downtown Hilo and
picked out a public telephone at random. Pecking out the
same "girlfriend"'s number, once he connected with her answering machine he spoke the code phrase that automatically
transferred his call to Hsen's office in Hong Kong.

Hsen was not there, said the Chinese beauty whose face
appeared on the tiny phone screen. She looked too perfect, too
flawless, to be anything but a computer graphic.

"Tell Hsen that Vanguard Industries has a secret operation
going on the Moon, a special base called Delphi, far out on
the Mare Imbrium."

The simulated woman smiled blandly and waited for more
information.

"Nobody on the board of directors knows about it,"

Tomasso went on, nervous, glancing out toward the balcony, as if expecting Jo herself to suddenly materialize there, desperately hoping he had not been followed by anyone. "Ms. Camerata and her husband . . . they're building a starship there. A ship that will be able to fly out of the solar system. I think they intend to send it back to the planet that the alien ship came from."

Lela Obiri spent every night in dread. Out in the forest, wrapped in her sleeping bag against the chill damp darkness, listening to the hootings and growls floating through the night, she slept fitfully if at all. Gradually she had grown accustomed to the natural sounds of the forest, and during the day she had come to love this emerald world with its mottled sunlight and clean sparkling streams. The thick foliage of the forest closed in like a green womb, surrounding her, enfolding her in its leafy arms. Each day she walked through this primeval universe, the only human being in a new Eden, alone with brilliant flashing birds and scampering chattering monkeys.

Yet she knew she was not really alone. Koku was shambling through the woods up ahead of her, sniffing the shrubs and pristine air, bringing scents to Lela's mind that she had never known before. Seeing the green world through Koku's eyes made it a true paradise, and she began to love the forest as he did.

Yet the night frightened her. Not because of the cold mist that condensed dripping from every leaf. Nor because of the predators that lurked in the darkness. Those she understood and accepted. They would never attack a human. Her sleeping bag was guarded by a tiny electronic transmitter that surrounded the area out to a dozen meters with a nerve-jangling field that would frighten off even a starving jackal.

There were other humans out there in the trees. That is what frightened Lela. There should be no one except herself in this sector of the reserve, yet she kept hearing the distant faint sounds of men talking, occasional clinks of metal on metal, even a whiff of tobacco smoke now and then.

They were stalking her. They had started by going after Koku, but now they were following Lela. They could never keep up with Koku once the gorilla was warned to stay away from them. So they were following Lela. Not merely following her, either, but constantly pushing between Lela and the territory that Koku was supposed to reach. They kept far enough away so that she could not see them. But at least once each day a stray breeze carried fresh proof of their presence.

Or am I being paranoid? Lela asked herself. Alone in the woods, city girl, and you see danger behind every bush. Once again she tried to radio back to headquarters, and once again she got nothing but screeching static on her hand-sized radio. Interference. Was the radio being jammed? How much safer she would feel if she could talk to Professor Yeboa or the captain in charge of the reserve's rangers. She longed to hear a helicopter thrumming high above, scanning the trees with its arrays of sensors.

Koku was well ahead of her, but still far from the territory where his mates were waiting for him. It was going to be difficult enough to have the tame-born young male take up a natural life in this habitat. Worrying about poachers made matters infinitely worse.

After days of inner turmoil, Lela finally made up her mind. Koku could take care of himself for a day or so. She would confront the poachers and make them know that they would be apprehended and jailed if they did not leave the reserve immediately. Inwardly she was frightened that they might kill her, but she forced such fears from her conscious mind. Nothing like that had happened in years, decades. Besides, both she and Koku were being tracked by locator satellites. Her voice radio might be jammed, but the beam of her locator transmitter was on an entirely different frequency. Even if someone jammed it, the loss of signal by the satellite would itself alert headquarters and a squad of rangers would start out immediately to search for her.

So she took her courage in her hands that morning and doubled back along the steep ridge she had been following. The rising sun was just starting to burn off the chill gray mist. The trail along the ridge was wet, the grass slippery.

Koku had awakened with the sunrise. When Lela closed her eyes she could see another part of the forest, taste the delicious leaves he delicately stripped from the *galium* vines around him, rejoice in the strength and freedom he felt.

Then she heard voices. Unmistakable. Her eyes wide open now, visions of Koku fading into the back of her mind, she ducked low and crept slowly, carefully through the thick enfolding bushes toward the sounds, as silent as she could be without stopping altogether. A tendril of smoke rose from behind the bushes off to her left. Lela's nose wrinkled at the smell of grease burning.

With newfound cunning she flattened herself on the damp grass and slithered around a thick clump of bush. There were four of them, two black men and two white. Just starting to break camp. One of the whites kicked loose dirt onto their small fire. They all wore khaki shirts and trousers, and each of them carried sidearms. Lela saw rifles stacked next to one of their sleeping bags. Five bags, she counted. Yet she saw only four men.

"What have we here?" a deep voice boomed out.

Lela scrambled to her feet. A big, ruddy-faced redheaded man was grinning at her, a huge rifle cradled in his bare arms.

The other four men dashed up to them.

"Well, well, well," said one of the other whites. "It's the bride of the gorilla herself!"

CHICAGO

FROM behind the roadblock, the TV news reporter quickly sprayed her hair so it would not blow untidily in the early autumn breeze.

It was an unusually warm October afternoon out on Interstate 80, ten miles beyond the city line. The sun shone serenely out of a pale blue sky washed by a morning shower. Off to the east puffy white clouds were building up by the lake shore. The woods on the far side of the highway were glorious in their autumnal reds and golds.

From the slight rise in the ground where the cameraman stood, I–80 stretched out to the horizon, a snarling metallic snake filled with fuming automobiles, vans, trucks, even school buses. Heat waves rose from the highway where the traffic stood tangled and stopped, glittering and growling in the sunlight. A roadblock of National Guard tanks parked shoulder to shoulder across the highway, median divider and all, had stopped the vehicles desperately trying to leave Chicago. National Guard soldiers in mottled camouflage uniforms, wearing their battle helmets and carrying assault rifles, were turning the cars around and heading them back toward the city.

The TV reporter, standing just outside the mobile news van with a big numeral nine painted on its side, made a final check of her appearance in the full-length mirror that hung on the inside of the open van door, then walked quickly up to the spot where the cameraman stood.

They made an almost laughable contrast. The reporter was neatly turned out in a pale silk blouse, pleated skirt, and beige jacket—and muddy, sturdy, comfortable jogging shoes. The Channel 9 pin on her jacket's lapel was actually her microphone, sensitive to a range of about three yards. The cameraman wore a grease-stained sweat shirt and jeans. He was bald, fat, and had tattoos on both his forearms. His camera was no larger than one of his ham-sized hands. Its monitoring screen was the size of a postage stamp.

"I got all the traffic footage I need," he said. Pointing toward a woman soldier bearing gold oak leaves on her shoulders, he said, "There's the major in charge of this mess. She's waitin' for you to interview her."

The major was gray-haired and had a face as hard as armor plate. She was not a happy person.

The reporter stood before the camera and put on her professional smile. "This is Becky Murtaugh on Interstate 80 about ten miles west of the city. With me is Major," she peered quickly at the major's name tag, "Wallinsky of the Illinois National Guard."

Turning slightly, but making certain her face was still on camera, the reporter asked, "Major, how do you feel about stopping all these people who want to leave the city?"

The major grimaced. "I feel like hell! But I got my orders. We're supposed to keep the city sealed off in order to stop the spread of the plague."

Someone started honking his car horn and almost instantly the miles-long pileup of vehicles began bleating, blaring their fear and frustration. The reporter had to shout to be heard over the din. "But only five cases of the Horror have been reported in Chicago so far. Why is everyone trying to run away?"

With a withering look, the major hollered back, "They're scared! They're afraid of catching it, of course. It's fatal. And extremely painful. There's no cure, no vaccine. Nobody wants to die."

"But the Army has sent out orders to prevent anyone from leaving the city?"

"The Surgeon General, actually. We're in a state of emergency. The governors of every state in the Union have called out the National Guard to help control road traffic and keep order."

"So you're turning back the desperately frightened people who want to get away from the Horror?"

"That's my job. We can't allow them to spread the plague into the countryside. The whole nation will be affected."

"But can't these people find alternate roads, side roads, to get out into the countryside?"

"Sure they can! That's what makes this job so frustrating. We can't put up roadblocks across every back road in the area. We don't have the manpower or the time!"

"So that means . . ." The reporter gasped. A sudden pain in her stomach, like a hot knife twisting. She recovered, knowing that the lapse could be edited out of the tape. "That means that just because five cases of the Horror have been reported in Chicago, the entire city of four million inhabitants is under quara . . ."

The pain struck again, more viciously. She doubled over, clutching her middle. The microphone pin slipped from her lapel to the grass, but still picked up her awful retching screams of pain.

The major bellowed in a voice of command, "Medic! Get a medic up here on the double."

The reporter writhed on the ground, blood bubbling from her mouth, eyes wild with agony. The cameraman bent over her and got every last second of her death throes on tape.

CHAPTER 25

THERE was no way around the robot that stood guard outside his door. His captors were too clever to face him; not even the squat serving robot appeared anymore. They had stopped feeding him.

I should have made them release me when I had the chance, Stoner thought ruefully. Now I'm stuck here.

We want to find out who they are working for, his star brother reminded him.

I know who they are, he replied.

The voices he had heard from the overhead speakers belonged to Janos and Ilona Lucacs. Stoner was certain of it. The man who had coldly stated that he intended to amputate Stoner's fingers to see if he could grow them back—that was Zoltan Janos.

Yes, said his star brother. But if he is no longer working for the president of Hungary, for whom is he working? Who built this laboratory? Why is he experimenting on us?

Ilona was with Janos, too. How did they leave Hawaii? How did they get away from Jo? Lying quietly on his cot in the dead of night, Stoner tried to expand his awareness past the locked door of his room, past the stupid hulking robot that stood guard outside, beyond the glimpse of hallway he had seen.

Ilona, are you there? he called silently. Can you sense my presence?

No response. He waited in the darkness, pretending to be asleep, but every sense in his body was straining to touch another human mind. He could feel the presence of many people, more than twelve of them, but dimly, too far away to reach and examine or control. This building is big, he realized. It must have been an army barracks or a dormitory at one time.

And he was trapped in it. None of the humans would dare come close enough for him even to begin to manipulate their minds. They hid away from him and sent their robots by day, controlling them remotely, and then turned them off so that Stoner had no chance to tinker with the machines mentally once their human controllers were finished with them. The only robot he could reach at night was the guard outside his door.

The damned stupid robot on the other side of that door! The perfect security guard, too inhuman to need a cup of coffee or to stretch its legs or move a millimeter from its assigned post. Its electronic brain was an old-fashioned hard-wired computer with limited program capacity, not one of the complex decision-capable neural networks that Stoner could manipulate. The damned machine was too moronic to be controlled or maneuvered or even to blink its electro-optical eyes . . .

Stoner almost bolted upright in the cot. Only rigid self-control kept him from moving. The robot can see! Maybe I can use its eyes.

Slowing his breathing, forcing himself to relax and concentrate all his mental energies, Stoner probed for the simple electrical patterns of the robot's computer.

And there it was, even simpler and less complicated than the brain patterns of a faithful dog. Stoner carefully traced his way through the command paths of the computer's programming. With enough time, he thought, maybe I could learn to control this beastie.

Time. That's the one thing I don't have. I've got to get out of here. And soon.

For the moment, though, he had to satisfy himself with nothing more than a look through the robot's eyes at the hallway outside his room.

There was not much to be seen.

The robot had four electro-optical sensors mounted in the bulbous projection at its top, four eyes in its head. Stoner saw the door to his own room, a scant two feet away. Without needing to move the robot's head he could see along the corridor in which it stood. It was a surprisingly wide hallway, and Stoner noticed that it was carpeted like the hall of a hotel. But the carpeting was faded, threadbare. There were even patches of fungus here and there.

Doors were spaced along one side of the broad hallway, all of them closed. The walls were cracked here and there; faint squares of lighter plaster showed where pictures had once hung. Dim bare bulbs glowed feebly from the ceiling, casting pools of grayish light along the mildewed carpet. The other wall of the hallway showed windows, boarded up. At the farthest point, where the hall should have ended, rough planks and slabs of plywood had been nailed up, as if the wall had crumbled away.

Stoner felt puzzled. It looked like an old hotel that had been abandoned. He wished the robot had electrochemical sniffers; he was certain he would smell the tang of salt sea air.

All the doors along the corridor were tightly closed, and the robot would not budge from its assigned post to investigate them. Ilona Lucacs was somewhere in this building, Stoner knew. Lying on a sagging ancient hotel bed, plugged in to her pleasure machine, oblivious to all the world.

She was his one hope. An addict who was in love with the man who was systematically torturing him.

For more than an hour Stoner wandered mentally through the programmed pathways in the robot's computer brain, learning slowly how he might override its commands and take control of the machine. It would take many hours of exertion.

Sleep, said his star brother.

No, we need to be able to move this hunk of tin!

In a few hours they will begin their experiments again. We will need all the strength we have. Sleep now, rest, prepare.

Stoner knew his star brother was right. Still, he wanted to learn how to control the robot. Before they started hacking off his fingers.

"With all due respect for her long years of fine service to this corporation," said Amanda Tilley from her seat across the circular table from Jo, "and with great sorrow for the loss of her daughter and kidnapping of her husband, I move that the board ask Ms. Camerata for her resignation."

Jo sat up rigidly in her chair. Since she had been elected chairman of the board she had insisted that the directors meet around a circular table. They had called it "Queen Jo's Round Table" at first, realizing that it was her way to stop the power games that the directors played. By emphasizing equality among the board, she also emphasized her own mastery of its members.

But now there was a motion on the table that would end her presidency of Vanguard Industries and chairmanship of the board. Jo studied Amanda Tilley: the woman was bone thin, her hair as white as cream, clipped short and neatly coiffed, her paisley frock conservative yet feminine. Her eyes shifted away from Jo's gaze uneasily. Her mouth was a tight, tense line in her drawn face.

How like Hsen to use a board member who had been one of

Jo's most faithful supporters. And to use Cathy's murder as the excuse to push me out. Jo held on to her blazing temper. Self-control had never been more vitally important. The subtle little oriental bastard had not dared to show up for the board meeting, not even in hologrammic projection.

Glancing around the table, Jo saw that none of the directors were surprised by Tilley's motion. Twenty-two men and women, nearly two dozen business people who sat on the boards of the world's most powerful corporations. Their clothes were quietly elegant; the women in one-of-a-kind frocks or day suits, the men in hand-tailored suits of gray or dark blue. Jo herself wore a sheath of black and beige feather print design; it clung to her figure just enough to be suggestive without being blatant. On the table before each member rested a computer keyboard with flat display screen built into the table top, and a gleaming stainless steel pitcher that held a pint of each director's preferred drink.

Some of the directors looked embarrassed at Tilley's motion, some distressed, others wire-taut. Sir Harold Epping was clearly angered. But no one was surprised.

"A motion that I resign has been put before the board," Jo said, mainly for the tape that was automatically recording the board meeting. "Is there a second?"

She turned her gaze toward Wilhelm Kruppmann and, sure enough, he muttered, "Second."

"Discussion?" asked Jo.

Several board members squirmed in their chairs. One of the older men cleared his throat, but then said nothing.

Molten hot anger seethed through Jo's every fiber. She deliberately waited for a long moment, waited while the other board members glanced at one another like guilty schoolchildren, waited while she fought for control over her fury.

At last she said, in a voice that was calm, quiet, and steel-hard, "I suppose I should open the discussion with a statement of my own. I have no intention of resigning the presidency of this corporation or the chairmanship of this board."

Several of the members nodded; a few even smiled, relieved.

"I believe," Jo continued, "that this attempt to use the murder of my daughter and the abduction of my husband as an excuse to remove me from office is a contemptible tactic, a return to the sexist maneuvering that was outlawed by the World Court decades ago."

That made almost all of them sit up: the threat of a discrimination suit in the World Court. No director in his or her right mind would want that.

"Moreover, we all know that this illegal sexist garbage is nothing but a front for the man who wants to take over this corporation. Amanda, I'm certain you don't realize it, but you are being *used* by Li-Po Hsen."

Tilley's mouth dropped open. "I never . . . this is something . . . Jo, you mustn't believe . . ." she sputtered.

But Jo had already swung her blazing eyes to Kruppmann. "Isn't that right, Wilhelm?"

She caught the Swiss banker as he was nervously gulping at a glass of sparkling water. He sputtered and his face reddened.

Before he could reply, Jo said, "Hsen wants to take over Vanguard, he's wanted to do it for years, and now he's using this pretext to try to get me out of his way. He's saying to you that I'm just an emotional woman, and the tragedy that's happened to my family has made me unfit to be your president. Well it's not true, and I refuse to stand aside and allow Hsen to . . . to gain control of this corporation—*especially when he's the one who had my daughter murdered and my husband kidnapped!*"

A shock wave went around the table. Jo smiled to herself. She had almost said that Hsen was trying to rape the corporation, but realized at the last instant that it would be too female a word to use.

"That is a very serious accusation," Kruppmann said, his voice quavering. "Where is your proof?"

"You are my proof, Wilhelm." Jo sprang the trap. "In the anteroom through the double doors is a team from my security division, ready to apply truth serum under medically supervised conditions. Will you submit to their examination?"

Kruppmann's face went white. "Now you accuse *me*?"

"You're damned right I do! You've been in this with Hsen from the beginning."

"I absolutely refuse to permit your Gestapo robots to interrogate me! You have no right . . ."

Jo cut him short. "As a member of this board you have agreed to periodic medical examinations. As president of the corporation and chairman of the board, I'm calling for an examination now."

Kruppmann looked wildly around the table, seeking support and finding none.

"This is illegal!" he blustered. "A violation of my rights!"

"Your rights," Jo mimicked, almost snarling. "You knew that Hsen was going to attack my home, my family, didn't you?"

Kruppmann's response was a strangled guttural growl. The other directors were staring at him, unconsciously leaning away from him, faces aghast. Amanda Tilley's eyes were wide, her blue-veined hands clenched before her chin.

"Didn't you?" Jo repeated, her voice hot enough to melt steel.

Kruppmann crumpled. His face sagged and he made a helpless gesture, eyes darting around the table as if for help. He looked like a man who suddenly realized he was going to be hauled before a firing squad.

"I didn't know . . ." he said in a tortured whisper. "I had no idea . . ."

Jo smiled grimly at him. Her scheme had worked. The pitcher of sparkling water on the table before Kruppmann had been laced with enough scopolamine to reduce his willpower almost to zero.

"Tell the board what you do know," she said softly. "Tell us of your own volition."

The Swiss banker began blubbering. The board members listened in growing horror as he hesitantly told them of Hsen's determination to take over Vanguard and to break up the International Investment Agency.

"What about my husband?" Jo demanded.

"That too," Kruppmann confessed. "Hsen wanted to capture Stoner to find out how he survived freezing. The man wants to live forever."

"Where is he now?"

Kruppmann heaved his massive shoulders. "I don't know. China, somewhere in China, I think. He knows you are after him. He has gone into hiding."

Jo pursed her lips and decided to let Kruppmann off the hook. He could be monitored electronically and by human surveillance teams. He was her best lead to Hsen's whereabouts.

"Very well," she said, her voice turned to ice. "Now we should return to the business of the board."

Amanda Tilley got unsteadily to her feet. "I would like to withdraw my motion," she said, her voice trembling.

The entire board clapped their hands loudly. All except Kruppmann, who sat dazedly, staring into emptiness. Jo accepted their applause with a tight smile. The cowardly bastards are too scared to throw me out now, she knew. But at least they've given me a free hand to deal with Hsen— whether they realize it or not. Now, with the board solidly behind me, *now* we start the moves to take over Pacific Commerce. And kill the murdering sonofabitch.

The voice from the ceiling speaker said almost casually, "We will not use an anesthetic, since we want to determine how well you are able to control the pain."

One of the many-armed robots had clamped Stoner's left hand in a grip of steel inches above a small table that was covered with absorbent surgical sheeting. Two of its other arms held Stoner's shoulders against the back of the chair on which he had been seated. A fourth steel-fingered hand pinned Stoner's right arm tightly against his side.

"If our sensors show you are in great pain," the voice went on, "naturally we will immediately inject you with a local anesthetic."

"Naturally," said Stoner through gritted teeth. Even though his star brother was controlling his fear, slowing the chemical secretions that produced the bodily sensations of terror, Stoner's mind still knew full well that in a few moments they were going to amputate one of his fingers.

Controlling fear is not the same as being fearless, Stoner realized. He could feel his heart thumping in his chest, feel perspiration beading his upper lip.

The second robot held two of its clawlike hands above Stoner's outstretched fingers. One hand gripped a pneumatic hypodermic syringe, its needle inches above Stoner's wrist. The other held a hair-thin optical fiber that wound back from the robot's delicate fingers to a compact surgical laser resting on a second table, closer to the door.

Stoner never heard a command given. The fiber suddenly glowed and a white-hot beam of light lanced across the base of his little finger. He knew that all sensations of pain were being shunted away, controlled by his star brother. But his breath still went ragged as he watched with staring eyes while the beam of light severed his little finger from his hand.

He heard a howling, bellowing noise and realized it was his own voice screaming not in pain but in savage, uncontrolled rage. His star brother was startled momentarily, but deep within his mind Stoner felt the alien presence agree that his primal scream was the simplest way to release the tension that racked his body.

The robots were totally unaffected by Stoner's feral roar. Their grip on his flesh did not tighten a millimeter. Or loosen. The laser light winked out and the finger dropped to the table top, disconnected, and rolled over slightly so that it lay askew, like a ship with a bad list. Stoner blinked and felt tears in his eyes. His throat was raw. There was a bit of bleeding but even that quickly stopped. The robot picked up the severed finger, its arm bending in ways impossible to a human, and deftly deposited it in a fluid-filled glass jar.

"We will preserve the finger," said Janos's voice from the ceiling speaker, "to compare its tissue composition with that of the new finger he grows."

"If he grows a new finger," said Ilona's voice.

"He will, I'm certain."

"Not without food," Stoner heard a voice reply. His own. Croaking, dry, harsh with brute anger and the rawness of his throat.

"What did you say, Dr. Stoner?"

"I won't be able to regenerate unless I get food. Any system needs an energy input."

"We must allow him food," Ilona's voice said.

"Tomorrow," replied Janos. "I want a baseline profile. Tomorrow morning we will go through the complete physical exams, plus a brain scan, and then he can be given food."

The robots released Stoner, gathered up their tools with quiet efficiency, and left the room. Stoner glimpsed the guard robot out in the hallway, massive as a small tank.

He flexed his left hand. The stub where his little finger had been was seared black. No blood, although a little clear liquid leaked through the burned skin. A tide of sullen, remorseless anger began to rise in him, only to be drained away by a coldly rational calm, like flames extinguished by a blast of icy water.

Let me have my anger, he snarled inwardly. Let me *feel* what a human being should feel!

His star brother replied silently, The most horrible things that human beings do, they do in anger.

Or in fear.

Or in fear, his star brother admitted. Anger is often the mask for fear.

"Bastards," he muttered aloud. But to himself, to both his selves, he said, We've got to find a way out of here.

Ilona, he called silently. Ilona, I need your help. He's going to kill me. You know that he won't stop until the ultimate test—to see if I can survive a fatal trauma.

He felt her presence, her own fear, her uncertainty. But he got no reply to his plea.

CHAPTER 26

FOR the first time in nearly two weeks Vic Tomasso leaned back and relaxed. He had been nervous throughout the Pacific Commerce flight from Hilo to Tokyo, wondering if Hsen had the balls to sabotage one of his own rocketplanes just to get rid of a man he no longer wanted alive. But the flight went smoothly and he transferred on the hovertrain to the spaceport out in the harbor, streaking along the superconducting rails that levitated the train on a cushion of magnetic force.

Now he sat back in a Pacific Commerce space shuttle, confident that if Hsen was too cheap to blow up one of his own aerospace planes he certainly would not destroy a much more expensive shuttle. Not just to assassinate me, Tomasso thought. And he wouldn't spend the money to take me to the Moon if he wanted to get rid of me. He could have had a couple of goons knock me off at the airport or on the train. Cheaper, by far.

So he felt reasonably confident that his information about the secret starship project had bought his life for him. Now all he had to do was lead Hsen's people to Delphi base out on the Mare Imbrium and let them take things from there.

After the shuttle took off from the harbor spaceport and angled steeply into the sky, Tomasso even managed to drift off into a restful sleep while the craft glided weightlessly toward the Vanguard space station that was the first stop on the way to the Moon.

In her office at Vanguard's headquarters Jo smiled humorlessly to herself as she studied the computer screen display. So it was Vic after all. The truth drug session had been a sham. I'll have to check on the doctor who handled the interrogation, she thought. I'll bet it was a woman.

The Hungarians should have been a tip-off, Jo realized with perfect hindsight. They disappeared the day after Cathy's murder and I never even paid any attention to it. No one but Vic could have gotten them out of the house, even in all that uproar. It's been him all along, the smiling traitorous murdering bastard.

Vic thought he was so clever, flying to Tokyo unannounced and getting onto a Moon-bound shuttle flight so quickly that no one could follow him.

What Vic did not know was that he carried imbedded beneath the skin on the back of his left shoulder a microscopic transmitter, powered by the heat of his own body, that faithfully beeped out a location signal every minute of the day and night. It had been implanted during Tomasso's very first physical examination by Vanguard medics when he had first been hired by the corporation. A routine procedure that no one, not even the chief of corporate security, knew about. No one except Jo and the medics who did the work. And the medics were bought off nicely with early retirements at huge pensions—and distant retirement homes.

The procedure had started years earlier as a security move against terrorism, when corporate executives were under constant threat of kidnapping or worse. Although such hazards had dwindled greatly Jo still found it convenient to be able to keep tabs on selected members of her staff—without their knowing it, of course.

Vanguard surveillance satellites routinely monitored only the location signals of the corporation's top executives. Jo had no need or desire to keep track of everyone, although there had been times when an individual attracted her attention enough to start the satellites searching. Since the murder of her daughter, they had been tracking Vic Tomasso. Jo wished bitterly that Keith had allowed her to implant a monitoring device in him, but he had refused with a grin.

"I've got enough going on under my skin, don't you think?" he had said. And she had reluctantly let him go unprotected.

Now she sat alone in her office late at night, the only light in the room coming from the glow of the display screen. Jo tried to put herself in Tomasso's position, tried to determine what he was up to. Clearly he was on the run. Probably to the Pacific Commerce mining center on the Sea of Tranquillity. He's a damned fool if he thinks I can't reach him there.

She eased back in her butter-soft leather recliner, thinking to herself, Vic will be out of range of the satellite sensors once he transfers to the lunar shuttle. I'll have to get somebody on the space station to lock onto him before he gets away. Which means I've got to act fast. Using the keyboard set into the armrest of her chair she asked the computer to locate Nunzio, her erstwhile bodyguard.

The dogged old Italian was on Taiwan, the screen told her, stubbornly tracking down rumors that Li-Po Hsen had retired to a fortified castle high in the island's central mountains. It was close to the dinner hour in Taipei. Jo put through a call.

It took a few minutes of computerized searching and switching, but finally Nunzio's craggy, wary-eyed face showed on her screen.

"*Si, Signora?*"

"Nunzio, I have a different task for you to do."

A man of few words, Nunzio said nothing, waiting for her to instruct him further. Jo transmitted Vic Tomasso's photograph and personnel dossier to him and told him to follow Vic to the Moon.

"*La Luna, Signora?*" For once, Nunzio's shaggy brows rose with surprise.

"You've never been in space, have you?"

"No, *Signora.*"

Jo quietly explained that everyone gets sick their first few hours in weightlessness, and it was nothing to be ashamed of. The spacecraft crew provides pills, but still he will feel nauseous.

Nunzio's face became an impassive mask. Finally he asked, "And this Tomasso . . . he is to be killed?"

"No. He is to be held until I can join you."

"And the Chinese, Hsen?"

"If you find Tomasso you will find Hsen also. I am certain of it."

"Su la Luna."

"Yes. If you do find Hsen there, you know what to do."

"Si, Signora." And almost as if he did not know what his hand was doing, Nunzio drew an extended finger across his throat.

That will take care of Vic, Jo said to herself once the call ended. Then she thought about sending some Vanguard security people to the Moon as backup for Nunzio. With a curt shake of her head she decided against it. Hsen's people would not recognize one gray-haired Italian tourist as a threat, but they would quickly sniff out a team of Vanguard professionals. Besides, Nunzio's honor was at stake. He had failed to protect his patroness and her family; he was working now to redeem himself. He would die before failing her, she knew.

She sighed deeply, looked around her darkened office, then got up to head for home. She wanted to be there when Rickie woke up in the morning. Her son was sleeping without nightmares now, but Jo was careful to be with him when he went to bed and to be there when he awoke, no matter how busy she might be during the business day.

During the nights she worked on her revenge.

Pretending to sleep, Stoner lay hungry and alert on his cot. For hours he had tried to make some kind of mental contact with Ilona Lucacs, but the young Hungarian scientist was either totally engrossed in her pleasure machine or simply too far away to feel his silent cries for help.

Then the lock on his door clicked. Stoner felt every nerve in him go taut as a bowstring. Slowly the door swung open. Feeble light from the hallway spilled onto the floor, marking out a dim rectangle with the figure of a woman framed within it. And the implacable guard robot behind her.

For a long moment neither one of them moved. Stoner lay on his cot, the woman stood silently in the doorway.

Then he got to his feet and called softly, "Ilona?"

She seemed to flinch, but finally entered the darkened room. "Are you . . . all right?" she whispered.

"I'm still alive," he said, pulling on his jeans.

"Your hand . . . ?"

"It will heal."

"And the finger will grow back?"

"Maybe. I don't really know."

Without closing the door she took a few more steps into the room. Instead of her customary tweeds she wore a pair of snug-fitting dark slacks and a man's tailored shirt, unbuttoned low enough to show considerable cleavage.

"Zoltan plans to leave you alone for a few days, to see what the finger does."

"And after that?"

She fell silent. Stoner deliberately stepped into the rectangle of light thrown across the floor from the hall; as he had expected, Ilona's eyes widened at the ugly red burn marks on his chest. But she quickly looked away. Beyond the door Stoner could see the obstinate robot standing on its unmoving treads.

"Can you get me past that robot?" he asked as he slipped on his shirt.

"No," she said.

Stoner walked up to her and, lifting her chin gently, looked deeply into her eyes.

"Before they find you in here, we've got to get away," he said softly.

But she pushed his hand away. "I am supposed to be the one on duty monitoring the video screens and other displays tonight. No one will see me here. You made me come in here to you, didn't you?"

"I called to you and you responded."

"Zoltan wants the powers you have. He's obsessed with the idea of becoming superhuman. I think he is going insane."

"We've got to get past that robot," Stoner insisted.

"I don't know how to change its programming. I don't even know how to shut it off. I can't help you. I'm useless to you, to Zoltan—even to myself."

Stoner turned away from her and went to sit on the bed. "Then he's going to kill me. He'll keep pushing my physical limitations until he kills me."

She said nothing.

"He's killing you, too, you know. With that electrical ecstasy machine of yours."

"Please, Dr. Stoner, no lectures."

"Are you going to let him murder me? Are you going to help him?"

"What can I do?" There was no fear or conflict in her voice. Merely the statement of someone who felt helpless. "We will all die soon enough. What difference does it make? I have nothing to live for."

She really believes that, Stoner saw. Her willpower, her individuality, is being sapped away like lifeblood trickling from a wound that won't heal. He looked at her more carefully. Her face was pale, eyes red with dark half-circles below them. She seemed to have lost weight. Like a vampire, the pleasure machine was sucking her life away a little more each night.

"Where are we?" Stoner asked. "How did you get here? Who's behind all this?"

Languidly, as if it took more effort than she could spare, Ilona went to the stiff wooden chair by the monitoring equipment and slowly sat on it.

"The morning after you were kidnapped and . . . and . . ."

"And my daughter killed," Stoner said grimly.

Ilona swallowed hard, then went on, "A security team from your wife's office took Zoltan and me out to a private airport and put us aboard a jet plane. We flew directly here with no stops. We refueled from tankers in mid-air. Twice."

"Here? Where?"

"Beirut. The old city."

Stoner nearly gasped with surprise. Old Beirut had been abandoned for decades. Shattered by a civil war that had lasted for a generation, bombed, gassed, blasted by rocket artillery, every wall in the old city pockmarked by machine gun bullets and shell fragments. Old Beirut had even been treated to the last nuclear explosion in the world.

The homemade plutonium bomb had gone off prematurely while still in the cargo hold of an Italian passenger liner. The waterfront area was flattened beneath a towering cloud of radioactive steam. Half a million people died, most of them in long-lingering cancerous agonies.

The world trembled with terror for days after that blast, then took the steps necessary to make it the *final* nuclear explosion in history. Old Beirut was abandoned and a new city, financed heavily by both Arabs and Israelis, with plenty of help from the superpowers, began to rise south of the once-embattled airport.

Old Beirut was left to stand as a shattered hulk, a reminder of the madness of war and terrorism. Abandoned to bleach under the hot Mediterranean sun, visited only by tourist helicopters that quickly flitted across the radioactive ruins while their pretaped lectures spoke of the horrors of war and their tourists took pictures of Earth's last battlefield.

"This hotel is well away from the harbor area," Ilona said. "The residual radioactivity has gone down almost to the background level."

But Stoner was working on another puzzle. "It couldn't have been a Vanguard Corporation team that brought you here. Not for this. Not for what you're doing to me."

Ilona said, "A Vanguard security executive took us to the plane. He had an Italian name: Tomasso, I think."

"Is Janos still working for the government of Hungary?"

"No, I don't think so. I don't know," Ilona replied. "What difference does it make?"

Stoner sat silently on the edge of the bed for several moments, trying to sort it all out. Finally he looked up at Ilona, waiting passively, and focused all his mental energies on her.

"You've got to find out who Janos is reporting to, and get a message to them. Tell them that instead of determining how I survived freezing, he's slowly killing me. Tell them that I'll be dead in a few more days if they don't stop him."

Ilona blinked slowly at him. "Zoltan would not kill you."

"Yes he would," Stoner answered, certain of it. "He'll keep pushing until he kills me just to see if I can repair myself and come alive again."

She nodded. He could not tell if she actually agreed or was merely unable to argue against him.

"If he kills me, his superiors—whoever they are—will be extremely unhappy with him. His usefulness to them will be at an end. They will murder him."

That made her dark-circled eyes widen slightly.

"You've got to save me. Otherwise Janos is going to die."

Stoner desperately hoped that she believed what he was saying, and still had enough volition in her to act on his words.

CHAPTER 27

KIRK Matthews cherished the simple life. No matter that he was in charge of a secret Vanguard Corporation base buried far out in Mare Imbrium. No matter that neither he nor the three dozen technicians living in the base knew what the hell was being created in the gigantic vat at the heart of the underground complex. The simple life was what he sought.

Back on Earth there were complexities. An ex-wife seeking every penny he earned. Lawyers hounding him. One of them nursing a broken jaw and several cracked ribs as the result of accosting him once too often.

Here on the Moon life should be simple. All he had to do was supervise thirty-six technicians whose job was to make certain the mysterious twenty-story-high crystalline vat was fed the prescribed chemicals and maintained at certain temperatures and pressures. The technicians were educated, well-balanced, eminently stable men and women. The pay was good, and it was piling up nicely, since there was no place to spend it. Living conditions were somewhat spartan, but much more comfortable than an Earthside courtroom. Or jail cell.

Liaisons among the men and women living in the underground complex were casual and easygoing. They all had signed up for the duration of the experiment at this remote site, knowing that it would take at least two years; they were all consenting adults who preferred not to make permanent attachments.

Matthews clasped his gnarled hands behind his graying crew cut and leaned far back in his desk chair. The simple life. Until this goddamned Latino wandered in.

Paulino Alvarado, as far as Matthews could tell, was neither a spy from another corporation nor a snoop from the International Astronautical Council. He seemed to be a genuinely lost soul, a Vanguard employee who got dangerously lost up there on the lunar surface and would have died if he hadn't stumbled onto Delphi base.

But now that he was here and had seen whatever the hell it was bubbling away inside the vat, Paulino could not be allowed to leave and blab to the outside world.

Worse still, the kid had a pocket full of Moondust pills. Matthews didn't believe that Paulino had the guts or personality to be a pusher. But a user was just as bad.

The simple life. Matthews had bucked the whole problem up the chain of command in a carefully coded message to his bosses, back at Archimedes. For days he had waited for a response, while Paulino wandered around the base, not exactly getting in anybody's way, but he sure enough made people nervous.

Apparently the problem had been directed all the way back to corporate headquarters, because Hilo was where the message resting on Matthews's desk had come from. The monomolecular-thin slip of reusable plastic bore a mere seven words, plus the name of the sender. An explosive seven words:

> HOLD THE INTRUDER UNTIL I GET THERE.
> JO CAMERATA.

* * *

Stoner sat impassively through all the medical tests that

the two tall, many-armed robots put him through. His mind, though, spent the whole morning probing the massive machine guarding the door to his room, tracing the pathways of its computer brain's programming. For hours he allowed the robots to take blood samples, test his reflexes, run him on the treadmill, check his eyesight and hearing.

They sprayed electrodes onto the skin of his chest, back, and legs. They minutely examined the charred stump of his little finger. They fitted a helmet over his tangled thick hair and connected it to a multichannel brainwave recorder.

Not a word from the ceiling speakers. The robots had been precisely programmed for these tests; no human direction was necessary. I could finagle these machines, Stoner said to himself. Their networks are complex enough to allow me to slip in and plant changes. They're not pre-programmed inflexible tin soldiers like the robot guarding the door.

Maybe I could even get one of them to turn off the guard robot, if I had enough time to tinker. Time. It always comes down to a matter of time.

Stoner could sense the presence of Zoltan Janos watching, could feel the tension of the Hungarian scientist as he studied the curves flickering across the display screens, taste the perspiration beading his lip.

He could not sense Ilona. She was not in the room with the monitoring equipment, where Janos was. Stoner could not feel her presence anywhere.

He returned his attention to the guard robot outside the door. The robot's computer was hard-wired; it contained one set of instructions and one only. It could not be reprogrammed unless you got inside and changed the wiring. The only way to prevent the robot from doing its job was to physically reach the circuit breakers on its back and shut off its power.

Stoner actually smiled, even though he saw nothing humorous. The robot was like the Varangian guards that Byzantine emperors hired: foreigners who understood only their duty to the emperor and nothing else, not even the language of the land they lived in. Utterly loyal because they knew nothing else.

At last the medical robots picked up all their equipment and trundled out of the room. As the lock clicked behind them, Stoner looked up to the ceiling speaker and asked, "When do I get some food?"

Janos's voice replied, "You feel hunger?"

"Damned right I do!"

A few moments of hesitation. Then, "Tonight, perhaps. More likely tomorrow morning. I must analyze the data from these tests first."

"And then what, another finger?"

"Perhaps. Perhaps not."

Stoner caught a fleeting impression of the robots clamping his head in their steel fingers while a laser beam deftly excised one of his eyes.

An electric current of fear shocked through him even before his star brother could damp it down. He felt his innards calm even while his mind screamed with outraged fury.

And he heard himself say coldly, "If you're thinking of injecting some of my blood into your own veins, remember what happened to Novotny."

No answer, but Stoner could sense the surprise and sudden fear that hit Janos.

"Once those symbiotes are in your blood," Stoner went on, "you can't look out at the world as you did before. You realize, every moment of every day, awake or asleep, that you are not alone. It's more than having another presence within your body and your mind. You begin to understand that you are not merely an individual. You start to see that you, as a single unit, are part of an entirety, a link between past and future, a member of a family."

Still Janos said nothing. He was listening, and Stoner could sense the tangle of curiosity and fear and burning ambition that swirled within him.

"That understanding drove Novotny into a collapse. What will it do to you? How do you think you'll feel about the experiments you've been doing on me, once you and I are linked as firmly as two cells of the same creature? What do you think it'll be like when you can feel what I feel, when you can sense my pain and anguish?"

"Thank you, Dr. Stoner," said Janos, in a very subdued voice. "Thank you for the warning. I was indeed tempted to inject myself to obtain your powers. I thought that what happened to Novotny was due to his age, perhaps, or his own psychological weaknesses."

Shaking his head, Stoner replied, "Novotny saw himself as a member of the human family for the first time since he'd been weaned."

"And have you led such a blameless life, that the alien symbiotes did not drive you insane?"

"Hardly," Stoner said to the ceiling speaker. "But I was aboard their ship for years, frozen in cryonic suspension. They had a long time to assimilate my memories, to make my unconscious mind grow accustomed to their presence."

"I see," said Janos thoughtfully. "I see."

"So you're out here to help that stupid ape get laid. That's cute."

Lela sat by the campfire, silently watching her five captors as they prepared their dinner. The utter darkness of the moonless night and the foliage pressing all around their simple camp made her feel terribly cut off from all civilization, all possible help. She felt the chill of the rising mist on her back and the heat of the licking flames on her face. Cold and hot, two kinds of fear that made her tremble and sweat at the same time.

"You must be some kind of sex pervert," the white man jeered at her. He was short, stocky, red-haired. "You have fantasies about making it with a gorilla, eh?"

"I can put on its head and skin, after we kill it. You like it that way?" one of the black men said.

The others all laughed.

So far they had not harmed her. So far. Their leader, the

blond one with the English accent, had made them keep their hands off Lela. But he could not stop their joking threats.

He came up to her now and sat on the rough log beside her, handing her a tin of stew.

"Just pull the top off," he said softly. "It heats by itself."

Sitting cross-legged, Lela kept her hands pressed firmly against the heavy twill of her trousers. She was afraid to let the men see how her hands would shake.

The blond placed the can before her, muttering, "Got to eat sometime, y'know."

"Why are you here?" Lela asked. "Why are you hunting the gorillas? No zoo will buy them from you; we have international agreements. No research laboratory will accept a grown primate."

The blond smiled sadly. "We're not hired to sell them, lady. We're just supposed to kill them. All of them."

Despite herself Lela clutched at the man. "Kill them? Kill them all? Why? *Why!*"

He held her wrists while the other men stared. "Calm down! Calm yourself."

"Why do you kill them?" Lela demanded.

"If the gorillas are gone, then there's no further purpose for this reserve, is there? The land can be sold to developers."

"Developers? To develop what?"

The blond shrugged. "New cities, I imagine. Kampala, Ruhengeri, Bukavu—all the old cities are bursting at their seams, aren't they? There's no place to put all the people. They're spreading out all across the countryside."

"But not here!" Lela snapped. "Not this far away . . ."

Patiently, almost like a schoolteacher, the blond explained, "There are people—powerful people—who want to build whole new cities. Cut down the forests and make more farmland. Build roads and airports and even spaceports."

"But the gorillas are *protected* by international agreement! They can't build here!"

"They can if the apes are all gone. In a few months they will be."

Lela was aghast. "You can't . . . the rangers . . . the World Court . . ."

The blond gave her a pitying look. "I told you, we're dealing with very powerful people here. Why do you think we can have a fire each night without the satellites reporting us to your rangers? We know you've got a locator beacon imbedded in your skin; the satellites are tracking you okay but the information isn't going to the rangers either."

"No! It cannot be!"

"Why not?" He pulled a slim dark brown cigar from the pocket of his shirt, clamped it in his teeth and lit it. Lela stared at its glowing tip, her mind racing.

"What you do is wrong," she said. "It is evil."

He blew a puff of gray smoke into the night. "Why should anybody care more about your stupid apes than they do about people? Human beings who need homes and jobs?"

"You don't have to wipe out the gorillas to make homes and jobs for people," Lela answered.

"That's a university graduate talking. My older brother went to university. I worked like a dog to help support him. Now he's off saving the bleeding whales somewhere up in the Arctic and I'm here, hunting down the last of the gorillas. Queer world, isn't it?"

Lela stared at him. He puffed on his cigar for a while, then started to look uncomfortable. Without another word he hauled himself to his feet and walked slowly to the four other men sitting close to the fire, grinning at Lela.

They're going to kill me, Lela realized. They can't let me go, not after what he's told me. They're going to kill me. When they're finished with me.

BOOK V

And so, to the end of history, murder shall
breed murder, always in the name of right and
honor and peace, until the gods are tired of
blood and create a race that can understand.

CHAPTER 28

"RICKIE, you and I are going to take a little vacation," Jo said brightly, with an enthusiasm she did not truly feel.

They were sitting at the breakfast table, set in a sunny glassed-in alcove off the kitchen.

Rickie looked up from his raisins and flakes. "A vacation? Where?"

"How would you like to see our center on the Moon?"

The ten-year-old's eyes widened. "The Moon! Wow!"

"You can ask a couple of your friends along, if you like."

"Can I? Can I *now*?"

"Sure. As long as you finish your breakfast after you've called them."

Rickie was off his chair and dashing to the phone in the kitchen before Jo could finish the sentence. She leaned her elbows on the glass-topped table and sipped at her steaming coffee. The psychologists said that Rickie was adjusting healthily to the traumatic shock he had gone through. He slept through the night now, and claimed that he no longer had nightmares. His appetite seemed normal enough, and the guardians that Jo had surrounded him with, in the guise of household servants, reported that he did not seem to be overly fearful or nervous.

Twice since that horrible night, Jo had taken her son to the Vanguard research laboratory where tissue from murdered Cathy's body was being treated in the plastic womb of a cloning tank. She carefully explained that Cathy was going to be born again, a new little baby who would grow up to be the sister he had known.

"She's not gone from us forever, Rickie. She'll come back to us."

Holding his mother's hand, Rickie had smiled up at Jo and said, "Only I'll be her big brother and she'll be my little sister, right, Mom?"

Jo had laughed. "Right."

His smile was replaced by a worried, "Will Dad come back to us, too?"

Jo felt her heart constrict within her. "Yes," she promised. "Your father will return to us."

"When?"

"I don't know, Rickie. All I know is that somehow he'll come back to us."

True to his word, Janos sent in the serving robot the next morning with a tray of breakfast.

"Good morning, Dr. Stoner. I trust you slept well," said the squat little robot, as if nothing had happened since the last time it had come into the room.

Stoner did not reply. The robot placed the breakfast tray on the little table in the corner of the room opposite the medical monitoring equipment and rolled out the door without another word. The guard stood out in the hallway; it had not moved a millimeter since Stoner had first challenged it more than a week earlier.

Eggs, sausages, half a melon, thick slabs of bread, a pot of honey, and a large glass of milk. Stoner broke his imposed fast with a will. The food disappeared quickly.

All morning long he was left alone in the room. No voices from the ceiling speakers. No robots coming in to test him. Or slice him up. Stoner probed with his mind but could sense no other human beings. Alone? he wondered. Have they packed up and left?

That didn't make sense. But for a few moments he pondered the possibility of being abandoned to die in the deserted emptiness of Old Beirut. Nobody left but me and that stupid, stubborn pile of transistors outside the door. It would be an odd way to die.

As he began to wonder if he could break through one of the

walls into another room, and get into the hallway and out of the hotel that way, the ceiling speaker crackled.

"Dr. Stoner," said Janos's voice, "I have news for you. We will be leaving this place shortly."

The Hungarian's voice sounded unhappy. He's being forced to stop his experiment, Stoner told himself. Ilona got to his boss, whoever that is, and now he's got to stop playing with me.

"Where are we going?" Stoner asked aloud.

"That is of no consequence to you."

Yes, Janos was definitely miffed. Stoner smiled. Wherever they were going, it would be better than this. And he might get an opportunity to get away from this maniac.

Hours passed, then finally one of the tall many-armed robots came into his room, pulled Stoner's arms behind his back and snapped a pair of handcuffs on his wrists. Then it slipped a burlap hood over Stoner's head. The bag smelled of coffee. It effectively blocked his vision, although the robot did not tie it tight around his neck, so some light filtered in and Stoner could see a sliver of the floor at his feet.

Almost immediately he realized what was happening. They have to move me, and it will probably be by plane. They won't have room for the robots. They'll have to come into fairly close contact with me. Janos is afraid that I'll be able to control him and the others, and he thinks that my ability to manipulate people depends on my being able to see them— like a hypnotist.

He almost danced down the hallway as the robot led him out of the room. That's Janos's mistake! He thinks he'll be safe as long as I can't see him. How wrong he is!

Relief and a strange, bitter form of elation flooded Stoner. I don't have to see him, I don't have to touch him. Just let me get close enough to talk to the sonofabitch without an intercom system between us. Just let me into the same room with him and I'll bend his brain into pretzels. I'll twist his guts inside out. I'll snap his bones, each and every one of them!

His star brother said nothing, but Stoner sensed the alien

presence's cool disapproval. Slowly, slowly as the robot led him carefully into an ancient elevator that wheezed and groaned as it descended and then out across a wide expanse that *must* have been the hotel's lobby and finally through a creaking set of boards that served as a door and into the hot brightness of real sunlight—slowly Stoner's exhilaration died away.

Patience, he told himself. Remember the story of the young bull and the old bull. He felt the touch of his star brother's curiosity. Smiling inwardly, Stoner explained, The young bull sees a herd of cows grazing in the distance and says to the old bull, "I'm going to run over there and grab a cow for myself." The old bull says, "Let's walk calmly and get all of them."

His star brother smiled back. Let Janos take us to his superiors. Then we will find out who is behind all this.

Yes, Stoner said. Let him take me to those who are responsible for Cathy's murder. He saw his daughter's body floating in the swimming pool again, saw her blood spreading across the lighted water. His elation turned to pain.

He was bundled into a car of some sort, probably a van from the way he had to climb up and slide into a padded bench. Not much light, despite the brilliantly sunny day. The van either had no windows in its rear or they had been painted over to conceal whoever sat in back. Couldn't be a limousine, Stoner told himself. Even blindfolded he knew that.

No one said a word to him, but he sensed the presence of Ilona Lucacs sitting in front of him. Stoner remained silent, realizing that Ilona had indeed called Janos's superiors as he had asked her to. Did Janos know that she had done this? Stoner sensed that he did, and he was furious with her.

Janos was not in this vehicle. Stoner made himself as comfortable as he could with his hands cuffed behind him as the van lurched and careened along the empty streets of Old Beirut. Soon they were on a highway, and within a quarter hour Stoner began to hear traffic noises. The shrill whine of a jet plane screeched overhead. They were approaching the airport.

Out to a big hangar they drove. Stoner heard an overhead door rattle shut behind them and, as they helped him out of the van, voices echoing inside the closed hangar. He smelled machine oil and the cold metallic tang of cryogenic piping and pumps that handled the liquid hydrogen used to fuel airplanes.

Standing in the midst of a small knot of people he counted six huddled around him, one of them Ilona, the others strangers. No robots. No Janos.

As he wondered what would happen next, the door clattered open again and another car drove in. Stoner sensed Janos, and then heard his voice speaking in English to the others. He felt an immense wave of relief. He wanted Janos with him.

They led him carefully up the aluminum ladder of a small transport plane and moved him back toward the rear. Without a word, the men who were guiding him pushed his head down slightly so he would not bump it on the narrowing ceiling panels. They went through a partition, sat him in a seat, and buckled a seat belt across his lap.

"Can't you take off these handcuffs?" Stoner asked through his burlap hood. "It's damned uncomfortable."

The two men with him said nothing. They left him alone, closing the partition door behind them.

The plane lurched into movement. Since the engines had not yet started, Stoner realized they were being towed to the runway. He heard voices through the flimsy partition, all of them speaking in English, although the accents told him none of the speakers were natives of the language.

That means they come from different countries, Stoner thought. Their native tongues differ, so they speak the international language: English. Which means that they're not all Hungarian. Whoever Janos is working for, it's not the president of Hungary anymore. Nor the Hungarian government.

Maybe it never was. The thought startled him.

Li-Po Hsen eased back in the sunken Japanese hot tub and allowed the nearly scalding water to cover him almost to his chin.

Of all the luxuries that one could have on the Moon, abundant water was still the most precious. The engineers could manufacture water out of oxygen from the lunar rocks and hydrogen from the solar wind, imbedded in the top few centimeters of the soil. But it took so much energy to harvest the hydrogen and to extract the oxygen that water was literally more expensive than titanium on the Moon.

Pacific Commerce had spaceport operations at each of the half-dozen bases on the Moon, no matter who owned the base itself. Hsen's only competition in space transportation came from Vanguard Industries, and even at Vanguard's facilities in Archimedes and elsewhere Pacific shared the transport franchise.

Hsen's own private retreat on the Moon was at Pacific Commerce's recreational facility at Hell, a twenty-mile-wide impact crater where Pacific had built a casino and posh tourist hotel that catered to mountain climbers and other kinds of gamblers.

It pleased Hsen that his safe retreat was in Hell, a crater named after a Jesuit astronomer, irony upon irony. He had built a modest home for himself there, deep underground, since he did not want to attract the attention of potential rivals and enemies. No one should suspect that the head of Pacific Commerce could live in comfort for as long as he wished on the Moon. Therefore his household staff was small, his quarters almost spartan when compared to his various homes on Earth.

The chambers were decorated in Japanese style, which seemed most appropriate for the setting. Spare, clean, the rooms almost empty of furniture. Except for the western conveniences such as a large, comfortable bed hidden behind wall panels. Instead of wood panelling and flooring, Hsen's quarters used plastic manufactured on the Moon, textured and painted to resemble wood. It was not that a man of Hsen's means could not afford to bring the necessary wood to the Moon; he used lunar plastic to avoid calling attention to a domicile he intended to keep secret.

Now he lay back in his steaming tub while two boyishly slim young women knelt at the tub's edge, naked and silent, waiting to administer to whatever whim possessed their master.

But Hsen's attention was focused on the screen of the telephone that had been placed on the floor at the edge of the sunken tub. Vic Tomasso's face looked wary, evasive. The man was smiling, but his eyes were cold. Tomasso was in the tourist hotel built into Hell's ringwall, above Hsen's deeply-buried quarters.

"Please give me a direct answer," Hsen said with the soft hiss of a dagger sliding out of its sheath. "Do you have the plan of Delphi base or do you not?"

"Not yet," Tomasso said.

"You will be able to get it? You realize that the information you have given me so far concerning this so-called secret base is useless without some actual proof of its existence."

"It's there, all right," Tomasso countered. "Hard to find, I know, but it's there."

"And the proof?"

"I can get it for you."

"How soon?"

Tomasso's eyes shifted away, then returned to Hsen's gaze again. "I don't like to be blunt, but—what's in it for me?"

Hsen nodded once, slightly, a movement that dipped his chin into the steaming water. "A reasonable question. At the moment you are being followed by an operative from Ms. Camerata's household—"

"What?"

Suppressing a smile of pleasure at the man's surprise, Hsen replied, "One of the Italians from her personal staff followed you from the space station to your hotel."

"I didn't see . . ." Tomasso's voice trailed off, his face went slightly pale.

"In payment for your information about Delphi—*complete* information about its location and layout—in return for that I will protect you from the bitch's personal assassin."

Tomasso licked his suddenly-dry lips and agreed to the bargain.

TOKYO

THE rioting had gone completely beyond all control. From the walls of the old imperial palace to the heart of the Ginza, hundreds of thousands of maddened Japanese battled the police, the army, each other. They howled and screamed. They threw stones and homemade fire bombs at the police, who crouched behind plastic riot shields as they were slowly forced to retreat. The tear gas that the police fired into the mob had no effect; there were simply too many people. Those who were gassed were trampled underfoot by those behind them.

Panic. Outright terror. The riot had started when a young woman had collapsed on the platform of a commuter train station, writhing and screaming in terrible agony. The Horror had struck once again.

But this time the others on the station platform made a mad rush for the exits. Fifty people were crushed to death in the panic. The terrified people spilled out into the streets of a heavily-trafficked shopping area, running blindly to escape the Horror.

Like an infectious agent of its own the panic swept the shopping area and spread onward at the speed of human sight and hearing. The Horror. The Horror is *here*! It is striking down people left and right. No one is safe. Run! Run!

It was the end of the working day, the time of the homeward-bound commuter rush, a time for catching a train or driving through the impossibly heavy traffic or just sitting down at a bar and trying to relax before going home or out to an evening's entertainment. Millions were in the streets. The word of the Horror spread like a brush fire and the millions of individual men and women, in their business suits and flowered dresses and working clothes, all those myriad minds and bodies became a single ferocious terrified wild animal desperately trying to escape the Horror and not knowing which way to run.

Within minutes riot police began pouring out into the streets, helmets buckled tight, electric stun wands and tear gas grenades clipped on their equipment harnesses. The many-faced feral animal of the mob swarmed them under. More police came out to do battle, then the army. Someone fired into the crowd, live ammunition that killed and maimed hundreds, and still the mob howled and brawled, smashing windows now, overturning cars and buses, burning and breaking in their blind fear and fury.

The huge video screens that rose ten stories high on virtually every street corner in downtown Tokyo showed the rioters scenes of themselves, taken from news helicopters buzzing overhead like busy insects seeking the nectar of sensation. The enormously enlarged video scenes pollinated the riot, nourished the mindless animal below with electronic feedback. Downtown Tokyo began to burn fiercely while the news cameras recorded its funeral pyres.

Abruptly all the news cameras turned to a single saffron-robed figure who stepped out of a police helicopter that had touched down on the lawn in front of the old imperial palace. While the police officers watched wide-eyed from behind their bulletproof visors, the slim, almost frail, saffron-robed man calmly walked across the wooden bridge that arched over the ancient moat and entered the swirling, maddened mob of terrified people.

It was as if a powerful extinguisher had been played against a rampaging fire. As if calming oil had been poured on raging waters. The rioters stopped where they were, clothing torn, faces scratched, breathing labored. The man in the saffron robe looked at them, his head turning right and then left, and raised one hand in benediction.

The people sank to their knees. A single murmur spread through the crowd. "Varahamihara." The huge video screens all around the city showed the same scene and everywhere the rioters stopped and gaped in awe.

"Varahamihara. Varahamihara."

The lama walked the whole distance from the palace to the Ginza, blessing all on his way. They dropped to their knees as he approached and watched with open-mouthed veneration as the Great Soul passed by them. When he moved too far to be seen they craned their necks to watch him on the video screens. He said nothing. He made no speech. He merely turned the terrified mindless mob back into individual human beings, who—tattered, bleeding, shame-faced—made their individual ways back to their individual homes.

CHAPTER 29

FROM his solitary seat in the rear of the plane, the burlap hood still over his head, Stoner closed his eyes and probed cautiously for the minds of those who were sitting on the other side of the partition.

It was uncomfortable sitting with his wrists tightly cuffed behind him, but his star brother constantly massaged the muscles of his arms and hands with microbursts of nerve impulses so that the blood circulated properly despite his enforced cramped position. Stoner paid no conscious attention to these ministrations; he took them for granted. All his attention was concentrated on reaching out mentally to touch the faint tendrils of fields generated by other human brains, the barely-discernible energy that comes with thought.

The human brain generates about two-hundredths of a watt of electrical power, he told himself. It would take a thousand people to light a twenty-watt bulb. His star brother replied, But it is the complexity of the fields that the brain generates, not their power, that counts. Stoner silently acknowledged the truth of it.

He felt Ilona Lucacs's presence, easy to detect because she wanted so desperately not to be alone. Janos was sitting beside her, separated by the aisle that ran down the middle of the compartment, separated from her by his own indifference and swelling cancerous ambition.

There were four others in the plane, plus the two pilots in the cockpit up front. Stoner thought about probing Janos's mind; he was curious to find who the Hungarian was actually working for. A good deal of money was behind Janos's research. Obviously the president of Hungary had been a cover, a straw man to hide the real source from view. But he feared alerting Janos, making him realize that this makeshift hood they had pulled over his face was not enough to protect him. So he did not probe Janos.

Instead Stoner caught fragments of conversation, the mental formulations that produced the sounds of speech. Two of the men were talking about something called the Horror. Something that killed with great pain. A disease. A new plague.

"We'll be safe from it on the Moon," said one of the men.

"I hope you're right," said the other.

The Moon! We're going to a lunar settlement, Stoner realized.

His surprise, though, was quickly smothered as he probed the speakers for information about this plague they called the Horror. Gradually, as the plane droned hour after hour southeastward, Stoner learned about the Horror.

And was horrified. A plague that strikes without warning. Incredibly painful, quickly fatal. Spreading across the world, particularly in the biggest cities, the megalopolises that had engulfed whole countrysides around them. Spread at supersonic speed by the airliners that jetted across the world. Killing women, mostly. Especially pregnant women. Carried by unsuspecting people flying from one major city to another, carrying death that burned their insides away and killed them in excruciating agony.

The only way to stop the Horror's spread was to stop all air traffic. Which would break down the world economy and cause a different kind of plague: hunger, starvation, actual famines in the poorest parts of the world. The kind of thing that Stoner had spent the past fifteen years struggling against.

And then a new realization broke upon him with all the terror and pain of a tidal wave crushing the life out of him.

The plague is man-made! Stoner knew it with a certainty that excluded all doubt. And his star brother silently, numbly agreed.

The world's medical researchers are looking for a virus, but the Horror is caused by—

His star brother shuddered within him. The Horror is caused by virus-sized devices that are parasites, rather than symbiotes. Some human being has started to create nanotechnology weapons. The thing we feared most of all is beginning to destroy the human race.

Stoner sat in shocked, stunned silence as the plane droned on across the Indian Ocean. Someone, somewhere, has discovered nanotechnology. Someone has produced nanometer-sized machines that kill. And there's no way on Earth for human medical knowledge to stop this Horror.

No way on Earth.

Nunzio Palestrina had the dogged patience of a thousand years of southern Italian peasantry bred deep into his bones. His family line stretched back to the days when Naples had been a kingdom, briefly independent, more often under the iron-handed control of Normans or Austrians or Spaniards or French. For generations Nunzio's peasant forebears had learned to be patient and to forget nothing. For generations they had waited for the darkness of night and the tenacity of blood ties to help them fight enemies too powerful to face in the daylight.

In a world at peace, where nations no longer fought or invaded one another, there was still work for a man of Nunzio's background. The family was always there, its bonds of blood and marriage stretching across oceans. *La Signora* was a distant cousin, born in New England and now living on a tropical island far from Italy. Like many a contessa before her, she had enemies. Her enemies were the enemies of Nunzio, by simple fact of family allegiance.

She paid well, and Nunzio was able to help his many sons and daughters to build homes of their own in the old country. His family grew stronger, thanks to the generosity of *La Signora*.

Now she had sent him to the Moon, of all places, to find *un' pezzo de merde* named Tomasso. And do what? Watch him. Nothing more. Simply watch him, without being seen. On the Moon. Watch and wait.

Nunzio shrugged and obeyed. He checked into the fancy hotel on the Moon, where the names were all diabolical: the hotel itself was called Hell's Haven; the casino was Dante's Inferno; even the restaurants had names such as Satan's Pit and The Devil's Den.

Nunzio found it very distasteful, perhaps blasphemous. He did not truly believe in the Church, of course, not the prancing effeminate men who sermonized against sin while they counted their gold in the Vatican. But still, it was not proper to make light of hell and its denizens.

Yet the hotel was very comfortable. Completely underground, but except for the fact that you had to wear special weighted boots unless you enjoyed hopping around like a fool, the place was not too different from windowless gamblers' hotels in Europe and America.

After three days of avoiding the casino and the women who smiled enticingly even at gray-haired old Italians, Nunzio began to think that Tomasso was never going to leave this place called Hell.

It was a total surprise when a baby-faced bellboy brought a complimentary breakfast into his room on the morning of his fourth day in the hotel and shot him with an air pistol that fired a lethally poisonous dart into his neck. Nunzio did not even have time to raise a hand. He slumped over in his chair by the TV wall, dead within seconds.

The bellboy stabbed at the telephone keyboard with the end of the teaspoon he had carried on the breakfast tray. He made two calls. One to Hsen's chief of security, to tell the woman that his task had been completed. The second was to the hotel's doctor, to tell him that an elderly Italian gentleman had apparently been taken by a heart attack.

The dart had melted away and its tiny puncture wound had closed by the time the puffing red-faced doctor arrived in the room.

Cliff Baker stayed semi-drunk all the way to the Moon. It was not too difficult to do, especially during the enforced layover at the Earth-orbiting space station. Everyone had to wait there twenty-four hours, the grisly incubation time of the Horror.

Acting more swiftly than Baker had ever thought they could, the World Health Organization's researchers had determined that it took no more than twenty-four hours between the time a person contracted the plague and the time when the Horror ripped out its victim's guts. Twenty-four hours from first contact to screaming excruciating death throes.

So everyone heading Moonward was detained for twenty-four hours at one of the space stations. Perfunctory medical exams were made by the largely automated diagnostic systems, and then the traveler waited.

The space stations took on a macabre holiday air. Their corridors and shopping arcades and restaurants were filled with brittle laughter and talk of "Eat, drink, and be merry . . ." It was like Halloween night, continuously. Sales of Edgar Allan Poe tapes skyrocketed. One enterprising shopkeeper even organized a bizarre party for all the tourists aboard the station based on "The Masque of the Red Death."

The station's supply of antihistamines was bought out immediately, no matter how quickly it was replenished by cargo shuttles from Earth. A single sneeze was enough to terrify everyone. Anyone who sneezed in public was immediately locked away in solitary confinement for twenty-four hours.

Baker walked uncertainly through the long sloping corridors of the space station, never fully sober, never entirely drunk. Just a pleasant haze, a crooked grin on his fleshy face.

What do they do when somebody comes down with the Horror? he asked himself. Pop 'em out an airlock? Wrap the body in plastic and ship it home? What happens to all the other people who're aboard the bloody station when the Horror strikes? They're all sent back Earthside, of course. Can't contaminate our space habitats. They've gotta be kept pristine pure. Safe havens in case the whole fucking world gets its guts ripped out by the Horror.

Baker laughed to himself, out loud. No one around him noticed or cared. They were all cloaked in their own forced gaiety, their own unavailing antidotes for terror.

I've got the answer to all the world's problems, Baker shouted at them silently. He weaved through the human traffic that constantly streamed along the station's main corridor, peering blearily into their faces.

I'm the savior of the human race, he said to himself, and they don't even know it.

It had all been so simple. The human race's big problem was overproduction. Population growth. Everybody and his brother was working furiously to reduce the birthrate. For years. For decades. Baker suspected that even Jo Camerata and her weird, alien husband were trying to do that—he more than she, he knew. Jo would help her fellow human beings only after she had helped herself. Long after.

But reducing the birthrate was a long, slow process that might not work, in the final account. How much easier to increase the death rate!

He giggled to himself as he reached for the flask at the belt of his coveralls and brought it to his lips. Pure unblended whisky. Those kilted sonsofbitches certainly knew how to get the best out of their barley.

Increase the death rate. And not among the poor, the hungry, the people at the bottom of the ladder. Kill the rich! Baker savored the idea once again. Slaughter the guilty, not the innocents. Strike down the ones who can travel by jet airliners. *Use* the jets as a vector for the disease. Kill the bitches who make the babies; get them first of all. Make them scream at just the thought of motherhood!

It was all going better than Baker had ever thought it could. The giant cities of the world, the great megalopolises with their proud towers, were starting to die. The plague was only the beginning. Already there was panic over the Horror, riots in the streets. The proud cities were starting to self-destruct.

And I'll be on the Moon, friends and neighbors, safe as houses, watching you kill yourselves. How's *that* for solving the world's problems?

The quarantine made no sense to Jo.

"It will take more than twenty-four hours to make the trip," she said impatiently as her captain held the WHO quarantine order in his hand. "If anyone aboard is going to come down with the Horror it will happen before we're ready to land at Archimedes."

The main compartment of the Vanguard spacecraft was fitted out like the interior of a luxurious business jet, except that there were no windows. Jo was buckled into one of the big padded seats, feeling slightly queasy in zero gravity despite the pills she had taken. The captain, who had something of a reputation for zero-gee sexual gymnastics, had strapped himself into the facing chair to talk with her.

Rickie was in the sleeping compartment, in the rear, enjoying the thrill of weightlessness for the first time in his life. Unlike adults, the boy seemed to suffer no symptoms of space sickness at all. When Jo had last looked in on him Rickie had been happily floating in mid-air, turning somersaults and twisting himself into pretzel shapes.

"Ma'am, the World Health Organization . . ."

Her captain was a young man, very competent, with a video star's rugged good looks and a record of solid reliability. He wore a Vanguard uniform of midnight blue with the stylized V of the corporate logo on the chest of his tunic. Briefly Jo wondered what it would be like to make love in zero gravity,

what he could do once he took the uniform off. She thought
of Keith, a pang of sudden guilt mixed with the worry and
dread she had carried inside her for nearly two weeks.

"Captain," said Jo, making herself smile, "I will not allow
my son to be exposed to god knows how many tourists and
workers for twenty-four hours at a space station. Any one of
them might have the Horror! And then what?"

The captain's brows knitted with concern. "We could sit
tight inside this craft while parked alongside the station. We
wouldn't even have to dock."

"No," Jo said firmly. "We will make our rendezvous with
the transfer rocket as scheduled and go on to Archimedes directly. You will file that flight plan, and if anyone from World
Health tries to interfere you will refer them to me."

The responsibility lifted from his shoulders, the captain
smiled at his boss, unbuckled his seat belt and floated up
from the chair.

Jo leaned her head back on the padded chair. I will not ex-
pose Rickie to the slightest chance of contracting the Horror.
Never! I'll keep him on the Moon or in one of the Lagrange
habitats until this plague is over. I don't care if it takes years.

She would protect her son. And her daughter. In the spacecraft's cargo hold, the delicate apparatus of an artificial womb
was tenderly held in thick shockproof webbing inside heavy
radiation shielding. The cloning team was coming up in a separate craft. They had assured Jo that a few days in zero gravity
would not affect the fetus that was growing inside the womb,
cloned from Cathy's cells. "It's effectively in zero gravity inside the womb anyway," said the chief medic. "It's floating in
the fluid like a little tadpole."

Jo had frowned at comparing her daughter to a tadpole, and
she frowned now as she recalled the bald medic's words. But
Cathy was with her, and Rickie, and she would see to it that
they were safe and beyond all harm.

But Keith. Where was Keith? When will I be with him again?

Yet even while she ached for her husband, Jo felt a tiny
undercurrent of seething anger. Once on the Moon, she in-

tended to squeeze Vic Tomasso until she learned all that he knew and then execute him for Cathy's murder. Then she would find Hsen, wherever he was hiding, and broil him over a slow fire. But she knew that Keith would never stand for that. He was too different, too alien, to feel the normal human hatred and thirst for vengeance that Jo felt.

Keith will try to stop me from killing them. He'll want to understand them, convert them, allow them to change their lives and their ways. Jo's fists clenched until the nails bit into her palms. I want them *dead*. They killed Cathy and I'm going to kill them, no matter what Keith wants.

It was not the first time she had faced the realization that if she were actually reunited with her husband, he would try to work against her.

Maybe it's better if I don't find him, Jo thought. Not just yet.

She tried to bury the guilt she felt over that. And she was successful, except that as she slept on the way to the Moon her dreams were filled with images of roasting her enemies over red-hot coals. And Keith was one of the men she tortured.

CHAPTER 30

THEY were getting closer to Koku. Lela sensed that the gorilla was near. No matter how urgently she warned him to flee from these murdering marauders, Koku seemed reluctant to run away.

As they struggled up the steep slope of a hill, the thick foliage so wet from the night's rain that they were all soaked through to the skin despite their heavy khaki clothing, Lela desperately tried to make Koku understand that he must run away.

But she could feel the young gorilla's confusion. The only humans that Koku had known had been at the university park, where men and women such as herself had lovingly tended the baby gorillas and reared them from infancy with all the care and affection of foster parents. Koku did not know that humans could kill.

"Take five," gasped the blond leader. The men flopped to the soaking ground, breathing hard from the punishing climb. The two blacks were up ahead of Lela, leading the way along a trail of flattened foliage so clear that even she could see it in the thick, dripping brush. Behind her was the redhead with the foul mouth and his silent friend. The leader stayed at Lela's side.

Her boots were soaked through and she could feel her feet blistering inside them. Sitting on the wet ground, she stared up at the menacing gray sky and wondered hopelessly what was going to happen to her.

And Koku.

Closing her eyes, she saw the world as the gorilla did. Koku was very near, she realized with a shock of fear.

He sniffed the breeze wafting across the steep hillside and smelled the faint tang of gun oil and tobacco. Koku put down the thorny blackberry branch he was nibbling on and hauled himself up on all fours. *Lela.* Lela afraid. Fear had a smell to it. From the biochip implanted in his brain Koku sensed Lela's terrible fear. And he vaguely saw men sitting on the ground, heard them speaking, saw one of them puffing on a slim white cigarette.

Dimly Koku remembered a man who had smoked in the house where he had been reared. Lela had pulled the cigarette from the man's mouth and shouted angrily at the man.

Now Lela was afraid. Koku felt her fear inside his own mind as he turned away from the men and from Lela and resumed his climb up to the crest of the ridge, shambling through the thick foliage in the characteristic knuckle-walking gorilla way, mashing the bushes and grass flat beneath his ponderous bulk.

Koku obeyed Lela's wordless warning. He moved away from the humans, away from Lela. But slowly, reluctantly.

*   *   *

The Pacific Commerce shuttle coasted weightlessly through the emptiness between the Earth and the Moon. Zippered into fiber mesh cocoons, the passengers slept and dreamed their separate dreams. All except Stoner, who lay awake, strapped into a sleep cocoon with the burlap hood still over his head and his wrists still cuffed behind his back.

Four pilots—two humans and two computers—monitored the spacecraft's flight up in the cockpit. Stoner knew that there was little for them to do in this stage of the journey. The craft was coasting on a trajectory that Isaac Newton could have predicted, as inert as a rock as it glided from one world to another in the frictionless vacuum of space.

Nature abhors a vacuum, Stoner mused to himself. The human pilots up front think that space is empty, but Stoner could feel the energies that pulsed all around them: particles streaming from the Sun, magnetic fields reverberating like the strings of a stupendous bass viol thrumming notes that no human ear could perceive, cosmic radiation singing of the death of stars and their rebirth.

Some people see a desert as a barren wasteland; others see life thriving there. Humans believe that space is a vacuum when it's actually the vibrant plasma of the universe, Stoner thought. How easy it would be to lose yourself eternally in this so-called emptiness; to go on and on forever, looking, listening, tasting the wonders of creation.

But there was work to do, he reminded himself. No time to swim among the star clouds. Not yet.

Ilona Lucacs was barely asleep, miserable and writhing inside her zippered mesh cocoon, alone and longing for the pleasure of her electronic stimulator. Stoner soothed her and she began to dream of her father. Her body relaxed as she saw the man she loved beyond all measure smiling at her approvingly. The man sometimes looked like her father, sometimes like Zoltan Janos. And now and again his face resembled the bearded visage of Keith Stoner.

Janos was deep in dreams, his eyes scanning rapidly back

and forth beneath their closed lids. With all of the Hungarian's conscious defenses down, it was easy for Stoner to look deeply into Janos's mind and to learn who was behind his abduction and the murder of his daughter.

Stoner's own eyes widened as he learned the truth. His hands behind his back clenched into fists powerful enough to snap the flimsy chain of the handcuffs. But he caught himself just in time.

It isn't the moment to strike. Not yet. Get them all together first. All of them. Until that moment, don't let them know what you can do. Let them keep on believing they're leading a lamb to slaughter. Don't show the wolf's teeth until you can get each and every one of them.

"Can't I go with you?"

Rickie said it in the semi-whine of a ten-year-old being told to come in from play and wash up for dinner. But Jo saw the fear in his eyes.

He had spent the day exploring the Archimedes facility under the watchful care of two security men, and now he sat unhappily in a big chair in his mother's office, looking to Jo like a little boy on the verge of tears.

Jo was sitting on the edge of the sofa next to her son. She made a bright smile for him. "It wouldn't be much fun for you. It's a business trip. You'll enjoy staying here at Archimedes more."

"I don't want you to go away," Rickie said.

Even on the Moon Jo had an apartment/office suite that was exactly like her suites at other Vanguard centers. The only difference here at Archimedes was that she wore special weighted boots to counter the gentle lunar gravity and save her from undignified stumbles and hops when she tried to walk.

Nearly everyone wore simple coveralls on the Moon. Most of the Vanguard employees' outfits were color-coded: tan for administration, coral red for security, yellow for engineering, pumpkin orange for maintenance, blue for research, apple green for safety. Jo was in a metallic silver zippered suit that bore only a faint resemblance to coveralls. And her weighted boots glittered stylishly.

Rickie enjoyed the low gravity. He bounced and leaped across furniture and up the walls. He never walked when he could hop like a kangaroo. Even when he did misjudge and stumble he could put out his hands and right himself before hitting the floor. In less than a day he had become a veteran lunar resident. He loved being on the Moon. But the thought of being separated from his mother clearly troubled him.

"It will only be for a day or two," Jo told her son. "Aunt Claudia and Max will be right here with you."

Rickie did not seem reassured. "What's so special about where you're going?"

"It's business, Rickie. Something mother's got to do."

"I want to go with you. I'll be good, I promise."

Jo got off the sofa and knelt on the carpeted floor. Wrapping her son in her arms, she said softly, "I know you'd be good, dearest. But this isn't the kind of trip that you'd enjoy. You'd be bored and very unhappy."

Rickie clung to her.

"Listen," she said. "While I'm gone, Max can take you up to the flying center. You can rent wings there and fly around the main dome. Would you like that?"

"Can I? And do high dives in the swimming pool?"

She hesitated. "You'll have to take a few classes in low-gee acrobatics before you can do that."

Rickie grinned at his mother and agreed to be a good boy while she was gone. She excused him and he dashed happily toward the door and his own room down the underground corridor from her office. There were wall-sized video screens there, and he could go exploring the Moon from the safety of a snug apartment more than twenty meters below the radiation-drenched airless lunar surface.

Claudia's like a she-wolf when it come to Rickie, she told herself. *And Max has two kids of his own back Earthside, so he'll know how to take care of him while I'm gone. Rickie will be all right.* Jo repeated that to herself several times until she almost believed it.

Then she went back in her swivel chair and began completing the arrangements to travel out to Delphi base. She thought about Nunzio. A fatal heart attack while sitting in his hotel room at Hell Crater. No one in that family had ever had heart problems. They died of cancer in their nineties, or shotgun blasts much earlier. Nunzio had been murdered. By Vic Tomasso or the man Vic worked for, Hsen.

Jo felt a brief twinge of guilt. Maybe Nunzio had become too old for such work. Maybe she should have sent a younger man, or at least some backup. But old or not he had located Vic for her, and that was what she had asked him to do. Of course, Vic could lose himself among the tourists coming and going at Hell. He might even double back to Earth. But she knew, and she knew *he* knew, that if he set foot on Earth there would be Vanguard people to track him down.

No, Jo said to herself, staring up at the featureless smooth ceiling of her office, Vic will stay here on the Moon. Under Hsen's protection. I've got to flush him out. Flush both of them out where I can deal with them. The ceiling was painted plastic sheeting that covered the bare lunar rock from which the room had been carved. Every day Vanguard security personnel checked her suite for electronic bugs. Jo had swept the office herself, with her own pocket-sized detector, barely an hour earlier.

Now she smiled and leaned across her desk to touch the keypad of her phone unit. She told the computerized voice that answered that she would need a cross-country tractor with a driver and two security men.

"I'm going to visit Delphi first thing tomorrow morning," Jo added. It was a serious breach of her own security regulations to give such information over an ordinary telephone link.

Then she buzzed the chief of Archimedes's security office and asked her to come to her office. In person. With no tappable communications links between them. Rickie's protection had to be absolutely foolproof. So did Cathy's.

They may call this place Hell, thought Vic Tomasso, but it's more like paradise to me.

He was living out an old fantasy, running up win after win at the craps table while the crowd grew and all eyes focused on him. White dinner jackets were *de rigueur* at the casino, even though it was permissible to wear baggy gym pants beneath them. Vic glimpsed himself in the big ceiling-high mirror behind the craps table: the lapelless jacket looked terrific with its padded shoulders and his pale-blue shirt with the bow tie painted on it.

He threw the dice again and watched in fascination as they tumbled slowly in the soft lunar gravity and came up eleven. The crowd gasped and applauded. The croupier chanted, "The man wins again!" and pushed a small mountain of chips toward Vic.

Gorgeous women in low-cut glittery gowns with warmly inviting smiles clustered around Vic. He took the dice in hand once more, but before he could throw again, someone tapped him firmly on his padded shoulder.

A blank-faced oriental, small and slight as a child, almost. Yet he looked mercilessly dangerous, the kind who used knives in the dark.

"Mr. Hsen wishes to see you immediately."

The stress on *immediately* was very slight, but very noticeable. Vic put down the dice and told the two women on either side of him to split his winnings between them. They squealed with delight.

"Plenty more where they came from," Vic said lightly to the oriental. The man did not reply.

Swiftly they went down the special elevator to Hsen's private quarters.

Li-Po Hsen was pacing back and forth in the spartan living room, hands clasped behind his back, so deep in furious thought that he paid no attention to the holograms of Ming vases and bronze horses that decorated the room. The plastic flooring and ceiling beams lovingly painted to resemble actual wood, the imitation oriental carpets and tapestries, the sweeping video window that showed the Great Wall snaking over hills as far as the eye could see—all were ignored.

"She's going to Delphi," Hsen snapped as Tomasso entered the breathtaking room.

"How do you know?" he replied automatically.

"She ordered a cross-country tractor for tomorrow morning."

"How do you know?" Tomasso repeated.

"The telephone lines!" Hsen nearly shouted. "Do you think I'm without my resources?"

Tomasso stopped a few paces before the Chinese. He knew that Hsen did not like to have taller men standing close to him. It pleased Tomasso to be taller than this powerful, ruthless oriental. But he took his pleasure sparingly; Hsen was obviously upset, and there was no sense turning that anger toward himself.

"I don't like it," Tomasso said. "Jo knows better than using phones . . ."

"Perhaps she feels safe at Archimedes."

With a shake of his head, "She must know that the old man is dead. Why should she feel safe?"

Gazing up at Tomasso, Hsen stroked his chin thoughtfully. "You suspect a trap?"

"Could be."

Hsen clasped his hands behind his back again and walked slowly across the carpeting of lunar imitation silk toward the holographic display of the Great Wall.

"What would Sun-tzu have done in a situation such as this?" he muttered.

"Sun-tzu?"

Hsen turned back toward Tomasso with a disdainful look on his face, almost a sneer. "A great general. The first of the great generals, twenty-five centuries ago."

Tomasso shrugged.

For several minutes Hsen stood stock-still, head bowed. Then he looked up and smiled thinly.

"When facing a trap," he said, "offer your enemy a piece of bait so that you may trap the trapper."

Oriental bullshit, Vic said to himself.

"Since you are familiar with the location and layout of this secret Vanguard facility," Hsen went on, his voice like a cobra's hiss, "you will follow Ms. Camerata tomorrow. You will spring her trap."

"Hey, wait a minute! She wants . . ."

"I will follow with a force large enough to destroy her. Have no fear, you will be perfectly safe at all times."

Vic Tomasso looked into Hsen's glittering eyes and knew there was no way to argue him out of his decision. He did not want to face Jo, of course, but he certainly had no way of saying no to Hsen.

BRASILIA

JOÃO de Sagres stood by the window of his office and looked out at the magnificent towers and sweeping curves of the buildings that comprised the capital of Brazil. In a few minutes the cabinet meeting would begin and he had to find an answer to the Horror that had begun its reign of terror in Latin America.

Once, many years ago, when he looked out this window he saw shacks made of hammered tin cans and cardboard huddling on the outskirts of the federal precinct. Now they were replaced by modern housing blocks, concrete, functional. The poor still existed, the problems of poverty and hunger still gnawed, but they were being solved—slowly, with patience. And with love.

De Sagres sighed heavily. Yes, love. It was impossible even to begin to approach the problems of the poor without love. That had been the great revelation: You must love your neighbor as yourself, and you must love yourself as you love your God. Otherwise you get bureaucrats and swindlers and opinion polls and computer-generated graphs in place of helping the needy. Cold impersonal bureaucracies do not solve problems. You must go out into the alleys, out among those old dilapidated shacks, among the poor and filthy and sick, just as did our Lord and Savior.

And now, as things were beginning to get better, just as de Sagres himself was finally understanding what had happened to him and what his true place in the world of his fellow human beings should be, now the Horror had reached its bloody fingers into the heart of Rio, São Paulo, Caracas.

It would reach Brasilia any day now. Unless he acted.

De Sagres squeezed his eyes shut and asked his star brother, What would Stoner do? The man had changed his life forever and then left him to face these crises alone, without help or guidance. What would Stoner do?

His star brother told him.

De Sagres's eyes popped open and he grinned to himself, almost sheepishly. He could see Stoner staring at him silently. What would Stoner do? He would tell me to stand on my own two feet and stop looking for a crutch.

The president of Brazil squared his shoulders and sighed like a man ready to face an unpleasant duty. He walked across the tiled floor of his office and threw open the double doors that led into the cabinet meeting chamber.

The cabinet members rose to their feet. He took his chair at the head of the table and announced without preamble:

"We must quarantine those who have been close enough to a victim of the Horror to have caught the disease. And we must quarantine all incoming passengers at every international airport and seaport for twenty-four hours, just as they do at the space stations."

That started a debate that took hours to settle. Cabinet ministers protested that such measures would cost too much, that there were not enough trained personnel to carry out such quarantines, that there were no facilities at the airports to hold incoming travelers for twenty-four hours, that the ports would be deserted and the economy would crash.

De Sagres heard them all, each minister, each objection, and invited them to use their wits to *solve* the problems they foresaw. Four and a half hours later they had hammered out a plan to contain the Horror. It would require a huge increase in paramedical personnel. It would require a massive rearrangement of the facilities at each of the international airports. It would require the cooperation of the media.

It would be done.

"This Horror comes from the pits of hell," de Sagres said, his voice trembling with emotion. "But we will show that men of good will and good sense can stop it. We will serve as an example to the rest of the world. We cannot cure the unfortunate wretch who is struck by this Devil's evil, but we can take the necessary steps to prevent its spread. With God's help, we will prevail."

Four of the cabinet members had training in medicine. Two of them had been practicing physicians and the other two research scientists before entering public service. None of them had thought to ask, that, though the incubation time for the disease was apparently less than twenty-four hours, could there be a dormant phase where the disease agent lay quietly within its human victim, waiting to spring up again at a later time?

CHAPTER 31

STONER knew that the spacecraft was heading for Hell Crater and the Pacific Commerce facility there. Janos had been working for Li-Po Hsen all along.

The president of Hungary had been a figurehead, like so many politicians. In this case, the power behind him was the immense financial and political clout of Pacific Commerce

Corporation. Li-Po Hsen. How many other governments did he control? Stoner wondered.

It had never been difficult to corrupt the average politician. Money and power are irresistible lures. And in an era where politics is played out on the media's screens, the most successful politicians are those who could perform before the cameras, those who reveal their need for adulation, their absolute willingness to say anything that the crowd wants to hear in return for the applause, the approval, the worship of the masses.

No wonder most politicians are emotional cripples, Stoner thought. No wonder an egomaniac like Novotny could be seduced by a powerful international corporation's money and influence. It took a rare person, a de Sagres or Nkona or Varahamihara, to rise above such lures.

Are they enough? he asked himself. His star brother replied, They might have been, if someone had not unleashed the Horror upon the world.

The sleepers were stirring. Stoner closed his eyes and saw their landing through the mind of the spacecraft's captain, up in the cockpit surrounded by panels of complex instrument displays as the pinpoint of light set in the dark lunar wasteland grew into a ring of brilliance, domes outlined in colors, landing pad marked with flashing beacons that grew larger and larger as they descended . . .

Stoner's mind suddenly filled with his last sight of his daughter floating in the lighted pool, her blood spreading across the crystal water as he was carried aloft by the kidnappers' rocket pack, her dead young body dwindling, dwindling as he rose higher, higher into the dark night.

Zoltan Janos bears responsibility for Cathy's death. More than him, though, is Li-Po Hsen. And then Stoner realized there was a third man involved: the traitor whose presence he had felt at his birthday party. Three men.

His star brother replied, At least three. There will undoubtedly be many more.

* * *

"How did you know I was here?" asked Cliff Baker. "I mean, you've got a big facility here and it seems to be jam-packed."

Jo sat tensely, straight upright in her powered chair. Her office at Archimedes was almost exactly like her offices at Hilo and elsewhere. The major difference was that, deep underground, this lunar office had video screens where windows would normally be. At the moment they showed camera views of the barren surface of Mare Imbrium.

She made herself smile at Baker. "I have a subroutine in my daily program that announces the arrival of VIPs."

"I'm a VIP?" Baker's blond eyebrows rose. He was sprawled on one of the small couches, arms spread across its back, slouched halfway down on his spine, booted legs crossed. Instead of the normal lunar coveralls he still wore a sports shirt and chino slacks.

"Don't be coy with me, Cliff." Jo was in metallic silver coveralls. Even the lowliest Vanguard employee at Archimedes could recognize her at a distance of a hundred meters.

"Alright, so I'm an important person. Good of you to let me have a suite at the hotel. I understand it's filled to capacity."

With a slightly nervous nod, Jo admitted, "Everybody who can afford the trip is trying to come here to get away from the Horror. That's why you're here, isn't it?"

"Royt as rayn," said Baker, emphasizing his outback accent. "The bloody plague is starting to wipe out whole cities down there."

"No one's found a way of stopping it yet?"

Baker shrugged. "National governments are starting to quarantine incoming people for twenty-four hours."

"I know. It raises hell with commerce."

"Sure. And it's *beautiful* when somebody who's quarantined at an airport comes down with the Horror. Talk about riots! Fuckin' troops have had to fire live ammunition into the mob. They're killing thousands every day, and not a peep of it gets into the media. Not even in the U.S.! States have declared martial law."

"It's . . ." Jo groped for a word. ". . . terrible."

"Not for us, though," said Baker cheerfully. "We can sit up here and watch the world tear itself apart, safe and sound. Just goes to prove that, rich or poor, it pays to have money."

Jo felt her nerves tightening. "That's my Cliff. Always ready with a snide remark."

He hunched forward, leaning his arms on his thighs, and almost snarled at her, "So what've you done to help? Run away to the Moon, that's what!"

"And you?"

"There's not much I *can* do to help, is there? You and your kind won't vote more money for the medics and you dash up here to avoid the consequences."

The bastard knows that Keith's been abducted, Jo said to herself. He knows Cathy was murdered and Hsen's out to get me. But he doesn't give a damn. He's too busy playing his stupid rich-vs.-poor game to care about actual people.

"So—" Baker leaned back in the couch once more, spread his arms again, "—how long d'you intend to stay up here, luv?"

"I've got work to do here," Jo said.

"Sure. Of course."

Suddenly her temper flared out of control. "You think I don't? You think all I've got to do is sit around here and wait for the plague to die down? You think I'm some kind of latter-day Nero?"

Baker grinned, a lopsided show of pleasure at Jo's pain. "I don't see any fiddle, but . . ."

Jo jumped to her feet. "Come on with me, Cliff. I'll show you what I've got to do! I'll show you things that'll wipe that damned smug smile off your face!"

An hour later Baker was sitting beside Jo in a converted lunar bus as it lumbered across the desolate Imbrium plain. Originally capable of taking a dozen tourists out across the lunar surface on journeys of a week or more, the bus now carried only the two passengers plus its normal crew of three. Her security troops were all still at Archimedes, waiting for her signal to board ballistic rockets that would loft them across the airless Mare Imbrium and land them at the secret base within minutes.

Rickie stayed at Archimedes. Jo was offering herself as bait to trap Hsen, and she did not want Rickie to be involved in more violence. So she left him behind, surrounded by dozens of security men and women, as safe as he could be in a world where private armies and mercenary commandos worked at the behest of giant multinational corporations.

She was certain that Vic Tomasso was on his way to the base, leading an assault force for Hsen. Maybe Hsen himself would come to Delphi base. No, she told herself, that would be too much to hope for. Tomasso would be there. That's enough. For now.

Briefly she wondered if it was smart to go to Delphi herself, to dangle herself as bait for the trap she wanted to spring on her enemies. There's no other way, she concluded. Hsen can't pass up the opportunity to get at me. Whether he suspects a trap or not he'll send Vic to Delphi to take me. She smiled to herself. Besides, I want to be there to see the bastard's face for myself.

The battle between her and Hsen was coming down to its final moves. There was no room in the solar system now for the two of them. Either he dies or I do, Jo told herself. And he knows that. It's gone beyond a corporate power struggle, beyond the battle to control most of the world's wealth and power. It's a personal war between the two of us. A vendetta.

Turning those thoughts over and over in her mind, Jo rode in the plushly furnished, windowless van toward Delphi base. How Nunzio would have been shocked to see a woman involved in a vendetta. Women were not supposed to fight. They could goad their men to fury, they could nourish the generations-long hatreds that set grandson against grandson, they could recite with bitter tears who murdered whom, but they were not expected to do the actual fighting. They stayed at home while the men slaughtered each other, tending to the wounded, keening dirges at the funerals, nursing the acid poison of vengeance all their lives.

Nunzio was dead, though. Murdered. Like Cathy. Killed without mercy or reason because Hsen wants my power and Keith's abilities. Is Keith dead too? She shook her head. Probably not. I just hope he keeps out of the picture until I've finished with Hsen. I don't want him trying to make me forgive the murdering bastard.

She closed her eyes and said to herself, Stay out of my way, Keith. Don't try to stop my revenge. If you force me to choose between you and Cathy, it'll destroy everything we've had together.

As soon as their spacecraft landed, a new team of security people replaced the burlap hood over Stoner's head with a sophisticated black blindfold and a pair of soundproof earphones. Stoner had a brief glimpse of the interior of a spaceport hangar and the solemn faces of strangers clustered around him and then the blindfold cut off all light from his eyes.

Blind and deaf, he was led to another vehicle, strong hands guiding him and then half-boosting him up a ladder and through a low hatch. Someone checked the handcuffs that still pinned his wrists behind his back; apparently satisfied that they were tight enough, the person pushed Stoner down onto a seat and fastened a safety harness across his lap and shoulders.

Stoner knew they were on the Moon. He recognized the gentle lunar gravity, and his star brother immediately helped him compensate his Earth-trained muscles to the lower pull. Then he felt the push of acceleration, like a rocket liftoff but much softer, almost ethereal. Before he could take a breath the acceleration died away and he felt weightless as the rocket craft soared across the airless lunar surface.

His physical senses cut off, Stoner probed with his mind to find out who else was in the rocket vehicle and where they were heading. He sensed Janos and Ilona, but they were the only ones among the eighteen people aboard whom he recognized. The others were all men, all strangers, except . . .

He felt the tingle of discovery: the same sensation he had felt at his birthday party. The same man was aboard this rocket, the traitor from Jo's headquarters. Stoner concentrated on his mind and found that Vic Tomasso knew where they were going and why.

They were heading for Delphi base, out in the bleak and empty Mare Imbrium where he and Jo were constructing the starship. Jo was already on her way there and they meant to trap her there.

Why are they taking me there? Probing deeper, he found the answer in Tomasso's mind. Li-Po Hsen planned to keep Stoner at the isolated base so that Janos could continue his experiments until he uncovered the secrets of Stoner's abilities. Hsen wanted those abilities for himself. Above all, he wanted immortality.

Stoner felt his teeth clenching together so hard that his jaws hurt. Hsen wants immortality for himself and death for Jo. He sees himself as a new Genghis Khan, absolute ruler of all the world, immortal and all-powerful. He wants to be a god.

CHAPTER 32

"WE'VE been thrashing around this bush long enough," muttered the blond leader of the hunters. "That damned gorilla is always ahead of us."

Lela sat on the damp ground and watched silently as the men shrugged out of their rifle straps and backpacks. The last slanting rays of the setting sun made the tree trunks glow almost orange while gray threatening clouds scudded so close that some of the taller trees up along the ridge crest were lost in their misty billows.

There was no dry wood to be found, so the men lit a tin of paraffin and tamped down their miniature cooking grill over its blue flame. One of the blacks started a pot of water boiling while the others laid out their sleeping bags.

The blond leader came over to Lela, who was sitting as far away from the men as she could, her back resting against the moss-covered trunk of a *Hagenia* tree. It had been a punishing day, climbing the steep, heavily wooded slope up past the ten-thousand-foot height, close to the territory where Koku's three females waited for him. Her chest hurt from exertion in the thin air.

The blond sagged wearily to the ground next to Lela. His voice too low for the others to hear, he said, "Now listen carefully. I know about the biochips. I know you're telling the gorilla to keep away from us. You've got to stop that."

"So you can kill him?" Lela wanted to sneer at the blond, but she was surprised to find that her voice was as much of a near-whisper as his.

"That's right. We're not leaving until we've done the job we've been paid to do. And the three females too."

"There is a team of students and rangers patrolling the territory where the females have been placed."

"We'll get past them without any trouble, never you fear."

"And kill them all."

"Just the apes. We're not here to kill people."

"And what about me?" Lela asked, struggling to keep her voice from trembling.

The blond glanced at the other four men, gathered around the minuscule fire.

"I'll make a deal with you," he said. "You stop telling the gorilla to stay away from us, and I'll see to it that you get back to your people safely."

"You want me to trade Koku's life for my own."

"Let us kill the damned ape and get it over with!"

Lela said nothing.

"They're going to rape you, y'know. A nice little gang bang before they kill you. I can protect you."

"Leave me alive to identify you afterward?"

"We'll be long gone from here by the time you get back to your friends. A chopper will pick us up once we send the signal."

She shook her head.

"For god's sake," the blond hissed, "are the gorillas more important to you than your own life?"

"I could ask you the same question."

"I'm offering to let you live if you'll stop protecting the damned animal."

Again Lela went silent. She did not know what to say. She did not believe him, no matter how sincere he sounded. The others would never let her live. They would strip her and rape her and then kill her. And him too, if he tried to stop them.

With a huffing sigh that almost sounded like a gorilla's grunt, the blond hauled himself up to his feet. "Think it over," he said, his voice still low. But now there was menace in it. "Once you're dead, y'know, we'll be able to track the ape down without much trouble."

Lela believed that. She knew it was true.

It was all coming together, like the threads of an ancient tapestry, thought Li-Po Hsen. Individually, each strand means little. But weave them together properly and a beautiful picture emerges. He sank back in his softly yielding recliner chair and twined all the threads together in his mind.

Stoner. The former astronaut. The man who had visited de Sagres and the other Great Souls. Stoner, the only man to survive being frozen, the only one to be reawakened after a sleep of years. The only man to defeat death itself.

From the Hungarian scientists Hsen had learned that Stoner carried within him the alien creature who had built the starship. Within his mind was all the knowledge of the alien technology, secrets that could span the unthinkable gulfs between the stars, secrets that had already provided fusion energy and invisible screens that protected cities from nuclear bombs. How much more did Stoner and the alien within him carry inside his skull? Immortality was merely *one* of the gifts he possessed!

From Tomasso he had learned that Stoner was building a new starship at the Vanguard base out on Mare Imbrium. All the secrets of the aliens were within Stoner's mind! Hsen knew he could not rest until he had all that knowledge for himself.

With such knowledge a man could become absolute ruler of the Earth, he knew. Emperor of emperors! The entire world would kneel at my feet!

But Stoner would never willingly share that knowledge. That is why, Hsen told himself, it is vitally important to have the bitch Camerata in my grasp. If I can control her I can control him.

He knew from the Hungarians and from the stories that Cliff Baker drunkenly reeled off that Stoner had impressive powers. But the Hungarians have learned to protect themselves against his mental abilities. And I will remain safely shielded from him.

Hsen smiled happily. It was all coming together at last. Nothing could stop him now, as long as he remained safely here in his protected headquarters while his trusted employees dangled Tomasso like a piece of bait.

Jo Camerata will snap up Tomasso, and I will have her. With her in my grasp I will have control of Stoner.

For good measure, Hsen thought, I should take the bitch's son. And the artificial womb in which she is trying to reproduce her daughter.

He laughed aloud. With her children in my grasp, I can even get her to bed with me, if I desire her. It was a pleasant thought. He closed his eyes and sank deeper into his enfolding chair, picturing Jo Camerata naked and helpless before him.

Twelve tourists just happened to meet in the lobby of the Vanguard Hotel shortly after Jo and Cliff Baker left Archimedes. Dressed in brightly colored coveralls that were decorated with jeweled clips and patterned scarves of lunar faux-silk, all twelve of them crowded into one of the lobby's elevators.

On the Moon, status was indicated by how many floors *down* one lived. While a penthouse indicated wealth and perhaps power on Earth, the most preferable quarters on the Moon were those furthest from the airless surface, where hard radiation and micrometeoroids constantly churned the lunar dust.

The hotel ran five levels down, but one of the tourists pulled a palm-sized electronic black box from her coverall pocket and applied it to the elevator's control board. With a barely-discernible click, the elevator plunged past the normal five floors, past the basement level where much of the life support equipment for Archimedes base was housed, and down to the sub-basement level that held nothing but the private quarters of the president of Vanguard Corporation.

When the elevator doors at last slid open, the twelve men and women leaped out, weapons in hands, balanced on the balls of their booted feet, ready to spray nontoxic gas from the nozzles of innocent-looking cosmetics cans.

The corridor in which they found themselves was empty.

Their leader, a solidly-built graying man with square shoulders, frowned slightly. No guards in the corridor, not even a robot. Nothing but the tiny red eyes of security cameras set up near the ceiling, and they had been short-circuited moments earlier.

These Vanguard people must be damned cocky about their security, the leader of the attack force thought.

With silent gestures he motioned eight of his force to the left, where the living quarters were, the remaining three to the other end of the corridor, where the makeshift laboratory had been established to hold the artificial womb and its associated apparatus. He himself went with the main body. There was bound to be resistance where they kept the boy.

The woman applied her electronic box to the lock of the living quarters' main door. It popped open and they poured through . . .

Into an empty room. Bare walls. No furniture. Nothing but an absolutely empty room.

"We've been screwed," the leader muttered.

Those were his last words. The air was pumped out of the room, out of the corridor, out of the entire sub-basement level. When a team of Vanguard security personnel came down to clean up, armored and helmeted, with robots leading their way, they found all twelve mercenaries piled in a jumble at the elevator door, their faces blue, tongues swollen in their gaping mouths, their eyes staring, their hands clawing desperately at the elevator door.

Half a mile away, Rickie played ping-pong with a Vanguard robot in the rec room of Archimedes's maintenance department office. Connected to all levels of the underground center by utilities tunnels, the maintenance facility was spacious enough to house several visitors from the security department with ease.

Rickie watched with fascination as the plastic ball arched lazily over the net. Ping-pong in low gravity was a very different game than it was on Earth: more deliberate, like slow motion. Through the open door of the rec room Rickie could see the jumble of equipment where his sister was slowly growing to the point where she would be a baby again.

Rickie paid no attention to the artificial womb. He and the squat little robot were tied, fifteen-all, and he was bending all his energies on winning his game.

The ballistic rocket in which Stoner rode with Vic Tomasso, the two Hungarian scientists, and an assault team of Pacific Commerce commandos did not at all resemble the sleek, slim boosters of Earth. On the airless Moon, the vehicle needed no streamlining. It was round and flat, like a saucer, with six awkward-looking legs sticking out and downward from its rim.

As it began its descent toward Delphi base, Tomasso slid into the seat to the right of the command pilot and buckled the light harness straps over his shoulders. The rocket had only one port, an oblong window of lunar glassteel that curved across the entire cockpit.

Vic still wore his sand-colored Vanguard coveralls, the front open low enough to show several strands of gold necklaces resting on his hairy chest. He slipped a communications headset over his thick curly hair and then, stabbing a forefinger at the comm console master switch, Tomasso said into the pinhead microphone:

"Security override. Access code one-one-eight-three-two, yellow."

A flat, uninflected computer-generated voice immediately replied, "Voiceprint identification accepted. Security override in effect."

"Delphi, this is Tomasso, from corporate headquarters. Approaching in ballistic vehicle. Require clearance to land."

A human voice, male, answered, "Clearance to land approved, Tomasso. This is Matthews. Why the security override and yellow alert?"

"I'll explain when I get down, Matthews. Expect arrival in . . ." Tomasso glanced at the pilot's control displays, ". . . seven minutes and twenty seconds."

"Okay. I'll be at the airlock."

With a nod and a grin, Tomasso shut off the radio. "Dumb bastard'll never know what hit him."

The saucer-shaped rocket landed slowly, its engines kicking up dust from the lunar surface. As it settled on its six spraddling legs, an access tube snaked from Delphi base's main airlock—little more than a rubble-covered dome on the pockmarked surface of Imbrium—and connected to the airlock of the saucer.

True to his word, Matthews was at the airlock in his frayed, faded blue coveralls. The expression on his face went from curiosity to outright shock as Tomasso and the dozen black-uniformed Pacific Commerce commandos poured through the access tube, guns in hands, and started down the power ladder toward the interior of the base.

"What the hell is this?" Matthews demanded.

Tomasso waved a slim automatic pistol in his face. "Stay cool, friend, and nobody will get hurt."

In less than ten minutes the commandos took control of Delphi's communications and life support centers. Tomasso led Matthews into his own office and took the seat behind Matthews's desk. The crew-cut administrator stood in front of the desk, fuming.

"I want to know what in hell you're doing!"

Tomasso was already pecking at the keyboard on the desk top. The display screen showed a list of the base's personnel.

Looking up at the older man, Tomasso said jovially, "This is a sort of corporate takeover, friend. This base is now the property of Pacific Commerce."

"Are you crazy? When Ms. Camerata hears about this . . ."

"She'll be here in another hour or so. She's going to become another Pacific Commerce acquisition."

Matthews's legs seemed to give way. He groped behind himself for the only other chair in the cubbyhole office and sank onto its creaking plastic seat.

Jabbing a thumb at the desktop display screen, Tomasso said, "I want you to assemble each and every member of the base's staff in the cafeteria. Now. I'm going to check them off against this list. If anybody's missing, those guys in the black uniforms are going to start shooting people. Starting with you."

Two levels further down, Paulino Alvarado looked out from the makeshift quarters Matthews had given him and saw strange men in black uniforms with machine pistols in their hands stalking up the corridor. They went right past his door, intent on some task, but Paulino knew they would come looking for him sooner or later.

Police! he thought. Or soldiers.

His pulse thudding in his ears, his palms suddenly clammy, Paulino desperately looked around the tiny cubicle for some means of escape.

Matthews had cleared out one of the small labs that was no longer being used and converted it into living quarters for

Paulino. A folding cot, a set of metal bookshelves that now held a few sets of coveralls, and a portable shower/sink/toilet unit plugged into the former lab's plumbing. Other employees had generously provided odd pieces of clothing, bedsheets, a blanket.

Trapped like a bird in a net! The tiny cubicle had only one door, and it led to the corridor and the armed soldiers. Paulino peeped out into the corridor and saw the men in black pushing a handful of blue-coveralled people back in his direction.

Very softly, but quickly, Paulino closed his door. Leaning against it, he heard the footsteps pass him by, heard a woman asking who the armed men were and what they wanted.

They want me, Paulino knew. I've got to get away.

His eyes darted back and forth across the bare little room. No way out. No escape.

Then he saw the grille covering the heating shaft up by the ceiling. With the strength of desperation he worked it loose and boosted himself on the shaky metal shelving to its level. It was a narrow square tunnel of smooth metal, too small for a man of Matthews's size.

But not too small for Paulino. He scrambled up into the shaft, scraping his knuckles and barking his shins, then wormed around and replaced the grille. It was slightly lop-sided and would fall to the floor if anyone as much as touched it. But it was the best he could do.

Slithering along the shaft, Paulino found himself looking through another grille out into the cafeteria. The whole staff of the base was there, sitting at the tables or standing glumly against the far wall. They looked bewildered, frightened. Like the people of my village must have looked when the soldiers came, Paulino thought.

The men in black uniforms did not start shooting, however. Another man, short, stocky, wearing crisp new coveralls of tan and gold chains around his neck, was calling out names and checking those who answered against a pocket computer he held in his hand.

Finally he said, "All right, that's the entire staff. Good. You people will be staying here until further notice."

Paulino saw Matthews take a step toward the man in the tan coveralls. Several of the soldiers leveled their guns at him.

"There's nothing for you to do, friend," said the man, "except relax and enjoy it."

Then he turned to one of the soldiers and said, "Okay, bring in Stoner and the Hungarians. Set him up the way they want him. Jo Camerata should be arriving in less than an hour."

CHAPTER 33

HUNCHING slightly as she stood behind the driver's seat, Jo saw through the tinted windshield of the lumbering bus the squat saucer shape of the rocket sitting on its spindly legs at Delphi base's main airlock. The saucer was unpainted, unmarked, but she knew that Vic Tomasso had brought an assault team of Pacific Commerce commandos in it to seize the base.

"Check Archimedes," she said curtly to the woman sitting at the driver's right.

The woman, in the coral jumpsuit of the security department, touched the comm panel in front of her with one hand while passing a headset to Jo with the other.

Jo received a terse report from the security chief at Archimedes. The attempt to kidnap Rickie had failed, and all the Pacific Commerce commandos were dead. Three platoons of paramilitary personnel were already aboard ballistic rockets, ready to take off for Delphi at Jo's signal.

"Good," said Jo tightly into the pin mike. "If I don't transmit a signal within half an hour, send the troops."

"Yes, ma'am," said the security chief's voice. He had been with Vanguard since boyhood, and Jo had investigated his background and actions so thoroughly that she knew him better than he knew himself. He was utterly reliable, she would stake her life on that.

I *am* staking my life on him, she told herself as the bus labored over the last small rise in the dust-covered rocky ground and finally groaned to a halt before the auxiliary airlock of Delphi base.

Jo walked down the length of the bus to its main hatch. Cliff Baker pulled himself up from his seat and joined her, a quizzical grin on his puffy face.

"So what's here that's so bloody important?" he asked Jo.

"You'll see soon enough."

It took a few minutes for the personnel inside the small rubble-covered dome to snake out the access tube and make the connection with the bus's main hatch.

At last the indicator light on the wall panel turned green and the hatch popped open with a little sigh. Jo's nose wrinkled at the slight odor of stale air and plastic as she pushed the hatch all the way out. Stepping into the access tube, she felt every sense heightened, every nerve straining taut.

Hsen's not here, she knew, but Vic is. He thinks I don't know he's taken over the base. He thinks he's trapping me.

As she walked slowly along the tube, Baker two steps behind her, she thought, And I think I'm trapping Vic. The kids are safe, so that card's been taken out of Hsen's hand. Even if I can't get to Hsen right away, I'll have Vic in my grasp. And I'm going to squeeze him until his damned traitor's eyes pop out.

She paid no attention to the fact that the two men working the airlock wore black uniforms rather than the blue coveralls of Delphi's staff. With Baker trailing behind her, Jo placed both her booted feet on the power ladder and grasped the rung at the level of her shoulders. It began to descend slowly, the faint hum of an electric motor the only sound in the cramped little dome. Baker followed her down.

Despite herself Jo was trembling inside. More than the anticipation of roasting Vic for his part in killing Cathy, there was something else gnawing at her innards. Not fear. Something else.

The ladder carried down past three landings to the lowest level of the underground base, ending at the juncture of five corridors. Vic was standing there, smiling brightly, as Jo stepped off. He was in the tan coveralls of a Vanguard administrator, the damned traitor, with the front unzipped halfway down his hairy chest to show off three ropes of gold.

"You don't look surprised," he said to Jo.

"Should I be?"

Baker stepped off the ladder, his lopsided grin fading into genuine puzzlement.

"Your bodyguard?" Tomasso asked.

"Hardly," said Jo. "This is Cliff Baker, chairman of the International Investment Agency. You're the one who needs a bodyguard, Vic."

"I've got one."

"They won't be enough. Rickie and Cathy are safe. The goons Hsen sent to take them are all dead."

Tomasso's smile faltered for only a heartbeat. "I didn't think that would work. Hsen wanted it for insurance, though."

"Where is Hsen?" Jo asked, her voice low and murderous.

Tomasso made his smile wider, showing lots of perfect teeth. "I thought you'd be more concerned about the whereabouts of your husband."

"Keith can take care of himself. There's nothing you can do to hurt him."

"Oh no?" Crooking a finger, Tomasso said, "You'd better take a look at this."

He led Jo down one of the corridors and into a small empty office. He pointed to the desktop computer and Jo stepped up to the desk and swivelled its display screen so she could see it.

Her face paled and she leaned heavily against the desk. Baker's mouth dropped open.

The screen showed Keith Stoner, blindfolded, strapped into

a stiff-backed chair, his bare torso showing a score of ugly burns, yellowing black against his pale skin. His head was slumped forward; he was obviously unconscious.

Jo kept herself from screaming. Barely. She realized that the tension, the odd sensation she had felt a few minutes earlier, had been a warning. The fear that she had kept bottled within her all these weeks finally erupted in a hot flame of anguish: Keith was helpless and in their hands. He was not the powerful, confident, capable superman she had told herself he was. He was just as vulnerable and defenseless as any ordinary man.

Jo realized now that she was vulnerable and defenseless, too.

Zoltan Janos had been carefully briefed by Tomasso. He and Ilona Lucacs had waited inside the rocket with the handcuffed and blindfolded Stoner until a black-clad Pacific Commerce commando returned to tell them that the base was securely in their hands. Then, following Tomasso's orders, Janos dispatched Ilona and two of the orientals to set up Stoner while he himself followed a third black-uniformed man to the base's communications center.

Ilona Lucacs had gone with two men who led Stoner, their hands tightly gripping his arms, down the base's only elevator to a small storeroom. There they ripped off his shirt and strapped him—still handcuffed—into a stiff chair. As Janos had told her to, Ilona then injected Stoner with a heavy dose of phenobarbital. He gave a little gasp, more of surprise than pain, when the needle went into his bare arm. Then his head lolled on his shoulders, and finally his chin sank to his chest.

Ilona stared at the unconscious Stoner for several moments, thinking, He wanted to help me. He wanted to be my friend, to be my father, almost. And all I've given him in return is pain.

She pulled off the earphones that were still tightly clamped to his head. He was completely limp, sagging against the straps that cut into the flesh of his chest and arms.

But it has to be this way, Ilona told herself. He is too important to be sentimental over. His offers to help me, to love me, they were nothing but bribes to make me do what he wanted. Janos and I must study him further, pry out all the secrets within him. He is an experimental subject, nothing more. An experimental subject.

Still, she knew that he had not volunteered for these experiments. And the only end to them that she could see was death.

The two silent orientals were waiting at the door. Carrying the earphones in one hand, Ilona walked out into the corridor. The two commandos shut the airtight storeroom door firmly; the rubberized gasket around its rim gave a sighing sound. They clicked its electronic lock and, for good measure, wedged a thick metal rod across it as a makeshift bolt.

Ilona took a deep breath and headed for the room that the man Tomasso had indicated she could use. Her pleasure machine was waiting for her there. Just a few minutes of it and she knew she would feel much better about everything.

Stoner remained limp and sagging against the straps that constrained him until he was certain that he was alone. His star brother had neutralized the sedative that Ilona had injected into him almost as quickly as the chemical had entered his bloodstream. But it wouldn't do to let them know we're perfectly conscious.

He sensed a camera over the room's only door, up by the ceiling. Originally installed to guard against pilfering, now it was watching him. He probed its mechanism and found that it could be overloaded and shorted out without much trouble.

Jo! He realized that she was in the base, watching the picture that the camera showed. Stay strong, Jo, he said silently. Stay strong. The real test is just beginning.

Paulino Alvarado wormed his way along the heating duct, desperately looking for a way to escape the soldiers who had taken over the base. He had seen Matthews and the others milling about angrily, worriedly, in the crowded cafeteria. If he could find them weapons, maybe they could fight their way out. There seemed to be only a dozen or so soldiers.

As silently as he could, Paulino slithered along the cold metal ducting. He had never seen guns or weapons of any kind in the many days he had spent at the base. But surely there must be something.

He stopped at one of the grilles. A beautiful young woman was sitting on the bed, an open suitcase full of electronic gear on the floor at her feet. Her face was exquisite, but so troubled that Paulino felt he had stumbled upon a princess in exile, like the stories he had read in childhood.

All the soldiers wore black uniforms and were orientals. This lovely young woman wore a tweed skirt and a wrinkled blouse that had once been white. Her hair was the color of thick honey and her skin was like flawless cream.

And she had a suitcase full of electronics. Maybe it was a radio. Maybe they could summon help. If she isn't one of the enemy. Paulino knew he had never seen her before. She did not wear the blue coveralls of the regular staff. Yet she was sad, perhaps even frightened, as she stared at the little suitcase on the floor.

And so beautiful. With the glandular wisdom of youth, Paulino decided that a woman of such beauty could not possibly be evil, or an enemy.

He tapped on the grille.

Ilona flinched and looked up toward the sound that startled her. A man was behind the grille set up in the wall near the ceiling.

"*Senorita*," he whispered hoarsely, "*por favor . . .*"

"Who are you?" she whispered back in English as she stood up.

"I need your help," the young man replied in accented English.

It took a few minutes of rummaging in her purse before Ilona found a nail file sturdy enough for the screws holding the grille. Standing on the room's only chair, she quickly got the grille off, then stepped down and watched Paulino slide stealthily to the chair and then the floor.

He looked something of a scarecrow, rail-thin, with frightened, darting eyes. The eyes were deeply dark, though, and his thin face with its sculpted cheekbones had an aesthetic look to it that was almost romantic. His pale orange coveralls were stained and rumpled, as if he had been living in them for days on end.

"I can help you," he whispered, once his feet were safely on the bare floor. "We must work together to get away from the soldiers."

Ilona heard herself answer, "Yes, but how?"

She was shocked at her own words, until she realized that she did indeed want to get away from these menacing orientals in black, away from the guns and the danger, away from Janos and what he was doing to Stoner.

But how?

CHAPTER 34

JO recovered her strength and her poise after only a moment. She tore her eyes away from the display screen, away from the picture of Keith helpless and unconscious, and faced Tomasso once again, unconsciously fingering the belt that cinched her glittering jumpsuit at the waist. Its jewelled buckle was an old family heirloom; it could be pulled free easily and used as a dagger.

Vic was trying to keep his face straight, trying not to smile, not to sneer. He almost succeeded. Jo, her mind filling with images of how his smile would turn to agonized screams, stepped away from the desk. Cliff Baker stood out in the hallway, goggle-eyed, trying to digest all that was happening.

"Your husband's in a storeroom," Vic explained, "and the air has been pumped out of the corridor on the other side of his door. If you don't cooperate, we'll have to pump the air out of the room he's in."

"I play ball or you kill him," Jo snapped.

Tomasso nodded. "That's it."

"What does Hsen want?"

Tomasso allowed himself a small grin. "Hey, what about what I want?"

Jo gave him a level stare, then replied, "Vic, you're nothing but a miserable little shit who's going to get his guts ripped out an inch at a time."

From the corridor, Baker made a guttural noise that might have been a suppressed laugh. Tomasso's grin vanished. "You oughtta watch your mouth, Jo."

"You talk as if you're in charge here," Jo said. "But it's Hsen who's calling the shots. What if I tell him that I'll cooperate—but only if he'll turn you over to me."

Tomasso frowned.

"Hsen knows you're a turncoat. Do you think he really trusts you? You've thrown away your only card. Now that you've helped him take over this base, what've you got left to bargain with?"

His face flushing with barely-suppressed anger, Tomasso snarled, "Never mind the big talk. You just call off the troops you've got ready to fly here or your old man starts breathing vacuum."

"Hsen won't let you kill Keith."

"Wanna bet? The medics can study his dead body. Be a lot easier than dealing with him alive."

Baker said, in a complaining tone, "Would one of you mind telling me what this is all about?"

"It's about a starship," Jo replied. "That's what you want to see, isn't it, Vic? Well come on, then. Let's go see it."

She swept past Tomasso, out into the corridor and past Baker, heading for the chamber where the starship was waiting, her finger stroking the razor-sharp edge of her belt buckle.

Li-Po Hsen paced nervously, almost frantically, across the imitation bare wood floor of his private quarters. Tomasso's reports from Delphi were all good, well-nigh perfect.

The base is securely in my hands, Hsen told himself. Stoner is incapacitated, ready for further examination. The bitch Camerata is my prisoner, and she has called off the counterattack that she had planned.

The only failure had been in the attempt to seize her children, but that is a minor matter. Jo Camerata is cooperating because she knows her husband is at my mercy. I can pick up her brats at any time now.

Hsen's head nearly swam with excitement. I can control Vanguard Industries! I can have the Hungarian scientists *make* Stoner reveal all the alien's secrets, because his wife is in my hands.

He clapped his hands gleefully and skipped right through a hologrammic reproduction of an ancient bronze horse to lean across his bare desk and tap the communications button.

Within a minute his dour-faced security chief entered the sparsely-furnished room.

"I have decided to go to Delphi base," Hsen told her, "to see this starship for myself."

The security chief bowed her head, but replied, "That is not part of our plan. It was agreed . . ."

Hsen snorted disdain. "The base is secure. There is nothing to fear."

"Sir, we still do not understand the extent of the man Stoner's powers."

"He is unconscious at present, is he not?"

"Yes, but . . ."

"And even when he awakes, he will be made to realize that his wife's well-being depends on his cooperation."

"Still, sir, it is my duty to point out that there may be unknown dangers in your personally going to the Vanguard base."

"Pah! It is *my* base now. I want to see the bitch and her husband for myself. I want to see this starship the alien has built for them. What kind of general sits quailing in his castle after his troops have conquered the enemy?"

A wise general, thought the security chief. But she dared not speak the words aloud.

Cliff Baker gaped in unabashed awe at the towering vat that bubbled and steamed, almost close enough to reach out and touch.

Vic Tomasso felt an uneasy sense of forces at work beyond his control or even his understanding.

The two men were standing with Jo on the grillwork catwalk that circled the vast underground chamber. The floor was lost in the mists, far below them. Many stories above, high-efficiency suction fans pulled the steam into special ducts where it was used to run turbines before cooling to the point where it condensed into pure potable water.

Jo was reciting woodenly, explaining the starship construction system as if she were a tour guide who had given this lecture a thousand times.

"The nanomachines are as small as viruses, but they are machines, not living creatures. Each one is programmed to do its specific task and no other. They can assemble individual atoms and fit them together like the pieces of a jigsaw puzzle. What they're doing now is taking the raw elements that are being fed into the vat in the gaseous stage through the hosing at the lowest level and picking out individual atoms to place them exactly where they need to be to build the ship."

"Individual atoms?" Tomasso asked, his voice somewhere between incredulity and astonishment.

Without changing the tone of her voice or the frozen expression on her face, Jo replied, "Yes. Individual atoms of aluminum, titanium, silicon. Quite a bit of silver. Some gold. Mostly carbon atoms for the ship's structure. The starship will be almost pure diamond, except for the guidance system and life support equipment."

Baker muttered, "It must be worth . . ."

"It costs less than a lunar shuttle," Jo said, with a little force. "The nanomachines are incredibly cheap; once you have a few master assemblers, they create all the other machines out of simple raw materials like carbon and silicon. Then the raw input for the ship itself is the same stuff, plus a bit of metal. Literally dirt cheap; we scoop most of it from the top few centimeters of the soil outside."

But as she spoke Jo was furiously thinking of how she could get out of this trap, how she could overcome Tomasso and the dozen or so military types who now controlled the base, how she could save Keith. No plan of action came to her mind. For once in her life she accepted the ancient wisdom of patience. The burning hatred still seethed in her heart. Every part of her wanted to tear Tomasso's flesh into bloody ribbons. But now her ancient blood counseled patience, so Jo kept her passions frozen within her and waited for the proper moment to strike.

For nearly an hour the three of them paced slowly around the catwalk, peering into the bubbling, frothing vat. Jo could make out a graceful curve of crystalline material through the steaming brew, but little more.

"And this ship is big enough to leave the solar system and go out to the stars?" Tomasso asked.

Jo replied, "This is only the propulsion and guidance unit. The living quarters and life support sections have already been completed. They're waiting in underground hangars, not far from here."

"What kind of propulsion does it use?" Baker asked.

"It taps magnetic fields when it's close enough to planets that have them," Jo said. "Don't ask me how, the physicists are still trying to figure it out. For the long-distance jumps between stars it scoops in hydrogen from the interstellar plasma to feed a fusion engine."

"And it can go from one star to another, all that distance . . ."

With a single nod, Jo said, "The nanomachines constantly maintain all the ship's systems. Keith told me they can even repair the erosion that micrometeors cause when they strike the hull."

Tomasso was about to ask another question, but his wrist communicator chimed softly. He held the unit to his ear for a moment. Jo saw his face go from surprise to pleasure.

"Hsen is coming over," he announced. With a wry smile, "You'll have a chance to show him your starship, Jo."

Jo kept her face expressionless. But her heart leaped within her. The murderer is coming here! And she knew exactly what she had to do. Kill the bastard. Throw him over the railing and let him drop fifteen stories to the concrete floor. Slice his throat open with the dagger built into my belt buckle. Jam my thumbs into his eyes and then kick his balls into his throat.

She clenched her hands to keep them from shaking with anticipation.

My babies are safe; he can't get to them now. I'll kill him. What happens to me afterward doesn't matter. What happens to Keith doesn't matter. I'll kill the sonofabitch with my bare hands.

Stoner, meanwhile, was still pretending to be unconscious while his mind explored the underground base. Reaching, probing, he sensed Jo with Tomasso and Baker, felt the fury of her mind blazing like a bonfire in the night. He recognized Matthews and many of the base's staff cooped together in the automated cafeteria. Delicately stealing along the silent underground corridors he realized that there were twelve professional soldiers present, half of them in the base's communications center, the others divided between the life support center and the docking facility.

Why the docking facility? Another rocket was on its way to the base, he found with a feathery touch on the mind of one of the orientals. Li-Po Hsen himself was coming to view his new conquest firsthand.

Stoner filed that information and pressed onward. Zoltan Janos was busily setting up equipment in one of the laboratories, getting ready to resume his experiments on Stoner. Where is Ilona?

He found her in one of the cubicles that served as quarters for the staff. There was a man with her; a stranger.

For several moments Stoner explored their minds, learning what he could without pressing hard enough for them to realize he was present. Then, realizing that he had no better choice, he called to the Hungarian scientist.

—Ilona. Ilona, can you hear me?

She stiffened with surprise, sitting on the bed. Paulino, primly ensconced on the room's only chair on the other side of the room, saw her face go pale.

"What is it?" he asked.

She silenced him with an upraised hand while replying aloud, "Yes, I can hear you."

—I need your help.

"There's nothing I can do."

Paulino saw that she was talking to thin air. His mother would have recognized a religious vision; his father would have twirled a finger against his temple. Paulino, however, had grown accustomed to electronics miracles and immediately assumed that Ilona was speaking to someone through a miniature communications device planted somewhere on her person.

"Who is it?" Paulino asked, getting up from his chair and crossing the room to sit beside Ilona on the bed. "Is it someone who can help us?"

And he heard in his mind: —Perhaps we can help each other.

CHAPTER 35

IT was night in the rugged mountains of the Fossey Preserve, along the border of Rwanda and the Congolese Republic.

Lela sat in a tight knot as far from the fire as she could, knees pulled up to her chin, thin black arms circling her legs. The blond had asked her for the final time if she would call Koku to them. She had refused.

Now the men were sharing liquor from a metal flask, laughing and eying her. The silvery flask gleamed in the firelight as they tilted it back. Lela could see their Adam's apples bobbing as they swallowed.

"I'm first," said the redhead. "I found her, so I go first." He had not shaved in the several days since he had discovered her; his rust-colored beard looked shaggy and vermin-infested.

Lela tried to block out their coarse jokes as the men swilled the liquor. All but the blond, who sat some distance away from the others, on the far side of the fire, his face looking tired and grim.

"Call the damned ape and save yourself!" he had hissed at her, only a few moments earlier. Now he sat staring at her the way an angry teacher would stare at a child who has gotten into mischief and must be punished.

The irony was that Lela could sense Koku. The young gorilla was near, very near. Lela wanted to command him to go away, to race as fast as he could to the territory where the females waited, protected by rangers and university students. But she could not. Her mind was filled with the terror of death staring her in the face, wearing the mask of a morose blond Englishman.

And the ordeal the others would put her through before they killed her. I could run, Lela thought. In the night I could probably get away from them.

But in the following day, she knew, they would track her down and find her. She would only be postponing the inevitable. Worse, Koku would probably seek her, linked by the biochips implanted in their skulls, and when the hunters found Lela they would also find the gorilla.

No, Lela told herself, hugging her shins tightly to keep from shaking like a wind-blown leaf, once I am dead Koku will go his own way. He will stay clear of these hunters. He knows enough to be afraid of them now. At least I have taught him that much.

Koku felt the swirl of emotions in Lela's mind. The young gorilla knew she was very near, and her growing terror filled him with a nameless fear. He could not build a sleeping nest. He could not sleep.

But he could not run away, either. His eyes saw nothing to be afraid of. His nose smelled the thin smoke of a campfire, but he felt no danger from that. The only sounds he heard were the normal hoots and shrills of the night. Yet Lela was afraid, and because she was, Koku felt fear also.

Fearful yet uncertain, wanting to run away yet unable to leave Lela, Koku paced back and forth on his knuckles, three hundred pounds of gorilla trying to deal with complexities that his brain had no way of unravelling.

But then a white-hot shriek of fright scalded his brain. Even without the biochip he heard Lela's scream. He charged off through the brush toward her.

The four men were all over Lela, their hands tearing at her clothing, gripping her flesh. She could smell their foul breaths and feel their fingers clutching at her. She screamed and struggled, and they laughed as they stripped her.

Twisting her arms painfully they pushed her to the ground. The redhead gripped her ankles and spread her legs apart.

A thundering roar. A blur of black smashed into the redhead and sent him sprawling, tumbling right into the campfire. He howled with pain and tried to get up but could not. The fire licked at the backs of his legs as he shrieked and yowled.

Koku's backhand slap knocked the two blacks away, and the other white man cowered and scrambled away, scuttling backwards, his eyes so wide Lela could see white all around the pupils.

Koku stood on his hind legs and roared at the men, slapping his palms against his stomach. It sounded like a huge drumbeat of doom.

"Koku, no!" shouted Lela. "Get away! Get away!"

She knew that the gorilla had done his worst. He could push strangers away from Lela, and his push could snap frail human bones. But he was not aggressive. Having moved the strangers away from Lela, Koku roared and threatened. But he could never attack.

The blond knew it. While his redheaded friend roasted in his own fire, his back broken, while Lela shouted and pleaded with Koku to run back into the safety of the trees, the blond calmly got to his feet, automatic rifle in his hands, and put the gun to his shoulder.

"Don't!" Lela's scream was lost in the roar of gunfire.

The burst of bullets stitched Koku's chest. He staggered backwards a few steps, then sank to his haunches. Lela saw blood gush from his mouth and he pitched forward. Lela crawled to him, sobbing. The gorilla reached out a massive hand toward her, but then his eyes froze and he went still. A final sigh, so much like a human, and Koku was dead.

Gasping, panting, crying, Lela sat frozen on the ground. The redhead and both blacks lay very still, bones broken, skin ripped open. The other white was on his hands and knees, eyes squeezed shut now, rocking back and forth like an autistic child.

Koku lay less than a meter from Lela. She crawled to him and lay her head on his hairy back, the bloody bullet holes already matting. She sobbed, crying as she had when her baby brother had died of fever so many years ago.

Through tear-filled eyes she looked up at the blond. He had slung the rifle over his shoulder and was picking up his backpack. Without a word, without looking back at her or the creature he had murdered, he walked off into the shadows of the forest.

Lela knew where he was heading. She stopped crying. Her entire body shook, but now it was not from fear. Pulling the tatters of her blouse around her, she got to her feet and went toward the sleeping bags. The redhead was muttering incoherently, his legs black and smoking in the fire, his hands twitching uselessly. She walked around him, reached the sleeping bags, and picked up one of the leather cases that held an automatic rifle.

Sliding the gun out of its protective casing, she briefly

looked it over, found the safety, and clicked it off. Then she worked the bolt as she had been taught to on hunting rifles.

Planting the plastic stock firmly on her hip, she shot the two blacks first. The blast shook her slim body and bellowed through the night like a stuttering lion. The blacks' bodies jerked and rolled as the bullets plowed through them.

Traitors, thought Lela. Thieves and murderers.

The redhead's eyes followed Lela as she stepped slightly toward him, then fired the gun again at the white who still hunched on hands and knees. He was knocked over sideways, gouts of blood and dust churned up by the bullets.

Lela looked down at the redhead. His face was contorting fiercely. He was trying to move but could not, his back broken.

She relaxed her grip on the rifle, let its muzzle point downward. "The jackals can deal with you," she said to him.

Then she put together a backpack, took a fresh, fully loaded rifle, and started after the blond.

Stoner knew the layout of Delphi base better than anyone else there, since he had directed its design and construction.

Strapped in the stiff-backed chair, still pretending unconsciousness, he instructed Ilona Lucacs and Paulino. The young Latin also had a fair knowledge of the base's layout; at least he knew where pressure suits were kept, and how to work inside a suit.

While Paulino and Ilona crept stealthily along a deserted corridor toward a set of lockers where the suits were, Stoner mentally examined the TV camera that was watching him. Probing the electromagnetic fields it generated, he traced the pattern of the picture it was sending back to the bored, half-asleep oriental who sat at the monitoring desk in the base communications center.

By the time Paulino and Ilona had zipped up their suits and begun plodding toward the evacuated corridor where Stoner's room was situated, he had altered the camera's inner workings so that it simply continued sending the same electrical transmission, no matter what its lens saw. The commando monitoring the camera continued to see Stoner slumped in his chair.

But Stoner slowly straightened up and flexed the muscles of his arms and torso. He was soaked with sweat from the effort of mentally jiggering the camera. How much easier it would have been to use physical tools instead of mental ones, he thought. The human race had developed physical tools instead of its rudimentary extrasensory abilities because a bone club worked much more surely than a mental death projection; for most humans, the club was more efficient and much easier to use.

The blindfold was a help rather than a hindrance. By eliminating all the thousands of bits of visual data his eyes provided every second, Stoner and his star brother were able to concentrate much more certainly on the mental tasks at hand.

Now for these handcuffs, he thought. There were many, many incidences of what the media and even the medical profession called hysterical strength: A mother sees her child pinned beneath an overturned car and lifts the car with her bare hands high enough to allow the child to wriggle free. A man being chased by a murderous mob leaps a wall that not even a top athlete could clear. Under certain conditions of stress, the human body is capable of fantastic feats of strength.

Stoner's star brother duplicated such conditions. A tremendous surge of adrenalin, a sudden flood of the phosphate and other compounds that energized the muscles, a wild light-headed moment as he strained to snap the chain that linked the cuffs together.

Stoner felt as if his arms would snap instead, but suddenly the chain broke with a sharp *crack!* and his hands pulled loose from behind his back.

He took several deep breaths while his star brother adjusted his body metabolism back to normal. His wrists were badly bruised, but free. He reached up and unbuckled the strap across his chest. Finally he undid the strap across his thighs and, on shaky legs, stood erect for the first time in hours.

He smiled grimly to himself. Like the old Frankenstein films when the monster breaks free of its chains and goes off to terrify the village.

For a few moments he puzzled over the mechanism of the locks on the cuffs. Once he clearly pictured the microscopic fields of the mechanism he easily moved them. The cuffs clicked open and fell languidly away from his raw bruised wrists in the gentle gravity of the Moon to clunk lightly on the concrete floor.

Stepping to the storeroom's only door, Stoner realized that its electronic lock was more complex. But the fields it generated were much easier to sense.

He sensed Ilona and Paulino entering the corridor through one of the airtight doors that separated all the corridors of the base just as watertight hatches separated the passageways of a warship. He directed them to his door until they were just on the other side.

"There is an electronic lock," said Ilona, her voice muffled by the door's thickness, "and a metal bar jammed across the doorway."

"Can you remove the bar?" he asked.

"Yes," said Paulino.

"Before you do, can you find the emergency pump and put air back into the corridor?"

"I don't know where the pump is."

"There's a control panel set into the wall next to each of the airtight doors. Emergency instructions are printed on it."

A moment's hesitation. "I don't read English . . ."

"That's all right," Ilona cut in. "I can."

Stoner heard their boots clumping down the corridor. He thought, If a section of corridor starts to leak air it sets off the alarms in the comm center. But there are no alarms if you refill a section with air. Just a set of monitoring lights on one of the consoles changing from red or yellow to green. Will the men in the comm center notice the change?

He decided that even if they did, it would be too late for them to do anything about it. Frankenstein's monster would be loose, and anyone who tried to stop him would be in for a shock.

The two came back and told him that the corridor was filled with air once more.

"I have raised the visor on my helmet," said Paulino. "The air is good."

"You shouldn't have taken that risk," Ilona said. Stoner sensed more admiration in her voice than admonition.

It took him a few seconds to spring the electronic lock. Stoner remembered a professor from his college days telling him, "The more complicated a device is, the more ways it can fail." Or be made to fail, he added mentally. That was the trouble with that damned guard robot in Beirut, he told himself. Too damned simple.

The door popped open with a little sigh of air and Stoner grabbed its edge and pulled it all the way back.

He felt astonishment from the two others.

"You are still blindfolded!" Ilona gasped.

"Oh!" With an almost embarrassed grin, Stoner tore the blindfold off and tossed it sailing back into the storeroom. He blinked several times before his eyes adjusted to the light of the fluorescent strips along the ceiling of the corridor.

"Come with me," he commanded Ilona and Paulino. With the scowl of an Old Testament patriarch on his bearded face, Stoner stalked off toward the chamber where the starship was being built, the chamber where his wife and Li-Po Hsen stood face-to-face.

The first hint of dawn was graying the sky when Lela caught up with the blond. He was working his way down a steep slope, long-leafed fronds of blackberry bushes slapping at him. Lela followed him down the heavily wooded ravine and then stopped, panting, while the blond continued up the next slope.

Her face and arms scratched bloody by the thistles she had

pushed through, Lela watched in the dim early light as the blond doggedly made his way to the top of the ridge. He is heading for the females, Lela told herself. He knows where they are and he knows how to slip past the rangers patrolling this area.

As the blond neared the top of the ridge, Lela unslung the heavy rifle she carried. Stretching out prone on the damp ground, she unhooked the gun's muzzle bipod and set it firmly on the ground. Squinting through the sights, she waited until the blond was clearly silhouetted against the milky sky. Then she squeezed the trigger. The gun blasted half a clip of ammunition before she could take her finger away.

Slowly, tiredly, Lela climbed the steep green slope. The blond lay sprawled on his face several meters down the other side, his back a mass of blood.

Lela slipped and half slid down to where he lay. She pulled him over onto his back.

His eyes were glazed with pain. Yet he smiled at her, raggedly. "You think more of those bloody apes than you do of human beings, don't you?" His voice was a harsh, bubbling whisper.

"Yes," said Lela as she watched him die. "Yes, I do."

CHAPTER 36

LI-PO Hsen walked onto the catwalk in the starship chamber only after six black-uniformed men armed with pistols and submachine guns stepped out and formed a silent menacing line along the metal railing. Then the head of Pacific Commerce came through the doorway. He was too short, Jo noticed, to need to duck his head. The only addition to his usual shortsleeved shirt and comfortable, baggy slacks were the weighted lunar boots he wore. To Jo they looked almost like the boots deep-sea divers had used a century earlier.

Behind him came Zoltan Janos, his antiquated business suit still buttoned tightly across his stocky torso, his round bearded face staring in awe at the huge bubbling vat that simmered and steamed almost within arm's reach of the catwalk.

Cliff Baker and Tomasso stood next to Jo, but their presences faded to nothing as she locked eyes with the man who had murdered her daughter.

Both of them tried their best to keep their faces from betraying the emotions that raged within them. Hsen felt the joy of long-awaited triumph. All the knowledge of the alien star-rovers is within Stoner's mind, and I have him in my grasp. He will cooperate once he understands what can happen to his wife if he does not. It might even be profitable to give him a little demonstration, show him how easy it is to make a woman beg for mercy. Jo would try to resist, of course. I wonder how much pain it will take to break her?

Jo saw the corners of Hsen's mouth twitch with the beginnings of a smile that he quickly suppressed. She allowed herself to smile back at him, and watched the surprise flash in his dark brown eyes.

That's not the only surprise I've got in store for you, she told her enemy silently. You think you're safe because you've got six goons with guns behind you. But just give me the opportunity to take my belt buckle off and I'll give you the last surprise of your life.

Does he want to go to bed with me? Jo asked herself. It would be just like his kind of barbaric thinking, fuck the woman you've conquered. Okay, just say the word, take me to your bed and tell me to strip. That's all I want from you now.

"I know what you are thinking," Hsen said.

"Do you?"

"You would like to kill me, wouldn't you?"

Jo said, "Wouldn't you?"

"No, not yet. Not for a long time. Perhaps not at all, if you are reasonable."

"You murdered my daughter," Jo said, her voice as flat and wooden as that of a woman who had given up all hope.

"A regrettable accident."

"You abducted my husband and tried to kidnap my son."

"Your husband is an extremely valuable property," Hsen replied. "As for your son, and the cloning apparatus that bears your daughter—I can take them, if I must, no matter what the cost. Or it might become necessary to destroy them. Archimedes has no nuclear shield, does it?"

Jo's teeth clenched. Kill him! her blood urged. Kill him as quickly as you can, before he kills your babies.

"You don't need to threaten me," she said, her right hand slowly going to her belt buckle. "You've won. I know that the game is over."

Hsen's eyes became wary. "You accept defeat?"

Toying with her belt buckle, Jo said, "I understand when the time has come to make an accommodation."

"Such as?"

Gesturing toward the steaming vat with her left hand, Jo answered, "You can control Vanguard through me. You can have access to all the technology of the aliens through my husband. As long," her voice hardened, "as you promise not to harm my children or my husband."

Despite himself, Hsen let his eagerness show. "Stoner will cooperate?"

"If I tell him that he must."

"Truly?"

"Why not ask me myself?"

They all turned and saw Stoner filling the metal doorway, his bare chest showing the ugly burns, his wrists skinned red, his beard and hair fiercely ragged. The guards levelled their guns at him.

"Keith!"

Jo ran to him, pushing past Hsen's slight form and the

shocked, gaping Janos to throw herself into his arms. He gripped her tightly.

"What have they done to you?"

"Not 'they,'" Stoner replied. "Him." He pointed at Janos with his left hand.

"Your finger!"

Stoner moved his accusing hand to point at Hsen. "Working for him."

"How did you get out . . ." Janos's voice choked off as Ilona clumped through the doorway, still in the pressure suit, followed by Paulino. Both of them had removed their helmets.

"Who are these people?" Hsen demanded.

Stoner made a wry smile. "Two lost souls."

Hsen folded his thin arms across his chest. "You are very clever, Dr. Stoner. But not clever enough to evade bullets, I trust."

"That won't be necessary," Stoner said. Then he saw Cliff Baker and Tomasso, still standing off a few paces along the catwalk.

For a long moment he said nothing. The only sounds in the huge underground chamber were the frothing hiss of the immense seething, steaming glassteel vat and the distant whirring hum of the suction fans high above.

Stoner recognized Tomasso and sensed the fear and tension that made the man's innards tremble. But no guilt. Not a shred of guilt. Tomasso felt no remorse for the role he had played in killing Cathy. He's convinced himself that it wasn't his fault, not his responsibility, Stoner sensed. Poor damned fool! All he fears is Jo's vengeance. If only he knew what he should really be afraid of.

Turning to Baker, Stoner asked, "What are you doing here, Cliff?"

But before Baker could answer, Stoner saw it flashing through the man's mind. He felt a sudden dizziness, a stomach-tumbling vertigo, as if the metal grillwork beneath his feet had given way and he was plunging in lunar slow motion down, down, down to the concrete floor fifteen stories below.

"My god, Cliff," Stoner gasped. "Why? Why did you do it?"

Baker made a lopsided smile. "Why not?"

"Do what?" Jo asked, still in Stoner's protective grasp.

"The Horror," said Stoner. "Cliff created the Horror."

Hsen and all the others stared at the Australian.

With a slight giggle, Baker said, "I didn't create it. The stuff came out of a Vanguard laboratory—your own lab, Jo. The one at Mt. Isa."

"That's not a biology lab!"

"The plague isn't biological," Stoner said. "It's caused by nanomachines. Virus-sized weapons specifically designed to destroy the cells of the stomach lining."

Baker's grin widened, became more twisted. "Two of Jo's very bright lads were working on the next step down in size from biochips. One of 'em was a drinking mate of mine. Instead of communications chips, he wanted to create machines that could work inside the human body. He got the idea of designing microminiaturized machines that could build even smaller machines."

"Down to nanometer dimensions," said Stoner. "The size of a virus."

"Right. The easiest one to build would be a machine that chewed up biological cells. That's what he wanted to do first. As an experiment."

"I've never seen a report about this work!" Jo said in an accusing voice.

"'Course not. They knew what they were doing could be turned into enormous profits for Vanguard. And power. That worried 'em."

Stoner saw Hsen's eyes glittering with the prospects of nanotechnology and the power it could yield.

"Being good lads, they let me talk 'em into quitting Vanguard before their work went beyond the theory stage. It was easy for me to convince 'em that no corporation could be trusted with this technology. So I got 'em both to come and work for the IIA. Gave 'em a lab of their own in Sydney and let 'em go ahead with their experiments."

"And then you killed them," said Stoner.

"I had to test the stuff, di'n't I?"

Hsen seemed wonder-struck. "And then you turned the plague loose on the world?"

"Right. Started my own population control program," Baker answered, almost laughing. "Women and children first, of course. Decent thing to do, don't you think?"

"It kills women preferentially," Stoner explained. "Especially pregnant women."

"Rich women," Baker corrected. "Kill the rich. Send the little buggers all across the world on airliners. Let the fat tourists and big-shot business people spread the plague among their own."

"But the Horror is killing millions of people—rich and poor!" Jo said.

"Can't be helped," Baker replied, shrugging. "Can't make an omelet without breaking eggs, y'know."

Ilona whispered, shocked, "But all those people . . ."

"What of it?" Baker snapped. "Maybe the plague will wipe out everybody except those of us who're clever enough to get off the planet. So what? There's too damned many people on Earth anyway, everybody knows that."

"If nanomachines cause the Horror," Hsen mused, one hand lightly stroking his chin, "then other nanomachines can be made to protect a person against the plague. Such protection would be priceless. Absolutely priceless!"

He turned to Stoner, "Is that not so?"

Stoner closed his eyes. Inoculate the whole population of Earth? Turn nanotechnology loose for everyone, all at once? The results could tear human society to shreds. Most human beings couldn't bear to see themselves as they truly are; it would hit them the way it hit Novotny. Half the world might go insane.

There is no other way, his star brother counselled. It is too late for gradual measures. Our deepest fears have come true. Humans have discovered nanotechnology and are using it for genocide, perhaps racial suicide. We have no choice now but to provide them with the means to protect themselves.

"Is it not so?" Hsen repeated, raising his voice angrily.

"Yes," Stoner answered. "It is true."

"The ultimate power!" Hsen said, half to himself. "The power of life and death. Over everyone! Over the entire world!"

Jo snapped, "You're acting as if the power is already yours."

"Of course it is! I control you, both of you. Dr. Stoner, you will begin by inoculating me, just as you inoculated de Sagres and the others."

Stoner stared at him for long moments, his gray eyes seeing beyond Hsen's jubilant face, beyond the starship being built atom by atom within the giant vat, beyond the confines of this world and time.

"Let me tell you about my star brother," he said, so softly that the others strained toward him slightly to hear.

It began nearly ten million years earlier, on a planet imbedded in a thick cluster of stars halfway across the Milky Way. They were originally created as weapons, Stoner told them. The nanomachines were first invented to serve as implements of death. "Almost the same way you're using them, Cliff," Stoner said.

Before they wiped themselves out, the race that invented the nanomachines sent a few of its kind into deep space. Their best scientists saw that they had committed planet-wide genocide and tried to save a few of their own. The stars in their cluster were so close together that it took only a few years for a spacecraft to reach another civilized world. But the nanomachines that they carried within them, built for nothing more than killing, began to destroy that race, too. Like an interstellar plague, the machines killed and killed and killed.

The second race's scientists worked feverishly to develop their own nanotechnology and counter the invading plague. They succeeded. They saved their species. For a while. They found that the nanomachines could be made to preserve the bodies they dwelled in, protect them against disease and cure injuries. Their lifespans lengthened incredibly. They became virtually immortal. But they did not know how to handle such godlike power. They allowed their numbers to grow beyond the ability of the planet to support them. The gift of life was turned into worldwide pollution that destroyed their biosphere. Again, a pitiful few were able to get away on spacecraft, but their race died in its own garbage and excrement.

And so it has gone. For millions of years, from one world to another, across the breadth of the Milky Way galaxy the nanomachines have spread. Over those eons the machines have gained incredible new capabilities as one race after another added different powers to them. Now they can be symbiotes, enhancing not only their hosts' physical well-being, but the hosts' mental abilities also. Yet not one race in a thousand has been wise enough to use them well. The race that sent them to Earth was one of those rare exceptions. Virtually every species to attain nanotechnology killed itself within a generation or two.

"The star brethren are a test," Stoner concluded. "The human race's ultimate test. Can we join with these symbiotes to move humanity to the next phase of our development, or will we use their powers to destroy ourselves?"

Hsen nodded as if he understood. "That is why this power must be restricted to the very few people who have the understanding and strength to direct all the others."

"Such as you?" Jo sneered.

"Don't you understand?" Stoner asked of them. "Don't any of you understand? We're talking about an evolutionary step as big as the invention of fire! Bigger! Even the biochips are trivial compared to nanotechnology."

"Yes," said Ilona. "I see. I understand."

Stoner went on, "At first, evolution works at the physical level, changing species over geological spans of time. Once a species achieves intelligence, though, evolution becomes social. Our societies change, and that becomes the driving force in our evolution. Social changes happen over centuries, generations, incredibly faster than physical evolution works. But when the species invents science, the big evolutionary changes come out of technology, and they come so swiftly that it's hard to keep up with them. The world begins to change in decades instead of generations."

The others stared at him in silence.

"Two or three decades ago," Stoner went on, "everybody was scared to death of nuclear weaponry. For the first time people realized that we had developed a technology that could wipe out all life on Earth. Politicians and scientists and diplomats worked out treaties to control nuclear weapons. But while they were doing that, our global technology was spewing out enough pollution to heat up the atmosphere and change the world's climate."

"And cutting down the rain forests," Ilona said.

"And manufacturing poison gas weapons," added Tomasso.

"That's just it," Stoner told them. "Our technology is *global* in its power. Unless we control it carefully it can destroy us in a thousand ways."

Jo said, "And nanotechnology is so big a step . . ."

Looking at her, Stoner said, "Right. Bigger than anything that's come before it. It's so big that it could shatter the human race before we learn to deal with it. That's what we've been trying to avoid. That's why we've worked to introduce nanotechnology gradually, carefully, with the least shock and pain to human society as possible."

He turned back to Baker. "But you've made that impossible, Cliff. You're forcing me to inoculate the world against your Horror. The consequences . . . god, I don't know *what* the consequences will be."

"That is of no importance at the moment," Hsen snapped. "You will inoculate me. Now!"

"No," said Stoner.

Hsen's thin lips curved upward slightly. "You are in no position to refuse me. Unless, of course, you do not care what happens to your wife."

Stoner thought swiftly. He's a strong personality, not like Novotny. And absolutely amoral. Like Vic, he doesn't feel guilt for anything he's done. A star brother might open his heart to the rest of humanity; or it might simply reinforce his existing personality. A man of that strength, of that ruthlessness, with a star brother? We can't take that chance, Stoner's star brother agreed.

"I won't do it," Stoner said.

Hsen let his fury show in his face. He pointed at Jo and said to the black-uniformed men behind him, "Pin her arms behind her back!"

Not a man moved. They stood staring at nothingness, their submachine guns slung over their shoulders.

"Do as I say!" Hsen shouted.

"They can't hear you," said Stoner softly. "They can't even see you."

His face contorting with rage, Hsen grabbed at the holster on the hip of the commando nearest him. Pulling the heavy black revolver from it, he levelled the gun at Stoner. The others backed away, but Jo clung tightly to her husband.

"You can control them but you can't control me!" he shouted.

"What makes you believe that?" asked Stoner mildly. "Do you really think that you're some sort of superior creature? Do you think that your ability to make money, to steal and lie and murder, places you above normal men?"

Hsen squeezed the trigger. Nothing happened. He brought up his other hand and pulled with both fingers. Beads of perspiration broke out on his forehead. His lips peeled back in the grimace of a hissing snake.

Ignoring him, Stoner turned to Baker. "Cliff, you're sick. Maybe you've always been this way. Maybe it's my fault. I don't know if a star brother can heal the scars in your mind. There's a chance that if you realize what you've done, truly understand the enormity of the evil you've unleashed—that realization might kill you. It's a chance you'll have to take."

Baker backed away, one hand sliding along the railing of the catwalk. "No you don't! You're not sticking those alien monsters in *me*!"

"Stop speaking!" Hsen screamed. "I'll kill you all!"

Without moving his arm from Jo's shoulders Stoner told him, "Be quiet, little man. Cliff is a psychopath, and he needs our help. But you are a deliberate, calculating murderer. You are a carrier of death; you belong with the dead."

"I'll kill you!"

Stoner's voice became as soft as the sweep of an angel's hovering wings. "There is only one person here that you can kill."

For a long moment Hsen stood absolutely still, holding the heavy revolver rigidly in both hands, pointed at Stoner's chest. Then his arms began to tremble and slowly, painfully, his hands turned the pistol inch by agonizing inch until it pointed at his own face. Hsen's entire body shook with the exertion. Rivulets of sweat ran down his face. His eyes were wide with horror as he stared directly into the yawning black depths of the gun's muzzle.

"Now," whispered Stoner, "if you truly want to kill someone, now you can pull the trigger."

Hsen screamed an incoherent animal screech. The gun went off with a shattering roar and the upper half of his head disappeared in an explosion of blood and bone and brain. His nearly headless body slammed against the catwalk railing, vaulted over it and fell slowly twisting to the steel flooring fifteen stories below. It finally hit with a sickening wet thump.

Jo's fingers tore into Stoner's flesh. She screamed, and so did Ilona. Baker stared, goggle-eyed. Tomasso and Janos stood frozen in slack-jawed shock. Behind him Stoner heard Paulino gag and retch in the corridor outside the doorway. Jo was clutching at his bare torso. He could feel her gulping for breath, her whole body wire-taut.

The six black-clad commandos still stood as if they had turned to statues.

"How does revenge feel, Jo?" he asked.

She swallowed hard. "Numb," she gasped. "I feel numb all over."

"You would have felt worse if you had killed him yourself. Vengeance is always bitter, Jo. Always."

Janos, his eyes nearly popping from their sockets, stuttered, "P-please . . . don't . . . don't kill me!"

Stoner stared at him.

"I didn't know . . . I didn't realize . . ."

"You knew," Stoner said calmly. Extending his left hand with its stump where a finger should have been, "You knew exactly what you were doing. You just never thought that you'd have to face the consequences."

The Hungarian fell to his knees and clutched Stoner's legs. "Don't kill me! *Please* don't kill me!"

Stoner reached out and grasped his quaking shoulder with his four-fingered hand. "Don't you think that I know the terror that lies deep in your heart? I feel it too, the terror of death, the fear that I will cease to be."

Janos raised his tear-streaked face.

"Hsen killed himself," said Stoner, "because he didn't have the courage to face a world in which he would be powerless. I simply allowed him to do it. I can't kill you—even if you deserved it."

"Thank you!" Janos blubbered. "Thank you!"

But Stoner raised his hand. "I'm going to do something to you that might be much worse. I'm going to give you a star brother. You saw what it did to your president. What it does to you will depend on your own inner strength, your own ability to expand your consciousness to envelop the entire human race."

"It'll protect us against the Horror?" Jo asked.

"Yes. And it will change the way you see the world, for as long as you live."

"What about me?" Tomasso asked, all in a rush. Stoner could see that it took every ounce of his courage to ask Jo the question. The muscles beneath the skin of his face were so rigid that he seemed to be wearing a mask of pain.

Jo looked up at her husband and then back at the traitor. "Just get out of my sight, Vic," she said wearily. "Go away and never let me see you again."

"Can . . ." Tomasso shifted his fearful eyes to Stoner. "Can I get it too, a star brother?"

Stoner nodded. "Will you share it with others? Will you return to Earth and help to inoculate your human brothers and sisters?"

"Ten billion people?" Tomasso's voice was slightly hollow with the challenge.

"Everyone," said Stoner.

"I'll try," he said.

"Good."

"You'll never do it in time," Baker said, almost snarling. "They're already starting to tear themselves apart down there. The human race is going to self-destruct!"

"You're wrong, Cliff," Stoner replied. "You've been wrong about almost everything."

"Everybody dies!" Baker nearly shouted it.

"Not anymore," Stoner said softly. "You almost had it right when you said that only those of us off-planet can survive the Horror. Space flight, the ability to live elsewhere than on the Earth, that's what guarantees the immortality of the human race. Even if we fail to beat the Horror, the human race can survive here on the Moon and in the Lagrange habitats. Our fate is no longer tied to the fate of the Earth."

"And star flight," Jo said, the realization of it filling her voice with wonder. "With star flight the human race can out-live the Sun!"

Stoner smiled at her and pointed to the enormous vat beyond the catwalk's railing. It had stopped bubbling. The steam was gone. Within its cylindrical glassteel walls they saw the graceful crystalline lines of the starship's propulsion and guidance section.

"It glitters like a diamond!" Ilona exclaimed. "An enormous diamond!"

Stoner said, "A lot of it is diamond, especially the structural segments and the hull. Nothing but carbon atoms, properly arranged by nanomachines."

Glancing down at the bloody remains of Hsen, Jo said, "That's what he wanted. The starship. All the knowledge that the aliens hold."

"There are no aliens," Stoner said. "Not anymore. They're our star brothers and sisters. Our symbiotes. We need each other to live."

"Like multicellular organisms," Ilona said. "Single-celled

creatures joined together billions of years ago to produce the earliest multicellular organisms. Now we are joining with the star creatures."

Stoner nodded. "First single cells, then aggregations of cells. Now we move on to a symbiosis that will create a new species, the next step in humankind's development."

"You're not sticking those alien machines in me!" Baker shouted, waving his fists in the air. "You're not going to turn me into an alien freak!"

Stoner took a step toward him. "Cliff, the symbiotes have made me more human, not less. There's nothing to fear."

Baker stared at him wildly.

"Believe me, Cliff," Stoner soothed, "we're all going to be more than human. You'll see."

The primitive fire in Baker's eyes calmed. His hands unclenched.

Will he be able to handle a star brother within him? Stoner wondered silently. His own star brother replied, That is a test that every human will have to face, now.

Paulino's timid voice came from the doorway. "Will we really be safe from the Horror?"

Stoner smiled at him. "And from addictions, too. Chemical and otherwise." He nodded to Ilona.

"Immortality?" Jo asked. "Will we truly be immortal?"

"Maybe. With the star symbiotes within us, who knows how long a human being can live? Long enough to go starroving, at least."

"It frightens me a little," said Ilona.

"It frightens me a lot," Stoner admitted. "This is going to change human society completely. The upheavals are going to be tremendous."

"But the alternative is the Horror," Jo said.

"Yes. That's the problem."

"Then what are we waiting for?" she asked, with newfound strength in her voice. "We've got a whole world of work to do. Let's get started. Now."

EPILOGUE

JOÃO de Sagres stood at the crest of the bare pebbly hill and watched, breathless in the high altitude of the Nazcan plain, as the Sun touched the horizon exactly at the point where the long straight line arrowed to reach it.

The star brother within him had never seen the figures before, scratched into the bare soil of Nazca so many centuries earlier. Neither had de Sagres. Together they thrilled at the artistry and determination that had covered the empty plain with human purpose.

De Sagres smiled inwardly. How my cabinet members would laugh if they saw me here, alone, in this faded old windbreaker and worn-thin slacks. *El Presidente* should always have his entourage around him; he should wear hand-tailored suits with razor-edge creases and elegant silk ties. At least, thought the president, they no longer expect their leader to wear a military uniform.

The breeze gusting across the treeless plain from the Andes was chilling. De Sagres knew it would get much colder once the Sun had dipped completely below the barren horizon. Still he waited at the hill's dusty summit. Waited and watched the sky darken.

Perhaps we should not have come alone, his star brother said to him. It's a long way to the nearest station on the highway.

I had to get away, he replied silently, away from the crowds and the ceremonies. Away from the work and the pain and the grief. This night of all nights, I must be by myself.

He sensed his star brother's hurt. Are we not one person? he rebuked mildly.

One person, my brother, admitted de Sagres.

It had been a long, hard year. The Horror was being brought under control, but slowly, ever so slowly. Nearly a quarter billion people had died in Latin America alone. A terrible, agonizing tragedy. De Sagres could feel the awful grief and misery that spanned the world. To him the deaths were not merely statistics; they were brothers and sisters who had perished, his blood, his kin. He had gazed deeply into the well of anguish. A lesser man would have given up hope and run away to hide.

But it has been only one year, his star brother replied. Less than a full year. And the death rate is dropping fast now.

De Sagres thought of the changes that were already taking place across Latin America and the rest of the world. Humans accepted the "alien" inoculations because they were terrified of the Horror. Then they found that they carried star brothers and star sisters within themselves.

Some went mad. Some seemed completely unchanged. But for most men and women, the star symbiotes seemed to make them more human than they had ever been. They could no longer look at another person as someone separate from themselves. They could not look at an animal or a tree or even a cloud in the sky as something outside their own existence.

Across Latin America, across the entire world, the human race was reaching toward a new level of existence. No one on Earth was untouched by the twin impacts of the Horror and the star symbiotes. There were no isolated human souls anymore. No one could stand alone and aloof, not once he acquired a star brother. Pushed by the Horror, pulled by the star brethren, all of humanity was swiftly becoming one huge interlinked family, brought together by ties of love and caring and—at long last—understanding.

The teachings of Christ are becoming the norm of human behavior, thought de Sagres. He smiled to himself. Even the Church is becoming Christian, at last.

Slowly the Moon rose from behind the sunset-tinged snowcaps of the Andes, enormous and full, pale and slightly sad looking.

De Sagres felt his heart thumping as he strained his eyes to see the lights of human settlements on the lopsided face of the Moon. And then he saw one single incredibly bright light, so brilliant that no one could miss it, rising up from near the edge of the Moon's disc, heading out into the darkness of the night sky, racing into the depths of black space, stretching into a streak of blazing light that crossed the dome of the heavens and then dwindled swiftly and was gone.

The sky seemed to shudder. Ghostly shimmering veils of delicate pale greens and pinks rippled across the encroaching darkness. The aurora, never seen at this latitude except when a starship taps the core of the Earth's magnetic field.

The dancing sheets of pastel colors seemed to be waving good-bye to the departing starship. A farewell from the planet. A farewell from all of humankind.

De Sagres waved too. Both his arms, like an eager child, until the light of the starship and the answering gleam of the aurora both disappeared and left the sky empty—except for thousands of glittering stars.

Dhouni Nkona stood outside his house and saw the silver arrow of light streak across the night sky of Africa. He watched, fascinated, as the aurora glowed the way it had thirty-three years earlier, when the alien's ship had first appeared in Earth's skies.

Beside the gray old man stood Lela Obiri, young, strong, slowly recovering from her ordeal of eight months earlier.

The star sister within her had confirmed what Nkona had tried years ago to teach her: that all living creatures are linked, united into a single form of life that spans Mother Earth. Yet her star sister expanded even that insight: all living creatures are linked even among the far-scattered stars. All life in the universe is one.

That vision had nearly destroyed Lela. The guilt and shame she felt over her murder of five men almost drove her insane. Almost. For months she could not face another human being. She lived in the preserve with the great apes while her star sister gradually, patiently helped her to understand her own depths of fear and hatred.

Now she stood beside Nkona, ready to take her place in the world of imperfect men and women once again. The old man gave her a fatherly smile. Lela was stronger now than she had ever been. The wound in her spirit was healing; the scar would always be there, but she would be all the stronger for having suffered the wounding and surviving. Men and women were imperfect, it was true; but they were striving toward perfection. Nkona believed with all the fierce passion in his soul that each human being was truly perfectible.

Less than fifty kilometers from where they stood, outside Nkona's modest home on the fringe of the university campus, several hundred gorillas lived in peaceful contentment at last. No one had even tried to bother them, not since the star brethren had shown all who received what Lela had known from the beginning.

In Bangladesh it was nearly morning. Walking slowly along the sandy shore, Chandra Varahamihara turned his gaze from the gently lapping sea to the dark forest that lined the beach with tall swaying coconut palms and thickly gnarled *goran* mangroves.

He was a lonely figure, this frail bald-shaved lama in his saffron robe. But he was not alone. Within him dwelled a star brother, and he sensed all the hundreds of millions, the billions of humans who also shared their blood with brethren from the stars.

Once this region where the five mighty rivers met the sea was called the Plain of Death. The rivers would flood and thousands who had no dwelling place except miserable shacks along their banks would be swept away. The sea would be heavy with drowned bodies for weeks afterward.

Now, in his mind's eye, Varahamihara could see the mighty dams far to the north in the mountains of Nepal that controlled the flow of the rivers. And the forests that had been planted to hold the moisture of the monsoon rains and prevent the erosion of the soil that the people needed to grow their food. Almost, he smiled. Nepal was becoming a rich nation, selling its hydroelectric power not only to Bangladesh but to India, China, and even the Soviet Union.

But the smile never came to his lips. The Horror had been particularly cruel in the great Indian subcontinent. Its ravages were diminishing as the visitors from the stars joined in the unity of life, but what a terrible, excruciating toll it had taken! Yet perhaps such pain was necessary. The wheel of life is lubricated with human blood, it seems. At least now the teachings of the Buddha were becoming the true frame of reference for all the people of Earth.

Yet he wondered. What changes will come when all men and women are linked with star brothers and sisters? We will survive the Horror, that much seems sure now. But can we survive the cure?

The lama lifted his worried face to the glowing dawn that touched the sea's horizon with pink.

A streak of brilliant light rose in that brightening sky and climbed across the heavens. Varahamihara watched the starship until it disappeared from sight, uttering a prayer of peace to those who were heading for the stars. And of thanks.

But most of all he prayed for understanding.

In the dimmed lighting of the starship's observation dome, Stoner and his son seemed to be standing on nothing, suspended in space, as the Earth dwindled to a mere point of light. Stoner rested one hand on Rickie's shoulder and realized that the boy was already chest-high to his father.

Wherever they looked the stars crowded thickly against the blackness of space, like sprinklings of brilliant gems that dazzled the eye.

"We're on our way!" Rickie shouted, a mixture of excitement and fear in his voice.

Stoner tousled his son's hair. "Yes, we are. This is going to be our home for a long, long time, Rick. You'll be a grown man before we return to Earth."

"How long will it take to get to the world where the star brothers came from?"

Stoner called up the figures in his mind. "It will seem like a couple of years to us."

"Cathy will be born by then, won't she? She'll be a little baby."

"You'll be her big brother, Rick. You'll help to take care of her, won't you?"

"Sure."

Stoner and his son walked back to the living quarters, where there were normal-looking walls and furniture. He had designed this part of the ship to look as much like their home in Hilo as possible, even down to the plant hangings and carpets.

Half the scientists of Earth had wanted to go along on this first human flight to the stars. Politely but with implacable firmness, Stoner had refused them all.

"The ship's sensor systems will be transmitting data to you constantly," he had said. "That will have to do until more starships are built."

The only other one aboard their ship, other than Jo and Stoner and their children, had been the dead and frozen body of Kirill Markov. The first duty that Stoner had performed once the ship had cleared the Earth/Moon region was to release Kir's sarcophagus and send it searching outward among the stars.

"Good-bye, old friend," Stoner had whispered. "May you find eager minds wherever you travel."

Now he lay in bed next to Jo, watching the stars through the transparent diamond ceiling above them.

"Just like home," Jo murmured.

"This is our home," he replied. "All the home we'll know."

"I'll miss seeing the Moon."

He smiled. "You'll have other sights to entertain you. Have you noticed that the stars aren't just pinpoints of light anymore?"

"No . . ." Jo stirred slightly beside him, as if concentrating her attention on the panoply of stars above them.

"See? They're like little oblate spheres. Almost like tear-drops."

"Oh yes! They're all that way."

"In another few days they'll look like streaks, smears that are red on one end and blue on the other," he told Jo.

She moved closer to him, pressed against his bare flesh. He slid an arm around her lovely shoulders. The scent of her hair was like jasmine.

Jo asked, "Are you certain we had to leave?"

He turned and looked at her in the light of the stars. "Helluva time to ask."

"We could always turn around." But she was grinning at him.

"*I* had to leave, Jo. Maybe you and the kids didn't, but I had to. I've done everything I could do. If we had stayed on Earth they'd start to treat me like some kind of royalty. Or worse, a deity."

"You wouldn't like to be worshipped?"

"I haven't done anything to be worshipped for," he said tightly. "I failed, really. I wanted to introduce the star brethren gradually, gently, give the human race enough time to absorb the changes that nanotechnology will bring. But I failed."

"It wasn't your fault."

"Still . . ."

"You did everything you could."

Stoner did not reply.

Propping herself on one elbow, Jo looked down at his starlit face and said, "I'm glad it worked out this way. If it hadn't, you'd have spent the next hundred years trying to ease them into nanotechnology. You'd have broken your heart trying to make things right for every last idiot on Earth. Now they've got to do it for themselves."

"But can they? Can they absorb this without destroying themselves?"

With a shrug of her bare shoulders, Jo answered, "We'll find out when we come back."

Stoner thought about it for a few moments. Then, "Maybe

you're right, Jo. I thought I could give them a new world, but maybe in the final analysis nobody can give the human race anything. They've got to make it for themselves."

"Sink or swim."

"Ten billion lives," he muttered.

"Less than that, after the Horror," Jo corrected.

Nodding absently, "Well, the human race has beaten other challenges in the past. The Ice Ages, wars, famines . . ."

"They'll make it," Jo said confidently. "By the time we return they'll have statues of you in every city on Earth."

"God forbid!"

She laughed.

"That's exactly what I wanted to avoid," Stoner said. "That's why we had to leave. If I had stayed on Earth they would have never left me alone. They would have wanted to . . . to . . ."

"To deify you. Or at least make you a saint." Jo lay back on the pillows. "Saint Keith of the Star Brethren. They'd hang your portrait in the Vatican."

"That's not funny." Despite himself he was grinning at her.

"No, it isn't. Especially when we both know you could have never said no to any of them. Never duck that damned sense of responsibility of yours."

Stoner changed the subject. "I know it was a lot to ask, Jo, bringing you and Rickie—taking you away from everything, away from home . . ."

"My home is with you, Keith."

"You won't miss Vanguard? The power?"

"I don't know. Maybe I will. But I want to be with you," she said, her eyes searching his.

"Even out to the stars?"

"Even out to the stars," Jo said. Then she added, "It *is* kind of scary, though."

"Scary?"

"Flying out to the stars aboard a ship completely unlike anything that's ever been built before. Don't you have any doubts? And questions?"

Stoner wrapped his arms around her. "I think it's time you received your very own star sister. Then you would understand much better than you do now."

"I don't need it now," Jo said. "There's no danger of the Horror here."

"There's no danger of anything here, except maybe an equipment failure. But the ship is self-repairing, self-regenerating. Just like me." He waggled the five fingers of his left hand.

Jo was quiet for a moment. Then, "Keith, I can't trust what I don't understand."

"But . . ."

"Let me finish." She touched a finger to his lips. "I trust you. If you think I should have a star sister, I'll do it. Not because I want it, but because you want me to."

Stoner kissed her. "I'll have to prick your finger."

"Can't you do it while we make love?"

He blinked with surprise. "I never thought of it . . ." His star brother smiled within him. "Yes, of course. If that's the way you want to, why not?"

"I'll get my star sister by injection," Jo teased.

Stoner laughed and kissed her again.

Nearly an hour later, as they lay side by side staring up at the stars, a sheen of perspiration on their naked skins, Jo said, "I don't feel any different."

"You will tomorrow. And all the tomorrows afterward. The next time we make love, you'll see."

"Really?"

"The symbiotes can damp down on your emotions, when it's necessary," he said, grinning. "But they can also enhance them. You'll see."

"So that's how . . ." Jo pursed her lips.

Stoner became serious again. "You'll start to understand why I couldn't let you kill Hsen."

"That would have been an execution," she snapped.

"It would have been a vendetta murder, and sooner or later you would have felt the full impact of its guilt."

"The last of the warlords," Jo muttered.

"What?"

"Hsen—he always reminded me of an old-fashioned oriental warlord."

Stoner smiled at her. "Good analogy. Only, he wasn't the last of the warlords, Jo. You were."

"Me?"

"Not all the warlords were evil," he quickly added. "Still . . . maybe it's a good thing that you're heading for the stars with me. You might have decided to make yourself empress of Earth."

For some while she did not reply. They lay together and watched the stars.

"I'm sure you would have made a good empress," Stoner offered.

Jo laughed softly. "Sure you are."

"Want to go back and try it?"

Instead of replying, she said, "Everything always changes, doesn't it? Whether we want it to or not."

Nodding in the starlight, Stoner answered, "Some changes we deliberately cause, some we have to adapt to because we can't avoid them."

"Keith," she asked, her voice suddenly urgent, "where does it all end? Where are we heading? What are we doing?"

He smiled at her. "We've helped the human race make the transition to the brotherhood of the stars, Jo. That's the greatest achievement we or anyone else could have accomplished."

"And now what?"

"And now we have the whole universe to play in. No matter what happens, we have each other and our children."

"And the stars," Jo said.

"And the stars," he agreed.

She turned toward him again. "Keith . . . you could have gone on this journey without us."

"Without you?"

"You left me once. For eighteen years."

"That was a long time ago. A lifetime ago. I couldn't leave you now. I love you, Jo. I want you beside me always."

She smiled in the starlight and twined her arms around his neck.

"That's what I wanted to hear," Jo said.

"You didn't know?"

"I still like to hear you say it."

Stoner kissed her lightly on the lips. Then he began to sing an old tune that Jo recognized from her student years. He's never sung to me before, she thought. And at that moment all her fears disappeared like a rime of frost evaporating in the morning sun. Jo smiled, content to be with this man and their children, wherever their destiny would take them.

And Stoner sang, in a surprisingly gentle and romantic voice:

"If the world should stop revolving, spinning slowly down to dust

"I'd spend the end with you,

"And when the world was through

"Then one by one the stars would all go out,

"Then you and I would simply fly away."

A Selected List of Science Fiction Available from Mandarin

While every effort is made to keep prices low, it is sometimes necessary to increase prices at short notice. Mandarin Paperbacks reserves the right to show new retail prices on covers which may differ from those previously advertised in the text or elsewhere.

The prices shown below were correct at the time of going to press.

All these books are available at your bookshop or newsagent, or can be ordered direct from the publisher. Just tick the titles you want and fill in the form below.

Mandarin Paperbacks, Cash Sales Department, PO Box 11, Falmouth, Cornwall TR10 9EN.

Please send cheque or postal order, no currency, for purchase price quoted and allow the following for postage and packing:

UK	80p for the first book, 20p for each additional book ordered to a maximum charge of £2.00.
BFPO	80p for the first book, 20p for each additional book.
Overseas including Eire	£1.50 for the first book, £1.00 for the second and 30p for each additional book thereafter.

NAME (Block letters) ....

ADDRESS ....

....

....